DIMENSIONS

THE GAME QUARKS PLAY

WHIT HANEY

DIMENSIONS
THE GAME QUARKS PLAY

iUniverse books may be ordered through booksellers or by contacting:

iUniverse
1663 Liberty Drive
Bloomington, IN 47403
www.iuniverse.com
844-349-9409

ISBN: 978-1-6632-0881-1 (sc)
ISBN: 978-1-6632-3497-1 (hc)
ISBN: 978-1-6632-0880-4 (e)

Library of Congress Control Number: 2022904521

Print information available on the last page.

iUniverse rev. date: 04/11/2022

To my wife, Louise, who is the epitome of patience and unconditional love to me, and my son Matthew, who inspired me to write down the story in my head that I talked about incessantly.

ACKNOWLEDGMENT

To all the people and experiences I have had in this
life, the essence that stimulates me to create.

THE BEGINNING

Summer, 4200 BCE
Ancient Ur in Modern Day Iraq
Sol Planet Three
Milky Way Dimension

A portal opened, and the warlord Kollindarrot's transport appeared on the star side of the asteroid belt. On this side of the asteroid belt were four smaller orbiting planets, one very small, one green, a red one closest to the portal, and the third one from the sun was a strange, alluring blue planet. He determined only the third one was inhabitable. While circling the planet, he took atmospheric and geological readings. When he landed, the warlord discovered a multitude of interdependent life forms.

Furthermore, two distinct types of intelligent beings strangely cohabitated with each other. One type was like him: taller, bulkier in the upper arms and shoulders. The other was distinct, smaller and with a different, appealing shape but curiously similar. He stayed to observe how these beings lived together. Instead of forming from quarks, as his kind did spontaneously, it took a combining of the two to create more life. All the creatures on this planet he studied had such a dual replicating process.

How do they replicate? For what it's worth, I feel an attraction to the more curved shaped of the pairs. I have never experienced this kind of visual stimulation. Why does my body react physically? Being around these creatures causes me to want more of this creature, the way I wish for greater power. My breathing changes. Why do I want to touch the curved being and not the other? I must study this further.

He told his lieutenant, "We need to be among them to learn more." They found a way to make clothes that compared to the fashions of the times and mingled with the local people. They discovered that the same yellow metal they had for component repairs was used as a store of value for commerce. This came in handy to recruit an unpaired smaller being. Once alone, light rings were used to render the recruit subdued and taken back to the cloaked transport for experimentation.

The two quarks stripped and held the being with light rings in the transport sleeping area. The warlord said, "We need to take samples of body chemicals." They extracted a fluid like theirs from its vein for testing. Noninvasive skin scrapes supplied more samples to analyze.

Surprising results came back. The astounded lieutenant reported, "Master Kollindarrot, these body samples are not much different than ours. This could suggest there is a universal chemistry for life."

The warlord snatched the report from the lieutenant's hand and read. He looked at the chemical profile and came to the same shocking conclusion. "We need to find a larger being that is shaped more like a quark."

That night the two saw a shepherd tending a flock alone. They captured and brought it back to the craft. They stripped them both and placed them on opposite sides of their holding room. While they studied the samples taken from the more prominent being, they observed the two's interactions. Kollindarrot reacted saying, "Lieutenant, the larger being has the same response we did around the other. His breathing looks shorter and, his posture is definitely changing."

They listened to the conversation through their translator device.

The larger being said, "I think we are going to die here."

The smaller one said, "I am scared out of all reason. I don't know if these devils are with us forever."

The larger said, "They are pure evil, and I hope they all die from God's wrath."

"I guess it is my fate, since I was lured to them by their gold. But you, a shepherd, you did nothing wrong. You should not be punished like this."

Kollindarrot said, "How about turning off the light rings so the two can get close and see what happens."

The two beings noticed they could now move toward each other. The larger being said, "I have never been with a woman like this. Have you ever been with a man?"

She said, "Yes, but my husband was killed, and I was thrown on the street. All I had left was my body. I am so scared. Please hold me."

The two embraced. The smaller being sweetly kissed the shepherd's chest, causing the man to press his body close. He closed his eyes and slightly opened his mouth. The passion of the moment overcame them. The smaller being then said, "Lay me down. Before we die, let me give you all I have left in this world." They made love while the quarks' eyes were frozen to the video feed.

After they finished, the lieutenant breathed heavily and said, "The larger being had tremendous excitement close to the other being. I even felt wanting the same thing."

The warlord said, "I hope it makes us feel that good. Get rid of the larger one and let us try the same thing ourselves with the smaller one." So they killed the shepherd and raped the woman multiple times. The woman screamed continuously until the quarks gave her a sedative.

Through his experimentation, Kollindarrot discovered that his body could have the same ecstasy by being forcibly together with them. He started clandestinely by capturing and raping more women to achieve his satisfaction. When he finished with them, they would be either eliminated or sent back to their home, whichever pleased him at the time. Kollindarrot thought to himself, *This is more fun than battling other quarks. I want more!*

His exhilaration was so intense, he did it more and went back to his dimension and brought others. It proved to be an excellent morale booster to his warriors, sending his fighters to every corner of the planet to have their pleasures. The hunger for these unusual beings became ravenous with demonic, addictive lust for sexual excitement; they raped indiscriminately whenever they felt the urge.

The quarks were more prominent in physical stature than the larger, more quark-like, of the two beings. Their technology overpowered the primitive beings with ease. This epic-scale invasion lasted for years. Over time, the warlord and his men discovered they could impregnate these attractive creatures and generate new life in multiple populations. This astounded and motivated Kollindarrot to create more through women.

The warlord and his companions began murdering men for their women with reckless abandon, striking fear in the world. Women would be taken through the portal to Kollindarrot's fiefdom. The quarks would use and abuse the women for their entertainment, abducting and using them for experiments and as sex toys. If one died, they would kidnap another. Other women committed suicide to stop the pain.

The beings on the third planet began hiding in caves and other places, not knowing what would come next.

As time went on, fewer were minding the fiefdom due to the crazed passions that bewitched its entire population. Once they had experienced these beings, discipline broke down, and officers became too wrapped up in themselves to care about compliance. Disorder grew within the ranks over years.

Spring, 4183 BCE
Space near Dimensional Portal
Kollindarrot Sector
Quark Dimension

This did not go unnoticed. Another warlord observed the dimensional travel and waited for the best time to take advantage of this distraction. While Kollindarrot and his warriors enjoyed the beauty and pleasures of the third planet, an observant rival lay in wait near the portal between the dimensions. As individuals came through, they were first being captured and tortured for information about defenses of the fiefdom as well as what was so enticing about the beings from this "third planet." Tol found that the other warlord and his hierarchy were smitten and drunk with physical pleasure by the fairer exotic beings, the "women," of this third planet. He initially dared not go for fear of the spell that infected his rival. He used this distraction against Kollindarrot to plan a campaign to conquer his fiefdom for his own.

Tol—who, being fond of conquest, loved the battle and the power over the fallen foe—first sent an attack force to assess the information the tortured souls gave. It was an impressive success, and whole areas of the sector were taken with minimal resistance over a year's time.

Now, it was time to finish off the negligent, grotesquely savage warlord and the other quarks accompanying him. Tol sent his lieutenant as a spy to contact the warlord before the attack. The purpose of warning Kollindarrot was to cause him to react about the pending doom of his sector. This finally awakened this wayward warlord out of his sexually active stupor, and he returned to the quark dimension to save his fiefdom. Tol's disinformation plan had succeeded, drawing Kollindarrot into his trap. He and the others came back through the portal only to be ambushed and captured or killed by the opportunistic attacker. Almost every quark was slaughtered in a complete rout.

Tol enjoyed executing the incompetent leader, who had been so easily led astray, and vowed to never fall under the same spell. He took Kollindarrot's ring to secure the sector and keep a reminder of the warlord's folly. He ordered the rest of his sector not to go to the third planet for its dangerous and beguiling forces. The population did not understand the nature of this warning but realized that the other sector conquest had been too easy for any fiefdom that was on guard. Upon Tol's return to his home sector's planet, he was hailed as a visionary leader who had almost doubled the size of his fiefdom in the dimension, a complete and near painless win.

Tol found Kollindarrot's research notes. He studied and assessed the warlord's detailed journal logs, which chronicled life in the other dimension. He decided to journey to the third planet to see what the outside exposure had done to the world and its inhabitants, knowing the pitfalls that could arise. He sedated and returned to the third planet the beings found captive in Kollindarrot's fiefdom. They were too dangerous to stay in the dimension. The trap Kollindarrot fell into would not be repeated.

To study this fascinating world, after leaving the women found in Kollindarrot's fiefdom on the other side of the planet, Tol chose a populated area to observe. It was very cold. He also made a facsimile of the local attire for himself. He landed his cloaked craft in a lonely place near two dwellings by a small lake. Quietly entering an isolated dwelling, he found a dead being with a wound that looked as if he'd been shot with a small blaster. He walked into the larger dwelling and saw two sets of clothing; he assessed that one would fit the dead being, but the other seemed quite different and colorful. He moved to another room that seemed to be for preparing food with a door to the back, thinking these beings had high intelligence. They used tools to work with and do other meaningful tasks. He concluded that these beings used logic when forming their living areas, just as quarks did, but were much less technologically advanced. Looking around, he noted the woven fabrics and colorful dishes. *These beings exhibit extreme intelligence early in their history. They will eventually advance rapidly in their technology. We must take care never to come here again.*

Suddenly, he heard two voices approaching outside, one higher pitched than the other. Tol hid, turned on his universal translator, and listened to the conversation, "Whoever those strangers were that ravaged you and other women seem to be gone now. I have not heard more about others being killed by those devils for at least a moon's full phase. I believe God has finally answered our prayers."

The smaller being said, "Yes, Enoch, we are all thankful for whatever stopped those heinous demons from killing men and abusing women. But the damage has been done with so many men gone and women pregnant and bearing children by those monsters. And many of the children born look like those devils that caused all this evil. My husband may have been the last killed by whatever they were. Luckily, the weather has been so cold his body has not smelled. When the ground thaws, we can give him a proper burial."

"It seems they all got in their magic flying dwellings and left. I am thankful they are gone."

Tol had heard enough to know that Kollindarrot's notes were accurate, and that his quarks had caused lasting changes to life on the third planet. But that was irrelevant since he was no longer alive or able to answer for himself. Since Tol had read the research, he was curious to learn more about how a powerful warlord would risk losing everything to have these pleasures.

The woman and Enoch came into the room to what turned out to be her deceased husband. She lifted one of the larger size pieces of clothing and kissed it, saying, "Efrem, my love and rock, is gone. I am now with no one and no way to keep this. What can I do now, Enoch?" The conversation continued until the woman broke down and cried.

Tol fiddled with his warlord's ring while witnessing the emotion of sadness for the first time, being caught up in the moment. Luckily, he could leave through the back door undetected and did so. Then he walked quickly back toward the cloaked ship. *I had better go now and not come back. I do not need to waste any more time here.*

When he was about three hundred meters from the house, there was a shout from behind. "You, stop! Who are you, and why are you here?"

And I was working on that cloaking suit prototype. Tol kept moving until an arrow zipped by his ear and landed a distance in front of him. He stopped and turned around to see a man with a bow and arrow ready to shoot again. He knew he was not able to ready his blaster in time to outshoot the arrow. The archer, the same Enoch from the house, approached him to see who or what he was. With his translator device, Tol began, "Please, I come in peace to see what devastation happened because of the evil warlord and his legion."

"How do I know you are telling me the truth? Also, I am going to assume that is a weapon on your side. I want you to slowly show it and put it on the ground. Then step back," the readied archer demanded.

Tol took his blaster belt off, slowly put it on the ground, raised his hands, and stepped back three paces. Enoch approached him and kicked the belt away. Tol said, "Sir, I mean no harm, and it was I who saw that this warlord had violated the portal from our dimension to this one and …"

"Silence. What kind of story is that? You will answer my questions. I want to hear where you came from and why you are here, not some wild nonsense."

Tol's stoic nature allowed him not to be upset with a lesser individual giving commands to a warlord in such a rude manner. "It is not nonsense. Watch." Tol uncloaked the spacecraft, which shocked Enoch so much he almost released the arrow.

"You are one of them! I should kill you now, Satan!" Enoch stood there considering his options. He darted his eyes back and forth, thinking of what to ask. He released the tension on the bow and said, "On with your story."

"Yes, the warlord Kollindarrot from my dimension caused this. I do not know why he initially came. Still, I believe he remained here smitten by the other half of your population, to satisfy certain urges brought on by the other binary beings among you. I noticed his distractions and was able to attack and conquer his fiefdom back in my dimension. I came to find the result of his reckless actions. Only time will tell of the harm he caused."

"Are you God?"

"No, I am a quark. We do not have binary life processes like you do. But, if you let me go back to where I came from, I will never come this way again. Also, I will do my best to keep my dimension from knowing the wickedness that was perpetrated on this world."

Enoch asked, "Sir, I will only believe you if I escort you into that thing you made appear, and we both go to where you came from. I want to make sure you are good to your word. I have lost all I have due to the evil and cry every day for God to deliver us from these times. I will give my life for an end to this madness. You will go, but I will keep my weapon on you as we leave together."

Tol breathed heavily and responded, "Your choice." So Enoch walked Tol onto the ship at knifepoint to his pilot's seat. Tol knew this being had no clue about how easily he could escape and turn the tables on the unknowing but brave and selfless being who was about to give his life for his fellow beings. The warlord had no desire to hurt any other life form in this dimension. He had thought that by uncloaking the craft, he would intimidate the being into submission and fear. Instead, he saw this primitive fellow's steely determination to do what he could to stop the carnage from the visitors. It made him respect the creature's tenacity more.

Tol made sure not to take off too quickly since he now had a knife at his neck. He made the liftoff as smooth as possible and exited into outer space, allowing Enoch to think he was in control. Once they were in outer space, Tol turned off the gravity stabilizer, causing Enoch to float, and then turned hard, which caused the unsuspecting man to drift away from him out of control.

Enoch yelled, "You devil! I will make sure you do not ever hurt my people again!"

Tol pulled out his light ring device and shot light rings to bind Enoch's hands and pin them to the wall, making him release the knife. Tol turned the gravity stabilizer back on and walked toward the shocked passenger. Undaunted, Enoch yelled again, "As long as I live, I will fight to protect my people!"

Tol saw the genuine fear through all the bluster. He put down the light ring device and calmly walked toward the man with his hands behind his back to study this being who wanted to continue to struggle and fight. He said, "Sir, I mean you no harm and am sorry to have taken advantage of you. But I came to this planet to see what the foolish warlord and his legion did to your world. I did not have to stay long to understand what horror they caused to all.

"But to limit our exposure to your world, I can't let you return. I am taking you back to my world, and you will be treated well for your bravery and suffering. You will stay and allow me to learn what happened and learn about you and your binary world. I also want to keep the knowledge of your world closely guarded, since your people are talented, crafty, and inventive. You did catch me by surprise, for which I applaud you. You earned my respect, and that is why you are still alive. From what I have learned, the warlord Kollindarrot inserted quark traits into your world, changing it forever. I would like to release you to talk about what I am planning for you when we reach my fiefdom. Agreed?"

Enoch slowly nodded in agreement, shaking with fear and emotion throughout Tol's conversation. Tol released the shell-shocked man from the light rings and allowed him to slowly pick up his knife, which he returned to its sheath, all the while watching Tol for any wrong move.

Enoch remarked, "You have given me an offer I cannot refuse."

Glancing out the window, Tol said, "You are correct. Look out this window and see where you came from. It is the last you will ever see of it."

Enoch swallowed, not knowing what to say. Knowing he had nothing to lose but his life, he looked at Tol and said, "May I have one wish granted?"

"What do I get in return?"

Enoch pressed his lips together. He began to shake. "I will be your unquestioning servant until the day I die. I will do anything you request even if it does me harm."

"Sounds like that is all you can give. Now, what is your wish?"

"That you pledge to me that none of your kind will ever come to Earth and hurt people again as long as you live. I give up myself for my home."

Tol thought this would be easy for a moment since he now controlled the portal leading into this solar system. *It is a small place that no one will ever find.* "Agreed, upon my life." No matter how insignificant, a warlord keeps his solemn pledge to anybody at all costs.

"What will happen now?"

"I control the access to your planet. There is very little possibility that anyone will visit it again. If anyone does, my pledge is to protect your planet so your kind may continue to exist."

Both smiled and sat down across from each other and talked about life on the third planet. Tol took detailed notes, being also an inventor and explorer. The conversations continued on and off until they arrived back at Tol's headquarters.

THE GAME

6/4/2018
Annapolis Rock
Appalachian Trail near Myersville, Maryland
Sol Planet Three
Milky Way Dimension

One weekend on the way to camping by himself, young Dr. Michael Townsend called his fiancée, Anne. "Hey there, beautiful."

She answered, "How are ya, big guy?"

He said, "Going camping by myself ain't the same since I found you. Now I want you to come with me every time."

Anne responded, "And I'd rather be with you than at Johns Hopkins."

Michael mournfully said, "Working's good, but sometimes …"

She groaned. "I know, and quit tempting me to call in sick and drive over there."

Michael chuckled and said, "There's always another day."

"Yeah, ya jerk. Rub it in some more."

"See you Sunday."

"Ya will if ya don't make me mad."

"Well, I better let you get ready for work. He-he."

Anne said, "Stop it, ya moron."

"I love ya—mean it."

"I love ya too. Bye."

Michael smiled and put his phone down in the cupholder as his car began the climb along the mountain road to the campsite.

Before Anne Wilson came into his life, he had always enjoyed being alone. He parked, got his gear, picked up the trail, and took off for the nearest mountain site, where he found a flat spot off the path near a stream. As an avid fisherman, Michael enjoyed fly fishing for his dinner. He set camp and cooked a nice trout over an open fire.

Michael loved the outdoors, anywhere he could be out in it. He grew up by the Low Country creeks of Charleston, South Carolina, hunting and fishing anytime he could. It was his respite from the pressure of his medical training, quiet and by himself.

However, this time he would not be alone; he was about to be linked to chaos. Michael was alerted by a change in the night sky that evening, a flash. He dismissed it as a nightbird passing by the moon rising in the east, illuminating the campsite with a misty glow. He had finished the dinner he cooked. Michael was proud to be self-sufficient in the wild while drinking his brewed coffee. He put out the fire to get ready for a relaxing night's sleep. The weather report called for a pristine night, with Saturn visible in the southern sky. Since the trees blocked the view, he gave up trying to see it. His camp light gave him about thirty minutes to relax, reading to settle his mind for the night. Checking his phone, Michael saw he was out of cell service. *I need to get a better provider.* He had bought a Tom Clancy novel from Amazon the week before, expecting a total escape from the reality of his condescending attending physician. He took a deep breath and put his book next to the sleeping bag.

Michael heard a strange sound like a jet landing in the distance. *Too used to city noises. There are no airports anywhere near here.* He wiped out the barbecue residue from the camping pan and threw the rest of his cup of water into the extinguished fire just to be safe. *Now for the best part, reading a book under the stars. I only wish Anne was here so I could read her eyes and share my sleeping bag.*

He began to settle down with his book and adjusted the pillows so he could read without making his neck sore. Just when he got comfortable, he heard small branches crack to his right. *I wonder what kind of animal that could be. It must be a deer.* He yelled, "Go away, shoo!" He got out of the sleeping bag, hiked his pants high enough to walk, and retrieved his holster from his backpack. *I'll enjoy sleeping with my Sig Sauer, just in case.* He took it out of the holster and went back to the sleeping bag.

He yelled one more time, "If y'all are human, how about moving on down the line? I've got my buddy Sig with a full clip." No response. He could sense something was watching him.

"Dudes, this ain't funny. Y'all go away now. I'm in no mood to give anyone an ass whooping, but I will if I need to." The sounds stopped. He waited a few minutes, then relaxed. He got back into the sleeping bag and thought to himself, *Big Sig will have to do tonight.* He drifted off to sleep five minutes into the book.

A bright light woke and froze him. He could not move or make a sound. His sleeping bag became like a cocoon around his body with only his head outside the bag. Something in a glass-shielded headgear touched him on the forehead. Next, a machine the size of a handheld vacuum cleaner appeared, then a blue pin light for twenty seconds, then a quick red flash. His body jerked.

It seemed like seconds later, he woke up and heard rustling brush to his right again. He got up with his pistol to look around, but it was gone. He looked around the campsite. Nothing was disturbed. *What a dream. It felt so real. Dream? No, a nightmare. I feel like I was kicked in the head by a mule.* He looked up and saw the moon passing its apex over his head. The planets had drifted beyond the western horizon. He closed his eyes, turning his face to the ground and thought, *I feel like I've been beaten up. I thought I left all this soreness in the NFL. What a horrible night of sleep so far.*

He looked around, not seeing anything move. The pistol was next to him for good measure. The last thing he wanted to do was use it and then have to explain to the authorities why there was a dead body. He searched his backpack and saw his wallet and phone were untouched and wondered what had happened. The evening had disturbed him so much that it was another two hours before he drifted off.

Minutes later, Michael had a horrible nightmare. He suddenly sat up and screamed. With his eyes wide open, he looked around to see whether he was still at his campsite. He was sweating and breathing heavily, so he took his pulse and counted 150 beats per minute.

Everyone has nightmares or bad dreams, but fire, destruction, and death? After a calming-down period, he went back to sleep. He woke up at dawn and tried to remember the dream, but he could not. It really bugged him—so much so, he took his flashlight and walked around for about five minutes. Then he came back to his sleeping bag and looked at his watch, *Three in the morning.*

He rubbed the back of his head, feeling a bump where he must have hit the ground hard, jerking his head. He got back in the sleeping bag but had trouble sleeping.

After three hours of tossing and turning, he gave up, got up, and looked at his morning rations. He felt so rotten that he didn't want to cook or deal with anything; instead, he broke camp.

Later while traveling home, he stopped at a Waffle House.

When he sat in the booth, the waitress came to him, "Hey there, darlin', coffee?"

He said, "Y'all got it in an IV?"

She giggled and said, "You're so silly."

He said, "I didn't sleep well camping last night."

She looked perplexed. "Neither did I, and I wasn't even camping. It was like something was flying around outside my house, looking for something. Strange. Now what can I getcha?"

"Wait. Do you think something was flying around? Where do you live?"

"Between here and Annapolis Rock. It was like every so often lights flashing. I just thought it was heat lightning or something."

Michael thought, *This is fixing to get weird.* He ordered breakfast.

The dreams disturbed him so much that he could not tear his thoughts from them. That Sunday afternoon, he went to the Orioles game, where he had a couple of beers. Then he went back to his apartment and fell asleep, wiped out. Anne got home after work and could not wake him. She got into bed and snuggled next to her "big guy."

That night Michael woke up to another nightmare, sweating and looking around, but he wrote down the dream this time. As he wrote, he shook his head and thought how wild all this was, and that he could write a short horror story about them.

Anne woke up and asked, "What's wrong? What's going on?"

He said, "My camping trip was a total bust, and I don't want to talk about it."

Anne pouted, gave him a kiss, and rubbed his temple. They went back to sleep after tossing and turning. He was eager to analyze the dream in the morning. Little did he know that as time went by, he would be visualizing more than he could imagine.

The following Monday morning, his friend Josh, who had grown close to him during their training, noticed that Michael was not himself. He usually did not drag in the morning. With the exceptions of the two grand rounds faux pas, he was on time or early. Even the attending physician, Dr. Bishop, stopped calling him out for his two lapses. The internship was about to end, and Michael turned into the go-to guy for tough clinical questions. He explained to Josh, "I didn't sleep well last weekend, and it's catching up to me. I am exhausted."

"Was Anne that good last weekend?"

"Dude!" He gave him a scathing look. "Nightmares have been waking me up." He then shook the cobwebs out of his brain, trying to be more alert.

"I know that you and Dr. Bishop have had a better time lately."

"They were not about Bishop."

"Then what?"

"They just recently started—let's pick this up another time, Bishop is about to speak. Catch you later."

Michael made it through grand rounds, determined not to speak up, since he was so tired. Anne got irritated at him for not noticing her as she walked by. He did not want to talk to anyone, and it showed. It was not like Michael to ignore her ever since their relationship had blossomed into a real romance. He didn't want to be bothered, so he wouldn't say anything stupid.

Anne came by before the shift ended and said, "Hi, big guy, who messed up your corn flakes?"

"Let's go over to the coffee shop. I need to talk to you about those dreams. Let me try to explain the horrible weekend of sleep I had."

Over coffee, Michael went over the vivid dreams, cutting the camping trip short, and how little sleep he had. Anne grimaced and paid. She said, "No gym tonight; seems to me you need the coffee so you can drive home."

9/19/2018
Heimerlich Coliseum
Zarsfon Planet Six
Heimerlich Fiefdom
Quark Dimension

Gimmish was outside Warlord Heimerlich's door when he heard the team captain's voice, "Team Heimerlich is at the very bottom of the rankings thanks to that Moonie Gimmish and his terrible essences. He was the wrong pick for the team, sir."

"I can see that, but I made a pact with him to choose what he wanted to do, since he saved my life in that assassination attempt. You know, if a warlord or any quark breaks their vow, he loses all trust and credibility anywhere in the dimension, period. That's the only thing that has been able to keep society progressing without destroying our civilization, save this attempt at peace. However, you know the worst thing that can happen is that he is sacrificed as the lowest-ranking quark. That's in the rules."

"I know. That is one way to cure the problem. The Game is fun to play; still, losing is depressing."

"Hold on. It's cut-and-dried. Gimmish is accountable for himself now. He can read the scoreboard as well as you. His newness is wearing off, and soon by game rules, he's accountable."

"If we had a better player, we would be winning at least some matches. He has not found a decent essence yet. We other three gamers hate losing and being the laughingstock of the Game. The announcers are already calling for a blowout and calling him out as the reason. It's horrible."

"I understand your passion. I have been in my viewing box every game to witness this disaster of a season. Gimmish has not acted as a team player. He focuses on himself and, in turn, looks foolish. Still, let's allow the season to play out. Also, remember, I am not holding you accountable for my decision."

After eavesdropping in on Heimerlich's conversation, Gimmish hurried off to the concession to pick up a drink before the match. He knew he had a new essence and didn't want to hear complaining about it until the last moment. *I think everybody is in for a surprise today.*

Tol's Dimension Game had been a success thus far. In its twelfth season, the Game had become a super event in every fiefdom, diverting the aggressive quark instincts from killing each other to using virtual gladiators in fights to the death. Even its initial critics enjoyed competing with other warlords for spoils. Only the irascible warlord Alchemy publicly said anything negative about it anymore.

Every large fiefdom had their home team, with game time celebrations and buildup. Still, Gimmish was not invited much to these other events, since it was known he was from a planet's moon and the butt of a joke dimension-wide. That was before today when he would introduce his latest essence discovery.

Minutes later, Gimmish strode into the gamer booth to the glares of his three teammates. The captain growled, "You have missed our pregame strategy session again."

Gimmish answered, "Something came up I had to deal with."

"What's new? That has been your excuse the last three times. You know we are on the bottom of the standings, and we can all see that you don't give a crap!"

"Yes, I know. This time will be different." He attached his Game device to the console to upload his essences for the match.

"How? Your first eight outings have been complete disasters."

"But that changes this time."

"That's what you said last time when you used that rock thing that was so slow, allowing the other team to cut us off and destroy us. We even got penalized points for not getting the thing to move off the court. We ended with a negative score. I did not even know that could happen."

"I got a new essence. I even killed a bad essence host to make room for this one."

"So what? If I only had your lineup of material, I would have shot them all and then myself. All of them were losers. There are highlight bloopers with your name on them."

"This one will impress everybody."

"It had better, because if we don't win today, we will be so far in the hole, we'll be permanently dead last with three to go. You know what happens then."

"Let's play the Game. You'll see." Gimmish saw the derisive looks of his teammates. They shook their heads and took their places.

Over the loudspeakers, the announcer called the arena to order. "To the quarks of the realm, welcome to round nine of this season's Game. Today's match has the visiting team Flashenol, at a record of seven and one against team Heimerlich at zero and eight. Please give a round of applause to our gamers."

The venue was built to a size that maximized the theater of four-on-four hand-to-hand combat. There was only enough space in the arena to seat twenty-eight thousand, which gave the venue an intense atmosphere. The cameras were positioned at every angle, giving the broadcast audiences the dimension-perfect views of every twist and turn during the event.

The camera scanned the gamer booths, announcing each gamer to the crowd. Gimmish's name was booed. With the last shot, the captain added, "You've not impressed one damn quark."

Taking a deep breath, Gimmish hung his head and thought, *I should find another team if this essence does what I think it will do.* The gamers got in their positions to begin.

The announcer came back to summarize the rules, "The players are in position, about to send their virtual gladiators into hand-to-hand combat. The basic rules bear repeating. To mitigate and satisfy the quark's raw passion to fight and kill each other into extinction, to fill these desires, we have created the Game to watch violent competition to the death. The rules are instituted to provide suitable drama to satisfy you, the audience. Each team of four avatar gladiators is equipped with an essence that each gamer has captured. The essences are derived from any living being that was not a quark. Each of the Game's four rounds is ended in ten minutes or when one team loses all four of their fighters. At the end of the period, any essence left can be used in the next round.

"Points are scored when one avatar destroys another at the time mark in that period. The number of minutes remaining is the score posted to the victor's team. If the victor defeats his adversary with six minutes remaining in the period, the team receives six points. There is no double-team or two gladiators striking one opponent simultaneously for quick points; however one fighter can divert another. Also, a gladiator cannot have eye contact with a team member unless an opponent is in the line of view. That is when a switch or diversion can occur."

The team captain again snarked at Gimmish, "Your gladiator won't quit on us like the last four times."

Gimmish ignored the comment. *This time will be different.*

The announcer continued, "This is hand-to-hand, with no projectile weapons such as blasters permitted. Any weapon must be handheld by the gladiator when it strikes its opponent. The defeated avatar then vanishes, clearing the arena floor."

Gimmish had heard the directions before. *Let's get this thing started.*

He watched as the eight gladiators walked onto the Game field. The dirt floor was standard for the footwork of the fighters. Their cleats would dig in while they fought in close quarters scrummaging in multiple player hand-to-hand fighting. They each wore a colorful uniform with a symbol on the back denoting which gamer controlled the avatar.

Over the loudspeaker: "Now it is time. From the Flashenol sector, the standing's leader." The four gladiators held their swords over their heads in unison to their crowd. Gimmish saw the confidence in the other side; clearly they thought this match would be easy. Then he noticed something new out of his fighter, reaction to the tension of the crowd. "Captain, my fighter is reacting that it's ready to go."

The captain responded, "It better be."

He looked and saw team Flashenol standing around like robots, not sizing up the arena, only waiting for orders. He turned to look at his team. Gimmish's essence gladiator looked to be active, analyzing the competition, pacing back and forth.

The announcer finished saying, "On my call, the first period begins. Teams, get ready. On my mark, begin!" Each team moved toward the other from their corners. Team Heimerlich's dark green was easily distinguishable from the Flashenol orange. The fans waved the colored pennons of their teams and began to cheer louder. Spectators started hurling epithets and small snacks at each other, rooting for their sides.

The captain turned to Gimmish, astonished, and said, "Your fighter is telling the others to stay in their lanes. What does that mean?" They both watched the four in a straight line touch each other's fists.

Gimmish answered, "It must be a strategy embedded in the essence." He turned back to the action, feeling slightly optimistic.

With more excitement, the captain said, "They are measuring their spacing! I didn't know we could do that."

Another gamer said, "They know where each other is without using their eyes. That's okay. There's no rule against it."

The other team moved toward the center, sizing up their opponent. They were a strong-looking foursome. Gimmish looked at the captain, who gave the order to engage. Heimerlich's team moved in unison as the crowd came to their feet, roaring their excitement at the start of the action. He then noticed Flashenol's gamers' expressions began to go from smiling to concern seeing the purpose and coordination his team had to their movements.

The gladiators engaged in the center. Since the Flashenol team was moving at different speeds, team Heimerlich reached the first three before the fourth Flashenol fighter reached the scrum, leaving a four-to-three advantage for the home team. Gimmish's essence avatar was on the end free, then reverse-spun into the middle spot, splitting the line, not looking at his engaged teammate per the rules, catching the opposing line off guard, and the team made quick work of two fighters in seconds. Two of the other gladiators took a swift in-and-out strategy on the third fighter to eliminate it.

Flashenol's last fighter made it in time to land a blow on the captain's fighter but lost to Gimmish's avatar in hand-to-hand combat. All of the action took 3.7 minutes for a score of 28.7 to 0.3.

The home crowd erupted with cheers at the impressive annihilation of the Game's number-one team. The captain yelled,

"Gimmish, your essence made that happen! Amazing!" He slapped Gimmish on the back and cheered. "That was magnificent!"

Gimmish sat stunned but smiling, looking at the home crowd wildly cheering for once.

The announcer came back on the loudspeaker and read the score with commentary. "After that short period one, Heimerlich 28.7 to 0.3."

The captain yelled, "That's the greatest one-quarter blowout in Game history!" He calmed down some and turned to Gimmish, "Your essence did it. Can it do it again?"

"I sure hope so."

"Hope so? We have five minutes before the next period. Your guy stole the show so far. What's the plan for a repeat?"

Gimmish had to think of something as opposed to letting the essence do it by itself. He said, "I'll take a different strategy; just watch." The captain looked at Gimmish, stunned, as if he did not know what to think. Gimmish had no idea what to do either. He looked down at the fighting foursome studying the landscape and being coached by Gimmish's surprising essence.

The horn sounded to give the one-minute signal. Both teams stood up, looking at their opposition. Gimmish's player again began to exhort his team to win. They lined up with his player on the other end, this time with his weapon drawn.

The public address announcer resumed: "We are about to begin period two. Rules as before: no double teaming, but still, one player can attack when another yields. As before, the period ends when one team has lost its fighters or after ten minutes, whichever is first." There was a brief pause; then, "Ready quarks? Begin!"

Again the Flashenol team began to walk together, but this time with more discipline. Gimmish's player moved the line forward faster this time. The captain yelled at Gimmish over the roar of the cheering crowd, "What are they doing? Don't you see the other team is more controlled this time?"

Gimmish could only think to say, "Just watch." He didn't know what would happen either. Then the line shifted, and Gimmish's essence aimed toward the inside fighter.

The captain screamed, "Your gladiator is going to commit suicide fighting against two. Stop him!"

One half second before Gimmish pushed the stop key, his fighter stopped and began to run backward, drawing two of the Flashenol warriors away from the other three Heimerlich players, not expecting the diversion. Gimmish saw the two chasing his player since the gladiator's eyes were trained on his two pursuers.

The captain said, "That's brilliant, Gimmish! Your guy has split their rank, giving us a three-on-two on the other end! Our guys will make short work of those two." Gimmish's essence kept moving and circling the scrum, keeping the attention of both fighters with diversions and head fakes.

Gimmish saw his dodging fighter watching for the time when the other subdued the two Flashenol players. When that happened, he turned to the middle to join the three left. Flashenol's warriors did not understand the tactic and chased the new essence. It ran past his teammates, charging. The team noticed that the other booth ordered the two remaining fighters to avoid the charge and use time playing defense. One of the two was caught and destroyed before the period ended.

Gimmish was amazed at his player's natural ability, speed, and instincts. The fighter was so agile and had such anticipation of his motions. The former waiter was so happy looking around and waving at cameras as they videoed the gamer's box. *Master Heimerlich had better be glad he gave me this position now.* The other three jumped for joy at seeing what was happening. The announcer came on the loudspeaker: "The score at the halfway mark, Heimerlich, 46.2 to team Flashenol's one. The third period will begin in twenty-five minutes."

Gimmish nudged the captain to look at the stunned faces of the opposing gamers. "Look at them! Look at them!" The team celebrated through the halftime break.

Four minutes before the beginning of the third period, the captain asked Gimmish, "Still a half to go. Got any ideas?"

"It looks like this essence instinctively understands attack patterns. We don't have much time to figure something fancy, so let your player follow mine." Gimmish turned and thought, *I'm letting this essence do the work as long as possible.* The one-minute warning alerted the arena that the third quarter was about to begin. The spectators and teams went to their seats to see if the number-one team in the cosmos could make an epic comeback.

The captain yelled, "Is everybody ready?"

The announcer came back over the address system, "Gladiators, begin!"

Team Flashenol formed in a diamond pattern so as not to tip off their strategy. Gimmish watched as they moved to the left in an oblique march. Then he saw his player slap his teammate on the shoulder to form a wedge. They were more tightly bunched with Gimmish's essence to one side inside the triangular arrow shape. They moved slowly, allowing the clock to wind down. The Heimerlich team moved back and forth, trying to bait their opponents. The crowd started to boo, wanting more action.

The captain asked Gimmish, "The crowd is booing. What do we do now?"

"Who cares? We are winning. Let's retreat some to goad them into making a move."

"Sounds good to me." The team slowly moved backward, giving more distance so they could react to a charge.

The minutes felt like an hour. The game clock in the corner became a distraction. *Faster, clock, faster!* At the 6.2-minute mark, the other team made their charge at the Heimerlich line. Gimmish's essence made another spin move that changed his position on the line and subdued the fighter that was to attack another player at the

5.9-minute mark. This left one Heimerlich fighter isolated from the other three. This again left a three-on-two scrum, advantage team Heimerlich. Now there were two fights in front of the crowd. Both sets of fans jumped up and down, shaking the whole coliseum.

The captain yelled, "This is the greatest day of my life!" Gimmish was also having fun for the first time.

As the time clock continued to run, the two isolated fighters had to continue their one-on-one to the death. Blow by blow, the crowd roared as they heard the weapons clanging and the essences struggling to stay alive. The scrum was brutal on both teams. A fighter from each team was lost, and Heimerlich captain's gladiator was injured close to the end. The crowd began to scream and stomp their feet. The Flashenol side came alive, waiting for a comeback. There had to be a last battle for the score. The captain yelled, "You better watch out; they're coming after you now. They don't want you in the last round."

Gimmish said, "If you want to protect me, you may need to watch my back."

At the 1.6-minute mark, Flashenol's best gladiator made a run at Gimmish's essence. In a sacrificial move, the captain had his wounded fighter cut in front of the charging enemy. Flashenol's gladiator killed the captain's fighter, and immediately Gimmish's fighter slashed and destroyed Flashenol's last chance.

The horn sounded to end the period. It was a much more competitive period. Still, team Heimerlich extended their lead. As theater goes, it was the most entertaining period, leaving only two Heimerlich fighters and one Flashenol player. The period went to team Heimerlich, and the score was sixty-two to 12.5.

The last-minute action kept the crowd cheering throughout the third break. Team Flashenol did not field their best fighters. It was also time for the Heimerlich team to try other essences. This time Gimmish was eliminated 3.8 minutes into the period. The quarks in the stands were howling with approval, knowing that they had new hope. The Flashenol team declared a moral victory in the fourth period, winning it by six points. The final score was eighty to 36.5. Flashenol and his gamers came to the booth and shook hands with all the Heimerlich team.

Gimmish was all smiles, knowing his new essence was the star of the coliseum that day. The other gamers knew it too, showing their appreciation and looking forward to the next match.

From his board chairmanship of the Game post, Warlord Tol watched the match, not expecting the result. *There is something very different about that gladiator. I believe I need to pay attention to this going forward.* He made notes and did not miss the next matches.

Beginning 5/10/1996
Tol HQ Compound
Areanosten Planet Five
Tol Fiefdom
Quark Dimension

The Game was created by Tol as a result of his observations and conclusions. With great study, he discovered that the dimension was formed by an expansion of super-condensed matter. As it expanded, energized particles collided, creating life in the cosmos. Intelligent life began to appear with the eventual quantity of atomic collisions.

As time passed, these beings called *quarks* began to covet what others possessed, growing more aggressive with each other, and organizing into fiefdoms for collective power and protection. After a time, hostilities began between fiefdoms, causing the death rate to surpass the generation rate.

In earlier times, quarks would simply be replaced by ordinary generation of matter. Then Tol sensed that the replacements were not being produced as quickly or as well as before. His hunch was correct.

After intense study, he found that with the same amount of matter, as the cosmos expanded, particle collisions occurred less frequently and efficiently, creating less life while hostilities took more and more lives. Tol quantified and concluded that the trend would cause the collapse of quark civilization.

The Game was Tol's best answer to channel quarks' lust for aggression, a diversion, a competition that generated tangible outcomes.

Sargen, a Tol ally and successful warlord, figured the analysis that took survival and food sources into account could be a unifying scenario in the dimension. Even the crafty and ambitious warlord, Alchemy, had to see the logic.

The job of convincing the warlords of this eventual catastrophe was airtight. The numbers and facts were meticulously presented to keep the most skeptical warlord from considering the analysis was done from a point of weakness. The two warlords came together and discussed the strategy. A list was presented with a ranking of warlords in the order of their perceived agreeability, putting Alchemy last. Charts of the expanding universe and timelines for action were available for all to keep copies of the predicted events and plan of action.

They began presenting to Philimar, who loved excess of anything, including food. Then Rezfen, Maldonate, Flashenol, on down the list to the irascible Alchemy. Maldonate was so astonished by the facts that he came along to meet with Alchemy to support the plan. Only upon realizing that he was the only holdout and that the entire legion of warlords had signed on to the peace agreement, and with the threat of annihilation as part of the effort, did Alchemy relent.

Now that every fiefdom in the dimension was on board, the Game was established with strict rules on governance. Not all the warlords enjoyed the idea of an elaborate game for such sobering times, but they did not have any better ideas that satisfied the other warlords.

Each Game season was a marathon that lasted for about two years from the third planet's perspective. The gamers could change their players by killing off the host that they came from in the universe. Gamers changed their essences so that they improved their sense of surprise and strategy. Most of the essences came from unintelligent animals, so they readily sacrificed them when changes were needed. Other life forms from other worlds that had intelligent consciousness provoked empathy when they had to be destroyed. Any one of them was expendable.

But Gimmish was about to ruin all the time and effort Tol and Sargen spent and instituted with one pivotal mistake.

4/27/2019
Gimmish's Workshop
Zarsfon Planet Six Moon Two
Heimerlich Fiefdom
Quark Dimension

The tall figure of Tol arrived at the faraway outpost to see how Gimmish had orchestrated his sixth team win in a row in the Game to end the season. He wanted to know what changes he made to achieve his recent successes, since before now, he was on the lowest-ranked team, the worst gamer on the team, and in danger of being sacrificed as punishment.

"Congratulations on your recent wins, Gimmish. I would like to personally commend you on your successful turnaround."

"Yes, Master Tol, I found a new character for the Game. It is a strong essence I found on that third planet by accident. I got lost in the other dimension and stumbled onto it."

"You mean the one I tell stories about? Didn't I tell you and everyone else it was dangerous to use essences from there?"

"Yes, but you never specifically said we couldn't, and no one ever said why. There are a lot of potential essences there that would make the Game even better."

Tol became concerned, "That may be so, still what you did is release a variable into this dimension you know nothing about. Those beings have free will and curiosity for knowledge that can be used for success in the Game, or they can corrupt and destroy it—or worse, turn on us and cause havoc."

Gimmish got down on his knees, pleading with the warlord. "But I am winning now. Please. I worked so hard to find and capture this essence. What can one of those do to us? They do not know they are being used. They do not know we exist, and we are superior."

"Gimmish, they are curious and savvy enough to possibly discover this dimension. They are the only creatures in either dimension known to be nearly as intelligent as we are." He did not tell him about Kollindarrot and his warriors having offspring with third-planet beings, giving the planet quark traits.

"How do you know?"

"I have periodically monitored them since I discovered them. These third-planet beings are rapidly advancing in science and reaching for the stars. They have telescopes that can now see far into their dimension. Luckily for us, portals are difficult to spot. They look more like small black holes."

"Why do we not just get rid of them by attacking them? Just destroy the entire planet?"

Tol thought for a moment. He did not want to reveal the pledge he had made with the third-planet being Enoch, so he said, "I do not want to waste that time and be diverted from protecting my fiefdom from someone like power-hungry Alchemy. The more we can keep him close, the less likely he will cause trouble for our dimension. Since I did not explicitly tell you not to go to the third planet, I recommend that you keep your recent gains, for you were honest and did not try to hide your actions. Your naivety shows you truly did not understand the pitfalls of your actions. However, I am ordering you to discreetly destroy that essence and find another to use from somewhere else at once. Now, get it done. Time is a factor."

"How do I destroy the essence without killing the host it came from? Once a life form is destroyed, only then does the essence die. And when he dies, others will see that he died, right?"

"You will need to kill the host by finding some sort of illness totally unique to that entire species that cannot be transmitted or cured, and the being must die. It will have to look like a slow, pernicious disease that developed, leaving no room for curiosity. You cannot make it look like a crime because that brings investigators. Blasters leave traces of evidence that would cause problems. You cannot be discovered with this, or it could destroy the Game and tear this universe apart."

"What do you mean by that? Why are you making it so hard for me to get rid of something so good?"

Tol glared at Gimmish and said, "You will do as I command you as an official of the Game. The alternative is to have you executed for cheating by going to the third planet. Do you understand?"

Completely flustered, Gimmish feel so his knees, elbows, and the top of his head touched the floor, and with his hands clasped on the back of his head, he quietly answered, "Yes, Master Tol."

"Now I must leave and log my report."

Tol got back into the transport and left. Gimmish rose and sat at his desk, shaken and distraught since his whole career with the Game—and possibly his life—was about to be vanquished without his third-planet essence. He wanted to know why there was so much caution since it was the first time he was moving up in the last five Games' standings, and now it was all gone. He was tired of being ridiculed by the other gamers as a loser before he found Michael. His essence was the reason for his latest successes, and he now had to get rid of it. He even pondered the thought that Heimerlich might have another favorite, and this was a setup.

7/14/2019
Zarsfon Heimerlich Research Library
Zarsfon Planet Six
Heimerlich Fiefdom
Quark Dimension

Gimmish didn't see anything wrong with using the essence and wondered what Tol was thinking about. Since he had finished the season strong, he would search for other essences for a time until he found out more. So he began the painful chore of researching diseases that would destroy his best player.

First, he searched records of past times to see what it was about the third planet that disturbed Tol so much. His team sponsor, Heimerlich, had given him the access code to the database as payment for saving his life years ago. He searched back to the beginning of the Game, where he found a redacted file area that was not supposed to be uncovered. Before the redacted pages was a description of the directions for going to the other, temporal dimension to harvest essences for the new Game. *Why doesn't anyone know about this portal?* However, after the redaction, this "third planet" was excluded from any essence hunting for the Game, a one-line afterthought. No reason was given, just the bare statement.

Gimmish traced the entry to an event chronicled over six thousand years earlier in the third planet's history. It took days, but he found references to supernatural beings written in religious history. He saw things referred to as dragons, to magical performers, and one reference to something called *giants* and *angels*. He dug deeper and found that a man named Enoch was mentioned who was said to have been "taken away." He did not understand all the writing, but he pieced together a theory that this had something to do with the warnings about the third planet.

Seeing enough to satisfy his curiosity, he now had to plan a way to kill his essence host with a unique, incurable illness. To find out more, he learned about these "human beings." They did not form from unstable quarks; instead, they were created from binary beings with a complex map of traits known as the "genetic code." *This code may be the key to getting rid of my problem.* He needed to change his replication process to make faulty genes slowly.

He stumbled on a disease that fit the scenario, amyotrophic lateral sclerosis or ALS, an incurable disease. He had to create a disease uniquely for the host that was 100 percent nontransferable to anyone else on the third planet, leaving no trace. He went to work.

It took weeks, but he had the resources. He found an idea from another planet that had overpopulated itself to the point where twenty billion beings lived on a planet with a surface area that would fit in a rectangle three thousand by two thousand kilometers. Most of the surface was covered with liquid that created insect-like creatures, which were modified and bioengineered as random vectors of illness and death by the leaders. He procured one of those vectors so he could use it for his plan to kill the host.

But he had to find a virus to change his essence's host genetic code slowly. He took the ALS model and, with the help of one of the gamers on his team, found someone who was able to create a vector organism. Gimmish and his friend, with a significant amount of research, found a synthetically produced organism with its own genome, very similar to a mutated virus. The unique organism was placed in the vector and taken to the third planet. The vector was a one-time use remote-controlled device with organic and inorganic parts.

Two months later, he traveled to the third planet carrying the weaponized vector in a custom-made case to end what he had started. The plan had no loose ends. The vector had worked before without the remote control, so all he had to do was aim and release. The vector was loaded with the weaponized DNA, and he was ready to get this over with.

7/18/2019
DNA Research Center
Cambridge, Massachusetts
Sol Planet Three
Milky Way Dimension

Dr. Ed Hatcher could not wait for this resident class of his genomic rotation to begin. Dr. Hatcher told others he had landed two of the most gifted minds in the country in Dr. Robin Grandy and Dr. Michael Townsend. They were at the top of their classes in undergrad and medical schools. They had received glowing praise from their previous rotations. Finally, they were the two most enthusiastic research candidates he had ever met, both wanting so much to find novel cures for stubbornly complex and deadly diseases.

Robin was the local Boston prodigy, via Dartmouth and Harvard Medical. Michael, the brilliant son of the South, hailed from Duke University, and a different class at Harvard Medical. That Monday morning, both reported to Dr. Hatcher's office for a meeting.

Hatcher opened the conversation by saying, "I am thrilled to welcome both of you to this genomic residency. We have work to do against many truly dreadful diseases. You both will be standing on the shoulders of others who have made progress in solving the riddles of human illnesses. I will demand your rigor to research and hope to solve the most vexing diseases in medicine. Now let me show you around."

The two residents were about to exit the office when Michael held the door, and with a smile, said to Robin, "Ladies first." Robin, with a curious smile, took the cue and coyly walked past.

Outside the office, walking in tandem behind Dr. Hatcher, she said to Michael, "My husband doesn't hold the door for me. I wish he had your manners."

Michael replied, "I'll take that as a compliment."

Ed spoke over his shoulder, saying, "Always professional, right?"

Both residents answered at the same time, "Right."

They reached their lab station, and Ed addressed Robin, "Dr. Grandy, I want you and Dr. Townsend to work together on a project that has intrigued me for years. Dr. Townsend has postulated in writings that a piece of DNA from one mammal can be used to be curative in another by selectively replacing snippets of specific genes into a human."

Robin said, "Fascinating."

Ed spoke further, "If you read the detailed explanation of his work, you will see its logic. It may not work, but it is better thought out than anything I have found thus far. We need to investigate it further."

Michael smiled and said, "I spent a lot of time using your genome mapping project as my starting point, Dr. Hatcher. I also read the research about the synthetic *E. coli* species created in England, which dovetailed with your mapping project. I took their ideas of creating life with DNA and then thought about changing lives by repairing DNA abnormalities, using the *E. coli* to produce the therapeutic compound."

Robin whispered to Michael, "Are all noses this brown down south?" Michael rolled his eyes and ignored the comment.

Ed continued, "Exactly! Dr. Townsend, I want you to lead this interspecies genome project. Dr. Grandy, your work with transport molecules has everything to do with targeting treatments in specific tissue layers. Together, I want you both to work on developing treatments that allow predisposed humans to turn off their ticking time bombs. Think of the breast cancer that could be cured without radical mastectomies. If we can fix the BRCA1 and BRCA2 genes, think of the other diseases that could be mitigated or eliminated."

Michael said, "I'm excited."

A smiling Dr. Hatcher clapped his hands and said, "It's three o'clock. For the next two hours, I want you both to set up your offices and make your spaces as conducive to creative thinking as you can. Then be at the alumni house down the street at six for the department welcome party. Now go."

After the first meeting, a two-week orientation began during which the two young doctors got to know each other better. Robin took Michael to a restaurant, letting him know about her history. "I tried psychiatry, but that turned out not to be my cup of tea. I did well, but felt I could contribute more by finding cures and letting others do the practice."

Michael said, "I'm too blunt to mold someone's head. Being a former linebacker, I'd rather crack it. I played pro ball for three years, but my heart wasn't in it for the long haul. Look here, if I were an animal, I would want to be a grizzly bear." She cut her eyes at him. "No, think about it. Bears and linebackers have a great deal in common. They're big, strong, and like to attack."

A hesitant Robin countered, "But you don't come across as aggressive, like my lawyer husband. Am I missing something?"

Michael smiled. "My parents taught me manners and how to control myself. And they said, if I were to do anything meaningful in life, I would need to leave the aggression on the football field."

Michael saw that Robin blushed. She cleared her throat and said, "Why medical science?"

He grinned and asked, "What do you mean?"

"Why did you go into medical science and not zoology if you liked bears so much?"

He answered, "I am fascinated by bears and what makes them tick. We have the same chemicals in our bodies, the same biological systems with a few variations, the same double-helix chemistry transcribing who and what we are. We have different illnesses; why? Which molecular code tells us to grow hands versus paws, hair versus fur, or color versus black-and-white vision? Also, an MD gets a better paycheck."

Robin looked surprised at the conversation. She asked, "Did you want to be a bear as a child?"

Michael chuckled at the question. He remarked, "Falling back on the psychiatry thing, aren't we?"

Robin retorted, "You began this conversation weirdly."

Michael raised his eyebrows and said, "Touché. Well, being a bear might have been cool for a while until I couldn't have my mother's cooking. Also, I would have never met my fiancé, Anne. She will be here in two weeks."

She sighed and said, "I also left psychiatry because I felt hypocritical. I was giving everyone else advice but could not solve my own problems."

Michael answered, "You know that the key to solving a problem is to look at it from an unbiased viewpoint. That's why it's okay to help others even while you struggle with your own demons."

She asked, "Are you trying to convince me to go back? And how do you know they are demons?"

He responded, "Just splainin'."

"Huh?"

"It's Southern for explaining."

"What about you being from Charleston? It's such a neat town."

"Yeah, I sure wish what I wanted to do could be done down there. But I guess that's what vacations are for."

"Okay, I guess the perspective is different, since I work in my hometown."

They continued to learn more about each other as time went on, adding to their ability to communicate their intricate scientific thoughts.

4/23/2020
Deep Wilderness
Near the Ninepipe National Wildlife Refuge, Montana
Sol Planet Three
Milky Way Dimension

Michael's research led him to bear country near the Flathead Indian Reservation in conjunction with the University of Montana in Missoula. There he worked with a Native American forester named Jim Longfield, whose passion was his native land. Their shared love of the outdoors began a lasting friendship.

One trip on a warmer-than-average spring day in the wilderness near McDonald Lake became eventful when Michael and Jim surveyed a group of female bears, one being very pregnant. Jim told Michael, "That female is going to deliver in the next two weeks. Notice how slow she is moving."

Michael replied, "Wow, I've only read and watched videos of this. But how do we retrieve the stem cells I need from them?"

Jim said, "That's the problem, my friend. When the mother gives birth, one thing she does is eat the placenta for nourishment and protein. To approach a hungry mother bear after giving birth is not a great idea."

"No kidding."

"We will need to hire someone who knows how to use a tranquilizer gun to come back. I know someone in Denver who's worked for me when we had a rogue."

"We need his number. We can call him when we get back to the lab."

They watched from downwind so as not to be noticed. The other females moved to the clearing quickly, and cubs came out of the brush to be close to their mothers. Michael said, "This is so cool."

They watched for about twenty minutes, every so often taking a picture of the majestic creatures. Michael went away in awe, talking about each bear and the traits he noticed from the observation.

They began to head back to the camp, marveling that they had seen so much and observed habits only studied or read about in the most esoteric literature or seen on channels like Animal Planet. Michael downloaded the photos from his cell phone onto his computer and made notes about the entire adventure. Michael and Jim decided to go back the next day to see if the bears were still in that area.

While walking back, they noticed broken branches and new footprints—newer than theirs from the day before. Jim also noticed something peculiar about the size of the prints. "This does not look good, Michael. These are boot prints from smaller feet than ours. I'm a size eleven, and your foot is bigger. This boot cannot be more than a size nine, which means we have company."

"Okay, you are the park ranger. What is going on?"

"Poaching; they are out for bear."

"Did you mean to be funny?"

"No, it just came out that way. We have got to be extra quiet since we are not in camouflage, and we may be mistaken for an animal, or they could be willing to shoot us to get rid of witnesses. The best thing we can do now is text the sheriff's department. Now we need to stay put and hide until help arrives."

"Where is a good place?"

"I know a cave I found by accident in the side of a mountain, off the path. The GPS will let the backup know where we are."

"Jim, do you have a weapon?"

"No, never carry one."

"Don't worry. I let the Southern redneck come out in me sometimes." Michael pulled his loaded Sig Sauer out of his backpack. "I use it to shoot snakes."

At that moment, two shots rang out in the direction of the clearing. Loud voices were yelling, and bears were growling. The words were indistinguishable. Then came sounds of bears roaring and more shots. The sounds of pandemonium rang through the trees lasting about two minutes. Both Michael and Jim thought the worst: something was dead, whether human, bear or both. Sounds like somebody running through the forest went by them as if danger was following the person.

Jim and Michael decided to slowly walk toward the clearing. They arrived to find one dead bear and one man mauled to death. The bear was shot in the back above the heart, so it had enough strength to attack and kill the shooter before it died from bleeding. These were inexperienced poachers using a deer rifle, not strong enough to stop a grizzly bear attack.

Jim called the station to see where the backup was. A man answered and said they were delayed by a man running out of the woods in panic, yelling and crying, "I told him not to do it! I told him not to do it!"

Jim said back, "Don't let him go. He needs to be prosecuted for poaching on federal lands. Also, I am here with two dead, one bear and one human, his poaching buddy that was not so lucky."

"Roger."

Michael said, "This was the mama bear near full term. Her cubs are still alive and will live on their own but need to be delivered before they suffocate in the womb. I'll do the quick surgery now, but I will need to contact a veterinarian to know what to do next."

Jim said, "Who do you know?"

He answered, "I have the number of a high school buddy, Charlie DuBosc, who is now the vet at the Creekside Zoo in South Carolina in charge of the large mammals. We used to hunt dove and fish together with our dads. I can call him to ask what to do next. We don't have much time before the cubs will be exposed, and the stem cells in the placenta will be rendered useless."

"I hope the reception is good out here. I do have a line of sight to the cell towers toward the reservation."

"Good. Now radio for a cooler so we can harvest the placenta or any other organs we need."

Michael took about ten minutes to open the dead bear's abdomen to extract the two preterm cubs. He then called and used speaker. A man answered, "Charles DuBosc. How can I help you, Michael?"

"Charlie, I need a professional consult. I'm in the Flathead National Forest in Montana. I came across a shot dead, pregnant female bear with two cubs still alive. I just delivered them by C-section so they wouldn't die from asphyxiation. I don't know how to keep them alive after birth delivered this way. And I want to save them so they can be released back into the wild."

"Daggum, Michael, what are you doing in Montana?"

"I have to do research here to study the genetics of mammals and their ... What do I do now?"

"Okay, first, bears are born hungry and drink mother's milk constantly. Usually they are born in the late winter or early spring and are kept warm, about our body temperature, wrapped up in the mother's arm, so get blankets as soon as you can. If you don't have bear milk, get fresh cow's milk, and mix it with baby formula for nutrients. Get unflavored protein powder and mix it in. You will need a lot of it. Just think, a mama bear will lose a third to two-thirds of a pound daily feeding the cubs. You need to know they will only be two or three pounds in four to six weeks. But just keep their body temps about the same as ours. Does that help?"

"Hell yeah, man."

"Keep them warm and fed, and don't worry how small they are now. That's normal, but I may want to come up to Boston later this spring and see you. Are you okay now?"

"Yes, I am, and thanks."

After the call, Michael looked at Jim's astonishment and said, "You never know when you're going to need a friend's help. Now pick your jaw up off the ground and help me. Radio for a cooler, blankets, and milk. We've got mouths to feed and a placenta to harvest." Michael took a canteen and towel out of his pack to wash off the newborn cubs.

Soon, two men with blankets, a cooler, and a half-gallon bottle of milk appeared, ready to help. One said to Jim, "We have a truck on the path over that small ridge about a hundred yards from here near the poacher's truck. We are questioning the one poacher and contacting the next of kin for the deceased. It looks like the other guy was trying to talk his buddy out of doing this. His rifle didn't discharge. The other met his maker doing something stupid."

Jim said, "Okay, have him talk to the authorities about this. We have cubs to save now. Michael, how are we doing?"

Michael said, "Not much longer with these two. They are small, so we need to wrap them up quickly and get them to an incubator fast. They can't stay out here long without warmth, or they will go hypothermic."

The men gave him the blankets, and he removed the cubs from the mother with great gentleness. He put the afterbirth in the cooler with ice, gave one cub to each of the men, and they hurried off to the trucks.

While walking to the trucks, he called the zoology department with the story of the poachers and the bears. He asked them to set up a makeshift incubator until they got hold of a real one from the local hospital. After they got the cubs situated that day and the placenta stored, Michael went to the hospital to pick up the incubator and went by the local Walmart for the protein powder, formula, and whole milk.

Michael was able to harvest the placenta for his genetic research. He took samples with him back to Cambridge to study, and the rest was left in cryogenic storage at the university.

THE ILLNESS

10/1/2020
The Appalachian Trail, Beartown State Park
The Berkshires, Massachusetts
Sol Planet Three
Milky Way Dimension

The last weekend in September was supposed to be an unusually warm weekend, so since it would be Anne's first weekend of the month to work, Michael decided to take an overnight in the Beartown State Forest to hike that part of the Appalachian Trail. He got there midmorning after seeing Anne off to work first thing. He was ready for a good escape from the closed-in lab. He hiked a trail three hours up a mountain and three hours back.

Just before he was to break down his gear at the campsite at dusk, he felt a bug bite him on his arm. *Damn, that almost felt like a hornet.* He thought it was a horsefly doing its last dive before the weather got cold, rubbing the back of his neck. *Can't even see it. It hurts like hell!*

He heard leaves moving behind him. *Funny, there's no wind, but something made noise. I guess it was an animal.* He remembered the last time he'd gone camping without Anne. It was the same feeling of something watching him. After he drew his weapon, he followed the sound into the brush. Still not finding anything, he went back to his campsite, took a deep breath, lay down, and snuggled into his sleeping bag.

43

When he heard a sudden whoosh overhead, he thought, *That was strange. Why am I getting a bad feeling about this?* It took him a while to fall asleep.

12/7/2020
Tol HQ Compound
Areanosten Planet Five
Tol Fiefdom
Quark Dimension

Gimmish wanted to tell Tol himself that he had accomplished the mission. He flew his small craft toward Tol's zone, wanting to get there as fast as he could. He had messed up so many times, he wanted Tol to see him as successfully doing something, anything. He arrived without incident and tried to keep from acting giddy. He knocked on the door while humming.

Tol was surprised and asked on the comm, "What are you doing here, and how did you get past the guards?"

Gimmish said, "I wanted to see you face-to-face to get your body language response." He ignored the second question.

"Why did you travel all the way here to tell me something that you could have done by video, wasting your time and mine? Well, you are not going to. You are a moron." He called the guard's office to come to get the "intruder."

Gimmish yelled through the communicator, "Your sector is on the way home."

Tol came back on the comm and said, "I do not care where you came from. You should not be here. Your escort will be with you in a moment."

Gimmish fumed and walked away. *I am no loser. I will show him I am the best gamer. Sure, I lost games in the beginning, but I've turned it around by using that third-planet essence for six matches in a row. And Tol sent me away. I don't know when or how, but he will regret how he treated me.*

A guard came up to him, drawing his sidearm, and asked, "Master Tol has ordered me to escort you. What are you doing here, and where are you from?"

"I am Gimmish, the gamer from the Heimerlich fiefdom."

"All right, that still doesn't tell me why you came all the way from Heimerlich's realm unannounced to see Master Tol. The warlord is not seeing anyone and is not receiving anyone at this time. You are trespassing."

"Oh, I was on the way home after taking care of a problem on the third planet," Gimmish said, hiding the thrill in his voice.

The official said, "Nobody from this dimension is to go there." He shot Gimmish with his sidearm, a light rings device, and bound his hands and feet. "You're going to jail."

With Gimmish bound in the rings, he was put in the car without issue even though he tried to struggle free. The light rings held him immobile the entire way to the station. He was brought in front of the magistrate and charged with violating a directive endangering the dimension and trespassing onto the warlord's premises. If he was found guilty, it could mean a life sentence, or if someone in this dimension died due to his negligence, the death penalty was to pay for the other's life. He was scared and asked if he could contact Tol, which was granted.

Tol, rubbing his ring, was betting to himself that it was Gimmish when his communicator alerted him. Tol breathed heavily, "What do you want?"

Gimmish said, "I wanted to personally tell you that our problem is taken care of. That's all."

Tol answered, "I want to impress upon you what a mistake it is to bother me. You are getting one chance to never do that again, or I will have you executed on the spot. The only reason I did not do it this time was that you are Heimerlich's gamer and now problem. Sleep on it." Tol slammed the communicator and went to rest.

The following morning, Tol called the station to have Gimmish released and escorted him directly to his craft to be at once expelled with a warning never to return unless on official business. His merciful act was now his nightmare if word of it got out to the other warlords about the third planet. He could have problems caused by the gamer's actions, since he had not made it clear while training him. Tol had to find a way to get rid of his predicament before it hurt him.

Gimmish went back to his home in the Heimerlich sector. When he got there, the workshop had been ransacked. Papers and drawers were thrown around as if someone was looking for information. Gimmish became nervous about who would be snooping around his workshop.

He had his essence device with him the entire time. *I bet a rival team broke in here looking for my essences.* He picked up the capture device that had Michael's extract in it so he could see how his plan was working. *Even better, why don't I give it to myself so no one else can steal it? If it gives me a benefit, fine. If not, I can make sure I do everything to make sure he dies of this illness. Still, if I'm guessing correctly, it may allow me to keep up with the host's health. When it dies, I'll know it and be free to use other essences.*

Turning the device to himself, he pulled the trigger and looked at the blue light entering his eye. It turned red and clicked. *There, done. Nobody else can get it. If it kills me, at least I've done it to myself.*

He was concerned that Michael was going to seek a remedy to figure out his problem. He wanted to see if this was a way to connect with Michael to monitor and affect his disease process until he died. Gimmish had to do something to get him away from any research people who might diagnose or cure his illness, not leaving anything to chance, or he would be held to account. He had to think of a plan.

4/14/2021
DNA Research Center
Cambridge, Massachusetts
Sol Planet Three
Milky Way Dimension

While writing the report about his trip to Montana, Michael made the mistake of updating his Windows software after lunch. *Daggum, why in the hell did I do that? Okay, smart people do dumb things too. It's been half an hour, and still, this thing is only 14 percent updated.* He read the comment on the screen, "Hmmm. 'This will take a while.'" *What an understatement.*

He got up from the desk, a little sorer than usual. He looked out the window at a gorgeous day. *I might as well get some fresh air and work off my lunch. If I stay here, I may put my fist through the screen. Maybe I will be inspired to look down another avenue for a fresh idea.*

He walked by Robin's office, knocked on the door frame, and said, "Going out for some fresh air."

Robin asked, "Need someone to walk with you?"

He answered, "I started an update on my computer. Now it's offline for an hour. I'm stuck in limbo and need to walk. Sure, come on."

As they were walking down the steps, Michael said, "I don't know what is going on with me. Anne said my gait has changed when I walk. The other day, I tripped over nothing. It was like my left leg quit working, and my right one kept on."

She reacted with concern. "That's odd. What could cause that?"

"I'm trying to research that. On a quick search, the first thing that came up was ALS, Lou Gehrig's disease. But …"

Robin interrupted, "Oh, there is no cure for that."

He continued, "Not now, but a new biotech company has come up with an experimental compound that inhibits the enzyme produced in people with the disease that degrades nervous tissue, causing the paralysis body-wide. That gives people time like donepezil does for Alzheimer's. At this point, I am self-diagnosing. It's me being paranoid."

"Oh, God help us, you don't want that."

"But what I want to do is to find the DNA link and use our research to fix the aberrant amino acid sequence and cure the disease."

"And I have been working on drug delivery technology to transport molecules that would normally be unstable in the body to their therapeutic sites."

"Right. It would be like fixing a computer program error. Your transport molecule would be delivering the correct DNA gene sequence throughout the entire body, installing the program fix. The key is telling the transport molecule where to go."

Before Robin could say anything in response, a disheveled individual appeared in front of them from nowhere. He came up to Michael holding a lotto ticket in his hand and said, "For food?"

Michael looked at this strange-looking person and held out his hand. The seemingly homeless person put the lotto ticket in his hand and repeated, "For food?" Michael did not say a word and gave a puzzled frown. It was a Powerball ticket that was powered up.

Robin said, "Give him some money to buy food." Michael shrugged his shoulders and gave him five dollars. The person in ragged clothing shook his head in pleasure and walked away down a side street.

Robin said, "That was nice. You gave him five dollars for a three-dollar ticket."

Michael replied, "He stood in line, so I didn't need to. I was going to buy a ticket after work anyway. Can't hurt to try."

Robin gave a pensive look and said, "Call it woman's intuition, but there is something strange about that person. He gave me the creeps, like he was stalking you to have that ticket."

In an exasperated tone, Michael said, "Aw, now you're acting paranoid. Why on Earth would anyone stalk someone with a lotto ticket, knowing that the odds of winning are only two hundred seventy-five million to one? Who in their wildest dreams would say that's plausible? He probably found it on the ground and wanted to try to sell it for beer money. You know what? There are greater odds for there to be intelligent life elsewhere in the universe than to win this lotto."

She answered, "Well, it seems you were the only person he offered it to with all these others around. He didn't offer it to me."

He answered back with a cheeky grin, "I would have offered it to a lovely lady like yourself since I am a smart man."

"And my husband says Southerners are dumb hicks. I must say that was a pretty smooth comeback."

He slowly shook his head and with an aw-shucks grin said, "Always professional. Let's go back to putting all that thinking you're doing into discussing your thoughts with me. I like the idea of your transport molecule." He put the ticket in his shirt pocket, and they both walked back to the office.

4/15/2021
Michael's Apartment
Cambridge, Massachusetts
Sol Planet Three
Milky Way Dimension

Michael and Anne were each about to leave for their respective jobs. She had found a nursing position in critical care at Mass General as a charge nurse. Intensely jumping into her professional role, every morning before going to work, she made sure to read something from any nursing journal to stay abreast of news on improving patient outcomes and enhancing the work environment.

After reading her journal, she came into the bathroom to brush her teeth. She moved Michael's shirt from the previous day off the bathtub side and noticed the lotto ticket in the shirt pocket. Coming into the bedroom, she said, "I didn't know ya played the lotto."

"Oh, that. Hey, tonight's jackpot is over five hundred million dollars. This homeless guy came up to me with the ticket, wanting to trade it for food. I gave him a five and took the lotto ticket."

"It probably isn't a winner, so ya did a good deed and helped the person out."

"I'll put it on my tin box and check it out later. Got to get in there after you and brush my teeth."

4/16/2021
DNA Research Center
Cambridge, Massachusetts
Sol Planet Three
Milky Way Dimension

Late that morning, Michael began to think about his dream, a research center near grizzly bear country. *Now I've got to do something to convince Anne this is not totally crazy.* He and Robin had teamed together to physiologically isolate specific genes responsible for bears' genetic advantages over humans. He looked up and smiled at the framed cover of the *New England Journal of Medicine* that contained the research letter that had produced worldwide interest in Robin's and his work. He knew he was on to something but needed a way to be close to the "action." *Now that I have found the specific gene sequence that allows bears to save water during hibernation, I need to search for other possible benefits humans can use. I need to do my research in bear country. I won't need to spend time searching for enough grant money.*

Robin knocked on the door. "Do you have a minute?"

He said, "Yeah, what's up?"

"Did you know that homeless guy who gave you the lotto ticket fits the description of the homeless guy that bought the winning ticket yesterday."

"Really?"

"Did you know the jackpot was over six hundred million?"

"No."

"Did you check the numbers this morning?"

"No."

"Then why do you have this grin plastered on your face since you got here? Are you trying to hide something from your partner?"

"No, but is that the real reason you are here?"

Robin stood quietly for a moment. Her facial expression turned sad with quivering lips as she closed the door.

He asked, "What wrong?"

She broke down, tears streaming down her face, and said, "My lawyer husband has found another woman! He said he didn't want someone who was married to their job!"

Michael watched her weeping, unable to speak. He asked, "Do you need to go home?"

She blurted, "To what? I have no home I want to go to. While we have been here doing gene research, he has been doing research in that woman's jeans."

"Oh, gosh!"

"And I don't dare go home and listen to my parents carp at me. They love their status enough to want me to beg the creep to take me back. What do I do?" She continued to cry.

Michael texted Anne for help. No answer. He suggested, "Why don't we take a walk outside in the fresh air? This way, we can breathe easier and not have people wondering what is going on in here. Let's go get some coffee."

Robin looked up quizzically. He said, "I mean, I don't want anyone to ask you questions until you feel better." Michael knew that, due to the success of their research, Ed Hatcher had given them more latitude when it came to time. Their collaborative success had exceeded his goals for his two residents. However, Michael knew others in the office would begin wondering what was happening if they stayed around the office. He did not want anything to cause questions.

Michael said, "Here, we'll go out for lunch at the bistro. I'll invite Anne if possible. I'll buy."

Robin said, "Maybe it will be good to speak in another place."

That evening at the kitchen table, Michael pondered the events of the past couple of days. He thought, *What other craziness is going to happen? I'm feeling sore and stumbling. Homeless guys selling me winning lotto tickets. My lab partner tells me about her husband cheating on her. I feel like I was the counselor listening to Robin pouring out her feelings and frustrations over her rotten six-year marriage. I didn't have Anne for backup. I may have said twenty words the entire lunch, including, "Check, please."*

He knew Robin needed to vent to process her anger and sadness. Luckily, the food was good, and the walk to the bistro was pleasant.

He saw on his voicemail ID a call from the University of Montana and hit redial. On the other end, a pleasant voice answered, "Department of Biology. This is Kate Horn. How can I assist you today?"

"This is Dr. Michael Townsend. I received a call …."

"Yes, sir, please, hold on for Dr. Dennis Bender."

"Okay."

Twenty seconds later, "Hello, Dr. Townsend. Dennis Bender here. I called you earlier to congratulate you on your article in the *New England Journal of Medicine.* Your passion for genetic research shows in your writing."

Michael answered, "Why, thank you, sir."

"Also, Jim Longfield spoke very highly of you after your research trip here."

"Jim is a fine man and a skilled woodsman."

"He is the finest ranger in the West."

"Now, how may I help you?"

"Dr. Townsend, as you observed during your last visit, the university has devoted substantial efforts into understanding the great creatures of the Rockies, predators and prey. Our long-term goal is to understand the needs of the natural order vis-à-vis human development, both environmentally and, in your interest, genetically, in comparing humans and bears. As you have written in your breakthrough research, you have uncovered genetic markers that determine these differences, which could aid in human development and medical breakthroughs, such as the ability of bears to conserve hydration during hibernation. If humans were to have this gene, think of the decreased need for water and its implications for the planet as our population increases. I want to make an offer for you to continue your research here."

Michael thought for a moment and said, "Dr. Bender, these are the ideas I have been pondering all of my collegiate career. Your appreciation for my research vision is flattering. However, what can you offer me that is compelling enough for me to leave the heart of medical research here in Boston?"

Dr. Bender answered with a deadly serious voice, "The university has authorized us to use land north of Missoula for a campus extension. The land is set aside to build the most advanced land mammalian research center in the world. I will offer you a seven-acre parcel for construction of the facility of your choice. We have a 180-million-dollar grant for construction on a set-aside seven-acre parcel. A seven-figure salary will come with the position. All of this was provided by an anonymous donor. Whatever money you can bring with your name will add to the size and scope of the project. Unlike Boston, we have the blank canvas, and you can be the da Vinci."

Michael dropped his jaw. *What will Anne say when I tell her?*

Dr. Bender continued, "I have spoken to Dr. Hatcher, who said you would be perfect for this project. He believes you have one of the most visionary research minds he has ever met. You have my number. Please call."

This day is getting crazier by the minute. It's like an alien or angel or fairy godmother is pouring all these events on me at once.

Michael sat at the kitchen table, shaking his head more. *I can't believe I won that lotto. Let me check the numbers.* He took his phone and searched Powerball winning numbers. He went into the bedroom to retrieve the ticket from the tin box, looked at the numbers on the phone to the ticket, and from the phone to the ticket again. He looked at the clock: 4:30. *I won. I won. Okay, I am going to put this down and walk out the apartment door and go downstairs.* He took five deep breaths to calm down. Then he got up and went out the door and into the hall.

He walked down the stairs and past the parking garage. He kept walking, forgetting to get his car to drive home. Ten minutes later, he stopped in midstride, and realized he was halfway to the hospital without his car. *Anne will have to drive me home.* He went to the hospital parking lot and waited for Anne to get her car.

Five minutes later, she walked around the corner, looked, and froze at seeing Michael. With a huge smile, he said, "Give me your keys. I'll drive you home."

At supper, Michael began, "How are things at the hospital?" He enjoyed seeing Anne not being able to know what question to ask first. It was time to spill the beans.

She answered, "Same old stuff, different day. Now, how about you?" She exaggerated her sentence, knowing he wanted to discuss a topic.

Michael smiled, noticing Anne's incredulous stare, and said, "I had an intriguing phone call from a university today."

She remarked, "Oh, wow."

"Yes, they are expanding their campus to establish a research center dedicated to comparative mammalian study. Thanks to my research successes, they want me to head their new genetics laboratory."

With an excited tone in her voice, she said, "Where is it? Texas? California? DC? Florida? Here in Boston?"

He answered, "The University of Montana in Missoula."

Her enthusiasm disappeared into a narrow stare. In a monotone, she said, "You're kidding me. Missoula, Montana? The middle of fricking nowhere? Why?"

He told her about the conversation he had with Dr. Bender and the project vision. He ended his pitch with "And it won't be the 'same old stuff, different day.'"

She replied, "It may be you doing it without me."

He squirmed a little while rubbing his face. Then, leaning back in his chair with his eyes closed, he tapped a finger on his lips, thinking of the best response. Then it came to him. He said, "How would you feel if we name the research building after your parents?" He looked up, using his right hand as if reading a marquee, and said, "Anne, how about 'The Wilson Center for Mammalian Genetic Research'?"

Any anger Anne showed vanished with the mention of her parents. "You can get that done? For my family?"

Michael felt better and said, "Dr. Dennis Bender told me I could have anything within reason."

"You also get me a beach house in the Caymans, and I'll do it."

He clapped his hands and said, "Done!" Michael felt the excitement building inside him.

"We can't afford that."

Michael pulled out the lotto ticket and quietly said, "Yes, we caaaaaa-an."

"It's the winner, and you have been holding it all day? And not telling me?"

"Check your phone for my call." Then he told her about everything else that happened.

"Wow, I thought it was not important. Poor Robin."

11/4/2021
University of Montana
Missoula, Montana
Sol Planet Three
Milky Way Dimension

Missoula, Montana, in November is always dicey weather-wise. This year was no exception; in fact, a snowstorm had moved through the upper Rockies days before Michael and Anne arrived from their month-long Cayman Island vacation. The university was surprised and delighted when Michael contacted them to propose his research and private funding. All of Missoula was abuzz about the new campus and planned to accommodate Michael's plans with open arms. They got off the jet to be met by the "red carpet" treatment.

Michael and Anne got the contracts and vendors chosen and onboard. After that came planning for construction. The architect and the contractor said groundbreaking would be at the first thaw in the spring. The real estate was purchased between Missoula and the Native American lands at the foot of the mountain range.

Interest in this project came from academia worldwide when Michael published his mission and vision statements in the scientific press. What was so unique was that the research center would focus on genetic disease research that expanded to cross-mammalian uses or finding cures for human diseases from the genetics of other mammals focusing on his findings in the bear genome.

Michael gained universal acceptance from the university community for his project after the twenty-million-dollar endowment gift from the Wilson Genome Foundation, funded by grants. It was given to the university to use the money for scholarships for science majors. The school began receiving more high-quality applicants in the life sciences, with the average college board scores increasing from the previous years.

The following spring, the new Wilson Science Center received its final touches as a six-story plus enlarged basement model of research and learning. The lab equipment arrived one day before the classes began in the fall. Everything was thought of, even a large private gym in the basement for the two of them to use, equipped with professional weights. Everyone worked through the night to install lab gear and safety tools in their proper place.

That night, after a marathon physical move-in before the semester began, Michael grabbed his knees and fell. Anne yelled, "Michael, what's wrong? Are ya hurt? Did you twist your knees?"

She ran to his side while he grimaced in pain. "I don't know what's going on. All I know is it feels like the cartilage in my knees collapsed as if it was a building weakened by an earthquake. My knees feel like they are swelling from a football injury."

"Let's get ya to a doctor fast. All that lifting ya do may have caused abnormal stress on your knees. You're not as young as ya were when ya were tackling running backs at Duke."

"Thanks for your glowing and adroit observation."

"I have been on ya since ya canceled that appointment last May. Ya should have taken care of it then."

"Yeah, but Dr. Hatcher sent me to that conference where I met Dr. Bender."

"I don't care. Now, look at ya."

"Okay, okay! You're right! With winning the lotto and everything else that has happened, I took my eye off the ball."

"Don't try to placate me. Your health is more important. I have every right to chew your butt about this, dammit!"

They went to the emergency room in town, where they got x-rays and bloodwork. The doctor came in after the x-rays were developed with a puzzled look on his face. He pushed up his cowboy hat and said, "This is the first time I have ever seen cartilage as sparse as yours. It's as if it is fading away. The lab results also point to a deficient collagen level in your body. More x-rays of other joints show the spaces in all your joints are in fact disappearing."

The emergency room doctor was an old fixture in the hospital who had treated football injuries for years in this university town. His bushy eyebrows pushed his glasses around when he raised them. He thought he had seen it all, but this was quite different. And with a baritone voice that sounded more like a spokesman from a pickup truck commercial, he said, "Well, son, you may have something to research in that fancy new building you built near campus. Before I came in here, I did a search about your cartilage symptoms and found nothing like it. But I do think it is a serious issue you need to deal with now. It looks like the density of the cartilage is decreasing all over your body. Have your shoulders been hurting lately?"

Michael answered, "Yes, sir. I thought it was an altitude thing since I lived all my life almost at sea level."

"Nope, that's not the case. I recommend you see a rheumatologist as soon as you can. Those are the guys that can tell if this is a rare autoimmune syndrome. That's not my specialty. But I can send you anywhere you want—Mayo, even Duke."

"Yes, I will go as soon as I can. I am not partial toward what hospital or clinic I choose to best treat me."

"Okay there. You do research, and get back to me, and I will write the referral to get this process started."

"Not a fun place to be," Anne said as she helped Michael move guardedly to the wheelchair, trying to avoid pain. The orderly came to help and finished the job. He wheeled Michael out to the SUV, got him in the passenger seat, and then put the wheelchair in back so it would be easy for Anne to manage.

On the drive home, Anne asked Michael, "The semester begins tomorrow," Anne said, a hint of worry creeping into her voice. "Can you manage your labs?"

"If I am going to have any credibility, I need your help to be there," he answered. "I will have to use knee braces for now, so I can stand and move around some. We will need a pair with the metal hinges like I used in college to protect my knees. We can go to Walmart to see if they have anything on a Sunday. Also, I will try to sit a lot."

So they got temporary braces, and within days he bought the metal hinge ones from the football athletic supplier. They seemed to work well during that semester. But the colder it got, the harder it was to move around without pain.

Even as his joints stiffened, he did not reveal his problems to anyone but his doctors. His research into the mammalian genome was bringing him attention from all over the world. His primary focus was using stem cells with augmented DNA to alter the placement of specific proteins in problematic areas of the body such as individual organs or glands. They also studied regenerated bone and ways to scale growth and production times. This research was to improve human longevity and quality of life.

He never thought he would need the research for himself. He and Anne were in their thirties and were thinking of starting a family. Everything was going better than they dreamt, except for Michael's deteriorating health.

1/25/2022
Gimmish's Workshop
Zarsfon Planet Six Moon Two
Heimerlich Fiefdom
Quark Dimension

It was time to check up on Gimmish again. Tol wanted to see how the third-planet essence was doing with the implanted disease. He saw that the essence in question was weaker but not weak enough to suggest that Gimmish had actually heeded his command. For Gimmish to keep up with his team, he needed to get rid of it before replacing it, since one of the Game's rules was to not have more than four essences registered at any one time. Also, Tol did not want any trace of an essence from the third planet to remain.

Tol arrived at Gimmish's station, coming from the left side, to see what he was working on at the time. Gimmish said, "Greetings, Master Tol! As you can see from our results, another one of my essences performed better than expected. After planning to eliminate the essence from the third planet, I used the same idea in the Game, to stay off the bottom. Being able to see a day ahead was a perfect way to see how these third-planet beings like to take chances with assets."

Tol asked, "So what else did you learn while you were there?"

"There is another peculiar trait they have. Beings there have mercy, which we consider weakness."

Tol responded, "Then what do you call my allowing you time to get rid of the third-planet being and not have you sacrificed immediately?"

Gimmish paused to think about the question. He continued, "But I have done everything you asked since then. My wish is to make things right again."

"That's good. The reason I came was to see where you are in eliminating the third-planet essence. As long as it lives, you are at a handicap, and the third planet stays in play, which can create a problem."

Gimmish replied, "I know the disease is progressing in the creature. His skeletal structure is to the point where he cannot move unaided and continues to decline. It will not be long until we can move on." He did not want to tell Tol that he tried to dispose of the essence by giving it to himself.

Tol asked, "What else did you learn while you were there?"

"I learned much about this third planet. I learned that this host and others have individual names just as we do. The host's name is Doctor Michael Townsend."

"Tell me more about the population of these beings."

"It is not a bad place, where they have fun doing things besides fighting and destruction. They are behind us in many aspects but live in large numbers in certain areas. They do not live as long. Half the creatures have certain traits and look similar to us, while the other half have complementary traits. They seem to pair well together in lives to create more life with each other, vastly different than us. And the half that do not look like us have extremely attractive essences, even to a quark like me. It is as if they were made for each other by design."

"Yes, Gimmish, that can be a large distraction for our dimension. Do not go back unless I tell you, or you will be infected by the atmosphere there."

Gimmish gave a puzzled look as if Tol was not telling him the whole story. When Tol turned to go, Gimmish asked one more question. "Master Tol, these third-planet creatures do seem very resourceful. What if this one finds a way to cure himself since he is trying so hard?"

"Sir, that would not be a good outcome for you." Tol walked up the ramp of his ship and took off, leaving Gimmish to think about his own well-being.

He needed to search for a replacement, since his teammates were still questioning why his best essence was not being used in practice. Last season, he had moved their rank in the standings off the bottom, for which they were grateful, but to continue this trend, the other team members were anxious about Gimmish's problem with his best essence. The team wanted each gamer to keep their essences at full strength for the push in the new season. The first five seasons of a ten-year period had ended, and thanks to his incompetence, team Heimerlich had hovered near the bottom for most of that time. They did not want any possibility of landing back in the cellar. If so, they wanted to let Gimmish know that he would be the odd quark out.

2/1/2022
The Wilson Center
Missoula, Montana
Sol Planet Three
Milky Way Dimension

By this time, Michael's disease had taken hold with a vengeance, keeping him in the lab all the time. He went for his follow-up to the rheumatologist, who confirmed after blood testing that his genetic code was missing molecules, unlike anything he saw before. As the doctors put it, it was as if something had spliced his DNA at the same point in every cell, leaving him to waste away in skin, bone, ligaments, and cartilage. The doctor estimated that without a miracle, his life would end in less than a year. Samples sent to Mayo Clinic and the Harvard genome lab confirmed this bleak finding.

He finally decided to reach out to Robin, who was now working at Cruncher Labs on gene therapy drug research. Their newly discovered molecule could add molecules to DNA that had genetic defects in diseases, like cystic fibrosis. He found that DNA strands from harvested stem cells matched his missing genes.

On his phone call to Robin, she said, "Remarkable. What can we do for you then?"

Michael said, "How much would it take for the company to release four treatments of this product under license so I can test it? I want to try it on myself, since without some intervention, I have been given maybe a year to live. I have an idea for treatment, but it is all theoretical. I would invest in the company to become a director or take a major stake. This would be considered under the Right to Try Act. We can do an AI run as our Phase I data. I have got to do something. I have too much to live for."

"Yes, you have just started to make your mark on this world. Research we did together has already saved lives. Now we need to save yours."

Robin called her bosses, letting them know of the situation. They developed an experimental compound that was so new that the patent application had not been completed yet. The company agreed to send the product with Robin to administer without revealing the molecular structure. The testing needed to be kept a trade secret so copycat drugs would not be discovered too soon and ruin the company's market potential.

An undisclosed sum was transferred to Cruncher Labs from the Wilson Foundation for a 5 percent stake in the company and a seat on the board of directors.

3/13/2022
Heimerlich Coliseum
Zarsfon Planet Six
Heimerlich Fiefdom
Quark Dimension

At the next practice, Gimmish told their team captain, "The essence has an illness. I don't want to use it in its weaker state since it may fail and lose the round for us."

Surprised, the captain said, "What, the best essence ever to play? That's too bad, but if it is sick, it needs to get well or die by the start of the season, and you need to find a new one just as good and fast. If we go back to being last, you know one of us must be sacrificed to the audience, and that, my friend, would be you. You did come through and get us off the bottom, but surprise wins will not last."

"Yes, I know. It won't be much longer."

"Why not now? The sixth and last season of the period is about to begin"

"The disease has not yet run its course."

"What disease?"

"Oh, the host has a disease that saps its ability to perform. But the host is weaker, and soon the illness will run its course."

"Okay, but if there is a way to speed up the process, do it now. I will keep the press at bay until the season starts. I have an interview with Drollis at Game Planet Central soon. I will keep this illness under wraps until I hear more from you."

The pressure was on for Gimmish. He needed to follow up with Michael's disease progress so he could plan for the new season. This imposed the need to find a new essence. He had to search this dimension for other beings. He looked for anything with a talent for battle in the arena.

4/12/2022
Uninhabited Rocky Plain
Polaris Planet Four
Milky Way Dimension

He went to another solar system to search for a replacement. He was frustrated since the life forms there were not very developed. He did not see that there were any talented beings, just ones with weird traits. One was an acid-spitting creature that would make its way through the ground by expectorating saliva to dig tunnels through rock. Nasty but effective. Smoke rose from the disintegrated ground, creating an awful sulfur stench that he smelled from a great distance. He had to get a new essence since Michael would eventually die, leaving room for another surprise essence that no one expected.

He checked his spacecraft. "Dammit, I forgot my stun weapon! I'll have to try without it because I don't want to lose this one. I don't know if it is all the stress, but since I found my workshop ransacked, I am not thinking straight. It is driving me insane with headaches every day."

Gimmish had to find out how to get around to see its eye to extract its essence. If this thing were to spit on him, he would lose any skin or body part it targeted. He put on shoes that caused no footprints. They were soft and made with a gravitation sensor that allowed him to walk silently one centimeter off the ground, leaving no footprints. It allowed him to move as if he was walking on the ground but not touch it.

Gimmish saw that the creature was about to go to sleep. Now was his chance, if ever. He did not know anything about this creature's resting habits. He saw it openly exposing itself, seemingly unafraid of any enemy. He had to take a chance.

He waited a few minutes to make sure the creature did not stir. He listened to the surrounding area for noises that were fitting for the area. The breeze came from Gimmish's front, letting him know that if the creature had a sense of smell, it would not notice his presence. He slowly and quietly crept toward the beast about fifty yards from his position, not making a sound on the small amount of grass that grew in the field. The surface was rocky, so he tried to avoid small stones that might knock together, making sounds to awaken this dangerous beast.

The creature was about his size, long with short legs, indicating it was not a fast runner over long distances. The door on the craft behind him was still open. He felt his blood flowing quicker until he felt increasing pain in his head from pressure. He went to the front to look at the creature's eyes, knowing he only had one shot at it. It was not likely that this wild animal slept as soundly as Michael. Luckily, the eyes were open enough to use the essence capture device. It took about twenty long, fearful seconds to copy its essence. When finished, the device clicked. Gimmish, who had been so quiet until then, realized he had forgotten about the device's sound that let him know the capture was complete.

The creature woke up and looked into Gimmish's fearful eyes. He sprinted back toward his craft before the creature could finish shaking the sleep out of its eyes. The beast ran after him, spitting acid in his direction, but missed because the wayward quark took a zigzag path.

He had never run so fast, kicking up dust along the way. His scream may have been the loudest sound ever on that planet as the creature chased him across the field, spitting in his direction, until

Gimmish was far enough away not to be a threat anymore. Out of breath, he leaped through the door of the craft and closed the door. He safely sank into his pilot's chair along with his prize and took off.

After stopping at more planets, Gimmish determined he could not find any other essences on the way to the third planet. Now to check on the third planet.

5/21/2022
Planetary Orbit
Sol Planet Three
Milky Way Dimension

Gimmish approached the third planet in stealth mode on approach to avoid detection. However, his was not the top-of-the-line craft, so he had to stay among the space junk so as not to be detected while he did observations. He still felt the weaker essence in him. It drew him to stay in orbit with the planet over a different part, a more rugged land area than before. The locator on the essence capture device verified his feelings. *This is very convenient to be able to find the host with an internal tracking system. It's also allowed me to understand communications around the planet readily. Let's see what I can find out about this being. I believe I will go down to see what they are doing.*

To his dismay, while hovering near Missoula for a day, he found out about Michael being a genetics researcher who had been studying the very same types of diseases that Gimmish had given him. He thought to himself, *Those crafty third-planet beings. This was what Tol feared—that they would not give up until no more could be done.* He studied more communication about his host, discovering how highly intelligent he was.

Gimmish ran out of time to learn more. His abdomen began to tighten with anxiety, fearing the worst.

Stressing all the way back to the other dimension with headaches, beating the steering levers until he hurts his hand, he put the craft on autopilot to get ice and medicine for his pain while heading toward the dimensional portal. He came back and settled into his seat with arms and legs crossed and eyes closed.

That was not his only problem. He had no clue how to use the spitting creature essence. He thought about going to another galaxy in this dimension but decided he didn't have the time. The next to the last phase of the Game was about to begin in a short time. *I hope that third-planet essence dies before it cures itself. I need to be full strength for my team. I cannot wait any longer.*

Ten days later, as he entered the quark dimension, a message signal appeared in the queue. *It's from the warlord Alchemy.* He opened the message.

Mr. Gimmish,

Greetings.

I wanted to congratulate you on your finish in the Game last year. I saw the first Game you won against Flashenol and wondered why you did not use that essence before. Then I learned about how you were treated by the others, ignored and banished to an isolated existence, readied to be sacrificed as the bottom gamer. Also, I found out you were from their moon and not from the planet. It fits. It is a way to send a message to all those from the "wrong" background to stay in their place.

You found a way to beat the odds and become a top gamer because of your tenacity and not anything given to you. I look for warriors with that mindset.

If you have an opportunity to travel, I would like to invite you to my headquarters for a meeting. I would like to hear your story.

Regards,
His High Excellency and Warlord of the Realm,
Alchemy

Wow, he gets it. It would be great to be on his team. He seems like a fearsome warrior who would not let me hang out to dry the way Heimerlich would. I'll keep that in mind.

6/1/2022
The Wilson Center
Missoula, Montana
Sol Planet Three
Milky Way Dimension

Michael sent a private jet to Boston to pick up Robin with the drug in dry ice. Jim Longfield picked her up from the airport and brought her to the Wilson Center that sunny afternoon.

Because Michael's knees and ankles were not functioning that day, his legs had to be secured in the wheelchair with Velcro ties to keep them in place. His skin was beginning to sag on his face, and he was unable to lift his withering hands above his shoulders. Anne wheeled him to the front door to greet Robin.

Robin looked at him in shock. "Oh, my gosh!" she said, not able to hide her horror or sadness. She remembered him as this huge, athletic man with a smile just as large.

Anne said, "Robin, we are so glad you came. Michael said you are the top in the field."

"Thanks to me," he jested. Everyone gave a nervous but relieved laugh, considering the moment. All went into the lab and shared old stories.

After about thirty minutes, Michael's expression became somber. "Thank you so much for coming, since without this, I have zero chance to live to next year. I can tell the symptoms of the disease are accelerating, and my pain grows each day. The sooner we try this, the better for any chance of recovery."

"What if it kills you?" Robin said.

"I'll die anyway, so this is the only chance for me to live. We have to try it."

Anne added, "We have made all the arrangements for transition to the university. And I ..." She broke down and sobbed. At that moment, Michael realized Anne knew that another woman admired him very much. She saw Robin's admiration and what her husband meant to others and continued sobbing and staggering from the weight of the situation. The possibility of being a billionaire and its responsibility without her love hit all at once. Jim caught her before she fell and helped her to a chair, where she continued to cry. Robin wiped the tears from her own eyes.

Then suddenly, Michael burst out, "Are we going to have a pity party, or are we going to get busy? There is no time to cry in lab work."

The two women looked at each other with annoyance and at the same time said, "Men!" Robin continued, "Why do we cry over them? They don't get it."

Cocking her eyebrow, Anne said to Robin, "Remember"—going for a deep voice—"he's a tough-guy football player. He's watched that Tom Hanks baseball movie, *A League of Their Own*, one too many times."

Michael responded, "Of course, wouldn't you love me any other way?"

Anne looked at him and said, "Try me. Sometimes you're just an inappropriate ass, and ya can't keep your mouth shut."

Michael got serious and continued, "Jim, I want you to be with me during the treatments so we can have a record keeper of the experiment. The two women will need the two hours of the infusion time to rest before the hard part. I will pay you for your time, since it's not going to be fun, and we expect you at dinner tonight too."

Jim protested, but Michael would have none of it. He said to Anne and Robin, "May I have a private word with Jim? Y'all could get me something to drink, please."

They begrudgingly agreed and stepped out of the room. Michael turned to Jim and said, "Jim, I have been in medical sciences ever since my schooling, but I never came across a man with more unique wisdom that allowed me to think so differently, which has helped my research. It is because of your inspiration I came up with this gene-splicing method that we will use tomorrow."

"Me?"

"Yes, you gave me the idea I am going to use in my drug cocktail. Be here at nine o'clock sharp tomorrow morning. Jim, don't look so puzzled. I learned from you on those research trips into the mountains. More than you realized."

Later that evening, after Anne got Michael in bed, she looked at him with a stern look and her fists on her hips. She started, "What kind of male chauvinistic crap were ya talking about earlier?"

He looked at her like a young boy, choked up, and said, "I don't want to die." He began to sob.

Anne realized that all the earlier banter was a façade to cover his real fear. She couldn't say another word. Her irritation melted away into her heartfelt consolation. She sat on the bed and hugged him, trying to calm his fear for an hour until he fell asleep from exhaustion.

6/2/2022
The Wilson Center
Missoula, Montana
Sol Planet Three
Milky Way Dimension

Jim arrived fifteen minutes early to the room with the hospital bed. Lying in the bed hooked up to monitors, a smiling Michael Townsend told him, "Jim, put on a white coat. Robin and Anne are preparing the drug cocktail for the IV solution. Anne is preparing the infusion for the gene molecule compound that will be transported to my cells by Robin's experimental drug."

The women were in the other room to prepare the IV solution to administer the combination. Only Michael knew the DNA combination, so the conditions of the drug company agreement were met.

The specific drug technology was two parts. The part Robin brought was the transport drug. This drug would be like a truck to take the unstable genetic proteins Michael had developed to the correct place on cellular DNA and then release them in the cell at the precise site to change the DNA. Without the transport drug, Michael knew his compound would be destroyed by the body before it reached the correct place on the affected DNA strand.

Robin and Anne walked into the room. Anne started, "Jim, if it gets the least bit much—"

Jim said, "You don't have to convince me. This is his idea."

Robin said, "Good." With that, she started the IV.

Michael looked at the two women without saying a word as they finished and walked out of the room.

Jim recorded Michael's pulse and blood pressure every ten minutes. The equipment made their sounds.

Michael leaned over to Jim and said, "I think we are safe now." They spoke about the wilderness trip and the cave Jim found. More than halfway through the administration, he said, "Until I say you can, don't tell anyone that I used the bear stem cell DNA to provide the needed molecules. I did not have enough time to find other matches for these doses and stay under the medical community's radar. I do not want Anne to know unless I tell her. You read me?"

"What? But, Michael, you know the downside to this."

"Of course, I am fighting for my life. Since it is beyond the point of no return, you needed to know that you are part of the estate if I do not make it."

"But why this? Also I don't need any money, I promise you!"

"Like I told Anne and Robin, if I did not do this, I would die anyway. I can feel the changes and the increasing pain in my muscles and joints from my wasting cartilage. I will die from that or commit suicide because of the intolerable pain from every joint in my body."

Jim begrudgingly agreed and thought to himself that Michael was a desperate man under that calm façade. Who would have ever done such a thing to himself if he knew there was no chance otherwise? Jim put his face in his hands, hiding his sorrow and surprise.

Michael gave a nervous smile because he understood Jim's feelings and the stakes of this trial. He said, "The next two hours will not be bad, but the drug will enter my cells and disrupt my DNA replication. During that third hour, I will have nausea and possibly severe vomiting with diarrhea. There are drugs on the side table for that. I want you to place the nausea tablet in my mouth if I pass out." Jim was getting nervous as Michael continued, "After my nausea stops, you are to call Anne and Robin to do the rest. And don't you dare tell the two women about the DNA source, please, as a favor. If I live, I will inform them." Jim agreed.

Like clockwork, two hours later, nausea and vomiting started. He was awake enough to open his mouth for the nausea drug. In minutes, the vomiting calmed down, but it drained much of his energy. He nodded and told Jim it was time to get the women. Jim was happy to do so. He gave the readings and history of the last two hours to the two professionals, who then rushed in to check on Michael. After a few more minutes, Michael told Anne to thank Jim and ask him to go home. Immediately after that, he lost consciousness.

Jim told Anne and Robin, "I will not let you be left alone."

Anne said, "How? People are not supposed to know about this."

Jim looked at Anne directly and said, "They won't." Then, as if on cue, four Native American women walked through the door. "These are your nurse's aides. They will be at your service."

Robin said, "But—"

Jim answered, "Trust me, it is all arranged. I will check with you later." He turned and walked away.

Stunned but thankful, the two medical professionals with the four aides went to work ministering to Michael's every need and side effect as day and night continued. Intermittent nausea, diarrhea, fever, and cold sweats lasted for over twenty-four hours. The situation was touch and go, with fevers spiking close to 106 degrees with seizures. Michael's eyes became inflamed, sometimes bleeding, while he faded in and out of consciousness due to fatigue. The aides held Michael's head while he cried in pain, cleaning his body after he unconsciously soiled himself.

Marveling at their skill, Robin said to Anne, "These are some of the best aides I have ever worked with."

Anne agreed, "They're amazing."

6/3/2022
The Wilson Center
Missoula, Montana
Sol Planet Three
Milky Way Dimension

At midnight, Michael went into cardiac arrest, and Anne showed she still had the savvy and instincts of a top cardiac nurse. The instant the monitor sounded, she yelled, "Doctor, need defib stat!" The aide already had the defibrillator in position with paddles ready for the doctor by the time she ran in the door.

Anne tore Michael's shirt off with all her strength. The defibrillator was charged and ready.

Robin yelled, "Paddles ready! Clear!"

The shock made Michael's body jump. Anne yelled, "Beginning CPR! One and two and three and …," it continued. The next ten minutes seemed like ten hours. The other aide began to notice, and as she put a piece of wood from her pocket in Michael's mouth, she yelled, "He is beginning to seize! Tongue uninjured." The other aide took the prefilled diazepam syringe for injection from the crash cart. A thankful but amazed Robin administered the diazepam IV to stop the seizure. He was put on the respirator to help his breathing.

Three minutes passed, and Michael's heart went back into sinus rhythm, and he began to breathe on his own with the oxygen. For the next hour, Robin and Anne took vitals and blood work. The lab had all the necessary tools that any emergency room had, down to a fully stocked emergency crash cart. Robin was amazed at the effort Michael had put into being self-sufficient in this top-flight laboratory.

Robin commented, "If this wasn't near the middle of nowhere, I might want to work here."

Anne responded, "That's why I have a condo in the Caymans, and I will fly to the Caribbean every other month in the winter."

"Smart."

Anne and Robin rested in two-hour shifts, maybe catching half that in naps.

Two days later, at ten in the morning, Michael stabilized with his fever reducing, allowing him to gain consciousness. His eyes were still closed. Then he whispered, "I heard y'all talking. How was y'all's evening? I feel like I got hit by a Mack truck."

Robin was on duty when she heard those words. She yelled, "Anne, he's alert! Come quick."

Anne rushed in, shaking her head and rubbing her face. Her hair and clothes were a mess from sleeping in a reclining chair. Robin wasn't much better, yawning the entire time.

Anne looked at him and spoke, "Boy, ya gave us one helluva night. You were sick as a dog and had every acute side effect in the book except death."

"I think I'll forgo that last one."

All smiled since they were too tired to laugh. Michael stayed awake for ten minutes before he fell unconscious again.

Michael continued in and out of consciousness for another five days, spiking fevers with seizures. Jim came by every day to check on the women, bring them whatever they needed, and document everything with Robin's approval.

Jim commented to Robin and Anne rhetorically, "I hope my friends have been of help."

Robin hugged him, saying, "Thank you."

Anne asked Jim, "Why did you not ask us if we needed help beforehand?"

Jim said, "I didn't give you a chance to refuse my offer."

6/3/2022
Space
Flashenol Sector Portal
Flashenol Fiefdom
Quark Dimension

Gimmish thought about the stress he was under and how his life had been altered by the Game. He originated from lower form quarks on a moon as opposed to the regular planetoid quark. The only way he could increase his status in life was to take a lower job with the warlord staff as a food server. *Because I saved Heimerlich's life by stopping the poisoning attempt, I get this opportunity to be a gamer. What does that get me? I fly through endless space looking for essences to use in this Game. And since I'm not a planetoid quark and just a*

"Moonie," the others have always looked down on me, not helping me when they went out together for their essences unless Heimerlich forces them to.

He got up and looked at the results from the last game match. Thinking about the Game he thought maybe Drollis would have something to say today. He turned on the broadcast to relieve the boredom of prolonged space travel.

"Hello, everybody. This is your highly trained and always on point broadcaster, Drollis, and welcome to Game Planet Central! This is the most anticipated time of year in the cosmos. The Game is about to kick off its last season of the period after a frantic finish to last season. All the chatter is about who can compete with team Heimerlich's fighting monster this season. As the cosmos knows, with six matches left in the last go-round, team Heimerlich was considered dead, last, and gone. Then the lowest-rated gamer, Gimmish, surprising the dimension, introduced the Game changer essence with six matches to go. The rest is history!

"No turnaround in fortune could be more dramatic. The introduction of a smarter, hungrier, quicker, more agile player made up for the stronger, more brutish gladiators they defeated. Gimmish also brought to the Game new strategic methods of brilliantly crafted maneuvers and formations to hide attacks and defenses, outsmarting all comers.

"Our colleagues around the dimension have spoken with the coaches and captains to see if they have found answers to counter the Heimerlich juggernaut. Take it away, Cosmo."

"Thank you, Drollis. The answer is a resounding no. There has been a feverish rush to find the essence that has the talent of team Heimerlich's. Gamer Gimmish has collected huge dividends and probably saved his own life from sacrifice by introducing what is to be known as the premier essence of all the Games. And even after knocking team Alchemy out of first place, causing a savage outbreak from the warlord, they still have no answer for the meteor that hit them in the last Game.

"Team Alchemy's coach Par had a message for the entire Game this year from the warlord. Quote: 'This will not stand.' The only thing is they need an essence that could complete with Gimmish's. That essence is somewhere in the universe."

Gimmish turned off the broadcast, apprehensive about how he would break the news to the team about his Game-changing essence and not finding one like it. During the off-season, he had been monitoring the progress of the disease he'd given Michael, the third-planet being, seeing it was weaker but not gone. The headaches and nightmares became more frequent as time went on, causing Gimmish to become paranoid; what trap would lurk behind the next planet he passed?

The word had not gotten to the press that the star essence was about to die. Gimmish knew the captain was becoming more anxious with each encounter. He had to think of something fast.

Walking up to the vessel holding the third-planet essence, he yelled, "Die, creature, die! You got me off the bottom, but it is now time for you to die, die, die!" The stress of the moment overcame him; he was hitting his head into the table and pulling his hair out, frantic for a solution. He began question-and-answer sessions with himself, laughing at the folly. "How did I ever get into this mess, Gimmish? Because I asked to. How funny!"

He lamented out loud, "My own teammates would not give me any ideas where to find good essences. Looking for my own essences all over the universe, I would find the only place that was off limits. Dammit, nobody told me, and now I am in this mess." He knew that it would be either the essence host or him—or both, if the new essence didn't work.

The worst-case scenario was that he could be exposed as a cheater, executed on the spot, and on top of that, every quark's ideas of Moonies as worthless lowlifes would be validated. He had to figure out something and soon.

Oh, these headaches have got to go! I can't think straight! The essence has got to die! He began to bang his head into the pilot's seat to relieve the pain.

Beginning 6/8/2022
The Wilson Center
Missoula, Montana
Sol Planet Three
Milky Way Dimension

Jim came by every day with supplies and any medicines needed to help his friend. Nothing was too small for him to jump in his truck with the singular mission to do whatever Anne or Robin asked him to do. The two women demonstrated true professionalism and became good friends.

Jim arranged continued help from the Reservation, which was a godsend. This would allow Robin and Anne to get things from the house and have some brief respite. Six days after the drug administration, Michael woke up and remained conscious for one or two hours at a time, finally able to eat something solid. A day later, the fever broke for good, and the seizures ended. He was going to live.

He lost twenty pounds that week with all the stress on his body. He began oral liquids and chicken soup on the eighth day saying it was the best food he had ever put in his mouth while smiling at the fact he hadn't killed himself.

Michael told Jim Robin's ideas and asked Jim to keep the DNA storage locked so no one could adulterate the doses.

Michael knew there needed to be a second administration of the transport vehicle to send the DNA stem cell codes to other places in his body necessary to fully target all his growth cells. Four weeks later, still in a wheelchair, he prepared the second dose of the DNA cocktail. Robin was always there to provide help and support. Jim was there while the experiments were going on to lock up after everything afterward.

As they worked together, Robin, noticing how resourceful Jim was, said, "I don't know how we could have survived under the radar this long had it not been for Jim. When something is needed, it is amazing how he can get it done."

Michael said in a quiet tone, "He surprises me almost every time I ask him about something."

THE CHANGE

7/8/2022
The Wilson Center
Missoula, Montana
Sol Planet Three
Milky Way Dimension

The next dose was planned for five weeks after the first when Michael's strength came back enough. A couple of days before that, Michael remarked to Jim, "My sense of smell is more acute, and certain things have more noticeable odors. Before, when I would prepare meat, I would not notice anything about its freshness unless it was discolored. Now, I can tell the difference between a fresh and thawed steak from the smell. I wonder if it was a side effect of the drug or my imagination."

Jim listened and pondered, not knowing what to think about that. The next day they went back to the lab with Anne and Robin to record all the issues that arose in what Robin classified as a clinical study. While reading the experience log, Robin was surprised at certain specific indicators. She said, "This is odd. Nowhere else in any other study is there any indication of olfactory stimulation. I will record this outcome as an outlier. This is interesting. We are achieving outcomes in Michael that do not fit with other trial patients. The only thing different is the DNA match and disease unique to Michael. Did they ever give a name or diagnosis to you, or should we call this Townsend Syndrome?"

That comment brought levity into a puzzling but promising situation that would be interrupted by the start of another administration the next day. The plan was set to start at eight in the morning, with IV administration given soon after. Michael took his nausea medicine before the reactions began to reduce the dehydration he suffered the first time, which had almost killed him.

That morning, everyone was in their place. Then Michael said, "Let the games begin!" And with that, Anne started the IV on a slow drip. Robin prepared and gave the transport drug and administered the DNA component; Jim wrote down the initial readings. Soon the two compounds were in Michael's bloodstream traveling to their appointed cells. Michael asked Jim to stay again to let the ladies go have breakfast and coffee.

"Here we go again. Jim, whatever happens this time, I want to thank you for walking with me on my journey. I have not discussed any of the DNA formula with anyone but you. I gave myself the same strain that I did last time, only twice as strong."

Jim said, "You almost died last time. Why would you risk so much when you had four doses you could have used? There is time to take it easy and give yourself time for your body to get used to the change and regeneration of your DNA."

"Normally, yes, but I have a feeling that something strange is going on with me, and it's more than I bargained for."

"Can you give me a clue what is so strange?"

"Yes. After the last dose, you know my sense of smell changed. There have been other things I have kept quiet about."

"Why? You would be a modern miracle and all of your research would then be validated. But why the double dose?"

"I have got to use as much as I can since there is a stability issue with the DNA compound, and it is a customized compound made for my body chemistry. It may not work the same over time, causing more damage than benefit. It would be like using out-of-date drugs. This drug is not that stable and goes out of date really quickly. I believe this treatment is going to work, but maybe not totally as planned."

"So why go forward and risk problems?"

"I want to take the complete treatment to get the end effects. I feel better than before the first treatment, and my appetite has returned, but my taste now responds differently to the same foods. I want to know where this goes."

"How so?"

"My mouth muscles feel different and swollen, larger in a weird way, but they don't hurt."

"How could your mouth change?"

"We'll find out. I want to get this over with because I do not want Robin or anyone else to discover that what I have done really works. I need to either die or use up the dose before someone gets to it. I believe I have discovered something that should never happen again because I am changing."

"You are scaring me, speaking such gibberish."

"I am already there, and I don't know what to think."

"If it had been me, I would not have taken that second treatment and instead destroyed the rest."

"But I'm not you."

The two-hour period where the treatment took hold came and went. Michael's reaction to the drugs was not nearly as severe as the last, just a slight queasiness and fatigue. The girls were late returning to the lab since they decided to go souvenir shopping in Missoula after breakfast. They breathlessly came into the lab apologizing because they had lost track of time wandering around a flea market looking at the Native American jewelry.

Michael laughed. "Typical women."

Both women's faces turned from concern to scowls, and they glared at him with all the feminist rage they could muster.

Anne remarked, "Will ya quit saying such stupid things? They ain't funny. We will hold back on concern for you from now on, ya pig." Robin shook her head in agreement. Both walked out of the treatment room to get their things out of the car. When they came back, Anne asked, "Okay, let's stop clowning around, Bozo. If ya weren't so sick, I'd kick ya to the curb. How are ya feeling?"

Michael said, "I am doing better but now want to rest because the nausea medicine is doing its trick. I am getting worn out. Jim, can you hang around for a little longer?"

He agreed, and the two ladies left them alone.

Michael started, "I haven't told you everything about what is going on inside of me. The other day, I noticed that my joints didn't hurt as bad, and my hips are getting wider. I can tell sitting in the wheelchair that it is getting tight. That is not normal."

Jim said, "You know it could be you are eating the same and not exercising."

"More than that. In a couple of days, Robin needs to go back to Boston, so Anne will be driving her to the airport. I have an x-ray machine and a small electron microscope here for research. I will need you to help me check things while Anne and Robin aren't around to see what is happening inside me that makes me feel these strange sensations. My strength is returning, and my nail beds feel like there is growth again, which means my joints and other protein-based body functions are returning. I believe this experiment is working, and we have done some medical magic. But I do not want to let anyone know until I am absolutely positive and show documentable proof of the results. No one will believe anything about using another species' DNA to cure human disease unless the proof is airtight, even after any previous research. We still don't know what the disease was."

With Jim's eyes as big as saucers, he responded, "What you are saying is that the Cruncher drug with the correct DNA cocktail will change medicine forever."

Michael nodded in agreement and presented a huge smile. They did a high-five but resumed their serious composure when the two women came in to check on them.

Robin said, "Jim, thanks so much, but it's our turn to take care of this fool," still miffed at Michael's boorish greeting.

Jim said, "I need to go to work now. The aides will arrive shortly. I need the rest of the day to ponder the ramifications of this miracle."

Robin added, "If this works, I'm going to stay for the party."

7/14/2022
The Wilson Center
Missoula, Montana
Sol Planet Three

The following week, Michael was feeling much better. Robin believed that she was ready to go back to Boston and discuss her results with her bosses. Anne agreed to take her back to the airport to send her off. That was when Michael discovered their lives would change forever.

Jim first drew Michael's blood and made microscope slides to check on the quality of the DNA match. Then they went to the x-ray room, where Jim received a crash radiology technician course, so he could take the films. Michael wanted films of all his major joints and spine. He was in a wheelchair the entire time since the disease had begun to worsen. But now, in the x-ray room, he finally stood up! Jim's jaw dropped, and he said, "Michael, what is going on, and how long have you been able to stand?"

Michael responded, "About three days now, but I did not want to reveal my recovery until I find out what growth is going on inside me. My legs and arms feel quite different—and look at my fingernails."

He showed Jim his hands, then Jim said, shaking, "It looks like the backs of your hands and fingers are getting larger and thicker. The nailbeds are getting rounder like the beginning of claws, not flat human fingernails. What else is going on?"

"No time to discuss. Let's get these x-rays done so we can get real answers." They took twenty-four views from head to foot. Then they read the films and discovered an amazing fact.

Michael said, "I've got new bones and cartilage growing, especially in my hips. They do not look totally human either. My leg and arm bones are getting wider with growth plates, which signals that I may start growing taller and bigger. Also, the spaces between my vertebrae—Oh, my!"

"What is it, boss?"

He gulped, took a deep breath, and said, "I may have made my DNA a bit too strong with the number of genes to change. Look at my mouth area."

He took his finger and pointed it at the space between his nose and mouth. "You see what I see?"

"Frankly, it looks like a bulge," Jim said.

"You are correct, a bulge that goes from my nose to my lower jaw. It's growing. My face is slightly protruding around the mouth. Anne said kissing has been a bit different, but I thought it was because we hadn't done much in the last six months."

Jim sat down, taking in the possibility that this man was not going to be totally human after some time. He had replaced too much of his human DNA with the bear DNA, and it was changing his whole body into something else, something new and unknown.

Jim asked, "What now?"

"Let's go down to the lab and destroy that last dose. We can never let this get out, or the world will never be the same." Michael left his wheelchair, not thinking that someone might see the quick progression of his recovery. He thought about only one thing, checking the locked refrigerator for the last dose.

Jim was stunned that Michael was able to stand to get out of his wheelchair. Then when Michael began to move with full mobility, he said, "This is almost as dramatic a recovery as in the Bible."

Michael said, "No time to think about that now." They trotted down the stairs, banged open the doors, and rushed into the DNA lab. They went to the fridge and locked to see if the door was unlocked. It was not, and the DNA dose was gone! They both said together, "Robin!"

Jim sat on the other side of Michael's desk. Michael continued to sit in the wheelchair to keep his recovery hidden from others in the program. After a silence, Jim said, "What do you think Robin will do with that last dose?"

Michael said, "If I were her, I would analyze the heck out of it."

Jim asked, "What are you going to do if she discovers what you did?"

Michael said, "Turn lemon into lemonade, talk to her, tell her the drug is out of date and too unstable to be used again, and spin it as our breakthrough." Suddenly, Michael jerked his head as if on alert. He sniffed the air.

Jim said, "What are you doing?"

"I'm getting up and smelling the air. I am beginning to notice scents. Anne's back."

"Wow. That's not a human trait."

"A few seconds and …."

"Oh my gosh, Michael, you're standing!" She rushed to his arms and hugged him with the love and surprise of Lazarus's family after his resurrection.

"Yes, Anne, the treatments worked. I am rapidly improving better and faster than I could have ever dreamed in a million years."

Anne backed away a step and looked concerned. "The tone in your voice …"

Michael said, "I want to show you a significant issue about my treatment and recovery outcome that may be a little more than unusual."

Jim asked, "Shall I go now?"

Michael nodded yes, and he and Anne went into the x-ray room. He told her, "On the way home, Jim always looks at those blue snowcapped mountains. He told me he is glad I will get to know them a whole lot more."

"What does that mean?" Anne's body language showed she was trying to respond while trying to tamp down her own anxiety. She breathed deeply, raising her hands to show her palms to chin high, then exhaling and lowering her hands palms-down at elbow level. Then she slowly asked him, "What is this all about? What did you not tell me?"

Michael breathed heavily and started, "Anne, the experiment worked. The whole outcome of my illness is a true miracle. I did not think it would work. I even suspected that after the first dose, there would not be another try, due to all the side effects."

Anne said, "That being said, we did a second treatment, and you're standing before me seemingly better. Is there something wrong?"

"Yes. About three weeks after the first dose, I could feel something stirring inside me. The good news is it was my body accepting the DNA."

Anne responded, "And that's a problem?"

Michael continued, "I didn't want to say anything around anyone else until I felt sure I was going to make it."

Anne gave Michael a stern look and asked, "What did ya not tell me?" She felt somewhat more settled and continued to listen.

Michael said, "I had the four doses under lock and key in the lab refrigerator for that reason and prepared a double dose of the DNA for the second treatment so that there was only one dose left. Somehow the—"

Anne went breathless, bringing her hand to her mouth, saying, "Robin wanted me to give her a tour of the lab so she could see how we stored experiments, and I opened the refrigerator. She asked if this was a dose of the drug. I said yes."

"If it is found out I actually used unregulated DNA on myself without clinical review, the ethical issues would be problematic, to put it mildly."

"Oh, Michael, What kind of ethical issues?"

"I made a choice and took the risk. Now for the rest of the story. I think the double dose will send the changes into overdrive, which allowed me to get out of the wheelchair so soon. But I need to tell you that there may be other changes that we will not know about until they happen."

"Whaddaya mean? Is this temporary, and you'll die?"

"No, something else. I want you to take this measuring tape and check my shirt sleeve size and tell me what it says, then measure me around the hips."

"I don't need to. I just bought ya those pants one year ago, and they loosened while the illness progressed. Quit beating around the bush and tell me."

"With all the regulations on human stem cell research, I wasn't able to find the correct human stem cell DNA to match the breaks in my chromosomes without appearing on the research community's radar, so I used the placenta of a grizzly bear to match the markers. They did, and I used them in the experiment. Now my body has started growing again, and on this x-ray, you can see that my growth plates are functioning again as if I were fifteen years old. And that is not all. My senses are changing, especially my sense of smell, which is now keener. That is why I greeted you coming in; I smelled you."

She asked, "What are ya saying? What's the bottom line, dammit?"

"I am noticing bear traits in my body."

And so, Michael continued to explain, telling his completely bewildered wife what he had spliced into his DNA and how it had done more than he bargained for. The man whose nickname in high school and college was "Bear" was taking on traits of a grizzly bear. The questions were how much he would change and how fast it would happen. Also, if Robin reported the contents of the DNA dose, it could draw ethical scrutiny and call into question the status of the research done at the Wilson Center.

Anne was so flabbergasted by the revelations she did not say another word for hours until she asked him what he wanted for dinner. The magnitude of an earthquake in her heart and mind did not allow her to respond to any stimulus. She walked around the house like a zombie. Her hands shook, knowing her world had taken a turn to the unknown. She tried cooking and broke an egg on the counter, missing the bowl and releasing a scream, "My husband, the bear!" then dissolved into loud sobbing. Michael picked her up off the floor and took her to the bedroom, where she cried herself to sleep. He put the palms of his changing hands to his face, shaking his head and wondering what would happen next.

No one at the university knew exactly about Michael's illness or the lengths he had gone to cure himself. The small staff at the Wilson Center was happy he was feeling better. He did more in the lab, to the surprise of his students. His local doctor cleared him to return to full work status that week and remarked about his remarkable recovery. On his first day back in class, he demonstrated DNA pairs and the science of the double-helix molecule. His strength and energy were coming back quickly, and his sense of smell became an asset when he smelled contraband coming into the class or lab, making people wonder how he did it.

A month later, he started going down to the weight room with the football players, evaluating the progress of his increased strength and stamina, remembering how strong he'd been when he played linebacker for Duke. He stopped using the school's facility when the trainers noticed him increasing his weightlifting to the standards of a midseason football player.

One of the trainers approached him, asking, "I know you played at Duke. What was your lifting max there?"

Michael deflected their observations by claiming he never stopped training until he became sick, and this recovery has been an extra incentive to work to his maximum ability. While doing this training, he added a back door to his first-class weight room in the Wilson Center basement so he could enter and exit unnoticed. Jim arranged the basement renovations with workers who could remain discreet, paying them in cryptocurrency.

Michael knew his time of anonymity was ending since the bear traits multiplied and were changing his physical structure. He wore a mask, feigning allergies, to cover up the growth beginning in his face. His hips started to rotate forward, and his shoulder joints enlarged. His arms grew as long and as large as his legs, making it easy to move around on all fours. People began to notice him growing into a bodybuilder and made comments. He told people that he and Anne had decided to push their bodies to the limits and make it part of the Wilson Center research. It was not worth fighting the changes, since the treatments had saved his life, so they trained together to maximize their physiques. This gave Michael an excuse about his changes for a little longer.

Four months after the treatments, Anne asked Michael, "How do ya feel about teaching with that mask on your face every day?"

He answered, "I let folks know my allergies to this area are horrible. As long as I have this N-95 mask, it covers the growth. But it's almost to the point where my face fills the inside of the largest mask I can get. I'm having to shave more of my face because my beard is growing almost to my eye sockets. I think I may make it to winter break. In any case, after that, I don't know how much longer I can look normal enough to pass as a human.

11/28/2022
Fire HQ Stadium
Feuerstat Planet Seven
Quark Dimension

Gimmish checked his essence stock, wondering when the third-party host would die so he could transition to the new creature. Instead of diminishing, however, he could feel that it had changed and was getting stronger! He tried to use it to access its energy but had trouble controlling anything about it. This was the worst outcome for him. Not only was he not able to switch to the new being, but he had also less and less control of the third-planet being's essence, rendering it basically useless. He began to tap the railing of the team box rapidly and nervously. His mouth tensed while his breathing got heavier, making his nostrils flare and his forehead pulsate with pain. Gimmish saw another gamer go over to the captain to point out his anxious appearance.

The captain came to Gimmish and asked him for an update. The only response was a blank stare. "Okay, Gimmish, what is the problem?"

Gimmish hesitated and then turned his head slowly to look his captain in the eyes. "We have a problem. My essence changed, and I am losing control of it. Instead of dying, it is adapting and growing stronger." He slowly turned away, wincing, knowing what response he would get.

"You moron! How in the world did you let this happen?"

"I knew it was smart enough to be the best player ever in the Game."

"Do you know that you can get our whole team eliminated because this is a change after the Game starts again? Once the essence host changes, the essence changes, and you will be disqualified."

"Yes, I know. I took that chance to win."

"Do you realize what will happen if we fall to the bottom again thanks to this? Let me explain something to you. There will be a sacrifice at the end, and you're it!"

The captain went to tell the others and left Gimmish to settle in with the news. All he wanted to do now was get in his craft with all his possessions and disappear into the farthest part of the universe. If not, he was a marked quark. He thought the only way to stay alive was to get up from his seat and head back to his craft, knowing what would happen when the facts were discovered. He had to make plans to get away now or die. He discreetly rose from his chair and left, saying he needed to be excused. Soon everyone would know of his great mistake, so the more of a head start he had, the better.

The captain saw Gimmish leave his seat. He asked him, "Where are you going?"

Gimmish said, "I need to go to my craft for a while. I have a raging headache."

The captain said, "You know the match begins in six hours. Get your stuff done and be back in time."

Gimmish ducked out the back of the stadium and calmly went back to his craft. He looked around at all the joyous fanfare, quarks in bright green Heimerlich jerseys happily cheering for their team, knowing it was ending in a matter of hours. He went to the craft parking area. Knowing that his ship would be his home for the rest of his life, he got comfortable in his pilot's seat. He took a deep breath, started the engine, and took off without drawing any notice. He flew below the radar over the horizon and then took off into space. As soon as he escaped the planet's orbit, he took the course towards Philimar's fiefdom to have the greatest chance to escape.

Two hours after engaging hyperdrive, he turned on the broadcast to listen to everything fall apart.

"It is almost Game time, and with you today, your highly trained and spot-on broadcast professional, Drollis, with you at Game Planet Central. Thirty minutes before the start of this season, and team Heimerlich is ready to start where they left off at the end of last season. We are anticipating a—uh, hold on. Something not planned is happening. There is an unscheduled meeting of team Heimerlich's captain at the umpire's desk. This is quite unusual.

"We are now looking at the team Heimerlich gamer booth and only see two others. Gamer Gimmish is missing! Last season's come-from-behind star has disappeared. Looking back at the umpire's desk, the tensions are beginning to rise—warlords are upset. There is finger-pointing. This is not good. We have a real problem."

"That was quick." Gimmish wanted to turn it off but did not. He had to know how long he had before becoming the dimension's most wanted criminal, dead or alive. He asked the navigational computer, "I need to know how much time I have left to get to the nearest portal to the third-planet dimension. That essence host has to be eliminated if there is any chance I can save my life." He looked again at his essence readings and found the third-planet being had survived the illness and was now strengthening. *I should never have listened to Tol and just blasted the thing. It's his fault I'm in trouble. If I have the chance, I'll make him pay.* He hurried back to listening to the broadcast in a panic.

"We need to know more details. Let's go down to our umpire booth reporter, Bage. Tell us more."

"Yes, Drollis. It seems as though the gamer Gimmish has abruptly left the coliseum, which, if true, would cause team Heimerlich to forfeit the match. The team captain has informed the umpires that he may have caused a Game-ending violation. I need to listen in on the discussions and will alert you when I know more. Back to you, Drollis."

"But Bage, why do you think the captain is giving up Gimmish so easily?"

"Remember, he is the only Moonie gamer on the team."

Gimmish couldn't think about the slur just now. He was focused on saving his life. He knew they were going to find out that his essence had become uncontrollable, which had never happened before and only happened if the essence's host adapted. The only beings that were storied to possibly adapt like this were from the third planet of Sol in the other dimension.

Then he heard Drollis's voice from the receiver.

"Bage, do you have more for us?"

"Yes, Drollis, a whole lot more. Heimerlich's team captain was moving his arms wildly in a heated discussion with the umpire. The umpire has halted the Game. He thanked the captain and then called together the other three judges, Alchemy, Contronto, and Maldonate, to confer and check the rules. They've concluded that the rules clearly state that no changes are allowed after the round begins unless an essence host dies—not a change. The Heimerlich team offending gamer should be disqualified, and the low member, the harvester of the changing essence, by rule, should be sacrificed as a result.

"There is more. The warlord Alchemy was interviewed for a statement. Here is the playback: 'This is an outrage! I knew that someone would try to cheat the system to save themselves. This only hurts others who are playing by the rules. Beyond all that has been stated, the fact remains that this entire Game was a farce from the beginning. So by the ring I wear, I proclaim that this gamer must be found and sacrificed, or this Game must be dissolved.'"

Gimmish sat in his pilot seat crying and banging the armrest, working on his navigational computer, searching the cosmos for a place to hide. He went the opposite way from Tol's and Sargen's sectors for safety toward the least-controlled sector, which belonged to Philimar, in a back corner on the edge of the expansion of the cosmos. Philimar had achieved warlord status by default, finding a sector no one claimed. And like Alchemy, he filled his defender ranks with outcasts of others. The sector was full of uninhabited areas that, with a little help, were able to support life. The broadcast caught his attention again.

"Alchemy has abruptly exited. The whole Game is halted due to the controversy over the essences. The venue is in chaos. The spectators in the arena are throwing objects onto the Game floor. Viewers all over the dimension are sending communications of their displeasure about the entire Game setup. For a bit of history on the Game, let's go to Roggert who is our expert on all things Game."

"Thanks, Drollis. This is the first and catastrophic crisis we have had since the Game created the Grand Truce. As most in the dimension know, the Game was instituted so we quarks would quit warring with each other but still have the entertainment of the fight. Alchemy was never a fan but went along since every other warlord had signed on to the premise. The word from off-the-record sources is that he has been bored with the Game's lack of sacrifices so far. The warlord has been looking for a reason to cause conflict again."

"Well, Roggert, he now has his chance. Let's go to the venue. Bage has an update. Go, Bage!"

"Drollis, we have another problem. Team Heimerlich has officially divulged that Gimmish's league-leading essence was from the so-called 'third planet.' And as previously reported, the warlord Alchemy has announced his departure from the Game, and other warlords are contemplating the same."

"Bage, do you know who they are?"

"Not exactly, but Contronto and Descrim have announced that they will make a joint statement about their future participation later. The warlord Buentos has not made a comment. Others just want to find Gimmish and hold him to account."

"What's that commotion behind you, Bage?"

"It is the warlord Alchemy getting ready to make another statement. Let's listen in."

"I am the warlord Alchemy with a message for the dimension. From the beginning, I have believed this concoction was ripe for cheating and failure, and no one believed me. Now we are faced with the realization that I was correct. Therefore I announce that everyone who does not live in my fiefdom will vacate the realm in three planetary rotations or face punishment. Those who stay are to pledge allegiance to my rule.

"The reason for this failed Game was that our dimension has expanded to the point where not enough quarks come together to replace those who die in battle. This entire Game charade put a soft bandage on the problem. We must find a better way to survive. I will find a better way."

"There you have it, Drollis. This is Bage sending it back to you."

Gimmish turned off the broadcast and ran to his waste station, where he heaved the contents of his digestive system.

11/28/2022
Tol HQ Compound
Areanosten Planet Five
Quark Dimension

Tol called Brandish. "Commander Brandish, I need you at once."

"Yes, sir, on the way." At the urgency in Tol's voice, Brandish ran to the warlord's Game office at the venue. Others in the hall jumped out of his way to avoid being pushed into the walls. Brandish was in a full sprint yelling at quarks to move out of the way. He turned the corner toward the office and saw the pair of wide-eyed guards assuming a defensive position. Brandish stopped ten feet before them with his hands out to show he was unarmed.

Then Tol's voice came through the intercom speaker: "Stand down, guards. I need to see Commander Brandish in my office. Let him pass."

With that, one guard moved away while the other opened the door to let Brandish in. Brandish, still out of breath, rushed in, saying, "Sir, I got here as soon as I could. Your voice told me there was something wrong, so I came running."

"You know me pretty well, Commander. I have a big problem, and I feel you are the best quark for the job. We must find the gamer Gimmish as soon as possible, at all cost, or war may break out in the universe with me as the target."

Brandish said, "Master Tol, no."

Tol gave Brandish a blunt assessment. "This will teach me to trust my instincts rather than be merciful to a moron gamer who breaks the rules. I have told you about that third planet in the other dimension. They call it Earth. It is a world vastly different than ours, with binary replicating beings that grow in numbers over time. They are behind us in development, but they are basically intelligent and adaptive learners, building up their knowledge over time."

"So what does that have to do with our problem?"

"Six thousand years ago, they were starting to form societies with a philosophy that considered attractions for the other set of beings unlike anything in our dimension. The entire world exists in a circular pattern of creation, growth, reproducing, and death."

"Could that be an answer to our problem?"

Tol continued, "Gimmish captured an essence from there for its intelligence, hoping to have his essence outsmart the other gamers' essences. That happened. Unfortunately, the risk of these third-planet beings discovering us cannot be sustained because they are smart enough to acquire our knowledge. Since we do not replicate, they could start a war of attrition and win by sheer numbers, thanks to replication. The fool picked one of the most brilliant beings on the planet. From the reports I am receiving, it had broken his essence bond before we were able to stealthily kill it, now tossing control of the Game into chaos and possibly causing the chance of war again."

Tol looked disappointed, hardly able to look Brandish in the eyes due to the gravity of his mistake. "Since the other gamers went to the other dimension for their essences, portals opened to our dimension, including the third planet. And since Gimmish's essence host spent so much time alone in wilderness areas, it was bad luck that Gimmish found him. Prepare for the most important mission of your existence. You must find and stop Gimmish at all cost before he does something that allows the third planet to find out about us."

1/1/2023
Missoula, Montana
Sol Planet Three
Milky Way Dimension

In mid-October, the hidden gym in the Wilson Center was complete with all the bells and whistles and a powerlifter's set of weights. The steel back door had been installed by laborers Jim had hired from the Reservation, who were conveniently forgetful about their work. Michael's appetite and nutrition needs were massive with all the growth. He bought a side of beef that he alone finished in one week. The development of his mouth allowed him to eat faster, more per bite. He did more online lectures to hide from the neck down while wearing more extensive masks and ball caps over his face and ears. He avoided meetings to keep questions from arising. He'd never been the social gadfly, so it was unremarkable for him to avoid parties and other social gatherings.

Anne had quit shopping for clothes for him. The eye-popping bills from the big and tall stores were getting whispers. Missoula was still not that big of a town, which made Anne nervous.

It was New Year's Day, and Michael took a break from watching football. He went into the kitchen, where Anne was putting lunch together. All of the changes were on both of their minds. Michael began, "Anne, I cannot believe that this has happened to you. You marry a guy, and he goes through all these changes."

"Yeah? Well, believe it. Your growth spurt pushed me out of bed last night. I wish this changing crap would end soon."

"You ain't the Lone Ranger."

"Ya know, if someone sees you now, our whole research enterprise is over. It will be the largest research scandal in history. The banner would read, 'The researcher changed himself into a monster.'"

"My life is now a bad horror movie. Call it *Frankenbear*."

"This is no time for jokes. What are we going to do?"

"You and I will be backpacking more to stay out of view."

Anne had more on her mind, feeling the pressure from the Wilson Center board about Michael's activities and whereabouts. She continued, "That's one helluva flippant remark. Ya know, lots of questions are being asked about ya. I know we have talked about this before. Still we don't have good answers."

Michael said, "The conference calls have helped, haven't they?"

"Yeah, but the board wants to see ya too. Shake your hand. That kind of stuff."

"Okay, you're going to the place in the Caymans with Robin next week for two weeks, right?"

"Yeah, part of the deal since she helped save your life. Why?"

"I'm going into the mountains to do research. If anyone sees me like this, they will put me in a cage."

"Your answer to everything is to hide in the mountains. You can't keep doing that kind of stuff. That's not going to stop the questions. I'm beginning to wake up with stomachaches at night."

"Look, I have had sleepless nights about this too."

"We have to do something. What is your plan?"

"Hibernate."

"What? This is no damn time for jokes. You are freaking me out!."

"I'm not joking. Look at me. I'm part bear. While y'all are enjoying the sunshine, I have got to go to the cave and set up the experiment on hibernation physiology. Also, while you are gone, no one can see me."

Anne stood there aghast at Michael's idea. She said, "Do you realize how close we are to a massive ethical scandal on our doorstep, and all you want to do is research your damn sleep? There will be hard questions raised about what you did if someone finds out. Sure, you saved your life, but at what cost? And if what you did were ever revealed, who else could try to change humans into other creatures? You've got to have a plan or our life, what we stand for, will crumble. This Pandora's box is about to be opened. Who knows? We can't even talk to a lawyer to see if we are in legal jeopardy. Right now, I'm glad Robin took that last dose. That means it's not around here."

"Right now, all I can think to do is hide in my research. If you have any ideas of something else to do, please let me know."

"Well, ya gotta help me. You're the smart guy, but you're acting like a dumbass. We've gotta think of something before the next meeting at the end of March."

"No, Anne, the sabbatical does not end until July, which means I get to miss the March meeting doing research."

Anne looked at the floor, shaking her head, knowing kicking the can down the road put more pressure on her. Angrily, she said,

"Please help me understand how ya can blithely stick your enlarging head in the sand like this. I'm not sure we didn't break the law. What if we end up in jail? I don't know how I can take the stress. Even if ya don't have to see the board, we have to answer to them. All you're doing is pushing the eventual exposure down the road three months. I've got to get away from you for a while. I don't know how much more of this I can take!" She got her coat, walked out to the car, and drove away.

Michael knew he had no answer. As time passed, he kept growing and changing, still without answers.

1/23/2023
Deep Wilderness
Near the Ninepipe National Wildlife Refuge, Montana
Sol Planet Three
Milky Way Dimension

His sabbatical began in time for him to hide the changes for five or six months. The day after grades were finalized and the semester's work was completed, Michael and Jim went to the cave in the forest to stage the area for the hibernation research. Michael's increased strength allowed him to pack over two hundred pounds of experimental gear on his back and comfortably trek into the mountains.

Jim said, "Michael, you've become one helluva pack mule. The only thing I need to do is feed you mass quantities."

Michael answered, "I would rather be like this than sick as I was. Imagine: a year ago, I was in a wheelchair, unable to lift my arms for more than a few seconds at a time. Now toting this pack seems almost effortless. I feel this amazing power flowing through my entire body. No matter what happens, I am alive and strong."

"Yeah, if some hunter doesn't shoot you first. I know it's none of my business, but if the truth about you is discovered, I know you did it as a last resort, but still, did you think about what could happen to the school if people find out about what you are now? You know I would do anything to help the university. But if anything goes south with the Wilson Center, it will hurt the rest of the school. Anne is right to worry about this. People get crazy with ideas, you know."

"I understand what you're saying, and I understand about the dilemma. I know this sounds selfish, but I am still alive. As long as I do not go to jail or lose Anne, everything will be fine. I will make the school whole. I'm sorry I seem so cavalier. My hope is to one day find a way to go back to being totally human again. But I don't know how to. I have even thought of disappearing, crossing the border into Canada, and living as a bear for good. Let everyone think I'm dead. Essentially the human Michael is gone." Michael took a moment, not able to control the emotions rising to the surface. He sat down next to a tree and cried.

Jim came over, knowing that Michael had finally come near the breaking point. "Michael—Dr. Townsend. As long as you can reason and love, you are human. Let's get to work."

After Michael calmed down, they set the experiment. Michael had the monitors placed on and around him at the prescribed places. He then settled down for his four-week winter nap. Jim was to monitor the data from the Wilson Center.

4/10/23
The Townsend Residence
North of Missoula, Montana
Milky Way Dimension

Anne came to terms with Michael's changes. Every night in the Caymans, she had missed sleeping next to his developing body. She still loved being Anne Townsend. In March, the board was satisfied with hearing Michael's voice during the meeting, which gave the two of them more time to figure something out.

Anne woke up and thought about it before she poked him in the side and said, "Hey, Yogi. Time to wake up. Jim will be here any minute."

Michael grumbled as he answered, "Well, all I've got to do is walk out the patio door."

Anne sat up, "What? Naked?"

Michael answered, "Okay, around these parts, what would look stranger, a naked bear or one dressed in a kilt?"

"Well, you're a big boy—uh, bear now."

"Now over seven hundred pounds of loving teddy bear, just for you."

Anne sighed. "I've got a bear of a husband. Ya know, every morning, I wake up with a different thing in bed with me. You've changed so much so rapidly. Ya hit me in bed with your damn snout the other night. Then ya started snoring! If ya hadn't juiced your doses so much, it would have been a whole lot less."

"Yeah, and if a bullfrog had wings, he wouldn't bump his ass."

"Don't be so flippant. I'm serious."

"I'm just lucky this sabbatical has allowed me to keep my changes under wraps. I physically have never felt better in my life. I am completely rid of the disease. My experiment has promise for many horrible diseases. And I have the strongest, most beautiful and impressive wife in the world."

Anne gave him a pained look and said, "Go outside and wait for Jim. I have to go to the Center to do my morning workout."

Michael rolled out of bed onto all fours and walked into the bathroom. After he brushed his teeth, he went to the refrigerator and ate a raw buffalo steak. A backpack was filled with two dozen hard-boiled eggs and a box of eighteen energy bars. He walked out onto the deck and around to the front of the house. He put the backpack down and then felt compelled to begin sniffing the ground around the hedge. *Interesting, things I've never noticed before.*

At that moment, Michael turned his head to see Jim driving toward the house. The vehicle stopped, but Jim didn't get out.

Why is he sitting there like a zombie? He waited for a moment, then waved. "Hey, Jim, you can get out now."

Jim flinched and blinked his eyes in disbelief, then got out of the truck and carefully walked toward him. "Look, guy, you look like a real bear now. Scared the hell out of me."

Michael looked down and around his fur-covered body. "Oh yeah. I guess I do look like a daggum bear now."

"Michael, I just realized you're too big to fit in my passenger seat. Even if you could, I'd cause a wreck with everyone looking at me driving down the road with a grizzly bear riding shotgun."

"Then what do I do?"

"You'll need to ride across the back seat."

Michael shook his head and stood hesitantly. He walked around to the back door, hesitated again, and then crawled into the back seat. "I can barely fit in here!"

Jim smiled and answered, "Not my fault. When I bought the truck, I didn't plan to tote grizzly bears." Michael grumbled but then hunkered down, getting as comfortable as he could for the hour-long drive.

The hunt was successful. They returned to the house where Michael effortlessly picked the five-hundred-pound elk cow from the truck bed and carried it to the shed in the back. Jim shook his head, saying, "I would not have believed it had I not seen it with my own eyes. I could not believe you picked up that elk from the back the way you did when we got it here."

Michael said, "Okay, get used to it. If my future life wasn't in jeopardy, I would enjoy the new me more. The only downside of today was having as much fur as that dead elk. If someone discovers me, my life's work is over. Maybe I'll claim to be Sasquatch or some other freak."

An agitated Jim snapped, "I've had it. You haven't got a plan, do you? I recommended that Bender call you in the first place. My real first love is this university. If this situation is exposed as a scandal, I won't forgive you if it hurts the school. Think about the impact you could have on this community. I'm losing my patience with your haphazard ways. I'm going home."

As Jim was walking out, Anne came into the room with a troubled look. She said, "Supper is ready. Let's sit down." Michael followed her inside and sat at the table.

Michael noticed and began. "You and I have been on the same wavelength almost from the first evening in the coffee shop after work."

Anne looked at him with her soft brown eyes, "I never would have dreamed any of this."

"Me either. I do not know how I got this disease or how I will live from now on as a man or whatever I am. Still, I am madly in love with you."

"Michael, I do not know where this is going. Let me say now, you have changed on the outside, but I will never give up on you. There is not one day that goes by when you do not thrill me somehow. Even last winter, when I was so mad at you, I could not get over the fact there is like this essence about you I cannot let go of. In any case, we have got to make a plan to come clean."

"If it were not for you keeping me motivated and lifting me up when I was down, I probably would have given up completely. Maybe I am trying to hold on to too much. I may need to let it all go."

Anne responded, "I would give up all the fame and fortune if holding on meant losing you."

Michael continued, "I am what I am now, one of the strongest creatures on Earth, being able to exercise this augmented body to lift nearly a ton over my head. I have bear genetics with human knowledge on how to maximize my muscle power. Selfishly, I have never felt better in my life, no pain at all."

Anne added, "And you have motivated and thrilled me with all this change. I have never looked this good in a bathing suit in my life. Still, I have been thinking about all the stress on us. I am thankful Robin got rid of that last dose because of how the contract was written."

"At least there will only be one monster in the world."

"I cannot believe who I am either. Thanks to you, I'm one of the most respected businesspeople in science, funding projects you have inspired all over the country. My life with you is incredible. I'm wondering what will happen when this all comes out in the open."

"I did something astonishing today when we were out hunting. When I saw the elk cow, something came over me. I remember something like another spirit, taking over inside me, to fall on all fours and dash after the elk."

"Ya mean you didn't shoot it?"

"No. When I caught it, I used the claws of my left hand to grab its neck and then bit its spinal cord above the shoulders. Then my right hand reached underneath to grab and tackle and break its front leg bringing the animal to the ground, killing it. I was a savage predator, yet it felt natural, like it was instinctive."

Anne only looked somewhat surprised and said, "Ya know, I have felt this coming too. I have seen some of that in your eyes when we're close."

"However, sometimes, when I feel these episodes, it leaves me to wonder how you are really feeling about being married to a freak. It is so difficult for me now, to believe any human would not be scared of me or could love me. I don't know what I would do without you." Michael choked up, knowing that was his greatest fear. The sun was setting over the mountains, which gave the vesper lighting on Anne's face. He saw her eyes moisten as the two tried to continue their conversation, producing no more than grunts as their food got cold.

After a while, Anne said, "I don't know anything about the future except I won't let you go, so let's sleep on it tonight and think about the future tomorrow. We can't hide this much longer."

Before bedtime, Michael noticed Anne watching him negotiate his electric toothbrush around his large canine teeth. In six months, he had grown a snout over twenty centimeters long and a tongue that hung out of his mouth while he brushed.

When they got in bed, Anne snuggled her body close to his chest, causing him the need to sweetly caress her exquisite frame. She began to quietly moan with comfort and security in total body comfort. He wanted nothing more than to be an old man when he died, holding her in his arms.

The following morning, Michael woke up at first light. He went into the kitchen, and while fixing breakfast, he looked out the window as the sun peaked over the mountains. His shoulders felt like they were being lifted to draw him to go into the high country with Anne that day. He brought her coffee to her bedside then looked at her as she smiled and gazed back. "After breakfast, I need to show you where I have been."

"Are you going to finally show me the cave?"

He smiled and said, "Yes, let's finish breakfast."

"Michael, I have been waiting for this. As you have changed, I have seen you become more comfortable about feeling your animal instincts. I feared they might overwhelm your humanity. Thank you for not leaving me alone."

Fifteen minutes later, when they finished, Michael said, "We are going now." He stood up and extended his hand. She stood up, and he led her to the back shed. He found a thick blanket and a long leather strap he wrapped around his neck and strapped down a blanket on his back. He got on all fours and told her, "Hop on and hold the straps. I'm going to start slowly, then you tell me when you're comfortable."

"Your back is broader than any horse I rode back on the farm."

He answered, "Okay, you can let me know how fast to go." They started.

In a few minutes, Anne got used to the blanket and soon told Michael, "Speed up. This is fun!" She forgot she was in her nightgown and began to feel the joy they had back in the Shenandoah Mountains on the backwoods trails. They reached Michael's cave in less than an hour.

Anne looked in and asked surprisingly, "You stayed here? You really did live like an animal."

"Yes, like this morning when I was cooking, a spirit or something was telling me to come. I realized you had to come too. Come in with me." He showed her where he slept.

Then she asked him to lie down and hold her. "Come here, animal. I want you to feel what all my strength training has done for me."

After a while, Michael said, "Let's take a walk."

"Where?"

"A special place where I have been able to think."

She hopped on his back and rode him to a large fallen tree next to a rushing mountain stream. Michael said, "I have gotten to know these woods fairly well. Still, when I am here, it never ceases to amaze me how new life is every time I am with you. I finally realized I cannot live this new life of mine without you."

Anne looked at him and said, "This may sound strange, but every day, I find something new and thrilling about you, giving me a reason to love you that much more."

Michael philosophized, "Not all the water that rushes down this mountain makes it to the Pacific Ocean. Just like life itself, it ends in different places. Nevertheless, each water molecule finds a destination in its travels."

Anne asked, "What's your point?"

Michael answered, "Even when the path is known, you never know how or when or where the journey will end."

Anne said, "I hope we make it to the ocean."

Michael responded, "Me too. But no river is straight."

Anne shook her head and said, "Boy, ya think too much. Let's go home. I've got to work in the morning."

They both stood up. Anne put her arm around Michael's lower back and said, "Ya know, I didn't realize how sexy bears were before now."

Michael said, "Yeah, you're not the bear. You're just married to one."

THE LOSS

4/13/2023
Approaching the Third Planet
Outer Space near Sol
Milky Way Dimension

G immish was figuring out that the idea of hiding in his dimension was not going to be successful. He could hear on the open communicator that he was a wanted quark. *I have a feeling, even if I fix the original problem and get rid of the essence, I still will be executed when found. In any case, I need the host dead to stop having all these headaches and nightmares before I lose my mind. While on the run from the other dimension, I have to find a way to eliminate the essence. I'm sick of it.*

The thing to do was stay in the other dimension and locate Michael. He continued to speed through space toward the third planet, thinking what he would do to eliminate Michael.

Gimmish had grown to hate this dimension.

What did I ever do wrong? Nothing! I did what everyone else did: find essences. All I did was find that stupid third planet that Tol seems so fond of. I went there and got a great essence that now I cannot use! He came to me even though I am on Heimerlich's team. That does not matter. Even my warlord is willing to sacrifice me. I earned this spot for saving him from the assassination attempt, the ingrate.

All for this idiotic Game Tol concocted. Ending warfare and replacing it with the Game to be a spectator sport. Warlord Alchemy is right that it was a damn farce. I would love to be on Alchemy's team now.

If I ever get a chance, Tol will pay for all this grief. After this, I am going to see if I can join Alchemy.

He knew where the third planet was. However, he did not know how to get there from where he was after exiting through the unfamiliar portal. It took him time to figure where he was in space in relation to the third planet. Gimmish found out he was four solar systems away, making his journey long, even for these ships that traveled much faster than light. This gave him ample time to become more enraged and bitter.

I wonder who will be coming after me since the warlords are having a grand time thinking of how to execute me. Hell, if it were me, I would have an armada with me and blow the entire planet into particles. But no. I'm out here to clean up a mess that should not matter. I don't care if those third-planet creatures know I've been there. I'm going to blast them and say the hell with it.

Gimmish thought back to how he found his essence, Dr. Michael Townsend. How quick and savvy he was during the Game. He saw him first when Michael played in a game on the third planet in a stadium that looked similar to the stadium where the Game was played.

Michael was the best player he saw on that field among the others engaged in the same third-planet game. Using his essence allowed his team to rise up out of last place. He was finally contributing to the team's performance. No whispers of "moron" when other quarks said his name. All of that gone, and now he was wanted for cheating. He yelled to the walls, "No fair! It's Tol's fault!" He thought about the conversation he had with Tol.

Why do they have that rule where you need the essence source dead before switching to another? It's a horrible rule. But now I am on my way to finish the job. I must get rid of the problem and maybe save myself from that essence feeling inside me. I need to quit having these visions, sounds, and feelings I cannot control. It's driving me insane. I have got to kill that essence host, or I am going to kill myself!

I'm almost there now. I can see the blue planet on this side of Sol.

4/13/2023
Orbiting the Third Planet
Sol Planet Three
Milky Way Dimension

This was Commander Brandish's first trip to the other dimension that he'd heard about for so long. He thought about how different the heavenly bodies were with ringed and colorful planets of red, green, and the blue third planet with brown, oddly shaped areas. It was a more beautiful planet than he had ever seen in all his travels in his dimension. He marked his place and time to judge one orbit around the planet and hid behind the horizon to wait. The debris circling the planet made it easy to observe when Gimmish approached without being detected.

Brandish took his assigned mission to find and bring back Gimmish with intensity. He had had enough time to think back on what he had done since the Game collapsed. But it was too late to forgive Gimmish. The damage to the dimension had been done, and the fallout was happening. Gimmish had to be caught and brought to account.

Over and over, the events of the Game venue went through his mind. He thought about going back to the tournament site picking up any clues about Gimmish's craft.

He remembered that the deserted site was a mess from the trash left behind by upset people the day earlier. He even saw a couple of broken windows and some fire damage. Bright green Heimerlich jerseys were burning on trash receptacles. Brandish chuckled since he knew a few quarks who would have been right there in the thick of the mayhem. No one had been near the stadium since the failed event. He was allowed to go into the booths and offices trying to see if Gimmish had left clues to where he was going. In the gamer booth were some notes in a trash can about the "third planet." He felt that was where Gimmish was headed.

He recalled leaving the building on the way to his craft, looking up at the venue, and shaking his head at the bare bones outside walls. It showed what Alchemy had thought of the Game from the beginning. He knew that Tol had a better arena. As he recalled walking to the spacecraft parking lot, the last of the ships were gone, allowing him to investigate Gimmish's spot without scrutiny from bystanders.

It took a while, but Brandish had finally found the parking lot assignments for the gamers and their ships. He found Gimmish's assigned parking spot to search for clues about his ship so he could pick up a trail to track him down. All he found was a piece of rope to anchor his craft, a piece of his metal, and a piece from a toiletry, apparently dropped during Gimmish's haste to pack—debris that could be tracked through tissue chemistry detection. He'd had to get it done quickly before the hot sun cooked the tissue evidence into the ground. *That planet was a miserable place.* He could still feel the sting of the windblown sand on the side of his face. *I am so happy I got out of there. I don't want to ever go back.*

Brandish looked at his notes to see if he had missed anything. They were the same notes he had looked at for months. The traffic control area was the most intriguing place on the planet to approach.

Looking around traffic control for exit routes and flight patterns, he had determined that Gimmish had left along the prescribed course so as not to cause scrutiny. He figured that Gimmish most likely escaped by way of the Philimar sector since it appeared to be the safest way to avoid contact with Tol's or Sargen's fiefdoms. Thanks to his rank in Tol's fiefdom, Brandish could access the automated tracking systems that projected travel of each craft coming and going. Gimmish's flight path was recorded automatically. *He did have to take a long way. I'm getting stir-crazy in this ship waiting for that Moonie.*

He had discovered that Gimmish had left before anyone knew, knowing that chaos would ensue if the rule's violations were found. When he found the signature of Gimmish's ship on the surveillance tracker, he took the clues he had and headed out into space.

Looking out his window at the third planet evoked memories of how ugly Alchemy's world was. *Sand, sand, ugly brown sand. There was barely any life on that planet. Why did Alchemy use that place for his headquarters? The only good thing is that he can see most of the other planets in his system. He's had to ship almost all of his supplies in from other planets. I am glad I left that place as soon as I could get the evidence.*

On the other hand, this planet is downright beautiful. I have never seen such an inviting place in all my travels. It was not the first time Brandish thought about the contrast since arriving.

All Brandish could do was his best for his master Tol, always ending by giving his salute, "My success is your success, but if I fail, only I am to blame." He would try to make a quick trip to the nearest portal to tell Tol about his status. He knew Tol had relented and given permission for Brandish to travel to the third planet's dimension since Gimmish's ship had not been sighted in their universe and thus was lost for the present. So he had arrived at the third planet well before Gimmish got there.

Brandish remembered Tol telling him, "I bet that moron went through a portal and is trying to find his essence host to kill it. If Gimmish makes a mistake and is discovered, the dimension, especially our technology, may be exposed to the third-planet beings. You must be careful too, Commander, for the properties of that world are bewitching and dangerous."

Brandish did as he was advised and hoped Tol's hunch was going to be correct. He remembered how easy it was to find the portal where Tol had instructed and travel through. Brandish did not even know about it. Looking at the guard routes, this area was never formally watched because it was off any routes.

But this was the day when the boredom would end. At last, Gimmish's ship was approaching from above the northern pole heading toward his victim. Brandish knew the essence host was on the planet but did not know where. Finally, Gimmish would come to take care of the host, then he could take care of Gimmish.

7:00 PM 4/13/2023
Inside the Residence of Michael and Anne Townsend
Outside of Missoula, Montana
Sol Planet Three
Milky Way Dimension

Michael sat across the table smiling at his wife. Anne was a stunning woman of pure muscle filling the shoulders of her athletic shirt. "The weightlifting has changed you into a goddess."

Anne rolled her eyes and said, "Just read the proposal before I knock ya in the head. Dr. Bender wanted me to have you review this proposal too."

After reading the proposal sent to the university, he exclaimed, "Wow! The research money is being matched by the CDC?"

Anne answered, "Yes, it is. Once we published your findings of stem cell therapy and its mechanism of action in neuromuscular diseases, the genetics world began raving about the new possibilities. It got me so excited presenting that when it came to handshaking, I almost broke a couple of the hands I shook."

Michael chuckled, "Between volumetric weight training, progressive overload, and that training table diet, you have become a rock. Benching over two hundred pounds for anyone is impressive, much less a woman doing it."

"It helps that I am six feet tall, grew up and worked on a farm, and was an athlete in college too. I have worked my body into peak performance. I need to stay this way, so ya don't break me, ya animal."

"It's all about having the right genetics. You are my awesome Mrs. Universe. I knew that from the moment I saw you. Do you remember how we met? I was such a doofus."

9:00 AM 10/9/2016
The Johns Hopkins Hospital
Baltimore, Maryland
Sol Planet Three
Milky Way Dimension

Michael missed grand rounds twice in three weeks losing track of time while reading genomics journals. The attending physician, the arrogant but brilliant Dr. Bishop, was not amused. He berated Michael in front of the entire staff, the second time warning him to make sure his "lazy Southern ass" did not miss another grand rounds.

The floor's new charge nurse was shocked at the attending's condescending comments. She was a registered nurse who also was a sharp woman with high regard for common courtesy.

"Are you okay? Bishop is such a condescending dick. What did ya do to stir that pot?"

He mumbled, "I deserved to be fussed at."

"Why? No one ever deserves that abuse."

He combed his hair with his fingers, wrinkled his nose, and with an embarrassed look replied, "I missed rounds for the second time in three weeks."

"What did ya do to miss grand rounds? That is a big one, but there is no excuse for his unprofessional behavior. Did ya oversleep?"

"Naw, I didn't oversleep. I just got caught up reading a medical journal." Michael turned around and saw a woman looking at him with an attitude he'd never seen in a woman. She looked like a woman who took nothing from anyone, no matter how big or smart or good-looking. It was as she was waiting for a plausible excuse and was not going anywhere until she heard one.

He said, "You wanna discuss this subject at another time?"

"No, now."

"Who do you think you are anyway? Why I missed the rounds is irrelevant. It happened. I did it. And now I'm fixin' to go to work on the floor."

"Fixing?"

"Yeah. It's like you're preparing. It's one of those 'southernisms.' And the g's on gerunds are silent down south."

She cocked her head to one side, arched her left eyebrow, gave a wry smile, and asked, "When do ya get off?"

Michael thought for a moment and took a good look at this woman, who was not much shorter than his six foot five and looked about the same age. Rather athletically built as if she worked out regularly (which she did) with brown hair and brown eyes that caused him to think, *Wow!*

"About five. I'm kind of a boring person. I mainly go from here to my flat and back."

"I am too, but I know this place a little better. You wanna meet me at a coffee shop called Ralph's?"

He was stunned by her forwardness. "Where's that?"

"Out the front door and across the street. Have you ever been there before?"

"I've never been out the front door."

"Ya kidding me?"

"No. I drive to work. Park the car in the parking garage, come in, work, go out to the garage, get into my car, and go home. I'm not from here. I don't know anyone here. I'm here for the education, nothing more."

"Now, instead of going out the back door this evening, why don't ya meet me at the front door so ya can get to know someone else in this boring town? Let me see your watch."

She took his wrist and turned the face of the watch her way. "Ya have a smartwatch, good."

"Why?"

She started touching the face to program it.

She began to speak now with a seductive lilt in her voice, "Ya seem like a guy who's very smart, extremely focused, and sticks to a rigid routine."

Michael nervously swallowed his saliva and asked, "What are you doing?"

"I'm setting a reminder in your watch for fifteen and thirty minutes before five this evening. I'd hate for ya to miss our date." She winked, "You'll find out I'm much more important than rounds. By the way, my name is Anne with an *e*."

Michael was a little embarrassed that he would allow this perfect stranger to start using his watch and touch him like this. He remembered in college how girls flirted, and he was so painfully shy to respond, making them think he was either a prude or a colossal snob. They would try to get close or offer favors to court his fancy, which made him feel uncomfortable and vulnerable to being used. Finally, he would stay at home or go to the library and read. Books did not try to tease him or want anything from him or want to use him. They just gave him knowledge and wonder. This huge football player in high school and in college was an emotional recluse. No one had been forward with him with the authoritative style this nurse had, which gave him a gut feeling she had something to give him that no one else had ever offered before.

"Now there. If ya don't show up on time at five, I'll know you're a complete dud. See ya at five."

Michael said nothing. He held up his hand to about shoulder height, smiled a half-smile, and waved at her with his fingers. He looked around and saw the other nurses turn their heads away and try to get busy. One snickered just loud enough for Michael to hear. He tapped at his forehead to try to remember what he was supposed to do that afternoon.

He remembered he needed the notes from grand rounds from somebody so he could see patients. One of the other doctors, Josh, came to Michael.

"I've waited for a moment to get a chance to ask her out for three weeks. She hasn't even looked my way. What the hell did you do?"

"Act like a doofus. Can I get your notes?"

Michael and Anne laughed until they cried at their story.

Anne said, "Ya know, after that therapy regimen you gave yourself, and the side effects that turned you into this monster, I wanted to do anything I could to keep up with ya."

Michael responded, "One of these days, I will need to come out of hiding. I'm going to do that when I figure out a good story. You know, if I reveal the risks I took, it's likely to negatively impact the Wilson Center's future reputation."

"But ya said it before. Ya did it to stay alive. Nothing else would have worked."

"The regulators would have made us go through major hoops if I were to use human stem cells. I had to act fast and use whatever I could or die. It was tricky enough to splice the DNA to combine with mine. But I think I overdid it."

Anne smirked and said, "That's the understatement of the century."

Michael continued, "And if it had not been for those poachers, we wouldn't have had those stem cells. And Robin bringing that experimental molecular transport drug and all the great work you two did keep me alive."

"We didn't know if you were going to make it through the first treatment."

"That was one hell of a time." Michael continued, "But I know there will always be those academics who will question, and the cloud will never go away. Plus, what if someone else tries this and really turns into a monster or gets hurt? I consider myself damn lucky to have survived this long. If I hadn't gone through with what I had, I would have died months ago. But now it is what it is, and we need to make a plan."

Anne said, "Wait a minute. Do you think that we can just explain your new self intellectually?"

Michael shrugged and said, "I only know about how beautiful you are to me tonight."

Everything was perfect for the evening except that someone was watching and waiting for their chance.

7:00 PM 4/13/2023
On the Property of Michael and Anne Townsend
Outside Missoula, Montana
Sol Planet Three
Milky Way Dimension

Brandish saw Gimmish arrive to try to solve his problem. Unbeknownst to the fugitive, the commander watched his every move, staying far enough away to avoid alerting his quarry, yet near the horizon.

As Brandish watched all of this take place, he knew full well that any wrong move would open the floodgates of inquisitive third-planet beings. He noticed the research being conducted in locations that Gimmish searched and saw aircraft looking at the stars for information and discovery. *These buildings look as sophisticated as Tol's research facilities.* He knew one time he was detected but got away quickly, which made him more conscious of the danger Gimmish had possibly unleashed. The commander monitored Gimmish's spacecraft as he landed near the mountain range for safety. He hit trees and animals with his clumsy piloting, leaving evidence. After he landed his cloaked spacecraft, Brandish saw that the desperate quark had changed into Earth clothing to exit his craft. Clearly he was trying to hide his intentions.

Brandish got into a cloaking suit and followed Gimmish's path to the Townsend house. The sunset over the mountains took Brandish's breath away with its beauty. He was able to see the topography looking like a big mouth to the stars with the mountains as teeth tempting him to stay and watch the sunset. But he knew he had to find the wayward quark before he did something else foolish. He saw where Gimmish had clipped the tree line, scattering branches, and then landed in a clear spot in the middle of the mess and tapped on his cloaked ship. Brandish saw footprints and followed them toward the house.

He turned the corner and saw Gimmish holding something hidden under his coat as he approached the door. When Gimmish touched the frame next to the door, something alerted the beings inside before they got up from their seats. He turned his translator on and heard a voice through his earpiece, "Sir, can I help you?"

Then Gimmish answered back, "I was expecting another, could you give me directions? I have a map that is hard to read. Is there any way I could get some help?"

Now hidden behind the hedge, Brandish was horrified that the desperate fool had made overt contact with third-planet beings. He held his breath and waited for the next move. Another stir inside let him know that someone was going to answer. He watched the door beginning to open and heard the voice start, "May I—"

Gimmish pulled a blaster out from under his coat and shot through the door as the doomed being began to open it, killing it immediately. It fell through the doorway onto the front stoop. Then he heard something roar with shock and rage, starting to run through the house after the blast and screams. From the anguished cry inside, he knew someone had seen the whole episode.

After Gimmish shot and killed the being at the door, Brandish noticed a vehicle turning to enter the driveway from a more significant strip of hard surfacing. *I'm trapped!* Brandish saw that Gimmish also noticed the vehicle. Gimmish then turned and ran around the house back toward his craft as fast as he could to avoid any chance of discovery or capture. Gimmish's head start allowed him to make it to the ship unseen. Brandish saw a beast-like specimen, like none he had ever seen, go through the door. The giant creature looked both ways looking for the assassin. It put the tip of its long face on the spot where the being's killer once stood and followed the direction the guilty quark took. Brandish was astounded at what he saw and froze in his position.

Meanwhile, from his vantage point, he saw Gimmish running back to the craft, not even looking back, for he thought Gimmish realized he killed the wrong being. If so, he knew Gimmish had made a huge mistake and probably wanted to get away before being caught.

Brandish saw him reach his ship and immediately power the craft to lift off, thinking that Gimmish probably knew his plan failed. He looked back to see the dead being had traces of an alien weapon that would allow the humans to question their existence.

The monster-sized being got to the place where the ship had landed. The creature saw it flying into the sky; thus it knew that whatever had killed its companion had gotten away in an alien craft heading into space. The giant being ran back to the house, where another different-looking being, more the size of a quark, got out of the vehicle that had come up the driveway holding a long menacing item that he assumed was a weapon. *No wonder Gimmish took off after seeing the transport machine.*

The being from the vehicle yelled, "Oh, my God, Michael! What happened?" The being saw the lifeless body with large wounds in the middle of its torso. The door had splintered at the powerful blast when it killed the fugitive quark's victim almost instantly. Brandish knew the being never saw the killer's eyes when it started opening the door.

A now the sobbing monster groaned, "Someone shot Anne! She's gone!" This hulk continued to cry uncontrollably and yelling, "I want to find the murderer and tear him to pieces." He went over to the dead body, still crying, and blood smeared onto him as he hugged the being.

Brandish knew he should act now. But he did not know how long he had before more locals would show up, possibly with more weapons. Any attempt to hide this mess would take too much time and risk discovery, capture, or being killed, exposing everything. Staying hidden would let Gimmish's deeds speak for themselves. He had to decide in seconds what to do.

In those seconds, while he was deciding, he became fixated on the scene in front of him. He had never witnessed such behavior in the other dimension. It was like something ending but more intense. Like something important that was missed that would never happen again. Still, he had not lost anything. The creature in front of him had.

He stayed motionless, irritated at himself. He had allowed himself to be caught up in the intense events happening in front of him. He was trapped behind the hedge, unable to tear himself from witnessing the crime, and could not ignore it. The moment overcame him. He felt a gripping, painful stimulus in his abdomen. Seconds later, he wept. *What about this is making me feel this way? Have I been infected by something?*

What horrified him was that there was no escaping that the third planet would know that aliens were real and had violent intentions. History had changed forever.

"Jim, it's all on camera. I watched while Anne came to the door and was shot without warning, like an assassination! The police are on the way now! Make a copy and show them the video."

"I am retrieving the video from my smartphone. Oh, my! That looks like a weapon from a sci-fi movie." The man looked at the massive beast next to the dead being uncontrollably crying.

Brandish understood that Tol and Sargen needed to know what Gimmish had done as soon as possible, since now the third planet had proof of alien life. He dared not approach the house since he saw Michael's strength in action and that his possible capture left nobody to report the damage. He waited until Michael and Jim went into the house to move back to his vessel.

Suddenly, Brandish thought, *Glad I didn't try to clean up*, when he heard sirens. He listened to the recent arrival yell, "Run! Hide, Michael! I see blue lights at the bottom of the road coming fast! Nobody can see you as you are now! They will interrogate you about the experiment, or you will be hunted down and possibly killed yourself! Run, now!"

The massive creature gently laid down the lifeless body and ran into the woods, still wailing with grief. Brandish cut his eyes, surveying the area. He decided to stay cloaked and motionless until the coast was clear.

4:00 AM 4/14/2023
Somewhere in the Ninepipe National Wildlife Refuge, Montana
Sol Planet Three
Milky Way Dimension

Michael settled down after running wildly over mountain trails and thick woods, looking for the cave he used in the past to hide from detection. He could not control his thoughts. His acquired bear instincts took him to his destination. No mapping was necessary for this man/animal to find his ultimate location. Once he arrived, he went to the back of the cave to hide from his sorrow, roaring and heaving in grief. But his mind brought him back to the dinner conversation, and what happened in Baltimore the first night he met Anne.

4:30 PM 10/9/2016
The Johns Hopkins Hospital
Baltimore, Maryland
Sol Planet Three
Milky Way Dimension

Since it was October, the cold winds started coming from the north, signaling the first frost of winter. In the last room of the day, Michael's watch alarm sounded. The nurse had programmed a piano alert tone. *Musical too.* He finished the patient and washed his hands.

Fifteen minutes later, the alarm played guitar strums. As he was walking out, he was caught by the attending physician who had berated him earlier.

Pointing his index finger at Michael, Dr. Bishop said, "Dr. Townsend, you know damn well that the grand rounds are mandatory! I want you in my office now. We need to have a, as you say down South, a 'come-to-Jesus meeting' about what happens the next time you pull that stunt."

Michael was in a panic. The only woman who had ever gotten past his defensive measures was going to be stood up! But he had to sit there and take his medicine from Dr. Bishop. "Dr. Bishop, please, I've got to get to an appointment at five. Can we speak another time?"

"Now, Dr. Townsend, you know how damn important grand rounds are."

"Yes, sir. I do."

"In my office."

"Sir, I'll miss my appointment."

"In my office or out of the program. Your choice."

Michael slumped his shoulders and walked into the office to sit down for his impromptu meeting.

Bishop began, "You know that when you are coming on the ward, you have got to know the progress of each patient in real time.

Critical things happen in a moment. You have got to be on top of this. Seconds count. Someone codes and you don't have your timely information, they die, and you are responsible. You want that?"

The lecture lasted for forty minutes. Dr. Bishop went on like a Marine Corps drill sergeant from Parris Island, letting him know that he would be terminated if he ever missed grand rounds again. Michael left the office shaking. He ran downstairs to the front door. It was 5:55 PM, and no nurse waiting.

The following morning, Michael arrived on the ward fifteen minutes before grand rounds. He saw the nurse and tried to catch her to explain. Then Dr. Bishop came, the nurse saw him, sneered, and turned down the hall. The attending began speaking about each patient on the ward.

He looked over at Michael and said. "Thanks for joining us, Dr. Townsend."

Michael only nodded, noting that Dr. Bishop's reputation as a brilliant but hot-headed physician was well-established. The nurse cut her eyes toward the group while Dr. Bishop kept needling Michael the entire grueling grand rounds. Other nurses noticed the verbal abuse but knew it was not the first or last time they would hear it; it was pure Bishop. Michael looked like a beaten dog by the end of the two-hour ordeal.

After it was over, he heard his friend Josh ask, "Are you all right, guy? How are you doing? I thought Bishop liked you since you have been nailing the diagnoses on every patient assigned to you."

"Don't miss grand rounds. Bishop had me in his office last evening right at a quarter to five. He took me into his office and dressed me up and down for an hour. I had a meeting at five that I missed that I really wanted to make. I didn't get to the front door until five minutes to six."

"That's awful. Now you have another doctor pissed off at you."

"Nope, a nurse."

"Oh, crap! Do you mean with that tall brunette? How did you screw that up?"

"I was supposed to meet her at five o'clock yesterday evening. Bishop put a wrench in that plan."

"You think I have a chance now?"

Michael looked at his colleague as if he was back playing linebacker at Duke about to tackle a running back. His lip started to curl, and he saw Michael's teeth clinching, making his jaw muscles flex.

The other resident held up his hands and stepped backward. "Just kidding, man! I was teasing."

Michael growled.

Josh then asked, "See you for lunch?"

Michael stepped towards him.

His friend turned and quickly exited with incredulous stares following him down the hall.

Michael realized this was one of the worst days of his life. He was more upset at missing the evening with the nurse than he was at getting dressed down by the attending who could boot him right out of the program. The nurse would not have anything to do with Michael and had stayed too mad to look his way. After two weeks, the two were passing each other on the ward as if their first encounter had never happened. By then, he felt it was a lost cause.

Then one morning, the loudspeaker sounded, "Code blue, room 523."

The nurse yelled through the intercom, "Bring the crash cart." Michael was at the nurse's station making notes when he heard the call. He dropped everything and ran. Dr. Bishop was close behind. Michael ran through the door to see the tall nurse starting the IV. Michael yelled, "Nurse! Status!"

"The patient is in v-fib. IV lidocaine started and no response."

Then the heart stopped and the monitor flatlined.

Michael asked, "Are the paddles ready? Stop the lidocaine and start D5W with bolus amiodarone three hundred milligrams, bolus forty units vasopressin now, and tell me when the drip is ready."

The nurse changed the IV in fifteen seconds, and smartly said, "Done!"

He then effortlessly tore off the man's hospital gown, moved him into position and yelled, "All clear!" Michael took the paddles and applied them to the man's chest. The man bounced on the bed in recoil from the shock. Nothing. "Initiating CPR!"

Thirty seconds went by.

Michael looked at the continuing flatline and yelled, "Paddles ready. Again, all clear!" A second shock was applied, and this time the monitor began to register a heartbeat, letting everybody know the patient had a chance. "Nurse, call the catheter lab now to transport this patient for immediate evaluation. Recorder, log treatment."

"Yes, doctor."

Dr. Bishop went to the patient's side to take the pulse.

"This patient might not have made it with any delay. Good job. I guess you won't be in my office tonight for an hour after work like two weeks ago."

The nurse spun around to see Michael's vindicated face.

"I guess you're not a dud."

"Well"—Michael closed one eye and looked up without moving his head—"the jury is still out on that."

"I should've let ya explain."

"Yes, but you can make it up to me."

She cut her eyes at him and raised her eyebrows.

He said, "How 'bout this evening—you, me, and a cup of coffee?"

Dr. Bishop left the room, and Michael turned to the nurse, "Programing the watch really helped."

"My name is Anne, you moron," she said with a wry smile.

"I'm Michael, and you're right. I'm a moron. See you this evening? Got to transport my patient."

They met each other in the front lobby all smiles, and that evening the coffee had never tasted better. Michael was the absolute—as they say—Southern gentleman, which impressed her since most northerners usually did not show the same manners. Other women noticed Michael opening the door for Anne. He helped her with her jacket. When they got up from their coffee, he reached out to offer his hand. She said, "I'm stunned. I feel like I'm back in an old movie, and you're Rhett Butler."

Michael said, "It's all that Charleston society training coming out."

They repeated their coffee run every night for the next week with increasing attraction.

All the memories flashed in his consciousness, the challenging, the good, and the best. He wanted to make many more, but they were all gone. Michael cried himself to sleep.

10:00 PM 4/14/2023
Outside on the property of Michael Townsend
Outside Missoula, Montana
Sol Planet Three
Milky Way Dimension

A thunderstorm the next night was Brandish's cover to start his craft to go back to the other dimension. The rolling thunder and brilliant lightning strikes allowed the noise of his engines to blend with the surrounding sounds. Before that, Brandish recorded every incredible detail of the previous night, Gimmish, the murder of the wrong person, the discovery, and especially this massive being with high intelligence that he guessed was the real target. He knew Gimmish had done something that the fugitive quark did not regret, except that he hadn't accomplish his mission, and his problem was still alive.

After Brandish cleared the atmosphere, he tried to find traces of matter from Gimmish's craft's waste in space around the planet. When he didn't, he traveled via the portal to the other dimension. He figured Gimmish was trying to lose himself and never be found again or come up with another plan for when the coast cleared. Either way, Brandish knew he had failed to capture the fugitive quark.

Early Morning 5/3/2023
Jim's House near St. Ignatius, Montana
Sol Planet Three
Milky Way Dimension

Michael peered out of the woods, searching for the right time to contact Jim. This was the fifth night in a row he sat at the tree line watching Jim's lamp turn on and off through the night. Thirty minutes later, he heard the door open, and Jim walked onto the deck, almost tripping on something, and sat in his Adirondack chair. Michael could tell Jim's anxiety level and sleepless nights dealing with the authorities and all the unanswered questions were sapping his ability to function. This night Michael exited the tree line, sauntered across the clear space, came up the stairs, and laid totally submissive in front of Jim.

All Jim could say was, "Hello, Michael. I thought you might have gone for good." Michael burst into tears again, putting his large face on the deck and covering it with his massive front arms that bulged with muscles so large that you could see their definition even with his fur. He was now the mightiest bear ever seen, with the worst broken heart on the planet.

After he collected himself, he told Jim in a melancholy voice, "I have been in the cave where we saw the poachers shoot the pregnant bear. I stayed there, only leaving to hunt and to come here. But I knew all the obligations that I had at the Wilson Center and came to my senses. I needed to talk to you about what we need to do now since I cannot be discovered like this. You know from Anne's copy of our will that I entrusted you with shepherding the Wilson Center if I was unable."

"Yes, I got that, but what the hell do I know about genomics? I do not know a tenth of what the board of directors is talking about. I never took Latin or medical terminology in school. All I know about is being a park ranger and living on the Reservation."

"But you know about the regional wildlife, their habitats, and the people who have lived here for thousands of years."

"How does that relate to running a board of directors?"

"You hire someone who can help you, like Dr. Robin Grandy."

"I guess you know me well because I spoke to her earlier today. I offered her one million dollars to come out here and help me. I told her that you were kidnapped by the same person that murdered Anne. I didn't want to say aliens because the government wants to keep the evidence under wraps."

Michael sighed then said, "Wonderful. I don't know what I would have said, but that can explain why nothing should be said in the obituaries."

"Yes, you are right."

"I will be nocturnal until further notice and will be using the basement gym for meetings when the need arises. The door is equipped with an optical scanner lock that only has Anne's and my eyes coded to unlock the door. I checked it last night. I will need to exercise in that room until I can find a way to arrange something else to continue my strength training."

"Don't you think our focus should be on the Wilson Center's future and not on exercise right now?"

"Both. We can meet, then I can exercise. We also can arrange times at the cave we found. I do not think that I have peaked in muscle development yet. I moved boulders up in the park, I think, greater in weight than I did in the gym. I need to measure the gains so I can record the progress."

"I believe you are beginning to enjoy your superhuman self and will be happy to be with you when you are pushing your limits. But this is going to take a lot of work on my part away from my day job."

"I know, but it's all I can do to someday find Anne's killer and rip him to pieces with these claws. I'm going to the gym to work out the anger. No matter who or what murdered Anne, I want to have enough strength to take on an army of them."

"I'm going back inside. See ya." Jim went to bed and fell asleep at three o'clock in the morning.

After his intense two-hour workout, Michael wrote a note and placed it in an envelope on Jim's back deck with the Wilson Center return address and his name without an address. He wrote that his suspicions were correct. His strength continued to accelerate with the extra workouts, and he mused about the capability of bears to do this if heavily trained. He finished with a request for Jim to meet him at the cave at noon today to hear an idea.

Michael knew Jim had to be at the airport at 6:45 in the evening to pick up Robin. *I bet Jim is stressed over the time issue. When he comes to the cave, he will be pushing it to pick up Robin at the airport on time. I know he wants to be presentable to the lady. Here he comes now. But he ain't going to like what I have to say either.*

Jim was huffing and puffing with a scowl on his face. "Make it quick. I don't have much time before I need to pick up Dr. Grandy."

Michael said, "They will be back. I saw a craft flying near the house when I ran into the woods to hide. It was a larger ship with different markings, but it moved the same way. I know they will come for me. I want to let you know I emailed all the documents signed on VeriSign that give you authority over all personnel decisions. I trust you and you alone to fulfill my wishes. If I am picked up by these folks, the fabrication we used will become fact. I do not know, even with my strength, if I will be able to withstand the technology they use, so I will let you see me send everything to you from this laptop.

I charged it up while at the basement gym. I will keep eating buffalo meat as long as I do not get caught, and with that I am now getting so massive that I need more advanced equipment. My hands are now a foot and a half long and can reach around a two-liter soda bottle. I wanted to let you know the fight is coming. I will do everything I can to make them pay for Anne's murder. I need you to be careful and take care of Robin. I will let you know the time for Robin to learn the truth, but not today. I gave you a passcode to have so you can record your eyes in the retinal locks for the basement. The code only works once for security reasons and is to be used only in emergencies. Only you and Robin can go there, and she cannot go without you."

Jim said, "I have to pick her up at the airport soon. I've gotta rush. Okay?"

"But not before I tell you what I've heard. I need you to look for triangular objects in the sky. They move erratically as if without propulsion. But they are fast and look like the same type of vehicle that I saw flying after Anne was murdered. If these are the same folks, they also have deadly weapons. They are probably looking for me. So for now, we will meet in the area near the cave where we saw the pregnant bear. Okay? Time to go get Robin."

Without another word, he grabbed Jim and set him on his own back. He twirled a leather belt-like strap around his neck so that the ends would work like reins. He gave them to Jim and said, "Hold on tight. I know you know how to ride horses. Grab the straps, and let's go."

Less than an hour later at the bottom of the mountain, Michael set Jim down and frowned at him, admonishing him, and saying, "Look, you knew I could do this, so get used to it. You need to clean up for the lady and don't be late. I need to go find something to eat. By the way, I am starting to really like fresh raw buffalo."

Then he headed back to the edge of the woods. He turned to see Jim's dumbfounded look. The urge came over Michael to run back into the woods on all fours. He stopped at the tree line and turned around. Then in a matter-of-fact tone of voice, the animal named Michael said, "You are going to be late for Dr. Grandy."

A startled Jim collected himself and went into the house to clean up.

7/14/2023
Tol HQ Compound
Areanosten Planet Five
Quark Dimension

Brandish returned as fast as he could to Areanosten Planet Five to inform Tol of the knowledge breach. He crossed the portal, casting his craft to fit into the slip that looked like a small black hole. Up close to the entrance, Brandish saw the light fade as the entrance connected to the other end and began to light up again, making it difficult to see even with a telescope that a portal was there. Once he exited on the other side, he put his craft on top speed to get to the sector.

It took him a couple of weeks, in third-planet time, to get back to the border of the fiefdom and feel safe again. Even though he was happy to be home, his face showed worry as he entered the headquarters door.

Brandish told the guard, "Tell Master Tol I've returned and want to tell him of my findings." The guard spoke into his microphone, and seconds later, the gate opened to let Brandish in. He walked straight to Tol's office, where he found the door was already opened. He entered to see Tol and Sargen at the desk, seriously thinking about what to do next.

Tol said, "Brandish, come in. What did you find in the other dimension? Was there any contact with that moron Gimmish?"

Brandish answered, "Yes, sir, but more than we bargained for. Gimmish exposed his presence to the third-planet beings and murdered the wrong one."

Sargen said, "Can't say I haven't done that before; kind of fun."

Tol banged his ring on the desk. "Go on, what happened?"

Brandish told them his experience at the third planet involving Michael, Anne, Jim, and the authorities. They wanted to hear more about the creature, Michael, and how inept Gimmish was in his assassination attempt. The three of them created a plan to keep the exposure damage at a minimum. The incident had raised questions the beings on the third planet could not ignore.

Sargen said, "Let's talk to Heimerlich since he chose that cretin to be on his team. What was he thinking, and why was he so insistent on keeping this guy?"

They sent a message to Heimerlich asking for communication. Their communication links had improved since the Game began. After the normalization of relations and the beginning of the Grand Truce, the communication devices were upgraded and connected to one other, so they could reach each other at light speed if any emergency or misunderstanding should occur.

The links did have a time delay. Tol spoke into his device, saying, "This is Warlord Tol. I am here with Warlord Sargen calling on an urgent matter. Your gamer Gimmish exposed our existence to Sol's third planet and murdered one of its beings with our technology. He also was discovered taking off from the third planet and left evidence, giving the planet's inhabitants clues about our existence. He was seen taking his blaster out as the being opened the door and shot it. Then a giant and intelligent creature was drawn to follow him to where he parked his craft. His work also drew the attention of investigating beings combing the area for clues, a total mess."

Sargen added, "Commander Brandish saw the entire episode in person. He obtained proof of Gimmish's incompetence and the trail of craft debris. Do you have any idea where this cretin went? And why did you choose him for your gamer team in the first place?" The message was sent, and the three took a break waiting for the response.

After a delay, Heimerlich answered, "Gimmish saved my life one time. I use Moonies as banquet servers. There was an assassin from another warlord who tried to kill me by lacing my food with poison. Gimmish saw the poison poured onto the food by the assassin before he served us all. The assassin told Gimmish if he said one word about anything, he would be next to die. Gimmish was to serve the head table where my staff and I were seated. He came out with the food and intentionally stumbled, dropping every plate on his tray, spreading the food all over the floor, and making such a scene that the assassin tried to escape without notice. Gimmish gave me a note about the assassin, so I could shut the gates and have him executed before he got away. I sent the assassin's head back to his master, Buentos, who of course denied knowledge of anything.

"I had to find him a better place since he had saved the lives of my staff and me, so I gave him a position as a gamer as a reward when the Game started. The other three gamers did not agree but said they would keep him from making too large a blunder. It turns out we were all wrong. What do we do now?" The communication asked for a reply.

Brandish started the recording, saying, "It seemed the large animal creature is what Gimmish was after when he made the big mistake. I know this because another being that arrived at the scene before the authorities seemed to know both of them very well, probably an aide. After listening to the quark-like being, I knew the deceased meant a lot to this monstrous being since it exhibited such a crestfallen, visceral response. When the authorities showed, it was apparent the large creature did not want to be discovered. It ran into the thick woods behind the house, leaving the person to deal with the number of others that came in marked vehicles with flashing blue lights, loud sirens, and accessories that also look like weapons.

"They asked questions and became very unnerved when they saw Gimmish's landing area and the toppled trees. I only witnessed these things because if I moved from my position, I would have been discovered. So in my opinion, the key to this entire problem is with the large creature. Only by contacting it can we understand why Gimmish was so interested in eliminating it."

Tol answered, "He needed to eliminate it for many reasons. The first was so he could use another essence in the Game. And, as you may have seen, the creature's murdered companion was very pleasing to see. I told him he needed to eliminate all traces of contact with the third planet. I agree we have to capture the creature and bring it to this dimension to keep what we did unknown to the rest of the third planet."

A surprised Sargen said, "That is a tall order—to capture a large creature like this without being discovered. How do you propose to accomplish this without an essence to track it down?"

Brandish answered, "The area in question is very rugged terrain without many beings in the area. We can land in a remote location and search for this creature. It may take time, but it is our only way to solve the problem. Once we capture the evidence of our contact, we stay away long enough that the memories of our contact fade away. Then after we come back here, notify the entire dimension that the third planet is off limits."

Sargen said, "We need to be wary of their advancing technology. We must decide how far along they are in preparing for the future. If too close, we may need to destroy them."

They sent their conversation and ended the communication with Heimerlich. The message was sent with no need to reply. They sat back in their chairs.

Tol said, "We cannot destroy the third planet."

Sargen asked, "Why not? We have destroyed other planets. What is the big deal with this one?"

"Because I gave my solemn word not to destroy it."

"You gave your solemn oath to who?"

Tol told Sargen and Brandish the story of Kollindarrot and Enoch. After he finished, Sargen said, "Well, I didn't swear to Enoch. Let me do it."

"Sargen, you swore to me to help save this dimension. The third planet may have our answer to this and other problems."

Brandish added, "They have research facilities like yours, Master Tol."

Sargen asked, "We will take that up later. What do we do about the idiot Gimmish? He is the root of all these problems. How do we find him, so he won't try something stupid and go back there and contact someone else for another essence to use for his own purposes? If he has learned how to use them in the Game and still possesses the equipment to capture more, he can learn to use them for other purposes. His naivety may get dangerous if he is nurtured the wrong way."

A grim realization filled the room where the three sat in silence for a minute or two, letting it soak in, which gave all a sense of urgency to fix the problem.

Tol said, "Does anyone have any ideas?"

Sargen said, "I was seeing if you had been thinking about the details of bringing such a specimen back to this dimension. First, we must guard that planet against Gimmish trying to return to the scene of his crime. I propose that we send four fully weaponized fighters to guard against any return and have Brandish show the team what direction Gimmish went in to escape to pay particular attention that way. Then, Brandish must go with a team in his craft to the third planet and land where there are no intelligent beings such as you witnessed and hide the craft. However, if this creature is as intelligent as you say, there is a good chance it will find you first, so you must keep on your guard, or you may not come back."

Before Brandish left, Tol said to Sargen, "I heard Alchemy may be planning something. If Gimmish comes back to our dimension, I am afraid Alchemy may give him safe harbor to learn about this planet."

7/14/2023
Alchemy HQ
Feuerstat Planet Seven
Quark Dimension

Tol's words were prophetic. Alchemy had already contacted Gimmish. Even from the farthest reaches of space, the encrypted message reached Gimmish when he came through the portal to meet his warlord Heimerlich. Instead, he took a path to Alchemy's sector to see what the deal would be. Through the chatter of other communication, he had learned that Heimerlich was furious with him and wanted to put him to death.

Gimmish kept his essences on board his ship for safekeeping and from other gamers. He had his four essences: the creature that spit acid, the numbers oracle or seer, a chameleon, and finally a shell-like specimen that never moved but was impenetrable, which meant that his essence play made him the butt of jokes in the Game. All anyone could do was to hide behind it. In the back of his mind, he thought, *They will pay for calling me a moron. I have not had any good luck until the third-planet being. No one else had the foresight to create and seek out the quality of my player. I had the best bar none. I know I will have my chance to be on top of more than just the Game.*

My problem now is I gave that essence to myself. Now I can't get rid of these headaches and nightmares unless I go back to destroy the host. The stronger it gets, the worse my headaches get. It must be destroyed!

He signaled his presence to the perimeter guards for onboard inspection of intent. The outer guards were not polite individuals, which matched Alchemy's personality. They came on board without asking permission, knocking over items, and pushing buttons they knew nothing about. Gimmish began to think this might not have been such a clever idea after all. A minute later, a message came hailing Gimmish to bring up his video feed.

Alchemy himself said, "Greetings, Mr. Gimmish. I hope my guards have not been too much of a bother with their inspections.

We cannot be too careful in these perilous times." The guards immediately stopped and stood at attention since Alchemy was ruthless to those who disobeyed his slightest wish. "I hear we have a mutual interest in surviving this expansion of space that led to the disastrous folly known as the Game. We were all duped by Tol and Sargen to give up protecting our fiefdoms with this silly plan. Look at what happened when you moved outside the rules trying to be creative; you received pain and ridicule. I have another idea that I would like to propose, and I need your experience to teach me. We will discuss it further when you get here, so, to my clumsy guards behind you, please escort Mr. Gimmish to my headquarters directly. We have much to talk about."

Gimmish's simplemindedness was all Alchemy needed to garner the information that would cause chaos to return not only to their dimension but to the third planet as well. When Gimmish landed in the hangar, he received a red-carpet treatment with the conniving warlord leading the way. "Mr. Gimmish, it is a pleasure to meet you in person. Even though I believed the Game was folly, I admired your recovery off the bottom of the standings. Let me show you to your quarters so you can get some rest before we go to work on a project I was pondering."

"That sounds great. I haven't been treated this well in a long time; thank you." Alchemy gave a satisfied smile.

The next day, Gimmish was escorted to Alchemy's office near the hangar. It was a large room with posters and star maps all over the walls. He had a great window that looked out into the stars toward Sargen's sector. The stars did not twinkle as they did on the third planet, since they were closer and did not reflect light; they all shone bright and constant.

Gimmish asked, "How can I help you?"

Alchemy answered, "Have a seat. We have much to talk about."

He asked about his experience on the third planet.

"As you know, as a gamer, my most important job is to obtain talent, essences for the Game. We had a losing streak going since I used an essence that was not the best, the impregnable rock. It was the only thing I found before the Game began since we needed four essences per team. I was having trouble finding essences worthy of play, so I only had three when the Game started.

"After staying on the bottom so long, I knew I had to do more for the team, and that was why I searched and found the third planet and observed and saw why we were told it was such a dangerous place to harvest. I noticed that the entire ecosystem was made of binary relationships of creatures coming in all shapes and sizes. The most interesting one was an intelligent life-form called humans. They came in multiple colors and statuses while living vastly different lives all over the planet.

"I was interested in a hyperintelligent being who, from his learning, became an essence with great value and was easier to obtain since it loved to be outdoors in isolation. I followed its progress and finally captured its essence, but was then discovered by Tol, that fool. He told me I had to find a way to destroy it without a trace so as to not make other humans curious of our existence."

"What did you try?"

"One of my other gamers was told by Tol to let me have a cell mutating virus so that it would no longer be able to move and then die. But it was taking too long, and I had to get rid of it sooner. So I had to go back and search the third planet to find and destroy the source of the essence and replace it with anything but a third-planet being. I found it in an isolated area and went to its door, but instead, a companion tried to open the door, and I blasted the wrong being, instantly killing it. I knew I had one shot at doing this because I did not want to be captured. But as I was taking off, I noticed it running after me. It changed into a huge monster about three or four times the original's size. It was the essence, but it had changed into this huge creature! I did not stay to see anything else."

"Wow, that is some story. But here is my question for you. Is this how the third-planet beings multiply to continue as entities?"

"Yes."

Alchemy added, "The story goes that many years ago, another warlord made a mistake and became so attracted to one side of these beings that he lost his mind to lust and left his fiefdom open to attack. The warlord who took advantage of the wayward warlord happened to be none other than Tol. He wiped out the warlord's whole sector and took it for himself."

"Wow!" Gimmish exclaimed. "That's why he was so hesitant when I told him about my third-planet essence."

Alchemy continued, "He also did not tell you that the warlord and the quarks he defeated were mating with these beings for a while, causing quark traits to be injected into their world. The fact is these third-planet beings are part quark! Their invasion of the planet has caused havoc to this day. They did not have quarks to generate life. We did until the cosmos expanded so that the quark particles could not collide as often. They don't need that. They have each other and do something called reproduction."

Gimmish responded, "Thus Tol's reasoning for the Game: quarks dying and not being replaced! So what should we do?"

Alchemy answered, "So now, my friend, what do you think about us going back and picking up some of those, I believe they are called women, from the third planet to give us another way to save ourselves? According to the experience, a much more private and fun way to increase our population.

"I want you to show me the way to this third planet without other warlords knowing. I want to secretly see this exotic world. Instead of us going over there and mating, we can bring some of them back here to increase our population," Alchemy replied.

Gimmish asked, "Would that not disrupt the balance of the dimension and expose us? If others find out about this, we may have a bigger problem with them wiping us out."

Alchemy leaned over the table, smiling. "Let me explain something to you in terms you can understand. I don't need to ransack your workshop anymore. You work for me now, and you will do what I ask, whether you like it or not."

Gimmish realized he had no choice. He also knew he was wanted by every other warlord in this dimension, so death was sure if he were to escape. He went back to his quarters, which had been redecorated with much more spartan furnishings. He walked in and saw another soldier who said, "I'm your new roommate; welcome." He shrugged, entered the room, and shook his hand, happy that at least he hadn't been thrown into a prison cell.

7/30/2023
Tol HQ Compound
Areanosten Planet Five
Quark Dimension

Brandish was worried because Gimmish had gone far in the other dimension; still, that did not guarantee he could not find a portal back to this one. The fugitive had made unauthorized trips to the third planet for years, learning what that world was like. He saw the beauty of the person shot by Gimmish and the power of the creature that came out to look for the other's murderer. He also saw all the other people looking around for clues to what had happened and felt lucky he could escape undetected.

He suddenly stopped, ran back to Tol's office, and burst through the doors saying, "Gimmish will return to the third planet for something bad. He did not kill the intended creature, and he found someone to sponsor him."

Tol and Sargen looked at each other and simultaneously yelled, "Alchemy!"

"Yes, I realized he was going in the direction of the portal in the other galaxy where he came from when I started following him. I think they have a plan to disrupt the entire planet the way that warlord did thousands of years ago on the third planet."

Tol said in horror, "He is going to mate with beings on the third planet to increase his fiefdom's population. This can open us to warfare and disease like the one we gave the essence holder during the Game to eliminate Gimmish's mistake."

Sargen said, "We have no damn time to relive past mistakes and do the what-if game. We have a problem to solve, and we're wasting time."

They all ran out of the room and down to the flight deck. Tol was running with a handheld intercom, telling the flight crew to prepare all ships for takeoff. Sargen was barking flight orders with his communicator, yelling for six ships back home to join them near the closest portal to this dimension.

By the time they realized the plan, Alchemy, Gimmish, and two of the three new allies, Buentos and Descrim, had gone through the portal into the other dimension, searching the third planet for Michael. Contronto, the intellect, stayed back to devise methods of managing the captives. Descrim's mission was to cover the flank from the closest solar system where Gimmish could escape. Buentos stayed close to serve as a backup if Contronto or Descrim failed in their mission.

Alchemy sent ships to remote locations to abduct females and kill their mates so that communication of the alien arrival would be as inconspicuous as possible. Their plan was to find about forty women to take back through the portal to their fiefdoms, ten for each warlord to experiment with. Alchemy's mission with Gimmish's help was to find and capture Michael.

THE CAPTURE

8/30/2023
Deep Wilderness near Ninepipe National Wildlife Refuge
North of Missoula, Montana
Sol Planet Three
Milky Way Dimension

Michael captured and killed an elk for food so all the bears could eat. The group came to like Michael since he was more successful in finding and sharing food, which is uncommon for male bears. He knew this was the day that Robin would find out the truth of his status. He had practiced a number of scenarios that could possibly work, but nothing was airtight.

He then noticed a strange sound rustling through the trees. Michael stood upright, smelling something in the breeze. He looked skyward to see a triangular flying object slowing over the ridge. *They're back. Mingle with the others.* He walked over to the other bears blithely gnawing on the elk's remains.

A minute later, one female bear with cubs became aware of the foreign scents and moved near her two cubs. Michael growled to get the attention of the others. He moved over to be among them.

Not long after, he noticed the smells becoming stronger. Then a group of strange-looking humanlike creatures appeared from the brush on the other side of the clearing, six in total. Michael moved back toward the woods. Then he realized, *That is the one that killed Anne!*

He froze, studying their movements, now knowing they were looking for him. He thought, *How did they find me? What do they want?*

Michael moved into the trees but still did not go far. He saw the female stay near the elk carcass with her cubs close by. The creature Michael recognized waved off the two that were about to shoot the mother bear. Michael then noticed the visitor was looking at a handheld vacuum-cleaner-size device determining the direction.

He saw the humanoid wave and make sounds in a strange language at the two others who were moving towards the female bear and pointed right at Michael. At that, he turned and ran on all fours deeper into the woods. He heard shots yet still ran trying to escape his pursuers. *My gun is back in the cave. I have got to go get it to defend myself.*

Minutes later, he heard the same sound from the sky. *How can they track me? What is going on?* A flash of light and an explosion cracked a rock ten feet in front of him. *Holy crap!* He turned left. Another bolt hit a tree in front of him, setting it on fire. *What did I do to deserve this?* He turned left only to miss another bolt of light. Then left, right, then left again and stopped behind a boulder.

He smelled a strange scent approaching from his right side. *I can't get to the cave unless I can avoid those strangers.* Michael went around the rock to see if he could do an end-run. Their scent kept following him. He thought, *Who are these guys?* He took a long way around the path, swerving over and under every obstacle possible. He knew the cave was not far now. He sprinted the last few meters until he ran into a clearing to see four humanoid creatures aiming what looked like weapons directly at him. The object in the air sent another flash behind him at the wood's edge. He was trapped.

The creature holding the device nodded its head, and another shot a small device that bound Michael's arms and legs and forced him to sit. Michael then realized where he was. *My second experience here with poachers, but now I am the catch.* He stayed still as all six visitors approached him with wonder. He knew, seeing their technology, that they did not want to kill him, or they would have done it sooner.

He then remembered that Jim was going to bring Robin here to see the changed Michael in person. *I let my instinct tell them to come here near the cave, big mistake.*

Then the one who looked like the leader turned on a small device about five centimeters long and placed it on Michael's forearm. "You can now understand what we say."

The shocked captive remained quiet. *These folks ain't from Earth.*

The one holding the handheld device said, "Master Alchemy, the essence matches the electromagnetic pulses. It's the one we came for." He said to Michael, "It was hard as cydomorpholous crystals to find you. We were looking for humans, not creatures like you." Michael began to struggle.

Alchemy said, "Not so fast, big one. Looks like we have you down where you cannot move. The rings use your energy to fuel their hold on your limbs. Now I am going to show you something. Good work with this one, Gimmish."

The rings lifted Michael to hover about ten centimeters off the ground and started moving toward the ship. Michael couldn't believe how these simple rings around his wrists and ankles held him so tightly. The light rings moved together, holding Michael, wrists and ankles touching with his back to the ground, like an animal roasting over a campfire.

At that moment, Jim came around the corner with Robin in the pickup truck and saw what was happening. Jim tried to put the truck in reverse, but the aliens saw them and incapacitated it, shooting out the tires. Michael heard Robin scream in horror at the entire scene. She yelled, "Where's Michael, and what are those things with those weapons? Let's get out of here!"

Jim yelled, "We can't now! They shot out the tires! It won't move!" Both sat in stunned shock, thinking this was their last moment.

Gimmish aimed his blaster at them, about to shoot them, then Alchemy said, "Stop. Let's take them with us. We have some more room. Check with the other ships to see if they captured enough of the women for the experiments; then we will leave quickly. Tell them to go back through the portal in the next solar system as fast as possible if they have forty. We can't be caught here and take too much time possibly fighting third-planet beings. We can always come back for more." The call was made. Two minutes later, Gimmish told Alchemy, "The other ships departed with thirty-nine women. We have this one more woman and these two others."

Robin and Jim were put in the rings and carried to the ship with Michael. All were placed in a hold in the back against the wall, unable to move. Jim told Michael, "I brought Robin to see you at the cave. I also wanted to let you also know that strange abductions of women were being reported all over the world where strange aircraft were sighted."

Robin yelled, "You are Michael? What in God's name happened?"

"The compound that saved my life went too far. I'll explain if we ever get out of this mess."

Michael heard Gimmish speaking in the other room. "Oh, Warlord Alchemy saw a nice-looking creature running this morning for fun. It looks like the other being brought her with him. I believe we got what we came for."

Michael remarked to Robin and Jim, "I do not know where we are going, but it's not good. Earth does not have a chance against a technology that disabled me so easily. These are some strong rings, and all we can do is see what's in store for us and pray for some way to escape."

Then Gimmish entered the room all smiles. "So we meet again. You have changed from the first time I saw you. You almost got me killed when I lost control of you. You did something to create a new you." A blood-curdling laugh made the three hostages wince with the painful knowledge that things were not going to turn out well. Gimmish continued, "I was the one who copied your specific traits to use for the disaster that cause the Game. It was a way to take our minds off not having the joy of fighting each other. One thing about us, we do not die unless we are killed or have an accident, so we can get pretty bored over time because we run out of things to do. So I found you in the stadium on your planet, hitting others in your game, and later sold you that lotto ticket."

Michael said, "I don't know or give a damn what the hell you're talking about."

Robin interrupted, "You were that homeless guy that sold Michael the ticket!"

Gimmish said, "Correct! But since the Game is over and I won't be needing them any longer, I need to find a host for the essences I have left and see if they are worth anything. Now open your eyes."

Michael yelled, "No, no, no!"

Gimmish pushed a button which froze Michael still and said, "Yes, yes, yes." And shot two of the essences into his eyes while holding them open. First was the acid shooting essence in the right eye and the rock creature in the left. Then he said to Jim, "Now for you, a chameleon in the left and a numbers oracle in the right."

Michael asked, "What did you do with my, my whatever?"

Gimmish answered, "Oh, that is part of the reason I gave you these. I gave yours to me, but it did nothing but give me headaches and nightmares, so I'm going to waste these things on you two so they can torture you. Gave you a good scare, didn't I? It was fun to see you squirm in fear. Such satisfaction for all the stress you've caused me." He let out another evil laugh.

Michael said, "That's how I got those winning numbers. You set me up with this plan."

"Yes, I did, and I also gave you that disease that almost killed you. But you were a tricky one. I didn't expect you to find a cure. Bravo!"

Michael spat and hit Gimmish in the face. The alien wiped the saliva away with the closest towel. He looked at all three and slapped Robin in the face as hard as he could.

The surprised Michael said, "I spat in your face. She didn't!"

Gimmish shrugged and replied, "I didn't know whether if I hit you, it would hurt you enough. I thought that hitting her would hurt you worse, knowing how fond the two types of being are of each other."

Michael growled at Gimmish, knowing he was right. He could see Robin's mouth quiver, the red slap mark and a stream of blood on her face, and tears of pain rolling down her cheeks.

Gimmish continued, "Another stunt like that, and she will get it worse." He slapped her again. She screamed and openly cried. "That was fun. It will be a shame to take you back to the headquarters and have experiments conducted on you and your friends. But that's the way it is. Now I am taking you three to the holding area where we keep you from bothering Alchemy, although he did say this third one was really nice to look at."

The three earthlings floated in the rings to the lower part of the vessel to a secure room that would hold all three. Robin said, "Michael, Jim, what is going on here? I have never been so scared in my life."

Jim said, "Robin, meet Anne's murderer."

Arrogant Gimmish smiled and left the hold to return to the flight deck, laughing until his voice faded in the background noise. They sat straddled to the seats, only able to turn their heads to look at each other. Jim felt different but did not think anything of it, so he said to Michael, "Let's get some shut-eye. I'm feeling kind of weird and tired." He agreed, and they both fell asleep.

Gimmish entered the bridge and sat down next to Alchemy, who asked, "How are our passengers doing in the hold? I did not know if those rings would be able to hold the big one, but they did."

Gimmish said, "Yes, he looks like he can do real damage if released. I don't want to be there if he does get loose."

Alchemy brushed aside Gimmish's concern and said, "That's not an option. He will have to stay in the holding cell at headquarters while we find out what the other warlords know of our plans. Among all our craft, we have forty of those attractive beings and the other two, the big one and the other, who is similar to us. I was told by the other ships that the best places to find these offspring bearers were in sparsely populated cold climates near the upper pole or in the center of the largest land area on the other side of the planet from where we were."

Gimmish added, "We did find a good one in the same place where the essence was found."

"Yes, a good variety. I believe the other warlords are going to be happy with the choices. From what I have seen, they seem to be attractive beings, conjuring up physical excitement. Good job. I may let you live a little longer."

"Yes, they did. I cannot wait to take an up-close and personal view of these beings. It may be quite pleasurable."

Alchemy cut his eyes to Gimmish and snarked, "Do you think any of this is for you? You are lucky I let you live."

An annoyed expression came to Gimmish's face. He looked around and then exited the bridge.

9/7/2023
Deep Wilderness near Ninepipe National Wildlife Refuge
North of Missoula, Montana
Sol Planet Three
Milky Way Dimension

Brandish landed in the area where he noticed disturbed vegetation and landing marks at a higher elevation near where he witnessed the murder. When he got out of his craft, he saw an old blast mark across the field where the bones of a freshly eaten elk were dried and dispersed. He said to his copilot, "I'm too late. They were here and did whatever they needed to do. I need to cloak the ship and listen to communication on every frequency."

Brandish monitored local communications and soon learned of the disappearance under mysterious circumstances of several third-planet beings called "women." The broadcasters didn't know the cause, but Brandish felt certain Gimmish was behind it. He listened to other broadcasts trying to obtain more details. However, all the evidence pointed to an alien invasion. He had to dial different settings on the translator when searching news on other parts of the planet.

Then on the radio frequency of a signal close by, a voice said, "Locally in the news, there are now three missing persons since the strange occurrences happened three months ago. Not only Dr. Michael Townsend who disappeared three months ago but now the whereabouts of Park Ranger Jim Longfield and the new head of research at the Wilson Center, Dr. Robin Grandy, are unknown. The authorities are searching the area for clues since they all have a stake in the Center. Other strange things have happened in other parts of the world. Remote regions worldwide, in Central Asia, Scandinavia, and Siberia, report that many couples' houses have been ransacked, with the men murdered and the woman disappearing."

Brandish said, *This sounds like more than Gimmish. He must have found another warlord to help him. I bet Alchemy is behind all of this.*

Brandish turned off the radio scanner and took off to head back and tell Tol and Sargen the bad news. He slipped into the portal and headed back to the sector. A surveillance drone sent by Descrim saw him go by. Alchemy's plan was complete.

9/30/2023
Alchemy HQ
Feuerstat Planet Seven
Quark Dimension

Gimmish entered the holding room and said to them, "Buentos, Contronto, and Descrim have arrived here, Alchemy's headquarters to inspect the women, which includes you." He pointed his finger at Robin. All of the women were crying and in shock at what had befallen them. Michael and Jim, in near shock, were taken from the ship by armed guards, holding the ring controller, going down the hall. The four warlords watched the two pass by as they were taken to the holding chamber. They were admiring Michael's size compared to Jim's and asked him who he was.

Michael answered, "I am the Knight Bear."

Jim snapped his head around and asked, "Where did that come from?

After seeing Jim's expression, Michael told him, "I made it up on the fly. I had to think of something to pass the time coming here. I thought I needed a goofy superhero name."

The warlords were amused that this arrogant thing had given itself such a title. Descrim shook his head.

Alchemy told Michael, "Mr. Knight Bear, your existence will soon be over. I hope you understand why I am going to eliminate you."

Michael replied, "Is it because I'm so good-looking?"

"Your insolence only makes me want to kill you more now, but I don't have time right now, and I want to experiment on you. You seem to be the only being from the third planet with enough power and knowledge to hinder my conquest of your dimension. I want to find out what you are made of.

"I thought Sargen and Tol were smarter than they turned out to be since they don't know anything about what I am going to do. They think I am coming for your world. Wrong! I want to see if

I can use your childbearing beings to create more warriors for our dwindling numbers."

"It didn't take a rocket scientist to figure that out when you only kidnapped women."

Alchemy yelled, "Gimmish, take them to the holding cell and pin them to the wall. I have better things to do than being insulted by this thing."

Gimmish took them down to a room with no windows and a heavy steel door that took two soldiers to open. The device that controlled the rings was placed on a desk on the opposite side of the room and hooked to a power source so it would maintain the ring's firm grip on their limbs. Then to keep them from squirming, the soldiers used more light bands around their waists. One device controlled each captive.

Michael yelled at Gimmish, "Looks like you're Alchemy's dog now." Michael smiled since he was getting under his skin, and Robin was not around to take the abuse.

Gimmish then took a strap and struck Jim across the back six times. Then he grabbed Jim's chin with his left hand like a tee and punched him right below his cheek bone twice. Michael watched Jim's head snap back with the blow.

When Gimmish and the soldiers left, Michael spat at the door in disgust. A puff of white vapor appeared from the metal where the saliva landed. Michael noticed the reaction and spat again. The metal began corroding. They looked at each other stunned. Jim was still reeling and groggily said, "Where did that come from? I knew bears had bad breath, but that is amazing."

Michael's eyes opened wide, and he said, "I believe ole Gimmish boy gave us a ticket out of here with those things he called essences. He said that he gave me an acid spitter, and I believe if I can get a good shot on that holding device, we can free ourselves if we can destroy them. Then I can tell if those folks are still around with this bear nose. Let's wait a bit, then try to free ourselves and find some way to escape."

10/1/2023
Alchemy HQ Auditorium
Feuerstat Planet Seven
Quark Dimension

A guard came into the room to feed the two prisoners. He took a whiff of the air and shrugged it off. He set the food on the floor thirty centimeters from their feet, then went to the rings and programmed something quickly into the side keyboard. The quark turned around to both of them and said, "Master Alchemy thought you both should stay alive until we get back. For fifteen minutes, the ring controller program will allow you to reach and pick up your food. The plates are held on the floor by magnets. If you pick the plate off the floor, the program stops, and you are pinned back on the wall. After fifteen minutes, the rings will snap back, pinning you to the wall again anyway. If either of you move quickly or try to move out of range of the device, the program will end, and you will be pinned before the fifteen minutes is up. Don't do anything rash. You are to be fed every ten hours to keep you alive." After giving the two prisoners the warning, he walked out of the room. Michael spat as he closed the door. Another plume of white corrosive vapor appeared where he hit.

Michael said, "I guess this is not the first time they've had prisoners."

Jim said, "Let's eat."

Michael added, "And wait for the right time."

Two days later, Michael and Jim woke up to the sound of the loudspeaker, "All quarks except guard garrison report to the flight deck for takeoff." Michael and Jim did not have a translator to understand what was said but knew something was happening.

Michael said, "I think it will be our chance to move soon. If we hear them leave, I will start spitting at the controller and make sure it's not a one-time thing. I do not know how it is connected to the security system or whether an alarm sounds if the rings go down, but we need to turn that thing off to make an escape. I believe this is our only option other than a miracle." On the counter across the room were the two light ring controllers, and behind them was another cabinet of flashing lights for unknown purposes.

"I used to win watermelon seed–spitting contests. With this new body, I think I have enough lung power to hit it from here. Here goes nothing." With the sound of crying women coming through the wall, he spat. The acid fell short but made a mark on the floor. "Daggum, missed. Got to use more oomph." He breathed heavily, collecting more saliva, and tried again, reaching the counter but missing the mark. Then he thought of something. "Maybe the essence of this thing he gave me used his mouth like a spitting cobra. Let's see if I can cause my oral glands to spit a stream." He opened his mouth then touched the tip of his tongue to the roof of his mouth, which pulled tension on the saliva glands underneath the tongue that shot a large stream of the saliva at the counter and hit one of the controllers. "Bingo!"

Smoke came from the controller, but it did not turn off the rings. It took another three hits with the saliva before he made a hole in the device that held Jim and finally made it short-circuit, causing the rings to loosen and fade out.

Michael yelled, "Yessir. How 'bout dat, y'all! Go turn the other one off, so I can get out of these things."

They were both free. Jim punched him in the stomach as a show of triumph and hurt his hand as if it hit a steel wall, "Damn, damn, damn, that hurt! You are hard as a rock now."

His two new essences were now part of him. So Jim had an idea and told Michael to look at the flashing lights on the cabinet. He concentrated on blending into the room like a chameleon. Michael turned around and saw only his clothes until he moved.

Michael said, "That Gimmish dude did us a huge favor. Now, no more play; we have work to do. Knock on the wall with 'shave and a haircut' to see if anyone hears." Jim started, *knock, knock-knock-knock,*

knock. In about ten seconds, someone on the other side of the wall rapped, *knock, knock.*

Michael said, "Yes, it's the women on the other side of the wall. I am going to spit on the lock so we can get out of here and rescue at least ten of the kidnapped folks." They left their room and went to the door of the next cell. He spat on the lock twice, but the lock did not dissolve readily. By now he was having trouble collecting enough moisture for another acid application. Robin came to the small window in the door. Michael said, "I'm trying to get y'all out of here."

Robin pointed to the side through the small opening and said, "Why don't you push that red button?"

Michael gave an embarrassed look, pushed the button, and heard the door unlock. Jim pulled the handle and opened the door.

Michael said, "Let's go. If any alarm sounds, you disappear like you just did and hide the women. Let me draw them away. I remember the flight deck is three stories up to the right after the elevator that took us here. Go up the stairs with the women one flight, then use another stairwell for the rest. We have to get off this floor."

Michael looked into the cell and asked, "Are y'all ready to get out of here?" The women froze silent in fear, not really believing what they saw when Michael looked into the cell. They stepped to the back of the cell, not knowing if they were going to be mauled by the bear. Robin, who just smiled and walked up to Michael, patted him on the snout and said, "Thanks, big guy. Now let's go home." Robin waved to the women to come on. The women hesitantly walked by the enormous monster, staying as far away as they could while they passed him.

In the next cell, another quark banged on the door waving to get attention. Jim said, "Michael, let's let him out. I bet he wants to escape too." He was released and came out speaking. No one could understand anything he said.

Suddenly the alarm sounded when the door to the quark's cell opened. Michael said, "Jim, hide the women across the hall in this utility closet. I will lead the guards away. Also, see if any of these other cells hold anybody." All the women fit into the closet, and Jim stripped off his clothes and used his newfound hiding ability to blend into his surroundings to scout for their escape while Michael led the guards on a chase. The quark prisoner waved for Michael to follow him. They ran down the hall, then turned into the stairwell and ran up a flight. They heard guards yelling and coming their way. They ducked into the entrance to the armory and crashed through the door. They saw one guard who tried to draw his weapon when Michael spit, hitting his hand. The man dropped his firearm and screamed in pain. Michael broke a case, picked up a blaster from the rack, and fired, killing the guard.

The released prisoner picked up the translator device and told Michael. "I'm Drudgen."

"I'm Michael."

"Pleasure."

"Let's go."

They picked up as many blasters and grenades as they could.

Seconds later, they heard the stampeding guards coming down the stairs and off the elevator. Two steps after Michael and Drudgen exited the armory, they understood the guards yelling, "They are going down the hall—after them!"

Michael saw a door, and they both went through, but it was a small room except for an air-handling vent above him. He opened his claws, and in a matter of seconds, ripped a hole large enough for Drudgen and him to jump through. He effortlessly pulled himself through the hole and crawled until there was enough room to run like a bear. Drudgen held up the rear. Michael yelled to him, "Watch my back."

Soldiers came through a utility passage in front of him as he approached. They were sliced with his claws and thrown behind him, just missing Drudgen, leaving a bloody mess that petrified the approaching guards. With Drudgen giving cover, Michael got to a wall, with shots missing him over his head, and ripped the wall down. He looked through the blast hole and saw the armory again and jumped through into the room.

"One damned circle. Where do we go now?" He looked around at all the stored weapons, broke more cases, and took four belts. He found grenades that he threw back through the hole in the wall with explosions that shook the headquarters. "Drudgen, do you know this place?"

Drudgen answered, "Some areas."

They heard what they thought was the entire headquarters guard contingent running toward the armory. Michael hoped Jim and the women had been able to sneak up the stairwell. Michael threw grenades through every hole he saw, making sure there was nothing behind the walls as explosions continued and more of the guard contingent became casualties.

Michael yelled to Drudgen, "Where do we go now?"

Drudgen answered, "This door—it's an auditorium."

They shot through the door and then opened it. A guard's body ready to shoot fell over a makeshift barrier on the other side of the door.

Michael said, "Whoa, he was waiting for us. Let's go." They ran onto a stage, dodging a quick burst of blaster fire before getting to the other side. They fired back and shot four quarks in the aisles coming toward them. They went to the other side, trying to set a post for the next guards they heard.

The hard-surfaced floors gave away approaching footsteps. They waited for sounds and then fired. Three more down.

Drudgen said, "There are supposed to be thirty guards in this garrison."

"How do you know?"

"I was a guard."

"Good, what are they supposed to do now?"

"What they do is seal off this floor then send knockout gas. It should have already been done, but Alchemy changed protocol since he wanted the smaller beings alive."

"Thank God for the women. I think we have neutralized eleven so far that we know. What would you do?"

"Set a diversion behind the stage. This floor is a story below the ground, but the metal bridge over the stage is ground level. Blow a hole up from the stage bridge to the outside. The ladder up is behind us here."

Michael said, "Lucky us. We don't have time to waste."

Four more guards came into the theater and saw their dead companions. They hid towards the back and sent another for reinforcements. Michael's sense of smell alerted him to their presence and he put his finger to his lips, whispering to Drudgen, "Quiet. They are in back getting others for an assault on us."

The quarks didn't dare follow Michael through the small door on the other side of the stage. They would be cut down in the open. They were massing in the seating area where they had cover. Drudgen knew that but then noticed, "Look through the edge of the door where you can see cases. Those are high explosives. I am going to shoot them and cause a chain reaction."

Michael heard the contingent around the wall planning and said, "Ten seconds before they start, shoot." Drudgen shot through the door and hit the explosives. The force blew the wall, crashing on the guards. Michael and Drudgen jumped from their hiding place and attacked the dazed guards digging themselves from under the rubble of the fallen wall.

Michael roared while shooting his blaster in his right hand and clawing and slicing with his left. He saw Drudgen shoot a particular quark more than once with purpose. After they finished, seventeen quarks lay dead.

Drudgen said, "Two more."

"Where?"

Robin said to Jim, "Is that really Michael Townsend? I analyzed the sample I, uh, took and discovered the bear stem cells in the dose."

Jim answered, "Yes, those were the only DNA stems he could get under the radar to use. The good news is that he's alive. The bad news is he's not totally human anymore. He's a hybrid, now more bear in many ways than human."

A stressed Robin said, "For our sake now, I am glad he is what he is."

Jim said, "I am going up to the flight deck to scout for a way out. You stay here and listen for my instructions."

The noise from below kept going for a while, telling Jim that Michael was holding his own. He saw a guard and stayed still. The guard was running toward the cells when Jim appeared from the wall and was able to grab the large quark in a chokehold. Jim did not let go even when the quark smashed him to the wall. Slowly the quark lost consciousness. A tired and banged up Jim climbed up the stairwell, hearing everything getting quieter, then *BOOM*. The building shook and the sound of explosions lasted for about fifteen minutes.

He put his pants back on and went back to the women. "It's time to move. Sounds like the whole place is going to come down!"

They opened one other cell, which released a small old quark. The little quark quickly smiled and shooed Jim away. Jim shrugged and began to guide the women to the flight deck.

Dust and other building material shook off the walls with every explosion in the building. As they were going up the first flight, the outside railing fell off when the side of the stairway cracked. Jim yelled, "Move! Move! Faster! Faster!" The women ran through the door holding their hands clasped over their heads for protection.

Jim was the last to get through the door. He yelled, "We need to find another stairwell to go up to the flight deck. The elevator is unsafe."

All the women began opening doors, looking for stairs. Halfway down the hall, one of the women yelled, "This way!" The eleven ran up two flights to the door of the flight deck. They ran in, and Jim saw a side room, "Stay in here until I say come. I will find us a way out." He saw the lone craft across the room. He looked up to see the open roof then walked next to the wall blending in for cover.

Michael ran up the steps and threw his last grenade behind him to ensure no one could follow. Then he burst through the door looking at the flight deck, tired but alive. He and Drudgen ran onto the flight deck and saw Jim. "Jim, where are the women?"

"Michael! The women are in the room to the left."

"Get them and let's get out of here!"

"No argument from me!" He opened the door.

First out was Robin, who said, "Hey, big guy, which way?"

Michael answered, "Go to the craft!" All ten women ran past Michael on a beeline to the ship's door, all with expressions of relief that there was an escape. The overhead door was still open since the rest of the spaceships were on their mission. The stars above shone with an inviting flicker leading their way to escape to parts that had never been seen before.

Jim said in a panic, "Who's going to fly this thing? The dials are in unintelligible symbols. I honestly have no idea what to do. Does anyone have an idea?"

Suddenly, a lone soldier came through the door not to shoot but ran into the control room.

Robin yelled, "Michael, do something!"

Drudgen said, "I am only a guard, but I can read, and the device will translate."

Michael said, "Is this buggy labeled where you can read the dials?"

He sat in the larger cockpit seat, squeezing in as best he could and pressed a button that Drudgen told him to. It lit up the cockpit. He pushed the button next to it, which did nothing. He saw a lever in the middle that wiggled but did nothing until he hit the switch behind it, making the craft turn on an outside light. He moved a lever on his left that made the ship move quicker. One of the Scandinavian women knew enough English to say, "The roof is closing!"

Michael asked Drudgen, "Where's the start button?"

Drudgen glanced at the console and pressed a button that started an engine sequence.

Michael thought to himself, *Well, Dookie, let's see if you can figure out this bucket of bolts.* He pushed the left lever, which shot a torpedo into the wall across the hangar.

Drudgen said, "Let me read the dial. Use the right lever."

Michael took the right lever all the way up, which made the ship rise up through the remaining space in the roof heading into the sky. Michael, who was now frazzled, moved the stick, making the ship go left, right, forward, and back. About three women came up to figure out the dashboard to control the ship well enough to get somewhere. They asked questions so fast Drudgen couldn't understand the translation from the computer. One woman pushed a button, and a radio signal started. Michael had had enough, "All y'all move back so Drudgen can read the panels!"

Drudgen synced the translator with the comm to understand the conversation on the communicator. They listened to find out that the four warlords had begun a battle with Heimerlich's sector and were executing a successful surprise attack.

Jim said, "The end game is for the four allied warlords to take out the others and reproduce with human women. The plan is insane. What do we do now since we have no idea where we are?"

Robin spoke up, "We are going to need to learn fast or die in space. Everyone look in every drawer for material, maps, or devices that may say something about these stars."

It was like twelve burglars ripping up a house to find loot. The flight deck was a mess, with papers and debris everywhere until someone found a diagram of the cockpit dashboard with directions. They were given to Drudgen to check for relevancy. Michael could control the craft much better after two hours of checking all the switches for their purpose with the recovered flight manual. They listened to the communication in the cosmos and understood that the four warlords were about to defeat Heimerlich before anyone could rescue him.

Then we heard a desperate voice speaking, "Why did you betray me, Gimmish? I gave you every chance …." The communication went dead.

Then Gimmish said over the comm, "Master Alchemy, your next wish is my command."

Alchemy responded, "That was masterful skullduggery. Gimmish, I think I'll keep you around."

Jim looked at everyone, saying, "We've witnessed treachery here as bad as anything that happened to my people. Thirty other women were captured for their reproductive abilities to satisfy these evil warlords' desires and population purposes. What can we do to stop it?"

Robin caught but did not respond to his comparison and thought, *Excellent subject, remember when we get home.* She then said, "We cannot do a darn thing to stop this by ourselves. There must be someone in this universe with some decency. These vile things will come back and invade Earth, and this time take over and stay. Did anyone find a map?"

One of the women who looked in the drawers to the right held up a star map with marked sections and stars. The screen on the dashboard had symbols and stars to represent borders. One of the stars seemed to look like one nearby so they were able to judge where they were using the computer's map coordinates in reference to other borders. They turned toward the closest border and went as fast as they could before being discovered.

Michael exclaimed, "This buggy moves like greased lightning! What kind of propulsion system can make objects move this fast? It's like the stars are blurs and we are moving at incredible speed. This may be fiction on Earth, but here it's the reality at our fingertips. Drudgen, is there any way on the control panel to tell where we are going? Fiddle with the panel on your side to see if there are any navigation features to this craft. I will keep my eyes out in front, so we don't fly into an asteroid or debris. You're the only one who can read this stuff. Robin, please check the other women out to see if they have recovered a bit from their experience, then come back here and help in the copilot seat while Jim works on navigation."

Michael was barking orders as if he were in the hospital where he and Anne had first met. Like a code blue cardiac emergency, he coolly took charge of the situation with the authority of a specialist in a life-or-death crisis. Minutes later, Robin returned from the back room of the ship to give Michael a status report on the passengers and their welfare and then asked if any of them spoke English well enough to understand commands without taking too long.

She said, "Surprisingly, they were taken from low population areas that did not have much exposure to other languages, but I was able to communicate fairly well through half of them. They said the others taken were in the same situation, so using them for anything will be a challenge."

Michael answered, "Well, we need to teach them a few key command words, about ten."

"Which ten?"

"Like in the military, right, left, forward, stop, go, up, down, back, run, come, and cover. That is actually eleven, all motion-type words that tell you something in minimal breath and easy to understand."

"Changing the subject, it is unusual to listen to someone seriously when they don't have any clothes on."

Michael turned around with a disgusted look, cutting his eyes, and said, "I am for all intents and purposes, a grizzly bear from the diaphragm down. With that said, frankly, as long as I have this much fur on my body looking like this, I don't give a damn whether I have a stitch of clothing on my body. Due to all my changes, I can't fit into anything without growing out of it within a month's time. I even do it in the woods like other bears, so let's get serious and find a way to get help and possibly live long enough to find the others and get home."

"Sorry," Robin said as she walked back to the giggling women. "I was trying to lighten the air a bit, so we don't seem so wound up, and I didn't make you a damn bear! By the way, it's kind of cute."

An irritated Michael shook his head and asked Jim, "Found anything yet?"

Drudgen instead replied, "Yes, but I did not want to interrupt your discussion, which was quite entertaining, to be honest. I found this booklet that looks to be the guide to this entire dashboard with pictures and arrows as if someone were flying who couldn't read."

"Well, that's the book for me since I can't make any sense of this language."

Michael read the pamphlet all the way through saying "hum" and "oh" with every page turned. Halfway through the booklet, Michael asked Jim to push a particular button on the dashboard, which produced an address book with a communication list of about forty names in seemingly alphabetical, or symbolic, order with stars noting the level of importance. He said to Jim, "Can you use that other essence thing that moron Gimmish gave you to find out which number is the best one to call?"

"Let me concentrate. Eenie, meany, minie, mo ...."

"Everybody wants to be a comedian. Just choose the best one, please!"

"Okay, this one. Sorry, Michael. I think we are losing our minds." Jim hit what looked like a dial search, and a voice came on saying, "Hello, this is Tol. Gimmish, is that you?"

Michael said, "No, sir. I was taken with forty-one others from Earth by that individual you just named and now find myself and twelve others lost in space heading from a place run by an individual named Alchemy. I do not know the arrangement, but they came to Earth and abducted forty women and my friend and myself for reasons I do not understand except what this evil guy named Alchemy said. I am in this craft you can probably zero in on, seeing we are by ourselves. I am flying this craft with my friend and ten of the forty women and a person we released from a cell when we escaped. The others were split with each friend taking their ten."

Tol said, "I need to hear about this conversation and your history in more detail, so I am going to send a party to greet you and escort you to my headquarters as soon as we stop this communication. This is not a secure channel, and I don't want anyone listening in. We do need to find out more about what he is planning. You also are in danger from another ship that could have randomly picked up this communication. I will see you soon."

In about eight hours, four craft looking like fighter planes circled and hailed Michael. Jim fumbled for the right switch and brought the picture of a person onto the screen, saying, "We have been ordered to accompany you to our headquarters. Please follow my lead." In a short but polite manner, the craft formed a triangle around the lonely vessel, with one in front leading the way.

Jim said, "It is nice to know that someone in this realm has some manners, but all we wanted was to go home and be left alone."

Michael replied to Jim, "No one gives a crap about us. They want information. Who knows, they may think Alchemy had a good idea and are luring us into a trap."

Michael turned to Drudgen and asked, "What are your thoughts now?"

Drudgen shrugged his shoulders which caused Michael to look up at the ceiling, shaking his head, and take a deep breath.

10/8/2023
Tol HQ Compound
Areanosten Planet Five
Quark Dimension

Gimmish's stolen transport arrived at the headquarters. Luckily, it did not need to land in a closed space. After a few bounces, they landed. Realizing they had made it in one piece, Michael and Jim slumped in their chairs and simultaneously gave a massive sigh of relief for everyone's safety. Drudgen made a fist pump, knowing he had escaped Alchemy for good.

Robin and the others came from the back, none the worse for wear but looking around, wondering where they were and what would happen next. Michael poked around the door for a way to open it and finally found a lever to pull. When he pulled it, the door opened like a drawbridge where the slats changed to become stairs.

Michael walked out to gasps from the guards, who were amazed at the massive specimen he was. Jim and Drudgen walked behind him, not being noticed. Then, the women walked out one by one to stares of wonder and attraction. The shoulders of the men slumped. They opened their eyes and mouths wide. The twelve earthlings and the quark came to a stop, wondering what to do next. In another moment, Tol and Brandish walked through the door, looking at them with pure curiosity.

Tol came to Michael and asked, "And who are you?"

"I am the Knight Bear. We contacted you to help the other thirty women and us so we can return home to Earth. We came here kidnapped by someone named Gimmish, who also shot and killed my wife, and I think his boss, Alchemy. This is Jim Longfield, a friend of mine from back home. This is my colleague Robin Grandy.

And this is Drudgen, who also was a prisoner at Alchemy's place and helped us escape."

Tol looked at Michael closely, taking in his entire frame. After a minute of nervous silence, he looked straight into his eyes and answered, "Interesting, Mister Knight Bear, I was expecting a fellow named Michael Townsend. I was the one that instructed the gamer Gimmish to give you that disease. I see you found a way around it to give yourself another chance."

"You wanted me dead? He succeeded in killing my wife. I now want to kill you, but I need to take these women back to Earth." Tol's guards immediately drew their weapons on the entire party.

Tol smiled and responded, saying, "Dr. Townsend, I know you are unlike any third-planet being I have ever seen. However, your blunt remark lets me know you are under stress, and I will dismiss it."

Michael looked around seeing that his whole group would be exterminated in seconds, if he did anything else. Michael had to use every ounce of his self-control not to attack and kill Tol that very second. He leaned toward the unflinching quark and asked with a growl, "Yes sir, but why did you instruct him to kill me?"

"Mister Gimmish made a horrible mistake that has had a terrible effect in this dimension. By coming to your planet and obtaining your essence, he violated a rule of the Game. This distraction was instituted to satisfy the natural predilection for violence and mayhem among us quarks. I told him to dispose of you before others found out. Not doing so would destroy the arranged peace so that warlords could quit fighting with one another to keep the population from dying. What has happened now is that your persons of childbearing ability were abducted in a scheme to populate the misguided warlord's fiefdom."

"How do you know that your kind and ours could procreate?"

"It has happened before, many of your years ago. I was the warlord that made it stop."

"That's a wild, unbelievable story."

"Do I have any reason to tell you anything but the truth? You remind me of this being I met named Enoch. Let's go in and talk further since we now have a common interest to stop their plans. Commander Brandish and your two men come with the guards and me. Show the women to their rooms on the top floor to give them a breather from their travels and make them comfortable. I bet you are hungry from all this travel and fighting. Let us get something to eat."

Michael said, "Please, I am famished."

While walking down the hall, Michael noticed Jim looking him over. Feeling a little self-conscious, he said, "Why are you looking at me like that?"

Jim said, "This is the first time I've really tried to study you closely, and you're drooling."

Michael replied, "You haven't seen a bear drool before? I'm still getting used to this big mouth and tongue of mine. It has been a trip to see my black nose at the end of my face. Often, I wake up thinking it's a dream but realize it's a nightmare."

"You still have blue eyes and your intelligence, which means your nervous DNA did not change much. But the growth of your snout in less than a year has been most impressive. But your ears really don't look bearish."

"I grew a beard to hide the new look, but that didn't last two months. One day I woke up and hit my nose thinking it was a bug. Damn, it hurt. Noticing some new change every day is a pain. I feel like I'm sixteen again. One day my shoes would fit. The next day they would be too small. Walking down this hall, I feel I am in a Hobbit house trying not to hit the walls with my shoulders which span two-thirds the width of this hall."

Tol interrupted, "Is it, Mister Townsend or Mister Knight Bear?"

Michael answered, "Whatever you want."

"That's fine. So Knight Bear it is. I did not expect to find you as you are."

"Me neither." Michael rolled his eyes.

"Through this door, please."

They walked into the room and looked at the large tray of food. Michael looked at the other four and said, "What are y'all going to eat?" and smiled.

Brandish and Tol did not quite get the point until Michael took a large meat shank, showed his teeth, and ate it in two bites.

Tol told Brandish, "Commander, order another tray."

Michael added, "Make it two trays, maybe three. I'm hungry."

Tol turned and spoke to Jim, "Your friend interested me with his size to the point of distraction. I did not have the wherewithal to ask you anything. While he continues to satisfy the needs of his frame, let me ask you what happened."

While Michael, now Knight Bear, ravaged the first food tray, he heard Jim tell Tol, "We mentioned a fellow named Alchemy who wanted Gimmish to lead him to Earth to capture forty women for his population scheme. Michael, now Knight Bear, and I were captured as an afterthought. His plan is to use Earth women to induce reproduction in his and the other three's fiefdoms to solve the problem."

Tol interrupted, "Who were the other three?"

"I only remember the first initial of their four names start with the letters A, B, C, and D. We were able to turn on the communicator after a while and heard someone named Heimerlich pleading with Gimmish for the reason he did what he did to which there was no answer and a halt midway through a sentence."

Tol said, "It was a surprise attack to wipe out someone who would be against their plans. Another warlord, Sargen, and I communicated with him about Gimmish, who was one of his gamers who probably asked to come, and Heimerlich let his defenses down ..."

Jim remarked, "Like a Trojan Horse."

Tol said, "I don't know what that is ... Anyway, if Heimerlich is gone and his sector taken over, that gives those four warlords more resources with which to create weaponry and one less ally for us."

A voice over the intercom sounded, "Warlord Sargen wishes to speak with you."

Tol said, "Patch him through." He pushed the lit button and said, "Tol here, Sargen. I think I know why you are calling."

Sargen replied, "We have a bigger problem now. Alchemy, Buentos, Contronto, and Descrim attacked and obliterated Heimerlich. Maldonate's sector borders Heimerlich and is now controlled by Buentos. Descrim borders him on the other side of his fiefdom. By taking over Heimerlich's territory, Alchemy will have one less flank to protect since we border him on this side. I have not spoken with Rezfen yet, but he is not going to be happy with this turn of events, to say the least."

Tol answered, "I know, and from what my visitors from the third planet from Sol—"

"What?"

"You heard me right, from the other dimension. Gimmish led those warlords there with Alchemy planning a horrible addition to this dimension, childbearing persons. The persons are not bad, but the warlords want to use them to increase their population and replace their casualties due to war or whatever. If this starts, they will feel emboldened to start more conflict, knowing they can produce replacements and go to the third planet and kidnap more."

Sargen answered, "That will throw our entire universe into imbalance, causing more destruction."

"Exactly."

Michael asked, "What in the world can Jim and I do to help stop this catastrophe?"

Sargen said, "Tol, I'm going to come there so we can plan a counter to those four. I must call for an emergency here and put my fighters on alert to safely come there. I will call Rezfen to travel your way too, to stop them and help Maldonate since he is now surrounded. Is there anything else I should know?"

Michael injected, "Yes, three of the four warlords, all but Alchemy, each have ten women, or childbearing beings as you call them."

Sargen asked, "Now who are you, and how do you know such details?"

Michael answered, "We were captured by Alchemy and taken to his headquarters. When he left to attack Heimerlich, my friend here and I escaped with some hostages in a craft left on the flight deck."

"Escaping from Alchemy is not an easy thing to do. You will need to let me know your story when I arrive. Tol, everyone, I will be there as fast as I can. Goodbye."

After the call was over, Tol remarked, "Indeed, I wish to also know how you escaped."

A few hours later, Michael accompanied Robin to her room. He opened the door for her and let her walk in first. "Becoming a bear hasn't stopped you from being a gentleman."

"It's still in my DNA." As they went over to the window and looked out, he remarked, "Not much to look at."

Robin turned and asked him, "Do you think we will ever get back home?"

Michael shook his head, bumping his snout on the window. He touched it with his hand, breathed heavily with frustration, and said, "Hell, I don't know. But I believe we need to think about everyone from Earth, all forty-two of us. It wouldn't be right just to abandon the other thirty. We've got to think about saving them too. Can you tell me about the others, where they are?"

Robin sat on the bed and looked up at Michael. "I'll tell you how it went. That Gimmish looked like he was so proud of himself. The four warlords sat in the second row of seats while the guards herded us, forty women, onto the stage. Contronto sat with his mouth gaping open. Descrim kept pointing and gesturing like he was determining who he would choose as if we were meat. Buentos squirmed like a horny thirteen-year-old boy. It would have been comical had it not been real.

"Before they chose, they used those light rings to force us to spread-eagle in midair and slowly spin us around to get a look from all sides. The one called Buentos even had a couple spread horizontal and wanted to have us stripped until the others said he was taking too much time. Alchemy chose me first. Then the others chose one each until the entire group was split into ten-person groups. Each warlord led their ten to their ships in light rings to take them back to their fiefdoms. You could probably hear the screaming and crying in fear throughout the entire building. The ten of us chosen by Alchemy were brought down to a holding chamber next door to you and Jim."

Michael immediately let his head hang, "That means we have to go all over an unknown galaxy fighting aliens to save the rest of our people."

"Really?"

"Yeah. If we don't do something and fight, it may turn into a full invasion of Earth. What would you do?"

She looked down, crinkling her face, and answered, "I guess we have to do something."

THE ATTACK

10/17/2023
Alchemy HQ
Feuerstat Planet Seven
Quark Dimension

Alchemy returned to his headquarters, shocked. Followed by Gimmish, he went straight to the holding cells and wondered how this happened, walking around the lower floor stepping over slashed and bloodied bodies. There were huge holes in the walls, arms cases torn apart, and debris everywhere.

They walked into the lecture theater to see the wall that had fallen and crushed the guards. Gimmish asked, "How did this happen? How did they get away? How did they fight with weapons?"

Alchemy released a scream of rage and cried, "How could one thing take out my entire guard detachment?"

Gimmish was behind, following the apoplectic Alchemy. They stepped through the charred armory, seeing twisted metal and broken glass everywhere. Windows were blown out, and debris covered the entire outside grounds.

They ran to where the ten women had been kept and saw that they were gone too. They looked in the cell that had held Drudgen. "That traitor helped them." They saw the open closet door and the dead guard down the hall. Alchemy took a blaster, shot Michael's empty place against the wall, and said, "I was going to come back and blast that Knight Bear into body parts." He reshot the wall, making charred marks.

He went to the little old prisoner who stayed in his cell. He raised the blaster and aimed. The old quark shook his head from side to side with his mouth open. The old quark yelled, "Please! Please! I did nothing! I stayed!"

Alchemy shot the quark's head into the back of the cell then gave the weapon to Gimmish. "Next time, no prisoners."

A voice came on his shoulder intercom: "Master Alchemy, please come to the control room."

They found one soldier alive, holding himself in a fetal position in the roof control room. Five minutes later, Alchemy stood over the whimpering soldier and yelled at him, "What happened here?"

"The big creature. Powerful. Deadly. Slashed with claws. No one was spared. Last one. Horrible. Escaped in the remaining craft."

"Corporal, he's useless. Put him out of his misery."

The corporal looked at the seething warlord. Alchemy screamed, "What are you waiting for? You want to be first?"

Gimmish saw that his handiwork had caused this carnage after he made the mistake of discarding his essences to Michael and Jim. He said nothing, but he did look and see that his ship was taken. The corporal swallowed then slowly pulled his trigger, executing the shell-shocked survivor with one shot. He holstered his blaster and said, "That was my roommate."

Alchemy responded, "Good. Less of a distraction for you." Alchemy saw Gimmish looking at him. He said, "What do you care? He let them steal your ship." The warlord pushed the corporal out of his way and walked out of the room.

They then went to the armory and saw the total obliteration of that side of the building from the inside. The warlord looked on the other side of the wall to see the demolished auditorium with concrete blocks on top of dead bodies. Alchemy marveled, "That Knight Bear set a deadly trap on the fly. It takes years of training to do what he did intuitively."

Alchemy ordered everyone to clean up the carnage and repair the walls that the one mutated and augmented animal-human hybrid could destroy when fully engaged in a fight.

"I can see why you chose him to be one of your essences, Gimmish. We have underestimated the craftiness of our third-planet creature, but not anymore. The next time we encounter him, we must eliminate him without fail when we have the opportunity." Alchemy turned on his communicator, "Sergeant, patch me through to the encrypted communicator. I need to send a message to warn the other warlords about this Knight Bear."

Alchemy called his three allies to speak with them in conference to have them come and meet to plan strategy because the dynamics had now changed with the escape of the Knight Bear and the other third-planet beings. He also knew that Tol and Sargen were on his border and assumed the escapees had made it to one or the other's fiefdom.

Gimmish went to his quarters, looked around, and realized he had the room to himself, thanks to the Knight Bear killing his roommate too. He remembered he had given the essences to Michael and Jim and realized the controller for the light bands that went into the circuit board had corroded, thus breaking the connection and the device. He was not going to tell Alchemy he was responsible for the entire escape. *I used that third-planet essence on me, and it did nothing but give me headaches. I waste them on the third-planet beings, and it works on them and gives me major headaches.* He thought more about what he'd given Michael and Jim and sank into his bed, dreading the moment anyone found out.

The first morning of the next week, Gimmish was awakened by a guard requesting him to come to the meeting room as the three warlords arrived. He got up to a sunny morning with the closest star shining bright without any obstruction in the sky. He sauntered down to the canteen, picked up breakfast, and continued to the meeting room where he saw the other three warlords walking to the room from the opposite way with Buentos in the rear. Gimmish was sore from working on the masonry crew lifting blocks to rebuild the walls. *At least today, I get to sit. All this manual labor reminds me why I took the waiter's job for Heimerlich.*

Buentos came in with a smile and a quick step right before Gimmish. Alchemy took notice. "What are you so chipper about? We are trying to conquer the universe, and you look like you have already done it."

Buentos answered, "I had a couple of my childbearing beings last week before I came here. They resisted but were not strong enough to keep me from enjoying myself. Having them strapped down gave me an even easier time. I assumed that was part of the body touching. Once I felt their warmth and softness, my entire body began to desire more of it. No wonder there are so many of those beings on one planet and all the other creatures too. My mind almost went out of control, and then it was over—though the aftermath feeling was superbly invigorating."

The others looked at him and rolled their eyes. Contronto spoke up, "Think back on the old story about Kollindarrot, who was wiped out by Tol for losing his mind with lust for those third-planet child-bearers. Now I see what effect it has on you."

Descrim asked Buentos, "Are you going to be able to focus on the plans in your present mental state? You seem worthless."

He answered, "I will surely try, but those nights were unforgettable and bear repeating over and over and over."

The warlords and Gimmish went into the meeting room and sat down at the table while the guard closed the door. The only one who smiled was Buentos. The other warlords were pondering their next move. Gimmish did not say a word.

Alchemy began, "Buentos, get with us. We must now plan as if there is no element of surprise because our prisoners escaped. Although they do not know how we conquered Heimerlich so easily, the word in the cosmos will spread quickly. Our next target must be Maldonate, since we now surround him, and he can only withstand so much before we overrun him. I will depend more on you both since the third-planet creature decimated my headquarters guard staff. I do not want that thing in a hand-to-hand combat situation."

Contronto questioned, "Your entire guard garrison? Are you sure?"

"Yes, I am sure. I can show you the carnage in the holding cell area on video, but back to planning. Gimmish understands that these beings are highly adaptable and think quickly when pressed with a dangerous scenario. Gimmish, please explain."

"I have been to the third planet a few times looking for ideas for the Game. I am the reason the Game dissolved because I obtained one of my essences from there, a brilliant being, strong and tall as if he was meant to be a warrior. But I was told by Warlord Tol to destroy the host to get rid of its essence. I needed to do it so that the people on the planet did not suspect anything out of the ordinary except for the fact that the disease I gave him was one of a kind and fatal. But the host, being as intelligent as he was, found a cure to keep himself alive. Somehow, what he did changed him into this huge creature. You know I was wanted by everybody for ruining the Game until I was able to seek refuge in Master Alchemy's fiefdom."

Alchemy told Gimmish, "You know we should kill you just for that."

Buentos interjected, "And you are the one who discovered these wonderful childbearing creatures. Although you saved Heimerlich the first time I tried to kill him, I may give you dispensation for finding these wonderful creatures."

Alchemy said, "You smitten fool. You could have waited until the campaign is done to get your mind fully engaged. You are damned worthless right now."

Alchemy rose to strike Buentos. Descrim grabbed his arm and said, "Cool down; we need him alive."

Alchemy looked at the four others, beginning to shake with anger. They continued their planning.

After the meeting, Alchemy and Gimmish went through the armory one more time to inspect the damage. Alchemy growled with rage, knowing that a single creature had done this damage to his well-trained soldiers. "Gimmish, I am going to make a pact with my warriors to avenge their deaths with the destruction of, first, the Knight Bear and then the third planet. I will hunt him down like a lignum, a low, slimy lignum, and kill him by slow, painful, grueling torture, then shoot his dead, dismembered body into space and let it rot or shrivel forever."

Gimmish said in return, "I wish to be there with you to witness your revenge."

Alchemy looked at him and said, "I'm getting to like you more each day."

10/19/2023
Tol HQ Compound
Areanosten Planet Five
Quark Dimension

The comm buzzed, alerting Tol. "Master Tol, Warlord Maldonate would like to open a comm link with you."

Tol Answered, "Let him know that Warlord Sargen will also be on the link."

"As you wish."

Minutes later, the link was established. The voice came through. "Tol, Sargen, I have a terrible feeling having these aggressive warlords around me I do not trust. Thanks to Heimerlich's defeat, I now have no ally on my border. My border patrol fighters report that Buentos has begun mining activity on a planet close to my border in Heimerlich's former sector. They reported that the excavation crew was mining rare metals used in weaponry but had no weapons. I have a strange feeling about this and told my fighters to keep monitoring their activity."

He continued, "Also, there is suspicious movement in Descrim's sector. He has recruited new pilots that were trained by Alchemy. These plans must have been in the works long before now.

"Another interesting issue is that the Heimerlich gamer has been gaining favor with Alchemy, who has promoted him to battle cruiser pilot. Before now, I have never been impressed with this Moonie's past. My information is that he maneuvers well in the halls of power."

Tol began, "Something has given him a crash course in judgment. He has not shown good decision making until now."

Michael interrupted and said, "Think folks, that Gimmish had a way to get to Heimerlich. When I heard the last transmission when I escaped Alchemy's planet, Gimmish must have known something that would have allowed the attackers to get the edge on him. They may be using him as a useful idiot. But I have a feeling he will surprise them."

Sargen said, "I think in any measure, we have underestimated this Moonie. I have always believed that there is a talent in being at the right place at the right time."

10/29/2023
Tol HQ Compound
Areanosten Planet Five
Quark Dimension

On day three before the attack, Michael, Sargen, Tol, Brandish, and Jim were huddled in the meeting room wondering what Alchemy would do next. The mood was dread since they knew many lives would be lost in the campaign with no natural way to replace the population, either by quark generation or binary reproduction. Being the doctor, Michael briefed Tol and Sargen on personal and sexual relationships on Earth. Both were amazed at the concept and had the desire to learn more later.

Sargen came to the point: "Gentlemen, the cosmos is in grave peril due to the actions of that person Gimmish who was given safe harbor with Alchemy. We don't know their exact plans. But Heimerlich did not believe Alchemy was working alone. I feel that Jim here had it right that Descrim and Buentos are at least involved in this plot to take over this universe. There is unusual activity in their sectors that I do not feel good about. Having a mining crew suddenly looking for minerals near Maldonate's border is very strange. At the same time, Descrim is activating his fighters to an unusually active degree for peacetime. If it is as you say that you killed all but one soldier at Alchemy's headquarters, that will probably motivate his men to fight harder for a cause. He will be down pilots and other ship personnel to replace the guards, so we will still have an advantage there. And I am not sure about Contronto. It's as if he is not doing a thing, and he is the 'C' in the letter group you told me about, Jim."

Tol took over, saying, "Sargen, you have analyzed the players well, so let's get to timing and strategy. Do we wait for them to attack somewhere, believing it is Maldonate, or do we preemptively attack Alchemy, weakening him to the point of surrender? I am against attacking because there are warlords still on the fence with all of this. If we attack, they might be alienated enough to join Alchemy and strengthen their alliance. As much as I believe there will be an attack, we cannot begin to seem like this 'peace,' if you will, is a way to plot overthrows of other warlords.

"Here's what I think. We have to move our forces to the forward position as a show of force to give all four warlords pause about beginning something."

Michael interjected, "Isn't there a middle option where we send aid to Maldonate and not leave him hanging in the middle of these predators? I know he is surrounded, but if hostilities break out, will you have time to save him? Back on Earth, this guy named Machiavelli had this kind of thinking, that the ends justify the means. Don't y'all think that saving him will help you?"

Tol answered, "I understand your calculus and why you think it is important. The ethos of this dimension is self-preservation and pragmatism. This seems easy to us without using feelings, such as you showed at the unfortunate murder of your mate. Maldonate's fate is out of our hands since we are at a strategic disadvantage from our positions compared to the enemy warlords. The result is that we cannot give any reason to the other warlords to sympathize with Alchemy and his allies. And we cannot stretch our forces with the possibilities of being counterattacked. He must initiate attacks to be seen as the aggressor. He has to be seen as the villain in this entire conflict even if it means sacrificing one who supports our cause."

Turning to the rest without a pause, Tol continued, "We need to send emissaries to Philimar, Flashenol, and Cooperon as soon as we finish here to express to them our outrage at Heimerlich's demise at the hands of their alliance, with the message that they may be next. Since Rezfen already knows the lurking danger, I will send him a summary communication explaining where we are in the planning.

"Brandish, you will lead my forces near the border so you can quickly respond to anything that happens. We will send extra men to help with the forward base so fewer guards will remain behind. Which leads me to you, Knight Bear. You will replace two-thirds of my guard since you have been so apt at defending and attacking soldiers in close quarters. Jim, you will stay with us.

"Sargen, how are you going to deploy your fighters?"

He answered, "I have already ordered them to my forward base on Alchemy's border. He sent all the other warlords and me, except Tol, a protest of my actions since I have not hidden my disgust with that vermin. Maldonate sent his letter of protest with Descrim and Alchemy too. Since Philimar and Cooperon are bordering me, I will send them my emissaries. Flashenol borders you and Contronto, so when you send your emissary you will need to be discreet because Contronto may try to intercept whoever you send."

Sargen and Tol went over to the three-dimensional chart of the cosmos, checking the borders and the fastest way to travel under all circumstances. Michael and Jim watched while the two of them pointed out planets and possible attack routes. Clearly, the two warlords were certain that, if they didn't win, there would be total chaos in both dimensions, with Earth pillaged and destroyed.

After they were finished, Sargen and Brandish discussed their defense and attack strategy working with their forces. Tol took the earthlings to another room to discuss the defense of the headquarters. Tol began, "Jim, you stay with us on the third floor in the command room since you do not know the building well. Commander Brandish will provide air defense. I want you, Knight Bear, to be deployed near the first-floor entrance to keep the lower floors secure. The women will be safe from bombardment protected by the ground." He showed a schematic of the building with entrances on each side and five floors drawn with rooms, stairwells, and hallways marked. The building hugged the side of a hill for defensive reasons. The first floor exited to the west side while the third floor exited to the east. The north and south had exits off the second floor. The complex had guest facilities on the top floor looking south and west with the coveted corner suite's view in two directions. The roof had a small landing area for top officials overlooking the more extensive field on the northside. Weapon turrets dotted the adjoining hill and the building. He gave them a grand tour so that Michael knew what each place contained, and they finally ended in his office.

Finishing, he said, "Michael Townsend, I am going to call you Knight Bear to designate your warrior status in my fiefdom. I want you to know how significant I believe your contribution will be to us. When I first saw you, I imagined your intelligence was low. However, you were impressive during the meeting with your explanations. Whatever happens, I am honored to have met you."

"Master Tol, I do not know how I impressed you so much in this short time, while not saying too much, but thank you. I will make it my purpose and passion to guard this headquarters."

When Jim and Michael returned to their room, Michael looked perplexed, scratching his head and holding his chin with his other hand. He was wondering what motivated someone like Tol to express such humility with him, seemingly wanting to say something that foreshadowed another future event, touching but odd.

"Hey, Jim, how about trying to use that numbers essence to see if something is going to happen tomorrow? Take the chance to see what you've got."

"Okay, Here goes nothing."

Jim sat down and leaned back in his chair, closing his eyes and clearing his mind. He went into a trance that lasted about ten minutes. Jim regained consciousness and shook his head. Michael asked, "Did you see anything?"

Jim took a deep breath and answered, "It took me to another world where strange-looking aliens stood around some kind of gambling table. Suddenly, another being approached me, telling me something in a language I did not understand. He pointed at a large pile of something that looked like chips or money. Then the aliens motioned for me to leave the hall. It was as if I were breaking the bank at a casino and being kicked out. I knew the numbers before the roll."

Michael chuckled, "That must have been a dream. Pretty good story."

Jim sat up and laughed. "I am going to try it again. I'm concentrating on opening my mind to whatever comes." He settled back again and again went into a trance. He began to shake and mutter something Michael could not understand. Jim woke up more quickly this time, saying, "I saw ships flying by, numbered, but where they were going, I could not tell. I tried to stay with the thought to see how long I could control it. These are short timetable visions that are only a few days before they happen. Michael, I think they are attacking very soon. I saw it in the number of fighters that flew by me in the vision. Tol has got to know what will happen."

Michael and Jim entered Tol's office as Tol was saying to Brandish, "Commander, you are going to lead a 180-ship armada to help Sargen if need be. On the way, I want some to peel off and destroy Alchemy's headquarters and his ability to attack anyone again."

Brandish responded, "Master Tol, are you not leaving yourself open on Contronto's flank and making it easy for him to attack us?"

"It is a risk I will take to rid our universe of Alchemy and his evil plans. Five star fighters and ground missiles should keep us safe enough to give you a transmission to come back. Alchemy has got to go."

"As you wish, Master Tol. But keep at least ten."

As they finished, Jim told Tol, "Master Tol, I had a next-day vision that the attacks will happen tomorrow. My visions are actionable in real time frames that allow you to change the events before they happen but only a day or two in advance, no long-range vision into the future. It was one of Gimmish's essences he got rid of by giving it to me unwillingly."

"What a moron. Why did he think that was a good idea?"

"I believe he was trying to get rid of them, so since we were bound by the light rings and put in holding cells, I guess he thought we would be executed before we had a chance to use them."

"Anything else?"

"Yes, he said he gave himself one of these things, and it gave him headaches and nightmares, torture to him. I believe he wanted to torture us too. But the vision all has to do with numbers of whatever the vision is about, not outcomes, as far as I can tell."

"Okay, thank you for the warning."

Jim argued, "But Master Tol, the enemy is coming within a few days. I promise you."

Tol looked at Jim, annoyed, and said, "My decision is final. Thank you for your concern. You may go now."

Michael said, "Listening to Jim would be erring on the side of caution, don't you think?"

Tol, motioning to the guard, said, "Again, you may go now." The guard got Jim's and Michael's attention and led them out of the office.

Jim said, "Tol is acting strangely, as if he is an alternate universe. It's as if he listened to you about Earth, and it changed his whole thinking as he feels he has something to atone for."

Michael added, "Whatever his reason, I must have said something meaningful to the point of changing his mind or even touched a nerve inside him that gave him an epiphany of some sort. Maybe that's why he complimented me as he did, and I have no clue what I said that was so powerful. Let's go to sleep because if you are right, tomorrow will be a stressful day."

11/7/2023
Tol HQ Compound
Areanosten Planet Five
Quark Dimension

Michael grabbed his equipment when he heard the warning sirens. He looked out the window to see blaster streaks shooting down from the sky. *This is not supposed to happen. The women must be protected.* He took a look at the building map to find where the women would be quartered, then charged out the door to the stairwell.

It was only a floor above him. He ran out of the stairwell yelling, "Robin, all y'all get out here, and follow me to the bomb shelter, now!" He went down the hall, beating on every door, smashing one of its hinges, wanting the ten women out in the hall. He yelled, "Robin, line them up so not to miss anybody!"

Robin said, "One's missing."

One of the women said, "She is in my room, that one."

Michael broke the door down to see a woman cowering in bed, crying. Picking her up with one hand like a baby, he said, "You're coming now." Then he yelled to the others, "Run down the stairs, all the way to the bomb shelter. We are under attack!"

The woman closed her eyes and clung to Michael's giant arm as he ran down the stairs yelling, "Go, go, go, go!"

Dust caused by the attack kept kicking up with every explosion. Everyone made it to the fortified bomb shelter with only a couple of scratches. Michael told the women, "Stay here."

Robin replied, "I'll keep them together."

Michael ran back up the stairs to the second-floor north entrance and waited. Other quarks lined up with him in defensive positions. He saw the outside ground troops try to hide from the bombardment but taking losses. The barricade was a steel plate that could defend against small blaster fire. He looked at it and thought it could be helpful. He strained but was able to move it across the floor. *Like a football sled.* "Quarks, follow me on signal!"

The enemy troops were charging the building under fire when Michael got behind the steel barricade and listened for the door to be breached. He heard the door and yelled, "Now!" He used the steel plate like a bulldozer running the oncoming troops with the quarks fighting in close quarters. The vicious hand-to-hand combat lasted longer than Michael expected. Of the forty who attacked, fifteen retreated to defensive positions. Ten dead or wounded were taken back to the building. The fighting continued, although the assault was thwarted.

On the south side of the building, another strike platoon advanced through the initial line. Michael was notified by the defending lieutenant that he was needed. Tol's defenders had been pushed back into the building when Michael got to the fighting. The attackers entered first, blasting everything in their path until they turned the corner and came up close and personal with the most ferocious creature they ever saw. He announced to them, "I am the Knight Bear," slashing with one hand and blasting with the other in an onslaught that caused every soldier to run and scream back to their ships. After Michael counted eight dead in a matter of thirty seconds, he heard Jim in his earpiece.

"The west entrance is being defended well. The building has been breached at the north entrance where Alchemy landed. He's entering the building from the north."

Michael turned around and caught the scents of Gimmish and Alchemy, and they were headed to Tol's office where he, Sargen, and Jim directed the battle. He said, "I just pushed that attack force out. I need to come back and do it again."

Before Michael could get back to the north side of the building, Alchemy burst into the door, followed by Gimmish. As if they had plans of the building, they ran straight for the war room where Tol, Sargen, and Jim were directing the operation. He entered the room and said, "Folks, I can't stay long, so I'm going to get this over quickly." Alchemy shot light rings at the three, binding them so they weren't able to move.

Jim disappeared and said, "Gimmish, thanks for those essences you gave us. They are coming in handy."

Alchemy yelled at Gimmish, "You moron, giving them a way to save themselves. Who did you give the spitting essence to?"

Michael yelled, "Me!" He used his huge claws to slice Alchemy down the back, at the same moment his weapon fired, hitting Tol in the abdomen. At the same time, explosions were heard outside, and the roof caved in, pinning Tol under the rubble. Michael tried to get to Gimmish, but a large beam and cement came between them. Gimmish looked down at the dismembered, fileted Alchemy. Without a beat, he took Alchemy's warlord ring and ran out the door, just out of Michael's reach.

Jim yelled, "Tol's injured! Need a doctor." Instinctively the doctor ran to the patient, forgetting about Gimmish and digging the rubble away. When he got to Tol, he found a piece of broken wood impaling him through his neck and spinal cord, causing him to lose blood at a rapid rate. His last words were, "Proclamation in top drawer; save ring." Michael tried to remove the stake, but more blood rushed out when it was released. He saw that the wound had severed Tol's spine and the ceiling beam administered a severe blunt injury to his skull.

Michael said, "He's dead," and walked over to Alchemy's severed head next to the light ring controller and crushed the apparatus between his hands. The rings disappeared, and Sargen and Jim rubbed their wrists, feeling the grip those things had on them. Michael watched Jim take Tol's warlord ring off his finger, then go over to the desk. He opened the top drawer, picked up the envelope with the word Sargen translated as *proclamation,* and gave them both to Sargen.

He said, "I cannot open this. It's none of my business to read another warlord's proclamation. That is the job of Commander Brandish."

Tol's soldiers came into the room. "Master Tol, Alchemy's lieutenant escaped. We shot him in the shoulder, but we were too far away to cause real damage."

Michael looked up with a scowl and said, "Master Tol is dead, killed by Alchemy. Let's go finish our job and beat 'em!"

He went outside and noticed Alchemy's forces were in full retreat, with Gimmish taking off in the lander. Michael watched again as his wife's murderer bolted into space. The explosions had stopped, and prisoners were marched into the holding chambers for processing. Michael gave them a growl that transfixed them in terror. Jim walked toward Michael, who waited until he was close and said, "Jim, I killed the wrong bad guy."

He returned to the wrecked office along with Jim and looked at Alchemy's lifeless body with three animal claw slices on the back of his head, neck, and back. He looked up to the ceiling and said to his wife's spirit, "I'll still get him, Anne." He fell to his knees, covered his eyes, and wept.

Jim knew he had to change Michael's focus, so he said, "Aren't we forgetting something?"

Michael perked up, remembering, "The women!" He ran down to the basement to find them scared but well. He said to them, "Y'all can come out now." He and Robin went to the office while six marveling quarks readily offered to help the other women to the nicer quarters that had not been damaged in the attack.

Robin said, "Michael, I am so glad to see you alive. This was an awful experience for everybody."

"No joke, but the guy who is responsible for this destruction got away, injuring his shoulder in the process. We also have to find out about the other thirty women with the other warlords."

They walked into the ravaged office to speak to Sargen. "Hey, Master Sargen, were your fighters instructed to rescue the women from the other warlords? I am going to contact Brandish to go by the warlord next to Tol's fiefdom."

Sargen answered, "No, Knight Bear, I told them to win the battle first. My concern now is to stop this calamity in this dimension. We can let you save your kind. We will help with supplies."

11/14/2023
Space
Leaving the Tol Sector
Quark Dimension

Gimmish sat in his sick bay, gritting his teeth as the medic tended to his wounds. He thought to himself, *I wear the ring. Let me act like Alchemy and take over the leadership. He and I both wanted that third-planet creature dead. If I pull this off, it will be my way to stay alive.*

The medic said, "Sir, this will only be temporary, so you will need to think about an extended time to take care of this. The debris from the battle took a large slice into your shoulder, cutting at least one muscle."

"Not until we defeat Sargen and Knight Bear. Master Alchemy is no longer with us. He was lost in battle and died a hero for the dimension. —Gee, that hurt!"

"Sorry, Gimmish."

He thought for a second, then said, "Until further notice, that's Master Gimmish. I wear the ring of the warlord now." Gimmish raised his left hand to show the medic the sign of authority.

The medic took a deep breath and said, "Master Gimmish. The pain medicine will soon take effect, but working on this arm cannot be delayed. You are still bleeding."

"Thank you. You can tell others I watched Master Alchemy die as a hero for the dimension when you finish. He gave me the ring so that we would continue his mission. I will make a formal announcement later this day." *It worked. Now stay calm.*

The medic bowed his head in respect for Gimmish's words, then said, "I was told that Sargen's forces have taken the headquarters, so we need to go to Buentos' for now."

Gimmish looked deflated and thought, *Oh! I have to now put up with him. He was worthless planning this strategy.*

The medic reported, "Contronto's fiefdom is under attack, and Descrim is too far away."

"Any word from them? I hope the other warlords haven't screwed up the plan. We gave those three all the interference we could to keep Tol and Sargen occupied."

Affirming Gimmish's comments, the medic replied, "Yes, and that Knight Bear had to defend Tol's headquarters instead of attacking somewhere else."

Gimmish nodded his head affirmatively and said, "We lost many good quarks today, but we did cripple those who wanted to stop us. Tol, the idiot that started that Game, is gone. I almost had Sargen, too, but that Knight Bear ... I want him dead; furthermore, I want to pluck his eyes out and have him dismembered limb by limb. I want his hide on my floor to step on more than anything in the universe. I will not rest until he's gone!"

"But you need to rest. We have got to get you some care."

Gimmish lay back, thinking about how he would announce his takeover of Alchemy's fiefdom for good. He had the warlord's ring. He now had to earn it. *For all Moonies and misfits everywhere, I will lead them.*

After his wounds were dressed, Gimmish returned to the battle cruiser's bridge. No one was saying a word outside of their duty purview. Alchemy's fiefdom worshipped him for his daring and swagger. Gimmish knew that to keep the warlord's ring, he had to speak first.

"Lieutenant, open a live video feed for broadcast, and give me the remote to end it." The lieutenant swirled around, looking at him with a scowl. Gimmish added, "Please."

The lieutenant gave him the remote, opened the feed, and said, "Broadcast link is live."

Gimmish looked at the screen and began, "This is battle cruiser commander Gimmish. It is with great regret that I must announce the death of a hero. Our warlord Alchemy died in battle, fighting to regenerate the quark spirit of independence and freedom to live as quarks were meant to live, as warriors. I was by his side to the last.

"He sacrificed his life to restore our lives to meaning from those who would call us just to be spectators for the rest of our existence. He was killed by the Game he warned us about by a creature named Knight Bear. The warlords Sargen and Tol used him against us. We cannot forget that our foes are stout, so we must be stronger! Master Alchemy knew that at the end when he told me his last words.

"Therefore, be it known that, as Alchemy's last words commanded me to do, I declare that I lead you onward. As confirmation of this, I wear the ring of the warlord Alchemy. I am now your warlord Gimmish." He held his hand so it would show the ring in the video as proof of his authority. "We will serve for Alchemy! We will fight on for Alchemy! We will win for Alchemy! Thank you." He clicked the remote to end the broadcast.

The bridge crew sat looking at him in stunned silence. They all saw the ring on his hand. Gimmish smiled and said, "Until further notice, out of respect for the position, the ring, and the warlord Alchemy, you will address me as 'Warlord.' Thank you. Lieutenant, take the bridge. Guard, come with me."

THE WAR

11/16/2023
Tol HQ Command
Areanosten Planet Five
Quark Dimension

Sargen sat in the less-damaged map room, staring up at the feed that came from Gimmish. "Knight Bear, what do you think about that?"

Michael seethed with anger saying, "That is a manipulative liar."

Jim said, "I'm sorry you missed him."

Sargen said, "You know, if it were not so consequential, it would have been entertaining." The two earthlings looked at the warlord, not appreciating the comment. "Call Brandish to see how he's doing against Contronto."

Michael initiated a call to Brandish, who answered, "Commander Brandish."

"Yes, Commander, this is Michael Townsend wanting to know if you were able to free the women who were in Contronto's keep. There are thirty more women out there split between the three other warlords in league with Alchemy. We need to get them out alive and keep them from becoming childbearing slaves. The ten we saved from Alchemy are here, a little bruised up but otherwise safe, and ready to go home."

Brandish said, "We are still not completely in control of Contronto's headquarters where we think they are being held. I don't think Contronto is here. He is leading the forces closer to Alchemy's former headquarters. They have a stalwart garrison that does not know when to quit, but after that, we will ask for their surrender and save the women."

Michael responded, "If they want to continue, have someone come get me, and I will tear them to pieces because where I come from, you don't hurt the women."

Gritting his teeth, Brandish said, "I'll have someone bring you so you can have some fun tearing up the place. Also, I can have some revenge in fighting vicariously through you. I want to witness you in your full kick-ass glory."

Michael growled and said, "Sounds good. Come and get me."

Minutes later, a pilot walked into the office. Robin and Sargen were sitting at the desk while Michael was psyching himself for the next fight. He said, "Commander Brandish sent me to …" Michael was out the door running before the pilot could finish. He even forgot about Jim.

The pilot followed Michael out the door, yelling, "To the right!" Michael turned around to look back at the pilot. The pilot pointed to show him that he would not find the transport if he kept on the same way. He changed direction and jumped through the doorway.

11/20/2023
Contronto HQ headquarters
Nishkofshine Planet Four
Quark Dimension

The pilot landed at dawn on Contronto's planet two miles from the target. Michael was equipped with full battle gear suited for hand-to-hand combat and plastic explosives with a translator and a body camera to record the action. Michael noticed the camera and said, "Brandish wasn't kidding about watching."

The equipment manager also instructed him, "You have twenty of these plastic explosives timed to detonate fifteen seconds after the easy-to-use package is opened. It will stick to the wall when applied by slapping it on the surface. Once it's applied, run. Also, a small drone controlled by your handler will be deployed with you to assist you with reconnaissance. You will not be alone. Commander Brandish and your friend Jim are with the fleet near the planet, so they will be watching in real time during your mission." Michael shook his head in acknowledgment.

After being instructed on the plan and weaponry and the translator technology, Michael took off running toward the city to the headquarters building. He stayed under cover of foliage as much as possible while approaching the central headquarters. Brandish and Jim watched the video in amazement while Michael reached the operations center and applied explosives to the wall to make holes while dodging blaster shots. His handler from the air shook his head and yelled into his mouthpiece, "Use more explosives in one place on the wall!"

Michael thought, *Need more training if I am going to be Rambo.* He looked for a crease in the fortification and found a weak spot where a rocket had previously hit and applied three explosives. He almost did not get away in time. The blast knocked him off his feet for a moment as it blew a hole in the wall big enough to run through. He entered the building through the hole on all fours, growling, clawing, smashing, and running over anything in his way. The drone followed. Two soldiers popped out from behind a corner too close to Michael. He slashed one's neck and grabbed the other by the throat. He demanded, "Tell me where the women are being held." He hesitated. Michael took one of his claws and put it up to his face, "Do you want to keep your nose."

The soldier said, "What are women?"

Michael said, "Ten folks that are not like you, in the jail, holding cell."

"Oh, those beings. It is one floor down toward the other end of the hall." Michael held the soldier by his shirt to lead the way, using him as a shield. The soldier, in fear, said, "Kill me now. I will be killed for being a coward anyway."

Michael told him, "Bud, I don't know who you are trying to fool. You are going with me to the holding cells now, and if they are not there, you will die as you wish."

Then Michael heard more soldiers running their way. Brandish saw the action from Michael's body camera, rooting for him as if he were watching a Game match.

Michael struck the soldier from behind the corner and growled as loud as he could, making all of them stop. The held soldier yelled, "Go now before—" The soldier's head was ripped off his shoulders, and the body was thrown sidearm at the group. The other soldiers froze in fear, believing that might happen to them. He waited momentarily after not hearing or smelling anyone close by. He looked around the corner to see the soldiers scurrying away, with a couple leaving their weapons and a pool of liquid behind on the floor. He picked up a couple more blasters and a handful of magazines and went in the direction of the holding cells.

Michael opened the door to the stairwell. A blaster shot missed his head and hit the drone. He fired back the way he'd come and threw a grenade stopping the guards' advance. He looked back, thinking, *There goes my backup.*

He ran down the stairs through the smoke to go to the cells. He heard female voices and followed them until he came to the right door and saw the automatic door lock. After a delay, the light flashed and four seconds later the lock unbolted. He yelled, "Back!" and then pulled the door open and yelled for them to come. The women did not know what to think of a talking bear until he said, "I am your ticket back to Earth. We must move now! Stay behind me!" Reluctantly they followed.

Michael used his sense of smell to find the path with the least resistance, holding one blaster and giving the others to the first volunteers. He found more weapons wherever he encountered and subdued enemy guards. Each time he found one, another woman was armed. He signaled the women to wait and investigate each room with hand signals while moving down the hall. Ahead was a fallen soldier near a blast hole in the wall made by an ordnance before Michael entered the building. He had a blaster and four grenades he gave to five other women. Now all were armed.

They kept walking carefully down the hall, peeking into an open area where they witnessed the equivalent of a squad sergeant dressing down his soldiers, "Quarks, we are fighting for our lives at this point. If we must die, we must die as warriors or be shamed forever."

They could have ambushed them then or let them march in the opposite direction. Unfortunately for them, they turned to come toward the earthlings. Without a flinch, the three women with blasters mowed down the entire quark team. Michael gave them the thumbs-up with a look of approval. The three women smiled but not for long. They heard a group of soldiers running down the halls toward them.

Michael said in a commanding voice, "Come, ready your weapons, and run up this stairwell!" The women followed Michael up the stairs and through the door, but one woman, the youngest, who had a hand grenade, stumbled midway up the stairs. The soldiers shot up the stairs and hit her in the back. Michael looked into her dying eyes when she said, "Kill them." She pulled the pin and blew herself and another quark to pieces.

This set off the rage of a linebacker and a grizzly bear in one monstrous package. The soldiers began to move for cover. As they did, Michael jumped into the group, shooting and slashing with his claws simultaneously. After all five soldiers were dead, he ran up the stairs. As he did that, another soldier came around the corner. One of the women shot him dead. One of the others tossed two grenades down on top of the pile to finish off the stairway, making it collapse down two floors. They had made it to the top floor with exits to the outside. They were almost free.

On the flat rooftop, they saw other soldiers, operating the anti-spacecraft gunnery. They had all they could manage with trying to slow the constant bombardment from Brandish and his attack wing.

Michael huddled the women and let the six armed attack craft fire on the main battery to the right. Michael, with four others who had blasters, went left.

One of the women looked through a window and stared at a burning fighter heading straight for the door. She yelled, "Everybody, get down!"

Michael yelled, "You know English?"

The woman said, "Yes, many of us speak English. Now get down!"

Michael was the last to take the warning but got down in time to shield himself and others from a blast that took the roof off and opened a massive hole to the outside. The others quickly ran out of the stairwell and onto the burning deck. They saw that the doomed fighter had taken out the two batteries. Michael thought about the unneeded plan and said to the women, "Never mind. Let's get out of here!"

Brandish flew cover for the nine remaining women and Michael after the dogfight that shot down the fighter that tore off the roof. They went down to the flight line. Michael looked for a transport. He got into the second one he tried and pushed the first button on the console. Luckily, its controls looked similar to Gimmish's. Michael pulled the correct lever and rose off the surface. Brandish provided flawless aircover, not allowing blaster fire to come in the transport's direction. Knowing that Michael had the women, Brandish sent in the ground forces to capture and secure the center while the group of now ten rocketed back to the safety of Tol's fiefdom.

On the way back, Michael asked, "Why didn't anyone tell me y'all knew English?

They giggled and said, "You didn't ask." An embarrassed Michael sat by himself the rest of the trip back to Tol's fiefdom.

They returned to Tol's sector and joined the other ten in a reunion of relief and hope for the others. Robin was an excellent doctor and friend, helping the women cope with the new reality of accepting the existence of aliens.

At their first private moment, a not-too-pleased Jim came up to Michael and said, "Next time, you ain't going to leave me. Remember, we're in this together."

11/24/2023
Buentos HQ Compound
Demarco Planet Four
Quark Dimension

Gimmish asked the lieutenant to assemble the crew for a talk. He did not trust Buentos completely, especially with their history. Before the gathering, Gimmish and the lieutenant had a private meeting. "Thanks for meeting with me before the gathering. I am sorry that I do not know your name."

"Master Gimmish, my name is Lieutenant Bort."

"Bort, I need you to help save Alchemy's legacy, the fiefdom, our fiefdom. I was with Master Alchemy when Knight Bear murdered him. He gave me his warlord's ring so that the realm, our realm, would continue. To remain one quark realm, independent, established, and unique, we must be unified under the ring, the one I wear. Do you want that too?"

"Yes, Warlord Gimmish. We must do it for Alchemy."

"We must do it for all of us, our comrades and warriors, the quarks that followed Alchemy in the first place."

"Yes, sir."

"I want you by my side when I speak to the others. I want this speech to be sent to all of our quarks so that I can announce your promotion. By helping me keep our fiefdom together, you would make Alchemy proud. Are you in?"

"Do I have an alternative?"

"Not a good one. Let's do it."

Twenty minutes later, the crew packed in on the shuttle deck. The assembled stood around, not knowing what was to happen next. First, Bort walked onto the cargo dock so the crowd could see him. He began, "Warriors, we must realize that Alchemy is no longer with us, a casualty of this fight. But the fiefdom, our fiefdom, must continue forward. Our warlord Gimmish"—the quarks gave a look of surprise—"wears the ring. He and I have discussed our situation and have agreed to work together. I want to now give the floor to our warlord, Master Gimmish."

Gimmish was pleased with Bort's remarks. He walked up the stairs and gave the group the plan for their stay. He wanted to warn everyone about being on their guard while they were there. He had told them all to keep their comm link open at all times in case of emergency and further instructions. The message was that they were to consider their situation to be dangerous. "In conclusion, watch your backs and stick together so we can all get out of here alive."

He went to his quarters to have some private time before experiencing the stress of meeting a warlord as a peer. He began to meditate on the events since the last season of the Game. Then it dawned on him. "After giving myself that third-planet being's essence, my thought process has improved. Also I am less self-conscious, making better decisions. The essences worked for that Knight Bear and his companion. Why not me? My problem now is getting another machine with essences. Still, I cannot allow the other warlords to know about this until I can trust them."

The comm alerted him. He answered, "Warlord Gimmish."

Buentos was on the other end of the call. He hesitated a moment, then said, "You are now the warlord?"

Gimmish confidently said, "Yes, I wear the ring of the warlord."

"Well then, welcome, Warlord Gimmish. I want to discuss where we go from here. One of my personal guards is outside your craft, and I have instructed him to show you to your quarters. I am presently"—he grunted—"oh, my … occupied and will have my guard escort you to my conference center after you rest."

Gimmish heard a muffled sound in the background and asked, "Is there something wrong in the background?"

Buentos wistfully said, "Ah, not at all. See you in the morning."

Gimmish looked around his quarters for any belongings he wanted to keep close. He rubbed his ring, feeling the ornate ridges that symbolized the history of the now fallen sector. "Irony, I achieve the rank of warlord but have no fiefdom left. I am now a leader in exile."

Gimmish and the guard sauntered to the nicest visitor's room. That night's sleep was not good. Gimmish knew that even though Alchemy's plans were instrumental in his exacting revenge on Tol, the chances of victory now were dire. *I hope Contronto and Descrim are also here. I am glad I still have my essence machine. It's empty now. However, if we escape this mess, I will find more to fill this device and see what I can do. I need to think of a plan.*

A knock on the door alerted him for breakfast. The guard said to press the signal when the warlord was ready, and he would be back. Gimmish hoped that Contronto was going to be there since there was history between him and his host. Gimmish told the guard that his lieutenant was to accompany him to the meeting.

The guard opened the meeting room door. "You are the first ones here. Take any seat you like."

Gimmish noticed the door was hinged to the right, opening to the outside so the guard could hold it for them. They walked into a large but spartan room, with maps of the dimension on the back wall. Large video screens were mounted on the wall at each end of the table, left and right from the door. Underneath both were small plants. Gimmish counted twenty chairs comfortably dispersed around the large meeting table. He sensed the good lighting made the room conducive to productive meetings. Next to the maps on the left was a door to another room. They took their seats across from the entrance.

The two sat in the room, looking around, not speaking for fear someone would hear their conversation. After a bit of time passed, the door opened again, allowing Contronto and another quark to enter. Stoned-faced, they both acknowledged Gimmish and Bort and took seats to the right of the door. Still, there was no sound made in the room. The body heat activated the ventilation system to blow air, causing the leaves of the two plants to slightly move in the breeze. The door opened from across the room, and a smiling Buentos briskly entered the room and took a chair. Two guards walked into the room from the hall behind Contronto.

Buentos began, "Welcome, Warlords Contronto and Gimmish. Under other circumstances, it would be a pleasure to see you both."

Contronto glared at Buentos with a disgusted look. "Alchemy convinces us to start this war, and you are acting gleeful?"

Buentos chuckled and said, "Oh, no. I'm extremely upset with Alchemy, but he's no longer here. Also, I would have killed Gimmish by now if he had not found these third-planet creatures. You would feel better had you had the chance to indulge."

Contronto closed his eyes while taking a deep breath. "I hope you are going to focus more this time than last, you besotted fool."

Gimmish broke in, quelling the tension. "If we kill each other in here, Sargen won't need to lose a quark. Is Descrim going to be here?"

Buentos said, "Thank you, Gimmish. No. From what I understand, Sargen is staging his invasion." He looked at Contronto and asked, "What happened to you, quark friend?"

"We underestimated how many of Tol's forces would be dedicated to attacking me. It seems that Tol allowed himself to be attacked in exchange for cutting me off from my headquarters and flanking my defense. Now two-thirds of my sector is under enemy control."

Gimmish said, "But Tol is dead, and his compound suffered heavy damage."

Contronto retorted, "But the Knight Bear is still alive. He single-handedly tore up my forces in my headquarters. And as you witnessed, if it were not for him, Tol's compound would have fallen, and Sargen would be dead too. How is that third-planet being so powerful? We must expect him to attack here."

Gimmish added, "And we must plan for the fight to come to us."

11/26/2023
Tol HQ Compound
Areanosten Planet Five
Quark Dimension

Brandish sent a fresh wave of fighters to relieve Sargen's pilots, who continued to battle through now Gimmish's fighters and Descrim's defenses. After securing Maldonate's headquarters and processing their surrender, Buentos sent the remainder of his fighters to join Descrim's dwindling force. Buentos came at Sargen's squadrons with his flank away from Alchemy's fiefdom to prevent Sargen's or Tol's reinforcements from surprising them. After Brandish's successful campaign against Contronto, routing his forces to the back third of his fiefdom, Buentos's path to the fight was easier.

Michael and Jim volunteered to go along for the ground assault to free each of the two sets of women still captive. He relished the chance to fight as if he were still on the football field. Jim said to Michael, "You ain't going to go alone this time. I'm going along this time to get Gimmish and to watch your back."

Now, Michael and Jim received formal training on piloting the transport, which gave both a feeling that going home was possible. Robin treated the women for any trauma and helped the women express their experiences, using her psychiatric background.

Michael came to her after a session and asked, "How are you holding up? It's as if I get this adrenaline rush every time I need to do something now. And I am sorry I almost bit your head off when you were teasing on the escape."

Robin answered, "You are more intense since I saw you last."

Michael responded, "A lot of crap has happened."

Robin counted with her fingers, "Contract an incurable disease, lose a wife, turn into a bear, get abducted by aliens, and fight in an intergalactic war."

Michael tried to downplay. "Wild stuff. You lost a husband."

She looked at him with a sour look. "All I did was divorce a spoiled mama's boy."

"We were abducted by aliens."

"One out of five for me. My point is that I want you as my knight. You have been our hero. Without you, Alchemy would have been successful."

Michael tried to get out of the conversation by saying, "I just want to go home."

"I wouldn't mind going home with you."

"Huh?"

"When we get back to Montana, I want to help you grieve."

"How?"

"Let me be with you and let the chips fall where they may." Then she sweetly kissed the side of his muzzle and said, "You do look kind of sexy with no clothes on." Then she patted his face and walked off.

Michael stood with his mouth open, not knowing what to say. He shook his head as if he was dreaming, stunned at what she had just professed to him. He thought, *How could any woman still be attracted to a freak like me? I miss Anne.* What Robin had said only made him miss Anne more. He forgot what he was supposed to do next, standing like the doofus Anne had called him before they had coffee together in Baltimore.

Then Michael heard Jim call him. "Are you coming, or have you changed your mind?"

"I'm coming." Michael trotted over where Jim was and apologized for the spectacle. The two walked down to the hangar to board their craft.

Jim warned Michael, "You need a clear mind for what lies ahead. Don't start losing focus."

Michael shook his head in agreement, trying to change the subject. He did not want to think about his feelings anymore, even though it helped him fight more viciously.

Michael sent a call request to Brandish, who answered, saying, "Commander Brandish."

Michael asked, "Where to, brother?"

After about ten seconds of silence, there was a reply. "What's a brother?"

"Okay, Commander Brandish, what is our destination?"

"I am not at liberty to say, but you are to follow me. At the right moment, I will give you further instructions. Stay in your position on the wing, and from now on, remain on radio silence until further notice."

Jim said, "You heard the boss man."

Michael then thought out loud, "I'm mad we didn't kill Gimmish when we had the chance. He now knows what can be done with essences. Just think how many gamers there were, and how many different traits can be created. You had twelve warlords with four gamers apiece who controlled four more essences, and they have the technology. At the peak, there were 184 essences out there, and we have no clue what they are, who has them, how to get them, or what they all can do. This is a monster of a problem, and the only other quark that knows this secret is Sargen. Gimmish started this whole mess!"

"I have not thought of that yet. What a horrible scenario. What we have to do is find every team or as many as possible. If they have not been lost in battle, there needs to be a way to find and convince them to either give up or destroy what they have." Both Michael and Jim sighed deeply at the same time.

Minutes later, the wing was commanded to take a forty-five-degree turn to the right that had them heading to the Descrim fiefdom. It would have been a good guess since Sargen's fighters had been fighting them as soon as they arrived in his territory. They had received no resistance from Alchemy's remaining fighters since they retreated to Heimerlich's old territory after Descrim was defeated. By the calculations made on their star chart, the flight time was only going to be another four days at full speed. For the next three days and twelve hours, they used a translator device to study the flight manuals of Gimmish's craft they had used to escape from Alchemy's headquarters. They learned how to steer correctly, how the protection shields worked when fired upon, and the ship's range and maneuverability.

Michael remarked about an hour into reading, "Hey, Jim, this thing doesn't come with roadside assistance."

Jim replied, "That comment can only have come from a doofus." They both laughed.

It then dawned on Michael, "Jim, we have no plan for attack. We don't know what kind of surprises they have for us."

Jim incredulously said, "And you're just thinking about that now?"

Michael, protesting, said, "Hey, I'm new at this hero stuff. Cut me a damn break!".

Jim retorted, "You know, Descrim's guards ain't going to cut us any damn break."

Michael did not respond. Instead, he signaled Brandish and asked, "Hey, boss man, do you have any intel on where we are going?"

Brandish answered, "Expect the worst, so you don't take it lightly." Then a message alert with an attachment appeared on Michael's dashboard. When he pressed the icon, a satellite map of the target area with the landing zone location appeared.

Jim said, "What's it look like?"

Michael thought for a moment and said, "It looks tropical with thick forest between the landing zone and the building. It'll take some doing to get through that thick stuff."

The two of them plotted scenarios and what-ifs to come up with their plan.

Minutes later, Brandish sent out the call. "Tol wing four, in thirty minutes we will engage the enemy fighters. Be on ready alert for an attack. The left-side wing will accompany the transport to the fourth planet beyond the great star until it makes a safe landing. Prepare for ground fire, and all be as safe as possible. The two attack platoons will engage with the enemy garrison, keeping them from blocking Knight Bear's mission. Hope all the third-planet beings are safe. Good luck!"

The fighter force consisted of sixty fighters split into three sections, left, center, and right. Twenty fighters surrounded Michael's transport and two platoon transports as they attempted to enter the planet's atmosphere. They traveled low enough to stay under the defenses below the horizon, then one of the fighters told them the landing coordinates to be as close to Descrim's position and headquarters. The first thing Michael said was, "All I care about is the welfare of the ten women. Capturing or killing Descrim is a secondary worry, leaving that to Brandish if I need to."

The small garrison near the headquarters on the far side of the thick woods looked for intruders. Michael was ready to go into killer linebacker mode as soon as he exited the craft. But his mission was to avoid the garrison and go to the headquarters. He was prepared with a blaster in hand and another on his belt. A leather strap full of grenades was strapped to his chest making him look like a grizzly bear commando. He placed the blaster in the other holster, got down on all fours, pulled out a thin leather strap, and wrapped it around his neck to use as reins. Jim, loaded with his weapons, got on his back, and Michael ran toward the city.

The trees were great cover from above the dirt path. The thick foliage blocked half the light, making the trail difficult to navigate in some places. About a third of the way through the forest, they approached a tree-lined stream with a purposely destroyed bridge to impede large-scale attacks. Michael tried to find a narrower place where a crossing would be easier with Jim on his back. At what looked like a good spot about one hundred yards from the road, Michael said, "Ready to go across?"

Jim started his sentence, "Ready as I'll—" and Michael felt Jim being knocked off his back.

A flying reptilian creature knocked Jim into the stream and attacked him, clawing him in his calf with its talons. He screamed in pain. As Michael was trying to help Jim, a giant monster snake tackled Michael from behind, making him fall into the stream face-first.

Jim yelled, trying to kick the animal off his other leg, "I'm caught!"

Michael yelled, struggling to get out of the water, "Me too!"

The speed of the animals had knocked both off balance. The snake seemed to trip Michael whenever he tried to get his footing. The creature pushed him headfirst into the water to keep Michael from anticipating the snake's next move. He kept falling face-first into the water, with the monster keeping his head underwater.

Jim screamed, "This thing has got my calf and is trying to fly away with me!" Jim was holding on to a tree as tightly as he could, trying to kick the snake with his free leg to save himself. The creature seemed to recognize Jim trying to reach for the weapon he had dropped while struggling, which kept the animal from flying with full force.

Then a second snake appeared to help attack and wrapped its tail around Michael's throat. Michael held his breath and rolled onto his back to use his front claws to rip at the snake choking him. The snake's grip slackened, but it held on and then wrapped itself around his arms to reduce the force of Michael's blows. The snakes worked together to restrict his movements while Michael thrashed, lifting his head above water long enough to take another breath.

Michael knew Jim could not hold on much longer. He looked up to see a blaster three feet from him. He rolled to the weapon and grabbed it with one hand to shoot at Jim's assailant, striking the predator at the top of his leg. It let go of Jim and flew away bleeding.

Jim picked up the blaster he dropped. A third snake out of the woods joined the fracas. Jim turned and shot at the third snake, which ducked into the woods. A fourth snake tackled Jim, beginning to pull him. Michael turned with the blaster and shot it in the head. Then Jim turned and shot the snake that held Michael around his neck. The third snake returned and attacked Jim from the woods, knocking the blaster into the water. The snake on Michael's neck went limp and died. The first snake kept holding Michael's legs, continually keeping him off balance and thrashing in the water.

Jim again yelled, "Help!"

Michael sank his claws into the first snake again and again until it went limp. Michael quickly got out of the bloodred water and saw where the snake had escaped with Jim. Michael screamed, "Yell, Jim!" He heard the cry going further into the woods. Michael began chasing, his nose to the ground, as he followed Jim's scent and listened to his screams. The snake seemed to know that it was being followed. It traveled a straight line in an attempt to reach its destination.

He caught them as the snake was reaching its burrow. As Jim was at the mouth of the hole in the snake's grasp using his arms and legs to keep from being dragged underground, Michael sank his claws into the snake's body just between the mouth of the hole and Jim. It thrashed wildly, throwing Jim off, then escaped down the hole.

Michael said, "Let's go someplace away from these critters and fix that wound. I see why they didn't use any defenses this way."

Jim said, "Also, let's stay near the road the rest of the way."

Michael said, "Yeah, we don't want to run out of ammo killing critters before we reach the headquarters."

The path they took seemed to have seen heavy use as it followed a roadway toward the city. They moved more cautiously the rest of the way. Michael took about three five-minute rest breaks before they got near the town. They saw the headquarters an hour later as they exited the forest. They viewed the antiaircraft fire, constantly sending explosive projectiles high overhead trying to hit anything moving while Sargen's and Tol's attackers kept hitting their stationary targets.

Michael observed, "This looks like a back entrance to the headquarters. I see that a moat does not go quite around the building. There is a low access point, but the windows are barred, much tougher to get into. We need to get Brandish to strafe the top of this side to knock out any weapons that could shoot down on us. Then when we see the vesper lights, we make our move. I will approach the building walking on all fours like a forest animal and climb to the window with a rope. I'll flash this penlight when it's dark enough, and you come when I make an opening. I'll grab you, and we'll enter the building."

Jim remarked, "That's the best plan you've made all day."

The message was sent to Brandish. About thirty minutes before the sunset, two fighters made bombing runs on the top of the building with incendiary bombs so the defenders would have difficulty regrouping.

Michael quietly said, "Jim, stay back and blend in with the trees. Use a bird call to warn me if the guards come." He then used a rope and a hook to throw and wrap the rope around the bars on the windows. Then he twirled the weighted hook and threw it to snag the bar. On his fourth try, he caught the bar and secured the anchor on the windowsill.

Looking back and forth, he climbed the wall by the rope the size of a gym battle rope. He quickly pulled himself up the wall and pulled the bars with his bare hands. But instead, Michael blasted the other window's bars out six feet to the side. He attached the rope to the other windowsill and repelled down. He motioned for Jim to get on his back, and they went up through the blasted window.

The room inside looked like one of Alchemy's armories, full of hand weapons ready for use. This time he broke the case, gave a couple of weapons to Jim, and took enough to arm the women if they found them. Michael looked out of the door into the hall and took a sniff. He came in and said, "The bear senses are useful here. The women are here in the building." Jim shook his head in approval and gave Michael the thumbs-up.

They listened and heard soldiers running down the hall toward the room. They got back and Jim blended into the wall laying the blaster on a counter with his hand on the trigger. Michael hid behind the door as the soldiers entered, six of them. They never had a chance. Michael mauled one with a swipe to his head and neck and blasted another at the same time while Jim took out two. One soldier tried to use his weapon. Michael grabbed his arm and tore it off at the shoulder before slashing his neck. The last soldier cowered in fear, waiting for his fate, when Michael commanded, "Tell me where the ten women prisoners are held, or I will slash you to pieces limb by limb until you agonizingly die."

"What will you do to me if I do tell you?"

"I won't slash you to pieces."

"They are two floors down on the other side of the building in two separate cells. Please, let me go now!"

"As you wish." Michael threw him out the window to land on the pavement headfirst to die.

Jim watched this merciless display of rage from one of the formerly kindest men he ever knew. It was the fury of a provoked grizzly bear ravaging the enemy that blocked his way to his goal. Jim said, "You did that so effortlessly, without a second thought."

Michael look at Jim and said, "They're not human."

Jim said back, "Well, you don't look human either."

Michael looked annoyed, and said, "We can discuss ethics when we get home."

Jim stripped the uniform from the soldier that looked like his size. They quietly walked out of the armory loaded with all the weapons they could carry plus a couple of extras, since Jim used the uniform belt to carry two more blasters. They immediately found the stairwell two doors down the hall. Pausing for a moment inside, Michael spoke to Jim about rescuing every women. He did not want to lose another human life to the aliens.

Going down the two floors was the easy part. They had two choices on the lower floor. One way was the main entrance to the headquarters; the other way was the soldier's canteen. The two decided to go back up a flight and work their way around. All the explosions outside drew the attention of the personnel, but they still had to be careful. The floor above was a busy infirmary. They chose to go the other way through storage areas. They went from doorway to doorway with Michael using his sense of smell to detect anyone coming. At one point, he whispered, "Hide in the office."

They jumped into the office with an officer with his head down behind a desk writing. He did not look up, but he asked, "What do you want, and why did you barge into my office?"

Michael undeterred placed four of his claws on the officer's neck, and said, "We don't need to knock. We want information."

The officer turned pale with fright and could not draw enough breath to make a sound. Michael continued, "You are going to tell me where the ten Earth beings are being held, and where Descrim is, or these claws will tear your head off." He brought his thumb around to take his thumb claw and poked the end of his nose, drawing blood. "See, my claws are sharp, and they have already been used today, so give me answers. First, where are the Earth women?"

The trembling officer whispered, "Go to the end of this hall and down the stairwell one floor, then left out of the stairwell to the left three doors down. They are in two holding chambers, five in each."

"That was excellent. Now, Descrim."

"I do not know exactly because he moves to the flight deck and sometimes goes into battle himself as he did yesterday. But his office is empty now because of air attacks damaging the wall near his office."

Michael said, "Wrong answer." And he ripped the officer's spine at the base of the skull. He looked at Jim saying, "He can't make a sound now."

They snuck out of the office and made it undetected to the stairwell and climbed down to the next floor. They looked to their right to see the canteen they had avoided earlier and darted to the first door.

Michael said, "They are in here." The doors to the cells were on the right, and the wall to the exterior was on the left. The cells were not reinforced like Contronto's cell. He said through the first door, "Back." They moved back, and Michael kicked the door open and said, "Come," motioning with his arms. Seeing Michael, the five women froze.

Jim stopped in his tracks and pressed a large button. "Look, Michael, all you need to do is look for these door buttons. Also, we're being watched." They looked up and saw a camera at the end of the dead-end hall. Michael aimed his weapon and blasted it. They turned around to see eight-inch diameter steel pillars drop from the hall ceiling and lock into cast footings, trapping them both behind bars. The poles were spaced four inches apart, enough to shoot escapees through.

Michael unsuccessfully tried to move a pole and said, "We're trapped!" Even with Michael's strength, they would not budge. Then they saw the guards run down the hall at them. Michael tore one door off its hinges to use as a shield. "Everyone, back in the room." The women went back to the rooms they had come from. The five women with Michael, upon seeing him, hid as best they could under their cots.

He yelled to them, "Hey, I'm the good guy trying to get y'all out of here!"

More guards congregated on the other side of the bars shooting into the blocked-off hall when they saw any movement. Michael saw the growing guard contingent and said to Jim, "Looks like we are going to need a miracle. Got any ideas?"

Jim added, "They aren't shooting much. Why don't they charge?" As Jim asked his question, the guards threw canisters of a gas that began to make the twelve earthlings cough and have a hard time breathing.

While coughing, Michael said, "Well, Jim, they know they can wait us out and let us give up or starve. I have an idea. Take your clothes off in chameleon mode. Walk against the wall with the blaster close to you, hidden from sight, to get to the other room."

"What about the bandage and bleeding wound from that damned flying thing?"

"Let me patch it, then make sure you move with the bandaged side away from view."

"I'll let them know we have a plan."

"What's the plan? What about the tear gas?"

"I'm still thinking." The guards took a couple of potshots at the cell door.

Jim gave Michael a disgusted look and blended into the wall, then took his clothes off and sarcastically said. "Let me know before tomorrow." Michael heard him move against the wall twisting and shimmying down the hall against the wall to the other cell, then ducked into the room.

One of the women got up and opened a speakeasy door between the rooms.

Then they heard Jim with his translator quietly say, "Ladies, we will get you out of here. We are going to need you to do exactly what we say." Seconds later, Jim returned to the room where Michael was.

Michael said, "I sent Brandish a signal where we were."

Surprised, Jim asked, "You can communicate with him in here? What can he do?"

Suddenly a blast hit the wall on the other side of the pole barrier where the guards were knocking them off their feet, killing many. They ran into the end cell. Michael affixed explosives to the wall then quietly said, "Everyone to the front cell, now."

All twelve were in the forward cell when the explosives blew a large hole in the wall. Michael and Jim went back to see the gap. Michael looked out and saw a moat with the same giant snakes they had escaped from earlier in the forest. "Oh, God, Jim. I hate those snakes."

Blaster fire rained down from the top of the wall, pinning them in the cell. Jim said, "When those poles dropped, it looked like it takes a lot of time to recoil them back which could give us some time to think of something." Jim looked at the hole again and saw one of the mammoth snakes begin to crawl into the room. He whirled with his blaster and shot the creature between the eyes, splattering his head against the wall. The rest of its body fell back out of the hole and into the moat.

An exasperated Jim said, "Let's just try to get the hell out of here with these women. What do we do now?"

Michael said, "We have a choice. We need to get through this hole and over that moat of snakes or else get around those bars and through the guards."

Jim said, "We can't see all the snakes in the dark, and the weapons fire from the top could get us too. Let's see what we can do with the guards."

They looked out the door to see that the guards were having their own problem keeping the snakes at bay. Michael said, "Now I know why they are in the moat. They will attack anything that stirs or makes noise. Well, we need to help the snakes take out some guards." He told Jim the plan. "Okay, go."

Jim became transparent and took a grenade belt and hiding it under him, crawled to the bars. He took two grenades and shoved them between the poles and then quickly crawled away. The guards saw the grenades roll toward them out of nowhere. They froze. The explosion rocked the hallway killing more quarks and scattering the rest. The snakes reacted to the commotion by becoming more aggressive to the guards. The guards ran away to avoid them leaving the twelve behind bars. Jim closed the end cell door to keep other snakes from attacking them. That left all twelve in the front cell, still trapped.

When Jim got back into the room he asked Michael, "What now?"

He answered, "We have to go through that hole."

One of the women, who minutes earlier, looked out the hole and saw the snake come through the hole in the wall, said, "I'm not going out there."

Jim asked, "You want to stay here and take your chances with the aliens?"

At that moment, a snake attempted to strike through the speakeasy door. Michael took the blaster and shot the snake, which fell back into the room. She started crying, which frustrated Jim. Jim said, "How about this wall? Doesn't the next room exit on the other side of the bars? We come out the other side with weapons blazing. Got any more explosives?"

Michael answered, "Yes, but we have to be fast here. You blast that wall, and they can come after us in here. Right now, they are allowing the snakes on the other side to keep us here. That gives us a chance to make a charge through the snakes in the hall."

Jim agreed, "We need to make it, so let's go!" They armed the women with the blasters and grenades they had left.

Michael said to the women, "We are going to attack them before they can fully regroup. I will lead. Jim, look out the door."

Jim said, pointing into the dark, "They are regrouping, but they're having trouble with snakes too. Michael, set the explosives in the room on the wall while I hold off the snakes and guards." Michael went into the room and set the explosives, then went back into the hall.

Michael ordered, "Everyone into the hall and up against the wall, now!" He set off the explosives. The explosion blew the wall clean. They ran through the open hole between the two rooms, exiting on the other side of the bars.

Michael yelled, "Charge!" They all ran as Jim fired through the bars in chameleon mode. The quarks only saw the end of the blaster.

Jim kept firing away as Michael got the ten women through the hole and attacked the guards and two aggressive snakes on the other side of the bars. Jim came last as Michael and the women picked up weapons from the fallen guards. Alarms began sounding, signifying the jailbreak. Michael and the women shot at anything that moved as they quickly moved toward the armory and freedom.

Tracing their earlier path, the now-clothed Jim entered the stairwell door while Michael was bringing up the rear. They motioned for the women to follow Jim up the stairway to the armory floor. Jim went ahead, blending into the wall and undressing again, scouting. After a winding route in and out of rooms and stairwells, Jim led them up the stairs to the armory floor, with Michael bringing up the rear. Jim looked out the door on that floor and saw a crowd of soldiers at the armory just now bringing out the five dead soldiers they had disposed of on the way in. Jim motioned everybody back into the stairwell, and all got to the top of the stairs wondering where to go now.

Jim started, "When we came in, this was the third story of the building, and we freed the ladies on the first floor, so—"

Michael said, "Yeah, if we blast a hole in the wall at the bottom of the stairwell, we can at least get out of here and have a chance to run for cover."

Jim responded, "But an explosion will attract attention and snakes. Also, how far does that moat come around the building? How many grenades do you have?"

Michael answered, "Hmm. Snakes. Four."

Jim said, "Okay, since I can hide well, why don't I go to the other end of the hall beyond where the cell was and, using two grenades, detonate two down there and run back. Then I'll wait a bit and detonate the other two here. We can blast the hole big enough to escape through and run for cover."

Michael thought for a moment and said, "I don't have a better idea right now. With all the sounds of explosions outside, that shows the fighters are still overhead, keeping their attention. I bet that is the reason we didn't have a mass attack from their soldiers. I say do it."

He watched Jim walk along the wall until he came to the other stairwell. He put a cloth on the ground, then pulled the pins of the grenades and ran out of the stairs. Five seconds later, the explosion rang through the building, causing soldiers to run toward the sound and drawing the squad from in front of the armory down the stairwell near those doors.

Jim returned to the third-floor door out of breath, asking what was next. Michael said, "Your plan worked better than we thought. Now the soldiers at the armory have left to tend to the explosion, and now the way is clear for us to go out the same way we came in. Put your clothes back on, and let's go."

Michael led the way, with Jim at the rear to hustle the women, who didn't need any reason not to. Michael closed and bolted the armory door so it would delay the quarks. He then sent a message on their position so that Brandish could send firepower to divert attention. He began to hear banging on the bolted door as if the quarks wanted to enter. Michael moved a large case to help fortify the barrier. Seconds later, he heard a blast that sounded like it was down the hall. The banging on the door stopped.

In the armory room, Michael saw Jim was guarding a quark who looked like an unarmed medical professional. In the meantime, the fighters descended on the headquarters wall not far from him. He felt the explosions hitting the wall, slowing the quarks' efforts to enter. Michael had mercy this time and grabbed him, telling him to be quiet if he wanted to live. Jim went down the outside wall to the ground. Michael instructed the practitioner to climb down the rope while both had blasters trained on him. Michael threw Jim a rope, tied his hands and feet, put him under a cover, then told him to be quiet. Jim pulled on the rope when he reached the bottom. One by one, the women came down the rope and ran under the trees at the wood's edge. They unhooked the rope and left the practitioner tied and gagged with a rag in his mouth.

While that was happening, again Michael communicated with Brandish leading the bombardment. "Brandish."

"Copy, Knight Bear."

"We are extracting the women from the building. Need more cover to stop the enemy from bombarding the escape route. Make sure enemy fire does not impede our group. Noise awakes the forest."

"What?"

"Large forest predators. We will advise when to begin."

"Copy."

Michael, Jim, and the ten women ran into the woods the same way Michael and Jim had come. The bombardment started on that side of the building, covering their escape. Michael warned, "All of you women need to watch for anything that moves. The same snakes in that moat where you were held also populate these woods and are triggered by noises. Those with blasters, be ready. The others, be ready with grenades to throw on my command."

They began down the path, walking as quickly and quietly as they could with weapons drawn. Michael said, "You are doing well with that alien flashlight. Keep it going ahead while I keep this lantern behind you."

One of the women asked, "What do we do if the snakes block us?"

Michael heard Jim answer, "That's what the blasters are for. Quiet now." Another two hundred meters down the path, they came to the stream they had crossed earlier. They stopped and made a plan to safely cross the creek, watching their back. Michael said, "Jim and I are going to help us get across two women at a time." He carried the first two across while the others watched up and down the stream for anything moving. Jim helped the second two, then Michael went back. At that time, some kind of missile struck near them, waking the forest.

Michael said, "We didn't need that." Seconds later, they heard movement from two directions coming towards them. "Everyone, close to the stream, back to back!"

Jim fired his blaster at a snake attacking from the woods. A second came from behind it, grabbing him on his injured leg. He yelled in pain, which caused more stirring in the woods. Jim and one of the women shot the snake, which let go and died.

Michael told the six left, "The forest knows we're here. Get across now, and I will protect the rear." Five women began to cross, but one stayed, telling Michael, "We go back-to-back to protect each other's rear." When the five were almost across, Michael and the last woman moved through the water.

A scream came from across the water, "Snake!" It grabbed the woman with Michael.

"Help!" she cried.

Michael jumped on the snake, wrestling its head underwater. It let go of the woman, who made it to shore while it struggled with the giant bear. Other snakes began to come out of the woods to attack those on the banks. Jim and three others began blasting the attackers, killing them, leaving Michael in close combat with a monster snake. It caught him at the leg again, knocking him underwater. It put its mouth over Michael's snout, trying to suffocate him. Those on the side could not be sure who they would hit with the blaster and held their fire.

He heard Jim yell, "Come on!"

Michael had no way to tell him to shoot anyway because the snake covered his mouth. It began to wrap its body around Michael's upper torso so he could not use his claws.

Jim took a grenade and tossed it as far as he could back in the direction of the compound. A couple of snakes left the women and headed towards the sound.

Jim wanted to yell at Michael, rooting him on, but did not want to attract any more snakes. He regretted his previous outburst.

One of the women asked, "Will he make it?"

Jim said, "He'd better, for our sakes."

Michael was getting lightheaded and trying to breathe. Seconds later, he thought, *Spit!* He touched the tip of his tongue to the roof of his mouth. The caustic acid went down the snake's throat, causing it to release Michael's head and allowing him to breathe fresh air. He slashed the snake's head and scurried to the banks while two of the women shot at the snake. Jim and other women kept taking potshots at movement in the brush.

While trying to inhale enough air, Michael took one more grenade and threw it downstream, causing an explosion to draw the giant vermin away. They quickly made their way further down the path. While moving, Michael called Brandish, saying, "We've got the women, but we need you to keep bombing the headquarters side of the stream to keep the forest away from us. Tell you why later." They were too scared to stop for breaks.

They blasted four more snakes and a sizable four-legged predator that approached them on the way. Three hours later, everyone reached the transport, worn out but alive. Brandish was radioed for take-off cover, and seven fighters swooped into position to protect the ascent.

After everyone was in and Michael sat with Jim as he opined, "I guess that's why there were no soldiers in the woods. The snakes did the job for them."

Michael took off and looked at his dashboard when an alarm sounded, "We've been spotted. They're coming after us."

Descrim's surface-to-air spotted the extraction team and initiated fire. Descrim's squad was alerted to the take-off and intercepted the extraction team and the transport. Brandish was signaled to come to rescue the extraction team.

Descrim's voice came over the comm, "I am going to blow you into quarks, Knight Bear."

Jim yelled, "Why is Descrim on our frequency? I see them coming from two o'clock high."

Michael yelled, "Shoot at them with whatever we have!"

The extraction team leader came on saying, "This is what we live for, Knight Bear. Team, two o'clock high!"

Michael yelled, "Go get 'em!"

Five of the seven exit squad fighters joined the battle with Descrim's larger wing. They were gallant and bought precious time for the escape. The sound from the comm roared out, "For Tol! For Tol!"

Jim was using the cannon atop the transport to shoot toward the oncoming enemy. Michael yelled, "Throw something at them, anything we've got! I'm trying to get us out of here!"

Descrim and his wingman broke free of the others to chase the transport. "I'm coming after you, Knight Bear!"

The women, hearing this, began to scream loudly, to which Michael responded, "Quiet, so I can think about flying this ship!" The sound died down to muddled apprehension.

Jim yelled, "We've been outflanked. We have no rear defense!"

An order from the comm yelled, "Turn!" The two fighters turned right while the transport turned left, to avoid being hit by fire.

Jim tried to shoot at Descrim, only the warlord stayed below the cannon fire line. Descrim moved around to the front while the other two fighters could not get around the wingman.

Descrim announced over the comm, "You single-handedly wrecked my headquarters, so I want to pay you back. Too bad I will not be able to keep the third-planet women. I wanted to be the one to destroy you. The other warlords are going to be jealous."

Grasping for anything to delay his demise, Michael tried to talk, "Hey warlord, you are going to shoot down an unarmed transport? Doesn't that seem a bit unsporting? We are sitting unarmed in the middle of space."

Descrim laughed and said, "You don't have anything left, Knight Bear, so let me blow you into a trillion parts." Descrim rubbed his hands, put his finger on the trigger, and said, "Goodbye, Knight—"

The fighter exploded in front of the transport. Another voice yelled out over the comm, "Goodbye, Descrim! Hey, Knight Bear, you're lucky I made it on time."

Michael yelled, "Boy, am I glad to see you!"

Everyone on board jumped for joy, yelling and screaming. Michael yelled, "Please, quiet so I can hear!"

Brandish admonished Michael, saying, "You almost got yourself killed not turning with the other two fighters."

Michael heard the displeasure in the commander's voice. Trying to deflect the seriousness, Michael said, "I guess you will need to give me fighter pilot lessons. Let's take these gals back to safety."

Brandish ended the transmission without acknowledgment. Michael sat back in the pilot's seat, blowing out a deep breath.

Once the forces on the planet knew Descrim was dead, the ground commander called for a surrender. Descrim's space fleet commander rallied the remaining forces to slow Sargen's and Brandish's advance on Buentos's sector even with the primary planet's loss.

The loss of life on both sides was tragic. Still, parochial pride ran deep in all quarks. They knew their fiefdom was lost, yet they fought on for their own honor. The continued spirited resistance slowed Sargen's and Brandish's momentum, allowing the fugitive warlords more time to prepare.

Buentos found out that Descrim had been killed in battle from the listening station set up by the fake mining expedition. Buentos collected Heimerlich's and Maldonate's essence technology before Sargen or Brandish could get there. About one-quarter of Contronto's fighters made it to Buentos's headquarters. The mood in the office was desperate, with thoughts of all the lives and hardware they had lost because warlords had listened to Alchemy.

12/18/2023
Areanosten Planet Five
Tol HQ Compound
Quark Dimension

Michael, Sargen, Robin, and Jim had a meeting about how they would proceed from here to recover the essences and the women. They knew that the final ten hostages were with Buentos, who had escaped the destruction so far. Brandish was due back soon to report on progress and losses and regroup for the final push.

Sargen said, "If I knew what you could do with those essences, I might have tried one on myself to see what happened. They did help you two."

Michael cut his eyes at Sargen and, without moving his head, said, "They come at a high cost."

Sargen continued, "Something else that hinders us is dealing with these women and not obliterating these planets to be done with it."

Michael wanted to stop this train of thought before it went to the next sentence. He pounded both hands on the table, causing it to crack. He leaned over, baring his teeth with his snout inches from the warlord's face. The guards aimed their blasters at Michael. In a slow, firm voice, Michael said, "Sargen, let me say before your guards try to shoot my ass, I saved your sorry life when Alchemy had his weapon trained on your head, about to pull the trigger. All I want to do in return is save ten more women, then go home and never see any of y'all again. You can then have this miserable dimension for your own."

Sargen held up his hand and said, "Stand down, guards. This meeting is adjourned until Commander Brandish returns to the sector with the troop strength numbers, information, and territory recovered. We are going to need Brandish's assessment of the space around that sector to plan the best assault route." He then spoke to

Michael directly. "You know, Knight Bear, that saving this last group will be the toughest. They know what you are coming for."

"So be it. I'm hungry." Michael slowly drew back, rose from his seat, and headed out the door. Jim and Robin followed.

The time had flown by, twelve weeks since their capture from Earth and their routine, unassuming lives, blissfully ignorant of the cosmos beyond their sight that had come stealing them away. Michael, Robin, and Jim made their way to the dining hall buffet. Knowing to look for Knight Bear, the staff made sure to give him a platter and extra-large utensils to nourish his frame. They went to their table fitted for Michael. The dining area still had repair scaffolding on the north side. Tol's portrait had come through the battle with only its frame damaged. Otherwise the hall seemed almost normal.

Michael began halfway through the meal, "You know, those last ten have been hostages for this whole time."

Robin said, "In my psychiatry days, I spent a year treating PTSD among victim groups. I can only imagine their desperation right now. This last group is going to need help on the ground when we encounter them. You need me to go with you to help."

Jim said, "Are you sure that's wise? Do you want to take that risk? It's not a sure thing that Michael and I will make it back."

Robin looked back sternly, saying, "What makes you think we are not all in this together?"

Michael answered, so Jim did not need to give in, "She's going with us when the fleet makes its push on Buentos. By the way, Robin, you look a little different."

Robin quipped, "Yes, I've been hungrier lately, stress. I may have put on a few pounds. Whatever. For so many years, you've only seen me in a lab coat anyway." She flashed a sheepish smile.

Michael reflected for a moment but dismissed it when Jim got his attention. Jim asked, "What about other machines like the one that Gimmish shot into our eyes? How many more of those things are there?"

Michael said to Jim and Robin, "What if Gimmish is there and lets the others know about what he did to us and tries to use whatever talents his essences have to augment his battle force? We need to ask those who watch this Game what kind of talents the gamers used from Buentos's, Heimerlich's, Maldonate's, and Controto's gamer teams. As we both found out, humans became receptive acquirers and users of these new, shall I say, powers. I know they will be experimenting with these traits on their troops and possibly the women they captured, especially if one or two became swayed in some 'Stockholm syndrome' sort of way. That's why Robin is needed to treat these poor people."

Jim added, "And Gimmish is crazy enough to try some sort of scheme like that. We must be careful not to distress those women when we are trying to free them. However, I don't believe these warlords have the subtle nature to persuade them, and none of them know about women."

Robin looked at Jim with a raised eyebrow, thought for a few seconds, and said, "If you were back on Earth, I would sense a bit of sarcasm in that statement. However, in the context of the present situation, your statement makes perfect sense."

Jim replied, "Maybe so, but we must think of all scenarios so that we aren't surprised."

Robin nodded in agreement and smiled. "We need Sargen's help to find these essence machines and account for them for their own protection. You never know what kind of essence you can find."

12/30/2023
Tol HQ Compound
Areanosten Planet Five
Quark Dimension

Sargen and Brandish knew that it was Tol and Heimerlich who had developed the essence extraction technology. The research was a secret that Tol had guarded in a place only he could biometrically access; therefore it was presumed lost. The essences and their capture devices needed to be retrieved as soon as possible to prevent their misuse.

A collection request was communicated along with the news report of Tol's death. Condolences came from all the neutral warlords with word that they would return their machines in his honor. Philimar and Cooperon accepted the promise and delivered their technology to Sargen's forces patrolling Heimerlich's former zone near Descrim's sector border. Flashenol destroyed his and sent the pieces in a box to Sargen's sector. Rezfen communicated, "Let the machines die along with their creators." That left at least nine devices and thirty-six essences left to account for, most likely held in Buentos's sector.

Brandish returned to the headquarters with intelligence about enemy preparations. The meeting began with him saying, "Sargen, Knight Bear, Jim, Robin, the enemy is building a solid defense that could take far more effort the longer we wait. Here is what they have now. To get to Buentos's headquarters, we need to pass or obliterate three planets in our path. This will be time-consuming."

Robin said, "No kidding. He had that many more life-sustaining planets in his sector?"

Sargen said, "No. Buentos has always had outposts. He was the one with the mining operation listening in on Maldonate."

Jim asked, "So how well fortified are these three planets?"

Brandish explained, "Two are run by outpost staff who are like sentries. They are in atmospheric pods dotted around the planet with central control communicating. To stop the threat, all must be destroyed."

Michael said, "Like blockchain."

Brandish said, "That may be what it is called on your planet. Now the third planet is a staging port for large attacks. It should be avoided if the mission wants to proceed quickly."

Sargen said, "So what do you propose? Or should I ask, is there an easier way?"

Brandish said, "Only with Rezfen's permission. We would need to travel through his sector."

Robin said, "Then get his permission. He is the one who showed the greatest empathy in regards to Master Tol's death. Couch it as a favor in his memory."

Sargen perked his head and remarked, "Now you're thinking like a quark."

When the three tellurians got to the transport, Brandish's lieutenant showed them the craft's weaponry and briefed them on their part of the plan, which did not include Robin. Michael informed the aide that she had to be onboard for prisoner debriefing and medical treatment. The aide gave her a puzzled look about her shape, since he had never seen a woman before. She shocked him when she introduced herself with a higher-pitched voice. The aide shook her hand and felt physical attraction.

· She said to him, "It is very nice to meet you, Lieutenant. I am looking forward to successfully completing this mission."

He smiled and continued with the briefing. "The plan is similar to the previous assault on Warlord Descrim's sector. We in the fleet are supposed to rain havoc on the enemy to neutralize their defenses and eliminate any means of escape for the enemy warlords. Your mission is to land on the surface and find and free the ten hostages. We expect this to be your toughest mission, since we assume the escaped warlords took refuge with Buentos, and they will know what we are coming for. We need to assume the enemy has proceeded down the learning curve."

Robin remarked, "That was an excellent use of a metaphor, Lieutenant."

The lieutenant blushed and could only mumble, "Thank you."

Michael said, "Continue, Lieutenant," and gave Robin an annoyed look since he knew she was flirting with the naïve alien.

"Warlord Sargen and Commander Brandish ordered all available personnel and hardware to be involved. A specific size defense force was readied to guard against raids back here in our sectors. All leaves were rescinded until the battle has been won and the cosmos secured. The first wave of fighters led by Sargen's flight commander and battle cruisers are ready to launch on their way to engage the enemy. The forces will include those warriors from Heimerlich and Maldonate who joined to avenge their fallen comrades who were attacked without provocation and their home planets destroyed. Commander Brandish will be leading the second wave, including your ship, in the landing force capable of bringing land cruisers and heavy weaponry provisions to land ten thousand fighters. We expect heavy casualties due to the desperate mindset of the enemy. Expect anything."

Then the lieutenant went to a table to show them a map. "Here is a satellite map of the area within a fifty-mile radius from the warlord's headquarters complex. You will notice that, unlike Descrim and Contronto, Buentos has a more heavily fortified, multilayered campus, so it is unknown where the holding cells are located. You will need heavy weaponry even to approach this fortress. The area is arid, so the vegetation does not provide good cover. The mission is going to depend much on cloaking technology. We will need to do it from space with the battle cruisers and overhead with fighters. We will need to land outside the range of the artillery from the fortress to set up our advancing forces. This does not mean we can land safely. We do not know what kind of ground army they have to greet us, so we need to be careful."

He pointed to a ridge of hills about thirty miles northeast of the headquarters city. "We will plan to land our forces behind this ridge to keep a barrier between us and the city. We can protect the camps easier while air cover allows us to take the high ground for scouting the city. Our first goal will be to secure the ridge. We hope the battle cruisers soften the battlefield where this ridge is to make our entry smoother. The initial battle group was instructed to fire from the southwest to disrupt their supply lines to our proposed landing area. The battle cruisers will cease their shelling when the ground informs the air the ridge is secure.

"The force will continue its bombardment of the fortress headquarters for the next period of light, softening their defenses for the battle. Knight Bear, you will be in the second group advancing to the fortress complex with those you choose. I suggest that you go in a five-person squad to be nimble yet have enough eyes to cover or alert you to attacks. I also suggest the doctor not go with you since it seems its stature is smaller than normal."

Michael retorted, "Does that include her ability to carry and fire a weapon? She can decide if she is up to this, but my instinct is to have a medical person where you need them the most, on the front line."

Robin graciously added, "Why, thank you, Michael, for letting me have a choice in this decision. Even though I spend my time now in labs, I did provide emergency medicine during my career."

Michael answered, "You're full of surprises, aren't you? Then you're going."

Robin sat back and smiled.

The lieutenant went on, "Now as we advance to the city on land cruisers, we will have air cover, but there is no guarantee you will not encounter resistance on the thirty-mile trek across an open plain. The six-passenger land cruisers will be armed with two gunneries on each end of the craft for self-defense. You will be in a formation with twenty other craft third from the right so not be in the center nor on the end, for your safety. The land cruisers can climb to a two-story altitude from the surface you travel over. You will approach the target quickly, but that does not mean you will not encounter resistance. For this purpose, the cruisers are equipped with forwarding shields to repel projectiles, so do not turn often and leave yourselves exposed during oncoming fire."

Michael whispered to Jim, "Do these people like to repeat themselves?"

Robin said, "Be quiet. He's doing it for emphasis."

Everyone agreed and made their way to the mobile armory to choose and fit weapons.

Michael chose the largest belts and gear so he could load up as much as possible. After he finished, he noticed Robin looking in a mirror fitting an ammo belt around her waist with the chest strap between her breasts, over her left shoulder, and down her back. She fixed grenades and magazines to her belt and strap and chose two weapons, one handgun-sized blaster and another with a long barrel.

Michael quipped to her, "Shall we get you a membership to the NRA when we get home? How about an NRA pinup girl?"

She smiled and said, "Maybe. My ex talked me into getting firearms trained. It's now coming in handy—and no pinup, although the compliment is flattering."

"Want to go hunting when we get back to Earth?"

"Will we be hunting for bear?"

"You had to say that."

"Yes, and I think you were flirting with me." The fur on Michael's face hid his blushing.

Jim said, "You two can load up all you want. I'm traveling light and concealable so I can blend in with the wall. A pistol and a knife make great weapons."

Michael's strength allowed him to carry enough armament for fifty soldiers, so enough for thirty was easy. All loaded their weaponry into the small transport with another eighty soldiers who boarded and filled the remaining seats. Everyone introduced themselves to each other and made ready for take-off. The assigned pilot listened and received the order to launch and slowly rose off the flight deck to join their twenty-ship wing of the armada.

Over the speaker, the voice of Sargen came through, saying, "To the entire fighting force, I wish for your safety and success. This will be the decisive battle of this campaign, so after we defeat the forces of the remaining rebel warlords, we will celebrate peace in the cosmos. However, many lives were and will be lost with this needless war given to us by these purveyors of the past. I daresay some of you may perish in this fight for liberation, but we must win the war, or more carnage will wreck the cosmos, affecting our lives for as long as we exist. They want domination of all to meet their evil needs. We are all that is in their way of bringing darkness and death to our universe. I choose life and peace so more can live. May your travels and trials be successful because the fate of the universe is in your hands."

With that, Commander Brandish ordered the fleet to head to the battle lines at hyper speed. As they traveled, they were told the battle group that had finished off Descrim, were keeping Buentos's fighters busy, pushing them back all the way to his sector. They knew that when the first wave of fighters arrived, they would be relieved to go back and be the defensive force to protect the rear. When the first wave came and released the fighters, they took refueling from a tanker and sped back to the sectors. As a part of the second wave, they passed them halfway through Alchemy's captured territory.

Brandish told the squad leader the plan and informed him of Master Tol's fate. The entire squad agreed to double their resolve to protect and defend the fiefdom. Brandish complimented them on their accomplishments with a light blaster salute on a nearby small asteroid, blowing it to pieces.

Rezfen allowed the armada to pass through, avoiding two outpost planets. The third was defeated with long-range asteroid buster missiles. This cleared the way for the attack on the enemy's main headquarters.

The first wave began their campaign with a blistering bombardment from all battle cruisers targeting the headquarters city. The population realized why Buentos had the underground dug so deep—although structures were decimated, and many turned to rubble, which helped shield the bunkers from cruiser bombardment. Anti-ship weapons fired from the surface, trying to hit any of these attackers. Fighters swooped toward the surface, engaging in combat with any comers. The decisive battle was beginning in earnest.

1/8/2024
Buentos HQ Compound
Demarco Planet Four
Quark Dimension

Contronto and Gimmish waited for Buentos to discuss the planet's defenses in the war room since the outer fortifications had been overwhelmed by Sargen's and Tol's forces plus the remnants of Heimerlich's and Maldonate's fighters. Gimmish's treachery to Heimerlich and the ambush of Maldonate's fiefdom had inspired their surviving warriors to perform beyond their skills out of sheer rage and revenge. The allied warlords knew it and were preparing to do what they could to save themselves.

Gimmish pointedly asked Buentos when he arrived late for the meeting, "Where the hell have you been? Don't you know if we don't find a way out of this, we all are dead?"

Buentos replied, "Yes, and I took liberties with another third-planet being to enjoy myself one more time before we fight. It was worth it. If we don't survive, I now have experienced something greater than power. My two best guards have brought her with them to allow us to feel more motivated." Light rings held the battered woman in a fetal position. Her clothes were in tatters from being forcibly removed repeatedly.

Gimmish asked, "And what might that be, you idiot?"

"Ah, something the third planet has used to populate their planet—sex, they call it."

Gimmish said, "You gave me a thought. They are coming, but they are not going to destroy this planet because the third-planet beings will try to rescue these ten hostages. We will either use them to destroy that Knight Bear, divert them, or deal them in a trade and escape.

"Let's plan for any scenario since it will be our only way out. Also, I learned something from that Knight Bear who sliced Alchemy to pieces and caused me to lose much of the use of my arm right now.

These essences we gamers used have powers for their games, but I dumped mine into that Bear thing and his third-planet buddy when we captured them the first time. They used them to escape and cause havoc in the headquarters. That thing, Bear or whatever, killed the entire guard less one with a fury never seen. It was unstoppable."

Contronto added, "That thing did a number on my headquarters too. I have never seen anything like it in all my years. It was all I could do to escape and come here. Not only did we deal with Sargen's and Tol's formidable forces, that monster-like creature also wrecked our whole inner area, destroying everything in its path, killing every soldier it could."

Buentos added, "I understand how Knight Bear can be so determined about these creatures. I now want them with me for the rest of my existence." The other two warlords were surprised at Buentos's seriousness.

1/9/2024
Light Battle Cruiser
Orbiting Demarco Planet Four
Quark Dimension

Jim asked Michael, "Can you get a hold of Brandish to see how things are going? It seems long."

Michael said, "I can see on the monitor that Buentos is prepared for us. He has knocked out one full battle cruiser and other transports that were part of the first wave. We need to get down on that planet and get those women before Sargen or Brandish pulls the plug on this landing and sends in the asteroid busters."

Robin came to Michael's side to look at the monitor and watch the destroyed battle cruiser break up as small explosions continued to detonate on the doomed ship. "All those lives!"

Jim said, "That's war. Ugly, universally ugly. I had an uncle who saw men die while holding a hill position during the Battle of the Bulge. He would never say anything more."

Michael said, "Let me call Brandish now. We need to get down there to see if the ten women are still alive. They should be accounted for for their families' sake."

Brandish answered the comm, "Can't talk now. Heavy fighting. Will call you when we are finished clearing the landing area."

After the call, Michael said, "I knew the job of the fighters was to knock out any infrastructure that enabled communication or transportation. The battle cruisers are pounding the ground constantly waiting for a sign of surrender, but there is no word."

Robin piped in, "I'm coming too. Women need to take care of each other."

Jim said with an incredulous tone, "How are you going to help this mission?"

Michael looked at her quizzically and said, "I don't remember you being this tall. The top of your head is further up my arm than it used to be. Is there something you are not telling us?""

Robin delayed then said, "Watch. When I found out your secret tricks and how you got them. I asked a guard to show me where you stored those essence devices."

Michael said, "No, you—"

"Yes, I did. I talked the guard into letting me into the room and found all sorts of things the gamers had, like this." Robin held her hand out, and all the light left the area around a chair, moving the light to another part of the room. "And I found all these traits to choose from. I used the device on myself."

Michael said, "Now what was that?"

Robin answered, "I can now bend light to stop entering a certain space and move it to another to use it as a diversion. And now watch this." The light separated into a rainbow and showed up on the wall, making the wall different colors as the light bent. "You're Knight Bear, I'm going to call myself Prism. I investigated more, but they were minimal in usefulness alone. I combined two essences so this could be useful in allowing me to move or block light in part or whole."

"How long did you stay in that room?"

"Oh, about three or four hours at a time on four occasions researching. They were labeled, so I was able to combine things to find a useful combination."

"You experimented on yourself?"

"I guess you can call it that, in a sense. But I knew the traits and calculated the worth to produce an optimal outcome for myself. You did it to yourself."

"You heard Tol. They gave me that disease without me knowing that it was supposed to kill me. I had to do something or die. I did it out of desperation, but now I am a freak forever. Did you really want to risk that?"

"I did it to help us save those ten women. I felt that we needed all the help we could get. I did it to win and help us go home. And you didn't even notice what I was wearing."

"Well, you look good, but not fitting right up top. No women's sizes in this dimension, I see?"

"True. Best I could do for my first time in battle. They said it was blaster-resistant, like Kevlar."

"What's done is done. Get ready." Michael left his seat, finding Robin more attractive. Without thinking, she moved around showing her more defined figure. Michael's heart jumped while he kept his eyes on her. As he was exiting the room, he knocked his head on the door frame, not looking ahead. "Crap."

Robin replied, "Karma. Is there anything to eat onboard?"

Jim remarked, "Robin, I agree with Michael. Still, even with our changes, we almost didn't make it back." Jim took a second look too.

Michael thought, *Hold your temper. One, two, three ….* He sat along the side of the cabin.

She noticed the look but did not react. Instead, the determined Robin looked Jim in the eyes, pointed at him with her opened hand with a bent elbow, and with a straight face quietly said, "I'm going to go and help save those ten women. You are going to be glad I did this. Trust me." Jim looked at her without saying a word.

The pilot, chuckling while listening in on the conversation, said, "Don't worry. I will arrange a meal when we get to the ground."

Two hours later, the comm drew Michael's attention. He said, "It's Brandish. This may be our cue."

"Knight Bear, we have landed behind the ridge. It's time for your group to land. Be advised, we landed under heavy fire."

"Jim is with the pilot now. I can't fit in the seat up there."

The pilot broke in, "Commander, they are training their fire on our entry points. Another transport has been hit, and the ship's escape pods have been deployed. I hope our shields can withstand a direct hit because they are getting close. What is your status on neutralizing those weapons?"

"A strike group is attacking the anti-craft battery as we speak. We should find out about their success in a very few minutes."

Jim stayed with the pilot to learn about entry procedures. They began to get ready for entry into the atmosphere. Ten minutes later, the vessel broke the stratospheric barrier. Jim yelled, "Here we go, folks! Hold on to your seats." At the same time, they drew fire as their group made its approach and fiery entry of the planet. They passed by a disabled transport that had entered twenty minutes earlier. They saw its emergency escape pods deploying. Another ship charged with collecting survivors passed beneath them toward the doomed ship. The flares of the explosions on the ridge were visible on approach. Much less flak exploded near the vehicle, letting them know the strike group was accomplishing their mission, but it still came.

An explosion knocked the craft off its descent trajectory. Michael saw a breach in the fuselage and yelled, "We've been hit on the port side. We are losing pressure." The edges of the hole became fiery red as the friction from the rapid descent caused the metal to glow. The cabin pressure rapidly dropped. Emergency oxygen was deployed.

Michael shoved struggling Robin into a seat behind the pilot to keep her from being sucked toward the breach.

He turned around to see a metal cabinet tearing off from the wall, all the equipment bouncing around in the cabin. A split second later, he ripped it loose from its last anchor and smashed it against the wall to cover the hole. The cabinet began fusing with the hot metal to partially seal the rupture. Michael, gasping, grabbed an air mask and took a deep breath.

Jim yelled, "What's the status?"

Michael answered, "I'm holding a cabinet against the opening to slow the cabin decompression so we can reach the ground in one piece. Get me something for my hands. This metal is getting hot!" Five soldiers from the back compartment came forward with fireproof equipment to join in the emergency.

The pilot yelled, "We are not clear yet!"

From another direction, new enemy fire shot up from the ground. As the vessel continued to approach the planet's surface, the pilot performed more evasive maneuvers that jerked the passengers in the cabin. Michael and three of the five soldiers held the cabinet in place as best they could against the g-forces. The pilot saw more ground fire. He yelled, "Incoming!" and jerked the transport to starboard. Everyone holding the cabinet was thrown off. One of the quarks hit his head on a support beam. Blood began to stream from his head. Robin got on the floor and crawled to tend to the unconscious soldier. All who could reach the cabinet grabbed and pushed it back to cover the opening again. Michael yelled, "How close are we?"

The pilot said, "Not as close as I want to be."

Another hit, this time in the back. The pilot yelled, "We only have one engine now!" Smoke began to come from the rear cabin. The front chamber became crowded with the soldiers trying to escape the smoke. Everyone passed around the emergency oxygen. Again the pilot yelled, "Here we go! The landing is going to be rough!"

On the ground, the landing area was a small road not meant for handling flying craft of any kind. As the ground grew closer, Jim looked around instinctively for any padding. The pilot's steely gaze showed he had every intention of finessing a successful landing.

Michael barked out, "We are as ready to land now as we will ever be. I think we can hold the cabin together. Tell us when you are going to make your move." *Lord, help us. Lord, help us—Lord, help us!*

Michael watched as the pilot gave the cockpit commands. "To be able to land without crashing, everyone needs to hold on tight where they are. Everyone ready? Five, four, three, two, one, *now!*" He pulled up the nose and barrel-rolled at the same time. He hit the throttle firing the one remaining engine as his brake. Half of the soldiers could not hold on and flew across the cabin. Robin slid across the floor from the injured soldier into Michael's ribcage with a thud. Robin said, "God, you're like hitting a boulder."

With the wheels deployed, the pilot powered down the engine with the nose still in the air. The craft came down on the rear landing gear and dropped the front hard enough to crack the top of the cabin like an egg. The nose fell to the ground. Then from the back, a soldier yelled, "Fire in the back!"

There was no time for words. They knew the fuselage was ruptured, causing the fuel cells to leak explosive gas and ignite. The pilot ordered, "Abandon ship, starboard side! We don't have much time." He knew the port side of the fuselage was too hot and could explode at any moment. The soldiers had practiced the drill. No one skipped a beat, trying to exit the ship as orderly and quickly as possible.

Michael picked up Robin and got in line like the others. As he passed the cockpit, Jim looked at the pilot sitting, watching the rest, and said, "Get up and get out of here."

The pilot said, "I'm last off. Go!" With one arm, Michael pulled Jim out of the seat and into line with Robin and him.

Michael said, "Quit arguing with him. The sooner we all get off, the sooner he will come. Let's go!" Michael looked back to see the fire beginning to spread. The three of them jumped out of the wreckage and ran to cover. All three looked back with Jim saying, "Pilot, come on, come on!" Finally they saw the pilot's hat poke out the nose.

Rooting for the pilot to survive, Robin called, "Please hurry. Hurry!" He got to the fuselage, and *boom!* The craft exploded in a fireball. Six other escaping soldiers became engulfed in flames and rolled around on the ground.

Michael yelled, "We've got to help!"

Robin said, "What will we use?"

Michael said, "Go get blankets and first aid. I have a thought. Watch!" Michael ran towards the soldiers and dug and threw soft dirt between his legs onto the burning warriors. He yelled, "Roll in the dirt." They did what they were told. The loose soil helped retard the flames enough to give time to other aid workers.

Jim, Robin, and other soldiers grabbed whatever they could from other vehicles to help save the blast victims, wrapping them in blankets when they arrived. Two of the six soldiers and the pilot died. The others were alive but badly burned.

Buentos's forces put up a stiff fight on the ridge. Still, the fire from the overhead battle cruisers gave the second wave an unfair advantage. After thinking about their own safety and that they were not going to survive the onslaught, many defenders surrendered to the initial forces on the ground.

Robin, Michael, and Jim walked to a ground transport that took them to the encampment. Battered and bruised, they were shown the quarters where all three were to stay.

Robin remarked, "I guess they assume there are no separate quarters for gender."

Jim said, "We won't look."

After settling in, they walked up to a table in the officers' tent to see the same map they saw when Brandish first gave them details of the rescue plan. They noticed there were more arrows and graphics written on the surface for presentation. Robin kept looking around the tent for food.

The officer began, "We all heard about Master Tol. The entire battalion wants me to offer our condolences to Commander Brandish and others who are deeply affected by his unfortunate demise."

Michael nodded to acknowledge his approval. The officer continued, "The first wave's mission is ready for the next and hazardous phase of traveling over the open plain for thirty kilometers to reach the enemy headquarters. The plan is for the cruisers overhead and fighters to provide covering fire to reduce the incoming fire from the enemy defenses. We may lose one-third of our attacking force in this charge. We will be exposed while moving, even with cloaking devices. They won't see individual targets, but the light will be moved, and they can shoot at the visual distortions. We think their remaining fighters may be diverted to the charge to show resolve that they will be tough to uproot, and we may be willing to retreat to avoid too many casualties. These arrows signify the best routes to move to attack across the plain because they have been prepared for us to arrive sooner rather than later. We will prepare for the charge at first light tomorrow. It may be the worst day of our lives. It's time for nourishment before we rest."

After the main briefing, Brandish took the three travelers aside to discuss their roles. "Knight Bear, Robin, Jim: for you to reach the target clandestinely, you will need to leave at first light. I will supply a cloaking hovercraft. Still, the faster you move, the easier it is to detect light distortions. Therefore it will take time to reach the landing point undetected. Once stopped, you are undetectable."

Jim asked, "Is there a guidance system that allows safe travel in darkness?"

Brandish answered, "Yes, but it is difficult to travel in wooded areas due to the density of obstructions. It is better to travel at first light when you can see where you are going. We will begin our advance soon after you. You will hear all commands over the secure comm link."

Michael added, "And we are to signal you of our progress when we can?"

Brandish said, "Correct. We need to know when to fully attack and finish this war. We are depending on you three having success. Now, let's all get something to eat, then get some rest."

At that moment, Robin sat straight in her chair with a blank distant look on her face. Jim noticed and asked, "What's wrong, Robin?"

She said, "Need to eat, now." She stood and abruptly walked out of the meeting.

Michael asked, "Where is she going?"

Jim said, "I think to the meal tent."

Michael said, "I think I'll join her."

The three followed Robin. Brandish asked, "Is she in a trance?"

Michael said, "Like a zombie. I knew something bad would happen when she told us she gave herself those essences."

An alarmed Brandish said, "She did what?"

Michael said, "I'm so damn mad. Let's catch up and get her something to eat before someone gets hurt."

Brandish went ahead to alert the staff to get a table ready.

Michael said, "We really don't need these distractions. The night before we attack, and she goes zombie!" He walked to the front of the line, grabbed a piece of bread, showed it to her, then tersely said, "Eat this now!" Heads turned at the words.

She took the bread and ate a two-inch-thick piece of bread in four bites. He gave her another, which she consumed just as fast.

After the second piece, Robin's eyes became less distant. Jim asked her, "Are you all right?"

She cut her eyes at Jim, looking embarrassed, and in a low voice said, "Still very hungry."

Walking through the dinner line, the mess servers behind the counter handed out the meal trays for the diners at each table. Most took two large trays to feed eight. Jim and Michael took two each for the four at the commander's table. Brandish sat first, directing the earthlings to their seats.

Michael noticed Brandish's puzzled look at the amount of food on the table. Robin sat down across from the commander, giving him an embarrassed smile, and started eating. Minutes later, Michael noticed her continued ravenous look as her second helping quickly disappeared and she served herself a larger third.

Michael quipped, "Robin, my dad used to say I had a hollow leg to fill with all the food I ate. It looks like you have two hollow legs."

Robin didn't say a word as she ate the third helping. When finished with that helping, she again reached for the serving spoon. Michael noticed and said, "We're going to get you a plate with some sideboards, either that or a feedbag." Michael gave her another look of feigned surprise.

She looked back and said, "Well, look how much you ate."

He let it fly, "I am as big as a grizzly bear. What's your excuse?" Jim and Brandish froze.

She threw the spoon into the serving tray, then stood up, leering at Michael. Her mouth quivered with anger. She grabbed the tray then and stormed out of the dining tent with it.

Jim, aghast at Michael's behavior, slammed his hand on the table. "Whatever she has done to herself, we can't change it, and we need her to help us. She has to live with her decision, so you didn't need to rub her face in it. By the way, brother, I didn't tell you to double that second stem cell DNA dose either." Jim finished with his meal, got up, and stalked out of the hall, following Robin.

Brandish sat back, crossing his arms, looking at Michael, and said, "That did not go well. Think now. Would any of us want to fight and possibly die with you now?" Michael's head popped back, his eyes becoming big as saucers. He continued, "You now have eight hours to repair the morale damage that an orbital frigate bombardment could not have inflicted. See me in my tent one hour before you leave, or I will have my forces lay Buentos's headquarters, to rubble."

Michael protested, "But you—"

Brandish stood and looked Michael straight in the eyes, put his hand up, and said, "To help you and the third planet was Tol's pledge, not mine. Disrespect one of my quarks like you did Robin, and I will leave your ass here." Brandish turned and walked out of the tent.

Michael took one more bite then left to walk to the tent. He arrived outside the tent to the sounds of sobbing. He took a deep breath and peeked in to see Robin with Jim consoling her and an empty serving tray to one side. Michael sat down on the ground outside, thinking, *Okay, smart guy. You got yourself into one hot mess.* He sat to the side where he would not be noticed for a while, trying to think of the right thing to do or say.

Jim tapped him on the shoulder, startling the brooding Knight Bear. "What are you doing out here?"

With the crestfallen look of a scolded puppy dog rather than a fierce bear, Michael said, "I was an obnoxious shit to Robin."

"Yes, you were. You hurt the lady."

"Yep, smart people do dumb things too. I never left my trash-talking on the football field."

He walked into the tent with his eyes to the ground. Robin looked at him with her tears and swollen face and said to him, "You think you can say sorry, and it will be all better? The only and I mean the *only* reason I don't stay here and try to go home are those ten women. I took the risk to myself because I felt I needed to better our chances of walking into a highly fortified compound of aliens who would kill us as soon as look at us."

Michael started, "I want to say—"

She interrupted, "Don't! After giving myself those essences, I have gained about forty pounds, grown three inches, eating whatever I can find, so my stomach doesn't cramp from hunger. I'm in this alien suit because I couldn't fit in my clothes any longer. This is the first time I phased out like I did. It scared the hell out of me. Then you go on your insult rant in front of others to stick your thumb in my eye. I will do my best, but it won't be for you." She looked the other way, saying, "Please leave."

Michael slinked out of the tent and saw Jim standing ten feet away with his arms crossed. With a stone face and a low voice, Jim said, "You're welcome." He passed Michael and entered the tent after knocking. He set his watch and found a spot behind the bushes at the tree line for three or four hours of sleep.

Without birds, there was no song in the woods. More explosions rumbled from the direction of their eventual destination. He was awakened by the guitar strumming from the same Apple watch that Anne had programmed before their coffee date at Ralph's near the hospital. He thought, *I hope God is taking better care of you since I didn't do such a great job.* Thinking of her choked him up.

Michael stood and brushed the dirt off his body, then walked over to Brandish's tent on all fours. He peered through the screen to see Brandish stretching out the morning stiffness. After he knocked on the door frame, Brandish said, "Enter."

Michael noticed the chair for him was too small. He told Brandish, "My rear end won't fit in this chair. I'll sit on the ground." He moved the chair and sat at the table. Michael's torso was large enough to function without a chair.

With a dead-serious face Brandish sat down and asked, "Are all three of you going?"

Michael said, "Yes."

Brandish said, "Your hovercraft is prepared for battle. We will be behind you monitoring your progress. Good luck. That is all." He got up from his chair and walked into another chamber.

Michael could tell that the events of the previous evening had soured their relationship. Suddenly, he felt very alone. He rolled onto all fours, sued his snout to open the door, and walked to the tent. Halfway there, he stopped, realizing he was walking instinctively like a bear. He thought about Jim calling out his hypocrisy. *How stupid of me doubling that second dose. I should have discarded it. Robin, I screwed up royally.*

Arriving at the tent, he saw Robin in a dimly illuminated corner combing her lengthening hair. He watched her flexing and moving her arm around, inspecting her noticeable body changes. She was larger, shoulders wider, more athletic like Anne. He could not tell whether she approved of herself or not. He did. He shook his head, not believing what he was thinking. *Minutes ago, I was thinking about Anne and now this. I am really scum.*

He cleared his throat and knocked on the door, looking away, ashamed of his thoughts. She said, "You can come in. Jim went to get some water for us."

Michael started, "I am truly sorry for my behavior last evening and how it hurt you. I am going to say when we get home—"

Robin interrupted, "Don't promise anything. Don't say anything. You may slip up and make it worse. I hurt, but I forgive you. Holding the anger will make it harder to survive today."

Jim walked in with the water. He handed Robin and Michael each a bottle. Robin finished hers without stopping and threw the empty container into the waste receptacle in one motion. She said, "I was thirsty." Michael offered his. She took it and repeated the action. She said, "Thanks." Both men were impressed.

Jim asked, "Are we ready?"

Michael answered, "Even if we weren't, we must leave in twenty minutes." Without another word, the three unintentional warriors took their gear and walked to the hovercraft. Brandish was waiting for them. When they stood next to their vehicle, Brandish said, "Before you leave, I want to wish you success. My aide will show you how to maneuver the ship. We will be listening for progress." With that, Brandish walked away toward his tent. The aide at the door silently asked them to enter the craft by tipping his head and pointing to the entrance with his hand.

After all four were on board, he closed the door and began teaching the earthlings the basics of the vehicle and the cloaking technology. He ended by saying, "Embedded in the technology is a voice-activated help application with a translator unit. Address the unit as 'Gome,' and then ask your question. Also, this craft has remote navigation. I am giving you each a sensor. You will be separated from your craft while completing your mission. You may need to escape a sudden danger. To activate the sensor, rapidly press the activator four times and the fifth time press and hold for four seconds. The craft will come to you wherever it can fit. If you press it twice and then four seconds, you can access Gome."

Michael asked, "Why didn't we get this information before now?"

He said, "This is the only craft like it. The technology is new and secret. Now I must leave. You are to begin your mission." With that, the stoic quark disembarked, closing and locking the entrance behind him.

Jim looked at the door after the aide left. "We have worn out our welcome. This is our last chance."

Robin looked at the two men. With a deep breath, she said. "We'd better go."

A larger pilot's seat had been installed for Michael, "Nice touch." In position, they started the vehicle. At once, the cloaking device engaged, making them invisible. A male voice emanated from the console, "My name is Gome. We are to navigate a preplanned route for this mission. At no time can this route be changed until the destination is reached. At that point, manual navigation systems will be enabled."

All three were speechless. Feeling the movement of the craft moving down the path, Michael said, "We had better learn about this gizmo and make a plan, knowing our only way home is through that alien compound."

1/10/2024
Buentos HQ Compound
Demarco Planet Four
Quark Dimension

Gimmish could not sleep that whole night. He thought about the stories from survivors about the fighting force they were about to encounter. The only good news was that Knight Bear was there, so he knew the hostages kept the attackers from leveling the compound with bombardments. He kept looking at the ceiling, searching for inspiration but finding only cracks. His shoulder hurt continually while his mind wandered with a dozen tangled thoughts.

He looked out the window to see the first light of dawn peer over the horizon. He looked at his ring, thinking, *I may have the record for the shortest reign of a warlord in history.* He sardonically chuckled.

He thought, *Buentos's forces are going to fail in the end. I need Bort to look at a transport to plan an escape.* He made the call.

Bort answered, "Yes, Warlord."

Gimmish liked the sound of the words. "Meet me at the flight deck within the hour. I need to go over something with you before you fly with your wing."

"I'll be there in less than half that time."

Gimmish hung up and walked down to the flight deck thinking, *Good thing Buentos left his ships cloaked.* They were scattered over the landscape away from the compound to escape the bombing. He continued to walk. When he got to the exit onto the flight deck, he reached for the handle. Bort opened the door from the other side, startling the fraudulent leader.

"Pardon me, Master Gimmish."

"That's fine. Let's plan. How soon do you expect to take off to fly cover?"

"Not long from now."

"Fine. I want you to use what pilots are left from our realm to help in case of an emergency. I need you to keep your comm open for my word and be ready to fall back on my command. I believe Alchemy's grand plan of conquest is destined to fail. They underestimated Sargen, Tol, and that Knight Bear. As the leader of the squadron, I will signal you by only saying your name once. When I do, order our force to return and run cover for our escape. I must now leave for a meeting. Good luck."

Gimmish and Bort saluted each other as they parted.

The meeting room was near the flight deck, which made for a short walk. He and Contronto met at the door simultaneously. Contronto said, "Good to see you. It's going to be a rough day." Both entered the room and sat in their chairs. Contronto added, "Buentos is late again."

Gimmish did not respond to the remark, instead asking, "How much of your squadron do you have? Sargen's frigates are pulverizing this planet. With all due respect, Alchemy underestimated our abilities. We need to think about our future."

Contronto's facial expression changed. "I know my emotions overrode my logic with Alchemy. My realm is gone. I don't think Sargen or Tol's replacement will have any mercy on us."

Gimmish said, "Let's plan where to use what we have in a defensive posture until Buentos arrives." The two desperate despots continued planning strategy.

A short time later, Buentos entered the room. He was the only one with a calm demeanor and a smile throughout the preparations. His two guards stood by, with an abused woman bound in light rings. She sat stone-faced, looking at the floor out of the one eye that was not swollen shut from beatings. The three warlords were informed of the landing and were able to guess the strategy to be used. As the cruisers continued their pounding of the complex, the defenses and shields held up reasonably well under the massive pressure, which they thought boded well for the morning.

Putting his best face on, Gimmish said, "I'm impressed with your stockpile of weapons, Warlord Buentos. We have enough here to make it a good fight against our foes and more. What made you secure all these weapons for good use?"

He answered, "I thought I would have needed them anytime Alchemy attacked me. I didn't trust him."

Gimmish smiled and remarked, "Fair." All three warlords got a chuckle out of that answer since Alchemy was always known as the most aggressive warlord.

Looking at the abused woman, Contronto asked Buentos, "Did you need to bring her? She has distracted you enough."

He replied, "She motivates me to work harder. Say it is a side effect of enjoying her body as much as I did. Also, she and the others are the reason we have the advantage and can predict the enemy's objective." The abused woman spit on the floor. "I like her moxie." He grabbed her face along the jawbone line holding it up for a good look. She snarled in defiance. He shoved her back onto the wall and laughed.

Gimmish said, "We need to redirect the defenses to point toward the plain before the mountains to have maximum fire trained on the formidable force. They are going to move against us. On the map of the plain's topography, I see the three ways a charge could be initiated toward the city."

Contronto said, "If they actually charge like we think, we will inflict high casualties with good aim. If I were them, I would not make a full charge from that point."

Gimmish answered, "Never underestimate the foolishness of the enemy to make a bad plan. You also must plan that this may be a huge decoy to move our thoughts away from the true plans. What else could an attack force do to charge this place?"

Buentos answered, "A more difficult approach can be made from the south and east of us, but we have no evidence of troop movement down there. All the landings took place on the other side of that ridge. I say they will be making a full-frontal charge, probably this morning at first light, knowing Sargen's history and tendencies."

Gimmish said, "It's unlike him to be so predictable. He must not be the commander of the forces on the ground. It has to do with trying to free the third-planet beings. First, they have not targeted our walls, I believe for their safety, and second, they do not know where in these walls the prisoners are. This poses an advantage for us using them as hostages. Let's split them into groups of two and disperse them around the building. What that does is force them to search longer and give us more time for us to pick them off."

Contronto said, "Good idea. Now, how and where?"

Gimmish asked Buentos, "Where are the difficult parts of the building to reach? I want to make one pair easy, to make them think that this mission will not go badly and set traps or hide the rest. Even if those two escape, the other eight will be harder to free. So you need to hide the pairs for the hardest searching paths with traps in place."

Buentos answered, "I know just where to place them and use the light rings to tie them to each spot. Now, I want both of you to guard two pairs. I will have a pair, with my guards protecting the other two pairs. I will tell them they can enjoy themselves with the captives if they succeed. You two will be near the getaway transport and come at the right time."

He turned to the guards and ordered, "The two of you, take this one and get the other nine. Bring them to us warlords so we can choose."

Contronto said, "I would like that."

Gimmish disagreed, "No, I need to ready the transport since I won't be that good in a fight with one arm." Little did the other two know Gimmish would not wait for anybody if it meant his skin. He had already lost effective use of an arm due to Michael the Knight Bear, and that was enough.

Buentos said, "Point taken. Okay, you do that. I will get other guards to take care of that pair."

Contronto asked, "How about surveillance? How can one monitor without power?"

Buentos cheerfully said, "Battery backup."

Gimmish said, "Good. I want to see that Knight Bear eliminated when he is caught."

They came to the holding cell, where the women were being held captive. The women were miserable in dirty tatters of clothing, unbathed and hungry. The food had been awful, and the only cleaning they were allowed was before Buentos was to have his pleasure with them.

Buentos chose two women he fancied; Contronto chose two Asians who attracted him. The guards took the last four, two each with a certain curiosity and expectation, and were led to their appointed places. Buentos primarily used two of the women given to the guards, one with a swollen face and broken, repeatedly hit for biting the warlord. The other was the abused woman who'd been brought to the meeting. Buentos then told the guards, "You two are some of the best quarks I have. Enjoy."

The five-story building had multiple places for holding captives, mainly for torture. One room was thought of as the easy hold. It was Buentos's main room, meant for experimentation and torture. It was set near a third-floor patio ledge where they thought the rescue party would enter. These hostages easy to rescue would require part of their group to escort them back to safety, leaving fewer to advance with the Knight Bear. Buentos hid his two in his office with a hidden door and an escape exit to the flight deck. Contronto held his in an office on the ground floor near an emergency exit with transport access. The chosen guards were stationed on the opposite side of the headquarters on the fourth and fifth floors. This dispersed the hostages far away from each other to make locating them as challenging as possible.

So, as the bombing was heard rising like thunder and the dust from the cracking walls filled rooms and hallways, the women were moved to their separate places as Buentos prescribed.

Gimmish heard the screaming and crying and asked Buentos, "With all that noise, is it still worth it?"

Buentos smiled and looked at his two new subjects. Quietly but firmly, he replied, "Yes, they are."

1/10/2024
The Approach to the Headquarters
Demarco Planet Four
Quark Dimension

As the earthlings left the encampment, Michael asked, "Gome, how do you know who the pilot is?"

The voice responded, "You have now activated the hovercraft's vehicle registration. I will now lead you through the process by asking specific requests. You will have access to the systems. The control panel on the dashboard is also a scanner. You will be asked one at a time to place both hands on the panel, look into the camera, and speak your name. Pilot, co-pilot, and navigator in that order." They followed directions. "You will now be trained on the critical systems of this craft."

Jim said, "I'm impressed."

Gome used holographic images to demonstrate the procedures and interactively train. Two hours later, Gome was finished with the introductory training course. The three marveled at the comprehensiveness of the instruction, which helped their confidence. Robin said, "That course reduced some of my anxiety."

Michael said, "You know we are the quark's guinea pigs. All this data is being transmitted back to their engineers for their use."

Robin said, "And they are learning how humans function under pressure. Whatever the outcome, they win."

Jim said, "Then let's give them a show. Gome, how soon until we reach our manual operation point?"

The voice responded, "You are not to know that until fifteen minutes beforehand."

Frustrated, Jim rapped his fingers on his chair arm.

Michael turned to the others and said, "Let's make a game plan. Robin, we need to know exactly what you can do, please."

Still stinging, Robin looked at Michael for a moment as if she resented answering his request. She blinked, holding back animus, and said, "Okay, here is something I worked on." She closed her eyes and faded out of sight. Seconds later, an item on the table disappeared. A moment later, she reappeared in two places. After that, one image merged into the other, after which Robin shook her head as if to become more alert.

Michael responded, "Wow. Anything else, Prism?"

She said, "Yes, there is." She walked next to Jim, and both disappeared for a moment and then reappeared on the other side of the vehicle.

Michael said, "Could you hide me too?"

"Let's try." She walked over to Michael, and again both disappeared. Michael felt more regretful than ever for his behavior. He took a big sniff to suck up his pride and said, "That was excellent. We are going to walk through the front door."

Jim said, "Gome, show us a map of the enemy campus."

The voice said, "Accessing." A map appeared in a three-dimensional hologram.

Michael said, "Gome, show us the target building and entrance." The headquarters building turned red with a yellow door signifying the main entrance.

Gome said, "Note, the headquarters is the fifth structure from the outer walls. The entire compound is encircled by various barriers that need to be crossed. The route with the highest probability of success is shown in green."

The voice from the console continued, "You will notice that you will disembark in an open space one hundred thirty meters in front of the main entrance at the shown point." A scaled, simulated hovercraft was shown on the display in red. "The probability to successfully enter the building from this route is 47 percent." All three were startled at the sound of the low odds.

Michael asked, "Gome, is there a way to increase the odds for success?"

Gome answered, "To do so, the fleet would need to change their bombardment scheme to provide cover and facilitate entry at dangerous points. The probability for success would increase to 76 percent. However, it could alert the enemy to your clandestine mission and delay your arrival and the attack force by one hour and twenty minutes."

Michael answered, "Gome, initiate a request for bombardment diversion. In that time, instruct us on the weapons capabilities of this craft."

The voice answered, "Request sent. Beyond the cloaking technology, systems were designed to defend in case of discovery. Access to these systems is guarded by your biometric signatures. Each of you put your right hand on the panel before we continue." All three complied and returned to their seats.

Holographic images appeared as instruction began. "Scans verified. First, there are eight medium blasters strong enough to break one meter of a wall with every four blasts. Four are mounted at the bow for frontal attacks and two on turrets, one mounted on either side of the craft. The intention of these weapons are defensive and to help in emergency escapes, creating exits from enclosed places.

"Second, the craft is equipped with compartmental shields. The Gome system calibrates breaches to divert energy to protect the integrity of the vehicle for escape. It will shed damaged devices that would hinder escape, such as an impaired or nonfunctional engine. It also diverts shields to more critical areas estimating need.

"Third, a portable system is the flash grenade. They can be launched from the ship to escape if the cloaking technology fails or carried as a soldier's personal weapon. The flash of light will injure the vision of all who see the flash with unprotected eyes. Special eye protection is to be used by the warrior. Otherwise, eyes must be covered."

Jim asked, "Gome, how many of these grenades do we have onboard?"

The voice said, "There are twelve, though only four can be taken from the craft. The grenades have a biometric lock that only allows you three to use them. This ensures that an enemy combatant cannot use them if lost. Look at the screen to see the weapon in action." A three-minute animated video showed both the hovercraft use and the personal warrior use, including the specific need for eye protection.

All three were impressed at the weaponry and the instruction.

Michael felt the hovercraft shift. "Gome, has the bombardment been adjusted for our arrival?"

"The change was approved. The compound barrier has been degraded enough to enter. Your chance of entering the building has increased to 72 percent based on the progress of the bombardment."

Robin asked, "Gome, compute the probability of us successfully completing our mission."

The computer delayed answering for fifteen seconds and then said, "The probability of achieving a successful mission is 14 percent."

The cabin went silent. The three humans looked at each other with dread. Michael said, "That's better than zero."

Robin shook her head. "We don't need your flippant crap. We have to plan."

This time, Michael spared them any comment. He continued, "We must stay undiscovered as long as possible while we are locating the women. I will need to stay with you, Robin, so you can hide me while we search. Jim can conceal himself while he searches. We will use Gome to communicate.

"From the hologram of the headquarters, it looks like there is a double entrance. One side for visitors, the other for workers. The continued bombardment will keep the locals inside, allowing us a better opportunity to reach the building. Gome will communicate our position to the quarks. When we get inside, the first thing is to find a place where we can eavesdrop for any information. It's going to be slow going. We don't know anything else about the place."

Jim said, "Let's get ready. You and I carry two of the flash grenades each."

The voice from the control panel said, "Fifteen minutes to destination. Manual navigational override allowed."

Michael said, "It's almost game time. Let's check our equipment. Gome, is all of our equipment ready?"

The voice said, "All equipment has been pretested. The sensors will record and transmit your progress to alert the main advance."

Robin asked, "Gome, once inside, will it be streaming, or do we transmit manually?"

"The sensor can do both. Press the sensor three seconds to toggle back and forth. A dim green circle will show when streaming. Approaching compound outer barrier."

All three turned to the monitor as they watched the craft navigate the pulverized barrier wall. The hovercraft piloted up and down in steepness as if going over swells on a choppy lake. Beyond the perimeter, they hugged the left side of the road heading south through the compound on the east side of the headquarters. They saw the bombardment rain down, hitting targets all around the moving craft as it glided toward its prescribed destination.

When it turned to the right, Gome announced, "Be advised we will reach the destination in two minutes." At that moment, Michael's thought went to the picture of the loaded troop carrier before it hit Normandy Beach on D-Day.

Jim said, "Here we go, sports fans."

The stone-faced warriors readied their gear as they felt the hovercraft come to a stop. The monitor showed an unobstructed view of the headquarters entrance. The door opened, and Michael said, "This is for the women and Earth's future."

Together Robin and Jim said, "Agreed." Able to move and stay hidden, they made their way toward the entrance.

1/10/2023
Walking to the Flight Deck
Demarco Planet Four
Quark Dimension

Gimmish walked down the hall toward the flight deck thinking, *These third-planet women change your thought process. I do not think Buentos could have developed such a formidable planet defense if he had these beings around all along. That is probably why, as smart as they are, they have not progressed as far as we have. He would have ended up like Kollindarrot.*

During the meeting, the intelligence reports showed cloaked troop movements from the northeast. He checked in with commander Bort. "Bort, status."

After a slight delay, he heard, "Master Gimmish, it is a war of attrition in orbit. We are making the enemy pay. Still, it is costly. We knocked out one of their light frigates, but it cost us four fighters. Our force is down to fifteen fighters and our frigate. I redeployed our small group to avoid the main battle and cover your escape."

He continued, "Buentos's fighters have interrupted the bombardment a few times with opportune strikes. However Contronto's force has been degraded by Tol's elite flight wing. The word is that High Commander Brandish is piloting with them. He owes Knight Bear for saving the fiefdom."

At the mention of the Knight Bear, Gimmish felt as if Michael were standing next to him. He quickly shook his head and said, "Wait, Knight Bear is here!"

"Sir, did you see him?"

"No, he is in the building. I feel him."

"How do you know that?"

"Trust me. I just know."

"Sir, we have all been under severe stress. The war is a great struggle."

"I did not sleep well. Yet I cannot explain this feeling." At that moment, Gimmish felt a stabbing pain from the wound on his left shoulder. He leaned against the wall groaning, unable to move.

Bort heard his distress, "Are you under attack?"

"No, I must get to the transport. One final thing: prepare yourself. The next time you hear my voice, I will only say your name once. That is your cue to cover our escape. Good luck, warrior."

Gimmish ended his call while crumpling to his knees, wincing in pain. He whispered to himself, "Townsend, I should have blown you away instead of giving you that disease. Screw Tol! May your quarks never coalesce into life again." He allowed the pain to subside and then pulled himself to his feet with his right hand. The sharp pain had subsided to a dull throbbing, which allowed him to make his way to the flight deck.

1/10/2024
Buentos's Headquarters Entrance
Demarco Planet Four
Quark Dimension

The rescuers arrived at the front entrance, not passing anyone on the way. The bombardment had forced all defenders to take shelter. The check-in station was staffed by a nervous quark pacing in the booth. No one was coming or going due to the bombardment. The lack of work only enhanced his anxiety. A shot from above shook the building. The guard avoided a piece of plaster that fell from the ceiling.

Robin said, "Let's move inside while the guard is distracted. Also, climb over the guardrail so as not to move any objects if possible. I am not sure being invisible will work if they use motion sensors."

Jim said, "Move slowly." Silently, their backs to the wall, all three crept past the guard. When they cleared the foyer, they turned toward the southeast corner to find an empty room.

The fourth door they tried was unlocked. Inside looked like a janitorial closet. Inside, Michael said, "This is where we need to split up. You find the top level and work down. We will work from the bottom up. Now go."

Jim exited the room. Robin and Michael waited about a minute before heading to the stairwell. Another blast hit the building, causing dust to rain from the ceiling. Michael noticed that the dust visually moved position when it came down on their heads. Michael whispered, "We need to stay clear of smoke and dust because it can expose your illusion."

Robin said, "Then tell Gome to have the constant blasting of this building stop while we are here." Michael did. They saw two quarks pass by them, looking around with concern. Robin said, "They are scared out of their minds."

Michael said, "I'm not thrilled either. Are you?"

Robin said, "Rhetorical question. Let's go."

Once they entered the stairwell at the southeast corner, they followed it down into a basement area. Michael whispered, "These floors are labeled, but we can't read it. My guess is that the holding cells are down here." They went further into the basement, ducking out of the way of oncoming quarks. They did find prisoner cells but no women.

They entered an open cell and looked around. Robin picked up an earring in the corner. "They were here."

Michael responded, "Now where?" They moved through the lower floor, avoiding soldiers as they walked by, with Michael jumping out of the way to avoid contact.

Robin said, "You are too big for this."

Michael said, "No argument."

They continued through the basement, listening to conversations, hoping for any clues. After a half hour of failed effort, Robin placed the earring on a table next to four quarks having a break. They moved away, exposing it outside of the light diversion. A soldier noticed it and said, "That is one of those third-planet being's ear hangings. How did it get here?"

Another said, "Maybe when they were moved around the building."

Michael had a sinking feeling while Robin gave a quiet groan of dread. They moved to an out-of-the-way place to discuss their next move. Robin said, "We need to let Jim know."

Michael activated the Gome sensor. "Jim, the women are not in the holding cells."

Jim answered, "I know. On the top floor, two are in a room with a guard. I will neutralize him." Jim ended.

Michael said, "We need to move. We have eight more to find." They searched every room possible for any others. They made it to an empty break room next to the stairwell on the northwest corner of the building.

The sensor alerted Michael. "It's Jim."

Jim reported, "We have one dead quark and two happy women. The issue is that the warlords ordered the women to be spread around the building to make it difficult in case someone like us showed up."

Robin said, "That's lovely. Do they have a clue where?"

Jim said, "I found these two in this torture unit strapped in those light rings. They were taken with two others who were dropped off on the third floor toward the front. But we are stuck unless we can hide somehow."

Michael said, "We're coming."

Jim said, "Room next to the northeast stairwell, out."

They carefully walked back across the building to reach the stairs. The dust had not been stirred since Gome had sent the message to divert the bombardment. However, getting across the building took time to dodge detection from bumping into soldiers. They had to pause once, waiting in an alcove for minutes while a group of soldiers had a meeting in their path.

Eventually they reached the stairwell. Upon entering, they encountered two quarks bounding down the stairs, who stopped. Michael and Robin froze in the corner. The quark that stopped first said to the other, "Where is the fire valve? Each floor has a fire valve in the corner of the stairwell except here." Michael and Robin noticed they were hiding it from view. The curious quarks moved closer to Robin's light-diverted space. Suddenly, two giant hands each grabbed a quark's head and crashed them together, cracking both skulls.

Robin asked, "What do we do with them now?"

Michael answered, "I will have to carry them upstairs with us." Michael threw them over his shoulders then began to climb the stairs. Robin walked behind him to keep him in the light-diverted area.

Robin said, "All of this extra effort is making me hungry."

Michael said, "You ain't the Lone Ranger."

Once they reached the fifth floor, Robin remarked, "I have got to take a quick break. This is wearing me out."

At that moment, Robin jumped, startled when Jim appeared from the wall without warning. Robin gave a quick cry of shock, to which Michael curtly said, "Quiet."

Robin quietly admonished Jim, "Don't do that again. You almost gave me a heart attack."

Jim cautioned her to be quiet by placing a finger to his lips. He then motioned for both to follow him. Making sure the coast was clear, all three crossed the hall to a room diagonally opposite the stairs.

Inside the room were two women in tattered clothing sitting at a table. The taller of the two looked badly beaten, one eye swollen shut. Her bloodstained shirt was torn on one side. Her lower body was bare except for underwear. The other woman was as unkempt, although less physically abused.

Their eyes doubled in size when Michael entered the room. He laid the two dead quarks on the floor. He then looked at the women and said, "I'm going to get y'all out of here."

Jim made the introductions, "Lovisa, Petra, this is Michael and Robin."

Robin said, "Pleasure, now let's get out of here."

Michael said, "Quick, we have two uniforms. I don't know how they will fit, but it's better than what y'all have now." Jim, Robin, and the two women took the shirts off the soldiers and put them on.

Lovisa said, "At least we are covered." Petra agreed.

Michael said, "Where to next?"

Lovisa said, "There's another torture room on the floor beneath here."

Robin asked, "How do you know?"

Lovisa answered, "I've been there."

Pointing to the ceiling corner, Michael said, "It looks like we are on camera. Jim, see if the hall is clear." They threw the dead quarks in a closet and moved into the hallway with Robin concealing them.

Coming back from inspecting the near stairwell, Jim said, "This stairwell is blocked. We need to go down the hall to the other stairwell now." All five deliberately moved down the east side hall to the other stairwell. Robin kept all four concealed while Jim scouted ahead. Michael kept searching the corridors for more cameras. Jim spoke through the sensor. "Everyone, flatten up to the wall."

Michael whispered, "Up against the wall." The four pressed against the wall as four armed quarks exited the southeast stairwell and ran past them. As they continued down the hall, Michael looked back to see the four quarks go into the room just as quarks exited the northeast stairwell to join them. They came back out of the room shouting to each other with perplexed looks, searching for something that was not there. All five reached the stairwell and went downstairs.

1/10/2024
The Flight Deck
Demarco Planet Four
Quark Dimension

Gimmish received the call from Buentos, "You were right. Knight Bear is in the building! The two third-planet beings are missing from the fifth floor, and three soldiers are dead. Do you have this extra sense from being a Moonie?"

Gimmish grimaced but ignored the insulting remark. "Okay. Now we need to prepare, for he is coming after us." A sinking feeling came over him. He could feel not only Michael's presence but his rage too. "Buentos, that Knight Bear has to be stopped, or he will destroy us."

"What do we do now?"

"And I thought you were an experienced warlord. This is your place. You know what you have available. Those third-planet things have screwed up your brain."

Buentos grew incensed, saying, "Screw you, Moonie!" and ended the call.

Gimmish smiled, for he knew Buentos was now a liability, giving him all the excuse he needed to escape. It was time to lay more seeds of deceit. He called Contronto. "Warlord, Knight Bear is here. He is now creating havoc in the headquarters, trying to free the hostages. You need to decide whether you want to confront him. He found the two on the fifth floor and is working his way down, I presume."

Contronto asked, "How do you know? I'm here in this side office without much communication."

"Buentos called me to let me know."

"I wonder why he did not call me."

"No matter. Buentos thinks he can do it all, so let him try. Think about escaping with me if things go wrong."

"Do you have any ideas?"

"Yes, I do. I am on the transport. The next time I call you, be ready to move." Gimmish stopped the call and thought, *I have really never had anything, so I have nothing to lose. I won't stay here to die.*

1/10/2024
Buentos's Headquarters Southeast Stairwell
Demarco Planet Four
Quark Dimension

The five quietly walked down the stairs to the fourth-floor exit. Michael determined there were no cameras in that part of the stairwell. "Robin, it's okay to drop the guard for a moment. Still, we need to listen for visitors. Petra, look through the window, and scout for company." Petra, grateful to be asked to help, quickly accepted the task. "Everyone, check your supplies."

Lovisa offered, "I was in the military. Let me help." Michael smiled and gave her and Petra blasters.

Michael heard noises in the stairwell from below. Michael whispered, "Is the floor clear?"

She answered, "There are soldiers down the south hall."

Michael said, "Sorry, Robin, we have to leave invisible." Robin took a deep breath and created another illusion. Jim stayed aside while the four walked out onto the floor. Before he exited the door, he tossed two explosive grenades to bounce down the steps as the soldiers made their way around the corner coming up the last flight. All five stood against the wall as the weapons detonated, blowing the stairwell door open. The soldiers on the south hall ran to the explosion along with the guards toward the fourth-floor chamber.

Lovisa moved her finger out of the illusion and touched the door, whispering, "Here." Jim went ahead looking for company. He came back and slid into the room where the others had gone without a sound. The two women, one Nordic, one Asian, were sitting despondently with their heads down in wooden chairs bound with light rings. Jim came up from behind and whispered to them, "Don't move a muscle. You are on camera." He saw the camera and moved where he would be out of view. Jim appeared and pointed above his head at the camera. Michael blasted the camera and then reached for the light rings. At about five centimeters from touching the controllers, Michael received an electrical shock.

Petra then looked from the door, saying, "They are coming back."

Michael said, "About how many?"

Petra answered, "Ten at least."

Michael did not respond but took a light grenade and said, "Cover your eyes tightly." Robin and Jim had glasses as Michael tossed the grenade out the door. Even with glasses, all he could see was white. For fifteen seconds, the world became indistinguishable. Screams of pain and shock filled the air as the quarks realized their world had gone dark. The whole group watched the horror of troops who were rendered blind in a flash. Michael shot the light ring controllers, and then the seven earthlings ran down the hall, passing the blinded soldiers who had no idea what had just happened to them.

Michael yelled, "Women, pick up a blaster."

They reached and entered the southeast stairwell to the third floor. As the earthlings ducked in, they heard troops from below. Michael said, "They know we are here. We need to fight now." As the soldiers turned the corner, the four former hostages fired, not waiting for prompting. Four quarks immediately died. Jim threw a grenade that ricocheted off the wall down the next flight and exploded, eliminating more. Michael jumped to the next level and began hand-to-hand combat; the others carefully followed him down to the third floor. A couple of quarks escaped and ran up the east hall to the north.

Michael yelled, "Cleared!" then noticed the south hall was clear at that moment. Jim blended into the wall and went ahead. Robin again covered the group and moved a couple of paces behind. About halfway down the hall, Michael looked back to see about five quarks looking around with their arms drawn. The end of the hall could not come sooner. He looked ahead at Jim, who had reached the corner. He motioned for them to come. They ducked into an empty room at the corner of the west hall.

Michael said, "Check your weapons." He counted. "We all have blasters. We have nine explosive grenades and three light grenades left. Be ready."

Jim looked and said, "Go."

They began to make their way up the west hall. Michael told Jim, "From everything I surmised thus far, most of the coordination is done on the north hall areas." Jim went ahead again.

When they got close to the northwest corner, Jim whispered, "Stop." He came back to Michael and reported, "It looks like they are massing right near where we want to go and waiting."

Michael got an idea. "Don't go around the corner. You women, cover the rear. Let me call Gome." He pulled the sensor from his waist pouch. "Gome, how long will it take you to get to my position?"

"Approximately four minutes."

"Gome, use your eight guns to open a large opening on the north wall one-third of the way from the western corner on the third floor. We will need a continuous blasting for two minutes or until I say otherwise. Advise me when you are in position. Gome, signal ready to resume bombardment upon the headquarters northeast corner."

The stage was set. The quarks knew the earthlings were coming for the hostages, waiting for their opportunity to exact revenge for their fallen comrades. One minute later, a giant blast hit the northwest corner of the building. The soldiers gravitated to the west. One of the women alerted the others, "They are coming from our rear."

Michael turned around to see a squad of quarks with weapons ready, charging up the west hall. He whispered to the women, "Stay up against the wall. Hide your eyes when I yell, 'Now.' Don't look until I say." He, Jim, and Robin were wearing their eye protection. The quarks got closer.

He heard his sensor, "Ready."

Michael jumped from the illusion, startling quarks and humans alike. "Gome, now!" The quarks pointed their blasters from both directions. The women hid their eyes, and Michael dropped the light grenade that produced enough light to white out two halls. The guns from the hovercraft blasted the side of the building, carving a large opening and spraying masonry over the blinded soldiers. Michael and Jim fired on any quark still holding a weapon in their direction. Two minutes after it began, Gome stopped, and Michael yelled, "Cleared." They charged through the rubble caused by the hovercraft armory to the double doors in the hall.

More soldiers came from the northwest stairwell, blasters firing. The four freed women kept firing as Robin used every ounce of strength and concentration to maintain their cover. The bewildered quarks could not see the targets to hit and were eliminated before they realized anything. The four women were relentless, firing at anything that moved.

Lovisa came to the double doors and yelled, "This is the room!" Michael gave a quick glance to see two frightened guards ducking behind the tables where the two women were lying on their backs, their arms and legs held down by light rings.

Robin said, "I can't hide light through the doors. Jim will need to go in there."

Michael motioned to Jim to disengage with the western hall advance and to come. He also noticed the double doors were east of the hole created by the hovercraft. Michael used the sensor again, "Gome, on my command, renew blasting from the previous spot and enlarge the area westward." Michael ran to the corner uncovered and roared. He ducked back as soon as they began to fire. They pursued him around the corner when Michael yelled, "Gome, fire!" The blaster fire started to hit quarks, who ran to the front too quickly. The masonry hit others as the blasting moved west to the end of the building. Michael and the four women were merciless in their barrage. Another blast hit the northeast corner of the building, collapsing the corner of the headquarters. All quarks died in the ambush.

Jim yelled, "Hurry, into the room. You know more will come."

Michael told the shivering guards, "Turn off the light rings and take off your shirts." Michael took the light rings, and the two women took the shirts. The other two women took shirts off two dead quarks.

Jim went to the west corner and immediately came back. "They are setting up another advance or waiting on us to come their way."

Michael said, "Gome, upload. To the wall opening, now." The cloaked hovercraft moved next to the wall.

Jim said, "Great idea." They put the two guards in the light rings and left. All nine jumped into the hovercraft and moved away.

Robin said, "What about the other four?"

Michael said, "Now that we are out of immediate danger, let Lovisa tell us where they probably are. You need a rest anyway. Great job." Robin fell back in her chair.

Michael turned to Lovisa. "Tell us about Buentos's office."

She answered, "There is access from the office to the flight deck, a door built into the tarmac area without handles. But there is a passcode box on the door with a cover. I know the code. He took me into space a couple of times to abuse me in space." She shuddered with revulsion and said, "There are nine buttons in a square. The code sequence is like an H. After you enter the code, the door opens automatically. There is a stairway that goes down to a tunnel and right into his office."

Gome interrupted, "Open comm."

They heard the voice of Brandish. "The major advance will begin on the compound in one hour. The bombardment will be intense, so you will need to finish, or you could become a casualty. Good luck."

Gome came back, "Comm closed."

Michael said, "Time is wasting. Gome, take us to the described door on the flight deck. Robin, Jim, and I—"

Lovisa said, "Me too!" Michael turned his head. "I want to end that scum's life."

Robin said, "There are four in two different spots."

Lovisa said, "Buentos first."

Jim remarked, "Hell hath no fury like a woman scorned."

Michael asked, "Shakespeare?"

Robin said, "No, William Congreve, *The Mourning Bride* in 1697."

Michael said, "Gome, take us to the flight deck door."

Without a sound, the hovercraft landed next to the tunnel door. Lovisa entered the code, and the door opened to reveal the stairs to the tunnel. Michael said, "Lovisa and Petra, grab weapons and come with us. You other four, stay here and help Gome protect the craft. Gome, keep us in communication. Let's go." The five went into the tunnel with the door closing behind them.

Jim looked up, saying, "Damn, there's a camera."

Michael reached up and tore it off the wall. He said, "Robin, do your thing."

Hidden, they moved further down the well-lit tunnel. About twenty meters from the door, a mammoth creature with a large weapon stepped in their path from a side door. There was no way to pass by him untouched. He shot his blaster down the center of the tunnel. It missed. "You third-planet beings hide well. I saw five of you come down the stairs; one I recognize well." Lovisa shot at the large alien. An invisible shield caused the shot to bounce away. He smiled and continued, "My master Buentos was expecting you, Knight Bear. From what we saw on camera, there is not enough room for you to get by me. So all I need to do now is not let you pass and seal you in this tunnel. This is too easy."

Michael touched everyone with his goggles. He whispered to them, "Hide your eyes." Jim and Robin put theirs on. Michael smiled at the bewildered look on the guard's face expecting more. He lightly tossed the grenade and yelled, "Now!" The tunnel filled with blinding light. The scream of agony echoed through the tunnel. The light triggered the force shield to drop, allowing Michael to grab and shove their obstacle into the room he'd come from. All five ran past, not knowing if there were any other guards.

They found the door to the office shut. Michael told the others to fire on the hinges. After ten seconds, the door blew off. Only two women strapped to two tables could be seen. A voice came from a hidden speaker. "Knight Bear, Gimmish told me you were resourceful. The two women you seek are in front of you in a place where I can enjoy them. The problem is you need to get through another shield, and I control the access."

Robin said, "I am about to puke."

Michael pressed the sensor, whispering, "Gome, can you see movement in the second-floor room near me?"

Gome responded, "There is at least one third-planet being like the others, strapped to a table."

Michael turned his attention, "Okay, Jim, go up to the force shield and see if you can scope enough to give us ideas. Robin"—she looked at Michael perplexed—"you are dynamite!"

She said, "Save it. Let's get out of here."

Michael spoke into the sensor, "Can you spot the camera?"

"Yes."

"Gome, destroy it."

"Maneuvering." Seconds later, a shot hit the camera from the side. "Target destroyed." Two seconds later, "Quark subject moving near the window."

"Gome, fire." The hovercraft blasters tore through one area of the second and first floors. Buentos jumped for his life while plaster and masonry flew through the room. Dust and plaster began dropping onto the bound and naked women on the tables.

Jim said, "The shield is fading."

Michael yelled, "Attack!" All five ran into the room with the shackled females. Michael ran to the tables to free the captives, but the light rings would not budge. A voice came from the other side of the room. "Knight Bear, I have the controllers. I want to make a deal."

"You don't have much time."

"You can ensure I have more."

"Yes, you are in a bad spot. In less than an hour, Commander Brandish is going to unleash his entire attack force on you."

"Then would you like to die with me?"

Gome broke in, "Knight Bear, there is movement on the flight deck."

"What?" he answered, pausing for a response.

Robin said, "Gome, what was that?" She then whispered to Michael, "Remember, you need to start by saying 'Gome.'"

Gome explained: "There is one quark with two third-planet beings in light rings entering a previously cloaked transport."

Michael yelled across the room, "Hey, Buentos, are you trying to leave?" He saw Lovisa with a sharp object in her hand crawling toward the warlord on the window side.

Buentos said back, "I know you don't want to stay here, but stay here you will!" He began firing blasters at their position. Michael and Jim fired back, noticing they were hitting a shielded area.

Slowing his speech to give Lovisa time, Michael lay on the floor and continued, "My dear Warlord Buentos, it is as if you and I ... have a substantial ... I mean very substantial difference in our wants, desires, and opinions."

"Knight Bear, no more talking!"

"Au contraire, almighty and highly esteemed ... warlord of the realm, Buentos. If you want something, you will listen. I block your escape."

Robin chuckled and shook her head at the over-the-top delay tactic. *So stupid, it's funny.*

"As long as I am here, I have the light rings on your beings strapped to the tables. If I escape, the light rings will fade when I reach a certain distance."

He saw Lovisa near the opening created by the hovercraft. She gave him a signal. Michael gave the punchline, "And now you can look out to see your other warlord and his two women … escaping in a cloaked transport without you."

Buentos moved outside his shield to look. Lovisa came from her hiding place, plunging her knife into Buentos at the diaphragm. She looked into his eyes and spit in his face as he went limp.

Michael yelled, "Turn off those controllers, and let's all get the hell out of here!"

Lovisa said, "The transport is taking off!"

Jim said, "Gimmish was there the whole time."

While Robin helped the women off their tables, Michael called the hovercraft. "Gome, park next to the tunnel entrance on the building's side." They all ran into the tunnel with Michael in the rear, watching for anything following. Lovisa tried to enter the code. She entered it wrong the first time, then a second. "The passcode may need reset. Please wait for assistance."

Jim took his blaster, yelling, "Stand back!" He shot at the lock until it crumbled. Michael then pushed the door open, holding it so the others could escape.

The hovercraft did a good job of hiding the smaller humans, yet Michael was taller than the angle of the cloaking. Weapons fired from the roof onto the flight deck at Michael. The hovercraft did not have good shields and began to sustain damage. Michael yelled, "Gome, move the hovercraft out of the compound, fast!" The hovercraft did what it was ordered to do and quickly moved.

Seeing that Michael would sacrifice himself to save everyone else, Robin ran to the door, jumped, and rolled onto the flight deck, turning invisible. She jumped on Michael's back while he was shooting and said. "Run to cover on all fours!" as they disappeared from sight. He ran up against a wall with Robin on his back, holding on by his leather strap.

Michael assumed Jim had regained control of the hovercraft in midair, aiming the blasters at the defenders and firing. The soldiers on the roof ran for cover, not knowing where to shoot.

Michael said to Robin, "You held on really well."

She answered, "I rode dressage in prep school. Let's keep moving."

Michael continued on all fours in a trot, going north on the road to the perimeter. The hovercraft flew down onto the road next to Michael and Robin to pick them up.

When Michael sat down in his pilot seat aboard the hovercraft, he said, "Gome, take us back to the launching area and call Commander Brandish." It was minutes later when the voice from the console said, "This is Commander Brandish, Knight Bear."

"I want to report that we have rescued eight of the ten women from the compound. Warlord Buentos is dead. Still, the warlord Contronto and Gimmish have escaped the compound in a transport with the last two as hostages. We are presently returning in the hovercraft to our camp. The compound is yours to attack unfettered."

Brandish asked, "Are your companions safe?"

Michael answered, "I would not have succeeded without them."

Brandish answered, "You are correct. Tell Jim he was right. He will know what I mean. I shall hail the enemy command with an offer for them to surrender."

Michael knew he had two more deeds to accomplish. Now, with all the distractions over, he had to save two more women and kill Anne's murderer.

Brandish said, "Knight Bear, a fast transport will be waiting for you at base camp with a fighter group for protection. Your success has saved many of our quarks. We will also provide fighter escort since they were seen leaving with nine fighters. You all are probably very hungry. The transport will have ample supplies. Lieutenant Carman will be your pilot."

"Let's go!"

It was going to take five hours to catch up with the enemy warlords, which gave the group little time to plan a rescue of two women from a ship they knew little about while traveling at hyperlight speed without killing all aboard in the process. Michael was a brilliant scientist who caught on to complex subjects, but ship-to-hostile-ship rescue and possible open fire was probably too much to negotiate on short notice. Nonetheless, that's what he had to do.

He and the pilot searched the computer for a diagram of Gimmish's transport specs in any database. They were too far from any headquarters to send a message for consult or opinions on this matter. They searched for information on enemy spacecraft through detailed databases to think of a logical way to make such a dangerous attempt possible.

After nearly an hour, the pilot said, "From a comparison of transports made in their sectors over the last few periods"—he pointed to a schematic on his screen—"I believe this one is the most logical and was his older craft that held about twenty persons. So, Knight Bear, when you were captured by Alchemy that time and were on board his transport, do you remember any details that could pinpoint what vehicle he used?"

Michael gave a shy smile thinking about the Knight Bear moniker sticking and answered, "Well, to the point, I do remember his chambers were separated from fore and aft by partitions, so no one saw the pilots from the back. The inside seating was along the sides, helping him utilize his light rings to hold me up against the wall. There was another chamber for sleeping behind the seating area, with the engine room behind that for a total of four different sections. The seating was like the paratrooper seating back on Earth, only with a jump door to the side."

The pilot did not ask for clarification and looked at the design. Listening to the description, he commented, "Indeed, this is almost the complete design for the entire transport since changes could be made to add options. There are details about the composition of the ship's outer wall and its purposes. Also, it looks like there are no top and bottom guns to worry about, so the best way is to go after this craft from below and avoid oncoming fire. Our fighters will overwhelm their protection to cover our approach, since we have minimal armament. We outnumber them and have better fighter craft and fresh pilots, so our cover will be as good as possible. This craft is designed to have a bottom and top gun that created a crease in the design that could be used to fit cannons in turrets. We could use those as pass-through portals, so the midspace rescue has a chance."

Robin asked, "How much of a chance? We'll need to pass through the vacuum of space. This is so risky. How can we safely board a hostile spacecraft and not be exposed to the elements?"

The pilot answered, "We have the good fortune to be in a modular transport with every compartment door capable of being an airlock."

Robin said, "Good design."

Late 1/10/2024
Two billion kilometers from Demarco Planet Four
Quark Dimension

Contronto spoke to Gimmish: "This is an older transport."

Gimmish said, "It was the only one on the flight deck. All the others were scattered around the compound, away from the buildings. I am pushing this thing as fast as it will go."

Contronto said, "I hope it will get us to Flashenol's sector before Sargen and Tol's forces can catch up with us. By the way, the hostages make it harder just to shoot us into particles."

"We have our fighter escort. If we had left those two beings back there, they would not have the same urgency to chase us. Knight Bear would have gotten what he wanted and would have left us alone to fight another day."

Contronto looked at Gimmish directly. Slowly he said, "I want the third-planet creatures for me. Once we reach Flashenol with our cargo, we are safe. Also, the third-planet beings sow conflict between Knight Bear and quarks."

"How so?"

"Knight Bear won't want them to kill the hostages. Sargen would tell him he got eight of the ten back. What is a couple extra? Also, Sargen would tell Flashenol to eat fallow worms if he got us."

"Okay, count on Knight Bear coming after us. I'll check on your hostages to see how they are doing."

Gimmish passed from the cockpit through to where the two women were held. The light rings bound them tightly to the wall. Their mouths were covered to keep them from making loud noises or biting him. The women looked at their captor with contempt.

He said to them, "You might as well get used to being with us. There is not much chance of ever returning home." Both women closed their weeping eyes as his voice processed through the translator. He went back to the cockpit, thinking about how his world had been changed recently. *Just think, this Moonie has lived for another day.* He looked at his warlord signate and smiled, thinking, *No moron could have ever gotten this far. Maybe not today, but I'm going to win one day.*

Contronto called back, "Gimmish, need to talk up here."

Gimmish got to the pilot's seat. "What's going on?"

Contronto took a deep breath, "I heard from Cranconish while he was retreating. Knight Bear was successful. Buentos is dead. His forces are either surrendering or fleeing into space."

Gimmish said, "Then we're alone. If we don't make it to Flashenol's border, we're dead too. Does he have any intelligence about their next move?"

Contronto shrugged. "He told me to expect them to try to catch us."

Gimmish thought, *They are after us, but those third-planet pests won't get me. I have got to think of a surprise.*

Early 1/11/2024
Two billion kilometers from Demarco Planet Four
Quark Dimension

Michael watched the monitor as they moved through space. He then broke the silence. "It's been three hours since we left Buentos's. It amazes me how fast these buggies are. How much time will we be in contact with their transport before they get to Flashenol's border?"

The pilot said, "By my calculations, based on that model of transport, we might have an hour to save your beings before the fiefdom border, probably less."

Michael asked the pilot, "What kind of equipment do you have for a spacewalk?"

He looked at the mammoth earthling, saying, "Nothing that will fit you, except maybe something for your head."

"That's enough. You won't believe how tough this bear's hide is."

"I thought we were going to kill the warlords and be done with it."

"That's not my plan."

The pilot dropped his jaw, looking at this third-planet being as if he was a lunatic. "That's crazy! Why would you risk your life for these beings you do not know?"

Michael smiled back. He laid a large hand on the pilot's shoulder and, in a sober tone, told him, "Lieutenant Carman, if I didn't, I would always regret it."

The pilot shrugged and shook his head. Grudgingly, he got up to show Michael what he had.

Robin saw the exchange and saw there was no second thought in Michael's mind. She said nothing, only pondered the exchange's genuineness.

Jim got up with the two to figure out what they would do. They went to the suit storage. The lieutenant said, "Knight Bear, try on this helmet. It's our largest." Michael put it on. However, his snout made the fit uncomfortable.

Robin came over and giggled when she saw Michael's snout pressed against the inside. "I'm sorry, Michael. I know this is not the right time, but you look so cute, like a puppy pressing his nose against the window. Let me try on a suit."

Jim looked at her quizzically while Michael quickly took the helmet off and cleaned the nose print with the closest wipe.

She continued, "You could use my concealment ability while trying to board another craft. If Jim goes, the spacesuit will render what he can do useless. Our advantage is they don't know what I can do."

Jim said, "Point taken." Michael agreed.

Robin tried a suit on and said, "Two weeks ago, I don't think I could have functioned in this thing. I can tell I will need a new wardrobe when we get home. Especially through the top." Michael nodded approvingly and kept his mouth shut.

Jim broke in, thinking this was Robin trying to test Michael's response, and asked, "What now?"

Michael looked at Jim's wry smile and saw approval in his eyes. A relieved Michael said, "I believe I am the only one who can get inside their craft. Only we will need to do it from the bottom. The good pilot has informed me of the probable design of the enemy craft. Since its main function is transporting goods, it has compartments with maintenance portals that can also be used as manual entryways on top and bottom. The trick is how fast we can break the locks, enter safely, and get out without total loss of cabin air pressure. That means I will need to carry two small suits and oxygen for the women."

Jim said, "The lieutenant is going to need the fighter support protecting our underbelly."

The lieutenant said, "That is my plan. Although the transport is an old model usually piloted by Moonies, their fighters are of a new design." The three earthlings were momentarily taken aback by the remark, then continued to plan. "The proposed entryway slides, exposing a square opening. Like this craft, the bay is compartmentalized to allow more than one type of cargo. If the women are in the first compartment, they have about twenty seconds before the air is sucked out of their lungs. Thus you must enter with the suits and oxygen ready. This leaves you exposed to close weapons fire upon your entry."

Michael said, "In that case, Robin—eh, Prism will ride on my back and hold the blaster to shoot while we are ready with the oxygen."

Robin said, "Thank you, Knight Bear." She gave him a sly smile.

Michael continued, "We will be returning fire with our blasters set on stun to lower the chance of hull breach. I am not sure the warlords are going to use the same caution."

Jim added, "They may use light rings. The only defense to that is those light grenades, but they're overkill. I should come too. They left in such haste, I don't know if they would be prepared for even one or at most two more."

Michael said, "Good thought. It looks like this transport has five space suits. That would be good if we cannot repressurize the compartment."

The pilot broke in, "The lead fighter has their transport on its sensor. I was right. We will catch up to them with less than one hour to spare. It will not be easy. We have to deal with their fighter escort."

1/10/2024
Three billion kilometers from Demarco Planet Four
Quark Dimension

Bort's voice came from the console, "Warlord, we have picked up a signal of someone following us."

Gimmish answered, "Yes, Commander, Knight Bear is coming for his fellow third-planet creatures. This is why I asked you to come with me. He will not stop until he can account for all the hostages. Your fighters will need to hold him off until we reach the border."

Bort observed, "From my sensors, it looks like they have a good complement of fighters with them too. We may be outnumbered."

To his own surprise, Gimmish calmly realized, "Yes. However, I know their blasters won't be blazing since they need to take into account our third-planet cargo. I have observed that their attraction for each other can be turned to their downfall."

"If your transport had been one of the newer designs, we would be at the border now, not needing to worry about this."

"If a bullfrog had wings, he wouldn't bump his ass."

Contronto and Bort said at the same time, "What?"

Contronto, still looking at Gimmish, said, "What a moronic statement."

Bort asked, "What's a bullfrog?"

Gimmish waved off the comment. "It is a third-planet saying. Never mind."

Contronto said, "How can you think of such stupid things with that Knight Bear on our trail?"

Gimmish pressed his point. "You have felt the attraction, and you have only been around these beings a short time. Imagine having these attractive creatures around all the time."

Contronto took a moment to ponder this strange concept.

One Hour Later 1/10/2024
3.5 billion kilometers from Demarco Planet Four
Quark Dimension

Lieutenant Carman yelled, "Got them on the screen!"

Michael said, "What's that?"

"I see nine fighters and one transport ahead of us racing toward the border."

"How soon will we reach them?"

"Within the hour; get ready."

Michael asked, "Have you gone over the attack plan with the fighters?"

The pilot turned to give him a disgusted look. "Does one form from quarks?"

Michael, feeling the rebuke, said, "Okay, this ain't my usual work. I'm sorry."

Robin looked at Michael and mimed zipping her lips.

The lieutenant continued, "Remember, you will have less than one hour to complete your mission before we reach the border and must disengage."

Michael asked, "Where is the best airlock to use for this ship-to-ship crossing?"

The pilot said, "The airlock in the middle hold has better clearance and a device that can surround and shield a breach on another ship's hull up to a certain size."

Michael said, "Is it like a jetway where it reaches out and touches flush to the side of the craft?"

The pilot let the translator complete the meaning of the phrase. When it finished, he understood and said, "Yes, and the end that fits at the end attaches with a sucking action to minimize air loss, but it is not perfect. We need to turn off the artificial gravity to use it."

Robin said, "I'm glad you warned us. I will tell the other women."

Michael said, "When he turns the gravity off, we will float through the tube with our equipment to get the job done."

Robin said, "I will ride your back with a ready blaster while Jim carries the equipment for the women."

Jim said, "I will follow with any need for reinforcement if they have any traps and then get the two women suited up as fast as possible."

The pilot said, "We have twenty minutes before we reach them. Let's get in our places."

The crewmate watching the console interrupted, "Lieutenant, there is a signal coming through from the enemy craft."

The pilot said, "Put it through."

Michael went over to the comm and answered. A voice came through the console, "Doctor Knight Bear Townsend, it is

DIMENSIONS

interesting that you would be out here in this lonely space. Why would you follow us, since it looked like you were having fun tearing up Buentos's headquarters?"

Michael thought, *This is one real asshole. I want to catch and kill him even more.*

Gimmish sarcastically continued, "Knight Bear—that is what you are called now, right? Well, unbeknownst to you, I have known about you since you were training on that green-striped area with bleachers all around on that third planet you call Earth. I was not supposed to visit your planet. Nevertheless, I did. Sig, what a stupid name for a weapon. Tol was the only reason I did not finish you off at that second campsite. He caused everything to go bad."

He continued, "And it is a shame about your third-planet mate. You should have answered the door so I could have killed you, not her, you coward. However, you need to know: if you try to kill us, consider your fellow third-planet people dead. Killing such attractive beings would be a shame." The call ended.

Robin said to Michael, "He wants you to lose your cool and make a mistake."

The pilot said, "You know Commander Brandish wants them dead."

Michael said, "I want them dead too, but I made a vow to save all the women possible. We rescue those last two, and you can take target practice."

The lead fighter alerted the transport, "The enemy is taking a defensive formation around their transport. It is thought that Commander Bort is leading the group of seasoned fighter pilots. We will prevail, but it won't be easy."

Lieutenant Carman answered back, "Change frequency to code 'two beta five.'" He changed the setting to the proper frequency. After ten seconds, he said, "Fighter leader."

"Roger."

"Set attack formation fifteen degrees, five Bender upper Areanosten."

"Copy."

Michael thought to himself, *Omaha, Omaha, hike.*

Ten fighters darted at a fifteen-degree angle, five pairs in a semicircular formation set to engage the enemy. The defending fighters flew into a diamond formation surrounding their warlord's transport. As the attacking forces from the above level angle, the lower fighters defending advanced to get a better angle underneath. While watching the movements, Lieutenant Carmen ordered, "Locate Bort if he is in the formation."

The flight leader answered, "By the markings, it looks like Bort's fighter is on the left center."

Lieutenant Carman ordered, "Pairs one and two left, dive right. Center, attack left center. Right one, attack center-right. Right two, attack lower right." The attack began with the right side of the defense being overrun. Still, Bort showed his prowess, avoiding the two-on-one and destroying one before moving with another to initiate a counterattack. Three on the right side of the defense were taken out with the first wave.

All the while, Michael, Jim, and Robin watched the action, giving their body English with every maneuver, rooting their forces on.

The warlord's defense heroically protected their leaders. Still, they retreated from the lightning-fast decisions Brandish's lieutenant instructed his pilots to perform. The enemy only had three fighters left while Lieutenant Carman canvassed ten fighters now ready to approach the fugitive warlord's transport. He looked at the guidance system. "My calculations say we have forty minutes to complete our mission. Ready. One minute to engaging enemy craft."

All three were ready with their equipment. Michael said, "Here we go!" The pilot turned off the gravity.

Michael and the pilot watched the monitor closely to make sure the tunnel would be in position. The crewmate at the controls reported, "Lieutenant Carman, the transfer tunnel is extending. You know they have to be watching us."

The pilot did not speak, remaining focused on the contact area on the enemy craft. The tunnel had come within three meters of the cargo door when the pilot yelled, "Enemy vessel turning!" Everyone looked at the enemy ship performing a barrel roll to avoid attachment.

The pilot ordered, "Use attaching anchor. We have to risk collision to be successful." Thanks to Gimmish's piloting skills, attachment at the correct maintenance hatch took another precious ten minutes. All the while, both ships sped closer to the border.

As soon as the tunnel connected, a message came from the enemy ship. Again Gimmish's voice resonated from the console. "Knight Bear, you might as well forget your plans. We have messaged the border patrol of the Flashenol sector to explain our situation. They again reiterated their ban on hostilities from other sectors. You will not have time to stop us. Give up, or more will die." The broadcast ended.

Michael ordered, "Tell us when the tunnel is ready. Time's wasting."

The pilot said, "Everything is in place. You have less than twenty minutes before the border."

Michael yelled, "Jump on, Robin. Y'all, let's go!" They got to the cargo maintenance hatch. Michael pointed to a spot and told Robin, "Shoot at this spot, then make us disappear." She did twice, and the lock broke.

She concentrated and said, "Done." The hatch opened, and blaster shots hit around the opening. One of the warlords was waiting. Then a voice, not Gimmish's, was heard. "Come out now."

While there was no fire, Michael thrust himself through the opening as Robin aimed for the warlord but missed. The warlord fired from the cockpit door wildly trying to hit anything. He fired at the tunnel, tearing part of the attachment and allowing air pressure to drop in the room.

Contronto yelled, "They're cloaked and shooting at me!"

Gimmish yelled back, "Get in here and close the door!"

Robin began firing at the door. A metallic reinforcement shield slammed down, further blocking the doorway.

Jim yelled, "The women are in the next room." He picked up the suits and oxygen and opened the door to the second storage area. Air began to rush out of the room. Michael jumped on the opening, plugging the hole. A voice sounded in Michael's earpiece. "Ten minutes to the border."

Michael spoke back, "Lieutenant, can a fighter help slow this transport down?"

The pilot said, "It would take three or four to do it with the high-risk maneuver. Also, Bort is still out there waiting for a chance. Faster you get out of there, the better chance we can blow it into quark particles."

"Copy." He then yelled orders, "Jim, tell me when the women are ready. Robin, keep blasting the door at full power."

Jim went into the room and saw the women in light rings. He yelled back, "Michael, I need to use the light grenade. Got to deactivate the light rings on these women." He took the gags off their mouths, tied them around their eyes, then told them to hold their eyes closed tight until he gave them the all clear. He yelled for the others to put on their goggles. When Robin and Michael signaled, the grenade was activated with fifteen seconds of penetrating light. The rings released from the women, allowing them to get into the suits.

The pilot's voice came through the earpiece. "Five minutes left. Now or we must disengage."

Michael, knowing all had oxygen, got up and began tearing at the cockpit door. "Gimmish, you die! Gimmish, you die!" The latch broke on the reinforced door. The door swung open. Michael saw the fear of the warlords looking into the face of a raging bear. Michael began to reach with his massive hand and claws extended.

Gimmish slammed his fist on a switch that made the entire transport jerk. With that, the cabin holding the earthlings began to detach from its anchor. Michael extended his arm as far as he could, swiping at the warlords as the cargo hold began to quickly drift away from the rest of the ship. Michael kept reaching for a handle to keep the cabin attached. However, the cargo hold was jettisoned away from the enemy craft with the quickly depressurizing tunnel connected to it.

Michael heard Lieutenant Carman yell through his earpiece, "Save those in the container!" The five earthlings rushed back through the damaged tunnel to the safety of their transport.

In the meantime, the two warlords escaped across the border with only their lives, Lieutenant Bort, and one other fighter. Back in their transport, Jim, the women, and the crew displayed huge smiles. Michael continued to look at the monitor, following the three remaining enemy craft speeding into the other sector. His eyes began to moisten, "I almost had him, Anne. I did put the fear of God in his eyes. I'm sorry, Anne. I didn't get him."

Jim noticed and walked over to Michael to look at the same screen. Jim said, "Think of it this way. You saved thirty-nine women from endless torture and slavery. Think how proud Anne is of you now."

Michael looked at Jim with his sad eyes. He slowly shook his head affirmatively and went into the other room without a sound to be alone.

1/22/2024
Tol HQ Compound
Areanosten Planet Four
Quark Dimension

The transport landed at Tol's headquarters ten days later to fanfare. Jim was uneasy with all the celebration. He enjoyed his solitude. Michael had never sought the adoration of the masses. But he had to tolerate the attention of the cheering crowds, happy that Alchemy and his allies were defeated. This war had brought about great carnage. The earthlings all had a private moment of silence for the woman who gave her life so everyone there could escape from Contronto's headquarters.

They then went to meet Sargen and Brandish. Jim gave Brandish the letter written to him found in Tol's desk. When he opened it, a melancholy smile came across his face. It read:

Commander Brandish,

You are only reading this because I died in this dreaded conflict started by Alchemy. This means the sector will need a new leader of sound judgment and intelligence. I believe you are that quark. You performed every task I set before you with excellence, usually done by seasoned trained professionals by using your gift of wisdom and patience. It may not be the proper handover, but I believe with all my strength that you will lead this fiefdom in peace and prosperity.

You can trust other warlords when they give you their word, speaking of Sargen. He is an intelligent, thoughtful warrior whom I have come to greatly admire because of his logical and rational decision-making. Ally with him to keep the cosmos at peace. Quarks are getting scarce.

If there are conquered sectors, lead them as you would your own since Alchemy began this bloodshed with his delusional plans for conquest. Fighting was not their choice.

Lastly, thank the Knight Bear and Jim for their work to stop Alchemy and save as many lives as they did. Do everything you can to return all the kidnapped people back to the third planet, where they may live and prosper in peace.

I also want to give my humble apology to Knight Bear. It was I who told Gimmish to infect him with the disease that began his journey through his unwanted transformation and took away his normal life for my selfish purpose. The Game was intended to save our dimension, not destroy his.

Finally, Commander Brandish, I officially hand over the title of Warlord of the Fiefdom to you. Wear the ring with honor.

Sincerely and best wishes,
Warlord Tol

The celebrations went on for six more days. Everyone relaxed, ate, and dreamed of going home. On the sixth day of celebration, Brandish called Jim, Michael, and Robin to his office for a chat. "I have my transport ready to take you all home tomorrow. It has been my good fortune to meet and fight with you to rid this universe of Alchemy and his allies."

Michael had to interject, "Hold on there. Alchemy's lackey Gimmish and Contronto are still alive. I do not trust that this is the last time we will have to deal with them, since they got away into Flashenol's sector."

Brandish answered, "Yes, and we will watch for him or his miscreants continually, with a bounty on their heads, dead or alive. However, you have to rebuild your lives, going back to that beautiful Montana."

"You have been there?"

"I witnessed the murder of your wife by Gimmish." When Michael heard this, he teared up, knowing her murderer had gotten away.

Brandish continued, "There is such strong attachment among beings on your planet. Your close partner didn't have a chance with Gimmish, which I truly regret for your sake. I want to take you and the others home myself to see you all one last time. The best outcome would be for us never to meet again, yet something inside me says we may. Still, for now, let's take you all home."

Jim and Michael went to say goodbye to Sargen, who thanked them for saving his life. He gave everyone gifts to show his appreciation. The following morning, the quarks, Michael, Jim, Robin, and the thirty-eight others, filled the transport and headed to Earth.

They began in Finland, dropping off eight of the ten women, except Petra and Lovisa, who stayed on board. Then, they went to Siberia, where all but one was happy to be home. Olga, a woman who had lost the only person she knew during the abduction, wanted to go to Montana with Michael and Jim. Then they took the Asian women home to western China and sped halfway around the world back to Montana. Michael gave every returning woman open invitations for all-expense paid visits to Missoula anytime.

Jim was never so happy in his life to see Flathead Lake again, acting as excited as an eight-year-old on Christmas morning. The crystal water reflected the sun's rays onto the bottom of the transport, coming through the clouds over the mountains. The expert pilot, Brandish, entered the Earth's atmosphere at the magnetic pole and stayed under the radar the entire flight. His only challenge was to negotiate the northern Rockies into the Flathead Reservation. After dark, he activated the cloaking device and landed a short distance from Jim's house.

The scanning sensors determined the area was clear of visitors. Everyone thanked the flight crews and Brandish for bringing them home safely. The quarks supplied rations and energy nodes for their comfort. As the quarks departed to return home, Robin wrapped her arms around Michael's waist and said, "I am so glad that is over."

He asked, "Are you still mad at me?"

She said, "I don't care. I'm just happy to be on Earth."

They walked to Jim's house since they knew no one would be there. It was dusty, with cobwebs throughout, and the food in the refrigerator was spoiled. But they were safe.

Jim asked, "What's the plan, Michael? We'd better have an amazing explanation for being gone so long and then appearing out of nowhere." The six went through ideas about what to say about being abducted by aliens and brought back. Robin volunteered to go to the public library down the road, search for stories, and come back with ideas. Jim had 125 dollars left in a clip he had hidden on a shelf before they were abducted; he gave it to her to use. In the meantime, the rest cleaned the house. Michael was kind enough to eat the spoiled food in the refrigerator.

Petra said, "Many hands make light work."

Lovisa said, "I am ready to do a normal woman's thing. At least I can see out of both eyes now."

Robin came back five hours later with lunch and copies of articles about the time they were abducted. Their disappearance was the big news story for weeks, confirming their decision to claim the aliens had caused all of Michael's changes.

After they finished Jim's house, Michael wanted to check the status of his house. Jim told him, "You can't fit in my car. My truck is still in the mountains. All that's here is my personal SUV and a trailer. We will need to drive to your house before dawn with you in the trailer covered by a tarp I have in the basement. Then, Robin, you, and I can go over to the house and inspect the premises."

The following morning at first light, they pulled up, and looked in the driveway. They saw a sign under the mailbox saying, "Life's a Beach." Michael said, "It didn't take much time to have someone take over."

Robin said, "The sign seems odd in Montana. Let me go into the house invisible to see what's going on."

Michael said, "Let me walk behind you a little so you will be safe. I want no one else hurt on this property."

She answered, "Given what I can do now, I would have an advantage. Still, you can't be too careful. There are bears in these woods." They smiled at each other.

Michael walked on all fours a bit behind while he watched her walk up to the opened patio door to the kitchen. He could see inside as Robin stayed hidden on the deck. He heard a man's voice yelled, "Shelley, could you please bring me my towel? I forgot it!"

A little girl at the kitchen table giggled and said, "Daddy forgot his towel again."

"Yes, honey." A woman came into the kitchen saying, "Your Uncle Michael did the same thing, only he would walk out of the shower wet to get his. Your grandmother would be furious."

That was all Michael needed to know. Robin appeared and turned around, looking at Michael with a shrug. She disappeared again.

When they returned to the truck, Michael told Jim, "My sister Shelley and her family live in the house now."

Robin said, "They are talking about Uncle Michael getting in trouble with his mother for forgetting his towel."

Michael said, "Yes, Shelley was in my will. Everybody must think I'm dead. How much money do we have left?"

Jim said, "This is not all. I have an emergency stash in a hidden place only I know, since I don't like banks."

Back at Jim's house, Michael said to the rest, "Okay, I have to stay here. Robin and you three"—the other women who had come back to Montana—"go buy a burner phone to use so I can call Shelley and let her know before she sees me."

Petra added, "What are you going to call your new selves, like the Knight Bear? I think it sounds nice."

Robin said, "Well, I will be Prism, since I can bend light and move it where I want."

Lovisa thought a minute and said, "Alien Warrior, I think it sounds pretty cool, but I can change it if I want to."

Olga said, "I'm just a regular girl with a Russian accent. I am nothing right now but normal."

Robin said, "Since you are normal, no one will look at you strangely when you go with me to the store and help buy food and other things." Olga smiled, nodding in agreement.

Petra asked, "How about you, Jim?"

"I like Jim."

The four women groaned as he shrugged, showing them how little he cared.

Michael changed the subject. "We need to know how much money you have."

"Over two thousand, and I'll go with you," Jim said.

Michael asked, "Don't you think people will recognize you?"

Jim thought for a moment and said, "True, I'll stay here."

Michael said, "I'll pay you back."

Michael made a list of items, including the phone, a large gas can, a small generator to run the refrigerator, and food the women wanted. The three were to fill the SUV with gas, go to the big-box store, and come back without being caught with no license. It took about five hours to shop and come back to the house, since they had to drive a distance to reach the store.

They returned with food staples, the generator, a full gas can, and most importantly, a smartphone hooked up to the internet. Michael said, "I'm going to call Shelley to warn her that we are back and to ask her what has happened for the last, I think, few months."

Robin said, "It was so strange using cash instead of plastic when we bought these things."

Jim said, "It works well, doesn't it?"

Michael said, "Okay, let's look at what has happened to us in the last few months, according to the press."

After searching, the press and police declared that aliens had abducted everyone and considered them dead. The coroner signed off on the declaration, and the wills were executed. Jim said, "We are going to give folks a big surprise, aren't we?"

Michael said to Jim and Robin, "We won't need to disclose the research that caused my changes to happen since we have proof of aliens."

They both agreed.

EPILOGUE

11/15/2026
Department Chair Office, The Wilson Center
Missoula, Montana
Sol Planet Three
Milky Way Dimension

Michael sat at the desk looking at the rough draft of his latest research article to submit to the *New England Journal of Medicine*. After about ten minutes, he closed his laptop and moved it to the side. The snowflakes piling on the windowpanes framed the pure, lovely scene on the hillside. Swiveling the custom leather desk chair side to side as he viewed the landscape, he opened his leather portfolio to a blank page of a legal pad. His eyes moistened as he counted the number of horizontal lines on the legal pad. He picked up a pen that he had thickly wrapped cloth tape around so he could grip it properly due to his enormous paw-like hands. Swallowing his emotion, he began to write.

Dear Anne,

I know you are doing well in paradise. If you don't already know, it is a lovely day here. As you can see, I still use the Coach portfolio you gave me on my first birthday while in residency. I will always believe it cost too much.

Still, I continue to wish to have one more day with you to look into your eyes and tell you how dearly I love you. Yet, that is not in the plan.

Last spring, the school chaplain asked me to meet with him at the coffee house. We talked about work and family. After about twenty minutes of rambling about how seriously I love you and how terribly I miss you, he asked if I had told you these things. I said that, of course, I did, every day.

He point-blank asked me, "Would Anne want you to be this lonely and miserable?"

The question surprised me at its directness. I asked, "Am I that transparent?"

He answered, "Afraid so. You are so clouded by your grief, you can't see what others quickly observe."

"Boy, you're really direct."

"You have to be when dealing with college students. But you need that too right now. I have known you since you came to Montana. You have been miserable since Anne was murdered. I get why. But what did Anne want for you when she was here?"

"Anne wanted me to be happy and enjoy life."

"Yes, then honor her wish. You are still sick with grief because you can't give her that love. She would want you to give your love to someone who can cherish it in this life."

"Yes, but—"

"You wanted to give her your love 'to have and to hold.' I knew her too. Since she cannot ever be with you again, she wouldn't want you to withhold your love and be miserable for the rest of your life.

She would want you to give your love to someone who will benefit from it here, don't you think?"

Knowing you, I had to tell the chaplain, yes. He said the right things that triggered me to release my grief. I didn't know a bear could cry so much. After five minutes of blubbering like a baby, I asked him how he knew so much about us.

He said, "Missoula is not that big of a town."

I went from tears to a smile of joy and relief.

I got up from the table and went to the office to ponder all the events of the last seven years. You were my rock up to the end. I will always love you.

As you know, Robin still loves and honors you. I finally realized she could have taken other positions, but she chose to stay with the Wilson Center this whole time. I then gave myself a chance to care about her. I have lost time by foolishly holding on and not accepting that you are in a better place now.

When I began to turn my attention to Robin, she opened her feelings to me. I now understand why she waited. I had to completely let you go before she could enter into my life.

I found a lady to hold, a new person to give the rest of my love to.

I hope this meets with your approval. You can always let me know. Just send me a message on my Apple Watch.

With love to you always,
Michael

He read the note, satisfied with how he avoided any selfish desires. Thinking back to the meeting with the chaplain, he thought about how patient Robin had been. Maybe he'd kept her at arm's length because it would not be professional. Keeping his attention on Anne, he allowed himself to be far too lonely. The bottom line was that Robin was still there, lonely too.

When he reached out to her, her quick acceptance surprised him. Since he was so large, he had not noticed that she had grown taller, becoming as tall as Anne, more reserved than he knew her before. They began to spend time in the mountains nearby alone, learning how their relationship could grow. Michael showed her the cave, part of his private world where he'd seen himself become who he was now.

Since Robin had risked her life giving herself the essences that helped save the women, she leaned on Michael's experience about accepting her changes. They coached each other to come to terms with themselves.

The university was pleased since enrollment and applications had tripled because everyone in the world knew about the Wilson Center and wanted to experience real heroes, not to mention the quality of one of the premier genetic research centers.

To celebrate all the accomplishments of the last three-plus years, Michael wanted to invite all who had made everything possible to a huge Thanksgiving Day feast. The group, his sister Shelley's family, Robin's parents, and other people from the university celebrated the Center's contributions to medical research.

After the last university guest was gone, Robin's father gave Michael a nod and escorted his wife to the other room. Jim and everyone else followed. Lovisa, one of the rescued, returned with two flutes of champagne and walked back out.

Michael smiled at Robin's questioning look. She asked, "This is strange. What's going on?"

Michael reached into his kilt pocket and pulled out a small box. Robin's hands began to shake. "Before I open this box, I want to tell you how sorry I am that it took me so long to see how much you mean to me. The only thing I can do now is to ask you to love this thick-headed bear for the rest of our lives. Will you marry me?" He opened the box with the diamond and placed the ring on her finger.

She jumped into his arms and yelled, "Of course, yes, yes, yes!" Everyone still in the other room walked in with their champagne flutes and toasted the engagement. After everybody left except Jim, she said, "No matter who or what you are now, I fell in love with you the first day I met you in Cambridge. The most disappointing day was when I met Anne because she was so in love with you too. I will honor her by loving you as much as she did, if not more, and will stay by your side as long as I live." The two embraced with Michael giving Robin the gentlest possible bear hug.

At that point, Jim said, smiling ear to ear, believing that this was a storybook ending, "You want to come to get the smoker for the barbeque tomorrow. We need both yours and mine for both of those hogs."

Michael let go of Robin and said, "Got to go with Jim, or we don't eat tomorrow. Faculty and staff are going to be hungry."

Robin patted him on the fanny and smiled in approval. "You know I'll be hungry."

Jim said, "The truck's ready, but you'll have to be in back."

Michael said, "No. I'll drive my truck. It cost me enough to customize it for my big butt."

Jim chuckled, knowing how Michael hated to ride in the truck bed. "Okay, just the grill."

When they got to Jim's place, their moods changed radically when they saw the light on inside. Jim said, "I know I turned that light off. That means there has to be someone in there."

Michael clenched his teeth and said, "Okay, let's give this numbskull a rude hello."

Michael pulled out his gun, and both slowly went in, turned around the corner, and heard, "Hello, Jim, Michael."

A dumbfounded Michael yelled, "What in the hell are you doing here?"

Brandish said, "So nice to see you too. But we have a problem, Gimmish and Contronto are back in this dimension, and they are coming after you."

ABOUT WHIT HANEY

Whit Haney is a pharmacist, author, and serial entrepreneur living large and loving life in Lexington, South Carolina.

He is a graduate of The Citadel, The Military College of South Carolina, the Medical University of South Carolina, and the University of North Carolina at Chapel Hill.

He has loved characters all his professional life, meeting them every day working mostly in retail pharmacy. This is the first time he has sat down and remembered these people from over the years to write a story, putting traits or essences of each in his characters.

You may wonder how a normal-looking medical professional could create this out-of-this-world saga. Normal is only skin deep. Life's perception of stimuli thrown his way and his reactions caused this author to scoff at normalcy. The result has created the universe of the tales of the Knight Bear.

Printed in the United States
by Baker & Taylor Publisher Services